Donald:

dition
ourney on the Wind)

le

The Vis

The Vision
Is Fulfilled

Kay L. McDonald

Walker and Company *New York*

Lovingly dedicated to my friends and fans and specifically to:
   My cousin Shirley, who cheered me when I was down,
   My mother-in-law, who makes many things possible,
   Tootie M. and her Silverton fan club,
   Donna R., who is deserving of happiness,
   My soul sister, Anne P., whose love is returned,
   Doris R., who reads for me,
   David D., whose suggestions to strengthen this work have
     been gratefully included,
   My first editor and agent, Jean N., who never lost faith,
And to all of you who have written or called for your patience, enthusiasm,
faith, and encouragement, my heartfelt thanks. You are the greatest fans in
the world.

Sincerely,
K. L. M.

First published in the United States of America in 1983 by the Walker Publishing
Company, Inc.

Published simultaneously in Canada by John Wiley & Sons Canada, Limited,
Rexdale, Ontario.

ISBN: 0-8027-4019-7

Library of Congress Catalog Card Number: 82-51303

Printed in the United States of America

10 9 8 7 6 5 4 3 2 1

Prologue

IN THE LAST month of winter in the year 1813 on the vast wind-swept northern prairie where unmelted snow still lay in the sheltered places, a child was born in a lodge of the Follow The Wind People, one of the small scattered bands of Nakota, called Sioux by their enemies. The child was white, born to a white woman known as Little Yellow Bird among the Indians, but christened Abigail by her white parents, Lucia and Elias Whitteker, a well-to-do banker in the small community of Riverwood in upstate New York. She delivered the child alone, afraid to let the Indian midwives see that her child was white and not born of her Indian captor Snow Cloud, chief of the Follow The Wind People. The child was a boy, and Abigail named him after his father, Ross Galligher, her Irish Catholic husband whom Snow Cloud had scalped and left for dead while he had been plowing a newly cleared patch of land on the Missouri frontier, where they had finally settled after many months of travel and hardship resulting from their elopement and marriage against both their families' wishes.

By the time Abigail's son was old enough to form his first words, Abigail had been subjected to all aspects of Indian life and was determined her son must have the choice of whether he would be Indian or white. Secretly, she began teaching him to read, write, and speak the English language, instilling in him the knowledge of his true heritage.

As the boy grew, he was also being schooled in the Indian culture of the band, and more and more he was gone from Abigail, spending hours with the elders learning the spiritual and tribal customs of the Indians and even more hours following and imitating the young warriors as they made weapons, hunted game, and competed for supremacy in all things they did, learn-

1

ing everything he needed to know to become the next chief of Snow Cloud's people.

The assimilation of the two cultures was confusing to the boy known as Holes In Face, and when he was old enough to seek his vision in the traditional Indian way, the vision he received did nothing to lessen his confusion. His vision, strangely different and perplexing to the Indians, showed him in vivid and unmistakable symbols that his mother would die, that he would go on to receive much honor and glory, and that the Indian woman he would take as his wife would also die, in childbirth. He was commanded by the voice of his vision to physically go in search of a white eagle's nest and procure its feathers as his totem, but he was made to understand, again symbolically, that this was also an eventual future achievement toward the fulfillment of his vision and, finally, that he would leave this future nest of the white eagle with another who appeared, again symbolically, to be the same as he.

This, then, was the legacy and the destiny of the young boy who would become the warrior White Eagle, as told in the *Vision of the Eagle*.

Thirteen years later, in the fall of the year 1842, a ship arrived at the Hudson's Bay outpost of Fort Vancouver in the vast, relatively uncivilized Oregon country. On the ship were eight people whose self-chosen mission was to find and chart mountain passes over the rugged Cascade Mountains through which wagons could be driven. The leader of the party was Joshua Brightwood, who brought with him his daughter Marlette and a small party of men capable of assessing the land through which they would travel in search of an easy route into the Willamette Valley, where the Methodist missionary Jason Lee had several years before begun a mission to the wild Indians of Oregon.

It was Jason Lee who had inspired the undertaking when he had gone east seeking reinforcements for his Willamette Mission. He had painted such a glowing picture of the Oregon country that Joshua Brightwood, along with hundreds of other disenchanted and restless people, was caught up in the excitement of Oregon fever, which was being fueled and spread by Lee and another Oregon promoter, Hall J. Kelley.

The Brightwood party found Dr. John McLoughlin, chief factor of the Hudson's Bay Company at Fort Vancouver, congenial but pessimistic about their expedition. Undaunted by McLough-

2

lin's lack of enthusiasm for their venture, they refused to abandon their expedition; McLoughlin, concerned for their safety if allowed to pursue their intention alone, introduced them to a man who was to become their guide. The man was Ross Chesnut, a quiet, self-assured, buckskin-clad man, appearing to be at least a half-breed, but with a surprising command of the English language. Marlette Brightwood viewed him with dislike and distrust, and so did most of the members of the party. But they had no other choice and hired the mysterious Chesnut, and their expedition through the wilderness began.

Their first destination was the Whitman Mission, 250 miles to the east along the Columbia River near another Hudson's Bay outpost, Fort Walla Walla. They little realized the dangers of the land or the Indians who were becoming hostile to the Whitmans. With equal naiveté, they underestimated the man who led them.

They arrived at the Whitman Mission just as Dr. Whitman was preparing to ride to the East Coast in an effort to change the order of the Mission Board to close down his station. No less a spur to his proposed trip was the recent party of settlers who had stopped at his mission for sustenance and rest on their way to the Willamette Valley. He felt that to close the mission at a time when it could offer a prominent place of succor on the Oregon Trail was failing to meet not only a Christian need, but also the needs of the United States. He wholly agreed with the expedition's intent and maintained that a route over the mountains was not only possible, but necessary as well.

The members of the expedition were advised by their guide against accompanying Dr. Whitman for any distance on his journey east because of the lateness of the season, so they started westward toward the Cascades on their mission of finding passes. Renegade Indians learning of their purpose in the Oregon country attacked the small party several times, but due to their superior weapons and the wisdom of their guide, they escaped with only minor injury. When it looked as if they might have eluded the Indians altogether, they were surprised in an ambush on the banks of a river they were preparing to cross, within the shadow of the Cascade Mountains. Only Marlette Brightwood and the guide, Chesnut, escaped.

Marlette, grief-stricken and afraid, had no choice but to stay with the man she distrusted as he led her into the mountains. But

3

they were still not safe, and a party of Indians caught up with them as they awoke one morning and took their horses and weapons with what food they had left. Because they knew Chesnut, they let them live, knowing there was little chance the man and woman would be able to get out of the mountains on foot before it snowed.

The snow came, cold and deadly, but again Chesnut was able to save them. Not far from the crest of the mountains was a cabin he shared in the winter with a French-Canadian trapper named Jacques. Here he brought the almost lifeless woman, and here they spent the winter. During their stay in the snowbound cabin, Ross told Marlette what little he knew of his mother and father and of his life among the Indians. Slowly, the mistrust she held for Ross changed to trust and the hate became love, and finally the day came when they could leave the cabin and continue their journey back to the Willamette Valley and safety.

On the trip downriver, their love was consummated, but Marlette had unfinished business in the East and felt compelled to return. They arrived at Champoeg the day the Americans voted to set up a Territorial Government and Marlette was asked to carry the petition to Washington. That night French-Canadians, fearing they would lose their land and their English benefactors— The Hudson's Bay Company—kidnapped Marlette and left Ross for dead. Though badly injured, Ross rescued Marlette and they were found and taken to Oregon City where Marlette stayed with Ross and Jacques, waiting for a ship to come that would take her East.

Ross, fearing he would never see her again if she left before he was well enough to go with her, asked her to marry him, hoping the vows given before a minister of her people would bind her to him and bring her back. Marlette, afraid she might be pregnant, agreed to the wedding. They were married in Oregon City only an hour before a boat arrived to take Marlette to Fort Vancouver and a waiting ship.

Once at Fort Vancouver, Marlette learned from Dr. John McLoughlin that Ross had been highly paid to protect her, but he was only to receive the money if Marlette returned to the Fort safely. Her word would release the payment to him or make it a reward for his life if she felt he had been responsible for the deaths of her father and the rest of the expedition. Feeling confused,

4

alone, and betrayed, she wondered if Ross had married her to protect himself. But there was no time to find out and she sailed for the East Coast, trying to deny the love she felt for the man she had married.

Once home to Philadelphia, she learned all she had thought she had to return to had been lost—ruined by the man left in charge. With debts to pay and only her home left to use as payment, Marlette had to build a new life, unable now to return to Ross, even if she had wanted to.

Three years later, the captain of the ship that had taken the Brightwood expedition to the Oregon country brings Marlette proof that Ross Chesnut had not used her to protect himself and still loved her and, against all odds, Marlette begins the journey westward to Independence, Missouri, to find the man she loves.

So ends *The Brightwood Expedition* (also titled, in paperback, *Journey on the Wind*).

1. Independence, Missouri— May 1846

Ross Chesnut leaned against a porch post, his narrowed eyes and impassive face belying the bewildered, almost frightened feeling he had experienced his first few days here as he stood alone, buffeted by the noisy, colorful throng of people milling up and down the ungraded streets of Independence, Missouri, in the muggy spring air. Now he just felt distaste for the pushing, sweating, bickering horde of movers waiting to take the trail west. He could even sympathize with the Indians, mountain men, bushwhackers, and the soldiers who tried to keep order to it all. They appeared just as overwhelmed as he felt now, watching and waiting with unapparent tenseness, his dark, thick-lashed eyes constantly searching the moving crowd, his ears alert for a voice that was only a memory in his mind.

He grew restless and tired of the oppressive din and humidity of the town, and was about ready to go on his daily search of the tent city spreading like a cancer on the surrounding plain, when a harsh expletive and the snort and squeal of sharply restrained horses in the adjacent side street caught his attention. He turned his eyes toward the disturbance as the driver yelled, "Hey, lady!"

Ross's body straightened away from the post in disbelief. Marlette was coming at a half run, her skirts lifted as she tried to avoid mud puddles and dodge the rearing horses belonging to the yelling man. He sprang off the high porch in one lithe leap, only to be confronted by a lumbering Conestoga wagon wheeling around the corner from the main street. It passed heaving through the squishy trough left by the last wagon, splattering his buckskins with globs of mud. He leaped across the settling mire and took

Marlette in his arms, the shuttered, withdrawn expression on his face replaced with one of unbelieving joy.

The total isolation of this moment of meeting was sweet but brief. Ross heard the shouts of encouragement from the halted wagons and onlooking people who had stopped to witness their reunion. He lifted Marlette in his arms and carried her to the porch where he had been standing. She clung to him, their eyes feasting on each other's faces, and in the same breath they asked, "Were you coming—?" and, laughing, answered as one, "Yes."

The crowd surged around them once more, and Ross closed out all the noise and people and just looked with deep, consuming happiness into Marlette's face. She looked as he remembered her when they had parted three years before. Her wide blue eyes had been brimming with tears then, too, but her tears then had been tears of sadness. Now she was smiling with joy.

A body in the moving crowd stopped behind Marlette, and Ross looked across the top of Marlette's head into a face that startled him with its familiarity. In a voice constricted with speculation, Ross asked, "Who is this?"

Marlette laughed happily and asked, "Do you recognize him?"

"It's like looking into a mirror."

"Ross, this is Cam Galligher, a son of your cousin."

A feeling of wonder and pleasure spread through him and lighted his face with a smile of amazement, the lines in his smooth-shaven cheeks turning into boyish dimples as his hand reached to take the slightly smaller replica of his own. "Is that what my name is—Galligher?"

Cam Galligher, smiling with pride, answered, "Yes, sir."

Ross couldn't quite believe what he saw. The boy was about eighteen and looked enough like him to be his brother instead of a distant cousin. He didn't want to let go of the boy's hand, wanting to hold onto this proof that somewhere he had roots and a heritage. In a voice more husky than usual, he asked, "Is he going home with us?"

Marlette nodded happily.

Clearing his throat in an effort to subdue the emotion so obvious in his voice, he said, "Well then, let's get started."

The tears spilled from Marlette's eyes again as she breathed, "Oh, Ross," overcome with joy, and buried her face against his chest. Ross held her, and Cam grinned self-consciously.

7

Ross grinned back and asked, "Has she been like this long?"

Cam shook his head. "Not a tear until now, sir."

Marlette pulled herself together and pushed away from Ross, swiping at the tears with the back of her hand. "I'm sorry to be so silly, but I'm just so happy I can't help it."

Ross touched her hair in a gesture of complete understanding. "Where were you going?"

"We were looking for a wagon-train leader or a guide, or even enough Oregon-bound wagons to join and make a company. The people we've talked to so far are going to California, and to hire a guide just for ourselves is more money than we have." She stopped abruptly and turned wide eyes on Cam. "Cam! We don't need a guide anymore. Ross can take us to Oregon!"

The light of truth flashed through Cam's eyes, and he grinned excitedly, "Hey! That's right! We don't need anyone else now."

Ross thought it was strange she was worried about money. The amount he had sent to her with Captain McNeal when he had passed through Fort Vancouver had surely been more than enough to get her this far, even with the boy. In his anxiousness to leave this crowded outpost and get them on the trail to Oregon, he didn't question her but asked instead, "Where are you staying? How did you get here?"

"Out there," she answered, indicating the field of canvas tents and wagon tops outside of town. "We came by boat most of the way."

He frowned. "Then you don't have horses?"

She smiled smugly. "We have everything—a wagon, horses, oxen, cows, chickens, provisions—everything."

He looked at her with dismay as he realized she had come prepared to travel with a wagon train, while he had only considered the two of them alone on horseback, traveling swiftly and lightly over the trail to Oregon. "I hadn't planned on taking a wagon to Oregon. It wouldn't be wise to set out with a wagon alone through Indian territory. If you've got two horses to ride, we can sell the rest easily enough here."

Marlette's face sobered as she explained, "But we can't do that. I'm traveling with another family. We have three wagons."

Losing hope for a quick start from Independence, he answered, "Even two or three wagons can't make it safely. You need at least

8

fifteen or twenty wagons to be safe. It would be best to go by horseback.''

She shook her head, the happiness at their meeting overshadowed by concerns and commitments he knew nothing of and had not even considered. Softly, she said, "No, it just isn't possible. I'm sorry.''

His arm went around her again and pulled her comfortingly close. "All right. We'll go by wagon. Take me to your camp. First of all, I need to see what you've got for equipment, and then we can find a company to travel with. The sooner we get started, the better.''

Her practical nature knew the truth of his words. "We're about a half mile out of town. The Jessups are with the wagons. I know they'll be as relieved to see you and meet you as I am.''

He smiled then, too, saying, "Cam, my horses and pack are at the livery stable down at the other end of the street.'' He reached under his belt and brought out a few coins. "Here's money to pay for their keep. Everything should be in the last three stalls on the left with a sorrel, a pinto, and a bay with one blind eye.''

Cam smiled and straightened with importance. There was a hero-worshipping eagerness already full bloom in the boy's eyes. "Yes, sir.'' He turned quickly away to do Ross's bidding.

Marlette looked up at him and smiled. "What do you think of him?''

"Do you need to ask? But I don't know if I can live up to what he thinks of me. How long have you been recounting my coups to him?''

She laughed and took his arm and turned in the direction she wished to lead him, and he walked with her. "For about two months.''

"Is that how long you've known him?''

"No, but that's about how long we've been traveling to get here. I found him, or rather his father—your cousin—almost two years ago. When I wrote and told Cam I was going west to be with you, he joined us.''

"*Us?*'' His heart skipped a beat, but logic returned, and he asked, "You mean the Jessups?''

"No,'' she answered.

He stopped and looked expectantly into Marlette's face, waiting for her answer.

9

She looked curiously at him, unaware of his excitement. "Martha, my housekeeper is with me."

His expectation faded as swiftly as it had come. The possibility that she had borne him a child had often occurred to him. This would have explained why she hadn't come back to him immediately. Feeling as much relief as disappointment, he said, "I want to hear more about Cam and how you found him. What about his family, and why didn't they come with him?"

She began walking again. "I was giving a lecture on Oregon in upstate New York, and Cam's father, Timothy Galligher, was at the meeting. I recognized him the way you recognized Cam. He strongly resembles you, as Cam does. Do you remember what you told me your mother said—that you couldn't go back? She was right, Ross. Your cousin and his mother talked to me, but they wouldn't admit anything concerning your father or mother. He drove me out to their farm, and from what Cam says, I'm sure it's where your father lived when he met your mother. Your cousin had Cam drive me back to town, and it was from Cam that I learned the truth. I told him about you, and the thought of you and the West obsessed him instantly. I knew he would try to find you when he was old enough to leave home. When I knew I was coming, I let him know, and he decided to join me. It's as simple as that."

Ross shook his head. "Not quite. There's so much more I want to know."

"Cam will tell you everything he knows. But that isn't a great deal. Just bits and pieces he overheard. You see, they didn't talk about your father—didn't acknowledge him at all. He was excommunicated from their family."

Ross was silent for a long moment, disturbed by the consequences Cam would suffer for his action, but there was little he could do now. Finally he asked, "Marlette, why did you wait so long to come back to me?"

Her eyes filled with distress, and her hand clutched his desperately. Then she turned away and spoke without looking at him. "How can I begin to tell you? So much has happened since I left you. I was wrong to leave you. I found that out too late. When I reached Philadelphia, everything I had felt I had to go back to was gone. The man my father left in charge, Martha's son Tom, had ruined the business and run away, leaving behind terrible debts. I

10

had to sell my home and find work. I had no means to come to you until you sent me the money Father left at Fort Vancouver for your pay.''

It was clear now why she had been worried about money. ''If only I had known. I never thought money was the problem. I should have come with you. I could have prevented all this.''

''All this and more, but it wasn't your fault. We're together now, and that's all that matters.''

He stopped her again and raised her chin until her troubled eyes met his, fearing what was still unsaid. Gently he asked, ''You'd better explain that more to me.''

''I will, but not now. There're our wagons ahead.''

They had walked to what had been the farthest edge of the city of wagons and tents only a few days ago, and already there were more wagons and more tents going up beyond them. The camp-fire Marlette was leading him to was being tended by two women.

The older woman, stout and gray-haired, spoke first. ''Where on earth—!''

Marlette answered excitedly, her face aglow again, ''He was here! He was coming for me!''

The woman scowled as she appraised him, clearly protective of Marlette. The other woman came forward, smiling warmly, her hand outstretched.

''Ross, this is Liz Jessup. And this is my companion, Martha Yates.''

While Martha made up her mind about him, Liz was saying in a rich, throaty, and strangely unfamiliar but not unpleasant accent, ''We are so happy to have you here, Mr. Chesnut. Marlette has told us so much about you.''

Ross said with a smile, ''I have the feeling she has been talking too much.''

Martha retorted crustily, ''Well, we'll soon find out.''

Cam came riding in with Ross's horses and gear. Ross turned to him, relieved, and asked, ''Did you have any trouble?''

''No. He was so busy, he didn't have time to notice I wasn't you. Do you want me to put your horses with ours?''

''Not yet. I'd better wait to see what the plans are first. Where is Mr. Jessup?''

Liz answered, ''John and the boys are out minding the stock.

11

Cam, would you go out and tell John Mr. Chesnut is here and that his supper's ready?"

Cam led the horses behind the wagons and tied them. Ross heard a girl's voice question him, followed by a brief, excited exchange. Then the girl came quickly out from behind the wagon with a big, red curly-haired dog at her side. She came forward hesitantly, and Liz said, "Jennifer, this is Marlette's husband, Mr. Chesnut, all the way from Oregon."

She curtsied, her eyes never leaving him. Then she said to Ross, "Everybody calls me Jenny. You can, too."

Ross smiled at her and said, "Hello, Jenny."

She looked at Marlette excitedly and said with reddening cheeks, "Cam does look like him!" She set down the bucket of milk and, picking up her tangling skirts, ran as fleet as a deer around the wagon in the direction Cam was taking, the dog bounding playfully after her.

Liz laughed, "I think you have impressed her, Mr. Chesnut."

"How old is she?"

"Fourteen, going on sixteen."

A man came into view, stepped over the wagon tongue, and stopped. He was somewhat slighter of build than Ross, with thinning brown hair.

Marlette introduced him to Ross. "Mr. Jessup, this is my husband."

The man came forward, and their hands met in a strong, friendly grasp. "Glad to meet you, Mr. Chesnut. We've been hoping we'd run on to you," he said, his voice quiet and drawling like his wife's.

"It's Ross or Chesnut, but not Mister."

Jessup smiled. "For me neither. I'm John to my friends." He turned to the onlooking women and shook his head with a good-natured smile. "You three remind me of a bunch of schoolgirls. Now quit your gapin' and serve us up some supper."

John pointed to a sturdy and well-used rocking chair set close to the fire. "Have a chair, Ross. I believe we've got a whole lot of talkin' to do."

"Thanks, but I'm not used to chairs. The ground is more comfortable to me."

Three boys came striding into the circle, looking over the new arrival with curious gazes. They were all handsome boys, combining the best features of their parents.

"Ross, these are my boys, Jonathan, Jeremy, and Joseph."

Ross shook each hand as they looked at him in awe and mumbled polite greetings.

Their father asked, "Who's mindin' the stock with you three here?"

Jeremy, the middle boy, who was about Cam's age, answered in the same drawl, "Cam is, but I'm going right back out to help him."

John smiled. "See that you do. You other two get washed up, and where's your sister?"

Jonathan, the oldest, grinned and said, "She's helpin' Cam."

They did a quick about-face, and Ross could hear the three of them chuckling as they went toward the wash pan.

Ross lowered himself to the ground, and John took what was obviously his chair. Liz poured them hot cups of coffee from the pot sitting close to the fire, and Ross felt less anxiety than he had for days. These were good people. He already felt he could count John and his boys, and most certainly Cam, as his friends; Martha would take a little winning.

John was saying, "Damn, I'm glad your here, Chesnut. I've heard so much talk and so many rumors about Indians and Mormons, I don't know who to believe or who to trust, and everybody's got a different opinion of what we need. Some say we should have mules because they're faster and take the heat better, and some say oxen are better on the long run and not as tough if you have to eat them. I'm almost afraid to ask your opinion, but what do you think?"

"The mules are better if you're just going to the mountains and no farther. Mules are all the traders used, but they were interested in speed. The trail to the mountains is fairly easy but sandy, and the oxen are better over sandy, rough roads. Once we're in the mountains, we'll have a lot of those, especially in the higher, drier desert country."

"I'm relieved to hear that. I was just about ready to trade my oxen. Your wife was smarter about wagons than I was, though; she's got a jointed tongue on hers. Do you think it would pay me to have mine changed?"

"Yes, if we can do it without too much delay. Tell me about the

13

rumors you've heard about the Indians. And what is a Mormon? I've not heard that word before."

John chuckled. "The Mormons are a who. They've decided they're God's chosen people and have been building communities in Missouri and Illinois. They've made their neighbors so fightin' mad there's been burnin's and murders, including the hangin' of their prophet. Now the whole kit and kaboodle of them are movin' out and going west, armed to the teeth. Rumor has it they'll plunder anybody who gets in their way. It makes the Indians out there waitin' to scalp and rob us sound like the lesser of two evils."

Marlette served them plates of hot roast beef and potatoes with Dutch oven biscuits. Ross hadn't smelled anything so good in days. He ate in silence, relishing the sumptuous meal. If nothing else, he had acquired a taste for the white man's cooking. Marlette came with her plate and sat on a block of wood beside him. He smiled at her and remarked, "I haven't eaten this good since you left me."

Her hand touched his shoulder, and their eyes met in a glance that spoke in silent eloquence the longing they felt.

Liz interrupted their thoughts. "Did you find any information on Oregon-bound parties in town today, Marlette?"

"I found out we couldn't afford a guide between us and not much else. Now with Ross here, we don't need a guide, but he thinks we do need to travel in a larger company for safety."

"Well, they been comin' and goin' all day. Shouldn't be too hard to find enough to make a company to travel with. How many wagons do you think we need?"

"Somewhere between fifteen and twenty or even thirty wagons would be a large enough party. You have fewer people to worry about, and you need less grass and water for a smaller party. Indians won't bother a fair-sized and well-armed group. We'll also be able to travel faster, and the faster we travel the better."

"What you say makes sense to me. How about going around and talking to some of the others after we get done eatin'? Maybe we can start gatherin' a few wagons together for Oregon."

"Yes. This dry weather won't hold. The sooner we can get on the trail, the better."

The evening was like nothing Ross had ever experienced before. Born and raised in an Indian camp, he had left the Indians and moved west to become part of what he had thought was a

14

white man's society, the trappers, traders, and men who ran the outposts of the Hudson's Bay Company. His sixteen years among the white men had not even begun to prepare him for the emigrants who had uprooted themselves and their families to build new lives in the West. These people were a diverse cross section of the American people: doctors, lawyers, clergymen, politicians, businessmen, teachers, laborers, and farmers outnumbering them all. He was overwhelmed and fearful of the impact these people would make on the West.

It was long after dark when Ross and John returned to their own camp. The acres of tents and wagons were hushed and ghostly in the last glowing embers of campfires. The last knots of debating movers were straggling off to bed. Ross's horses whickered softly at his coming, and he stopped long enough to notice that someone—he suspected Cam—had taken care of them. It reminded him that he wanted to be included in their night duty.

"Call me when it's my turn to watch the stock."

John smiled and waved his request away. "Not tonight. I'm in trouble already for keepin' you so late. Tonight you better spend with your wife."

Ross went willingly toward Marlette's tent. He smelled dampness in the westerly wind, which was rising with gathering force, and he knew it would be raining by morning. He ducked into the black interior of Marlette's tent and stood still, afraid to move until the clouds drifted out from in front of the moon and he could discern her bed. He undressed and knew she was awake, sensing the breathless expectancy in the tent as she waited for him.

He crouched to find the blankets, lifted them, and slid in beside her, whispering, "Are you awake?"

She stirred and turned. He reached to take her in his arms. He had waited a long time for this moment. There were questions to be answered later, but there was no time for words now. Their melded lips and eager bodies allowed nothing but the ultimate satisfaction of the need that had been unfulfilled for so long.

And then the moment was reached in lightning swiftness and gone just as quickly. He held Marlette close, stroking the satin smoothness of her hair.

"Oh, Ross," she sobbed, "I don't deserve your love. Can you ever forgive me?"

15

"Forgive you for what? The blame is mine. I should never have let you go without me."

She was silent a moment, brushing the tears away as she tried to control the emotions that wracked her. "You don't understand. Oh, I'm so ashamed of myself! I loved you so much, and I doubted you so much—" Her voice broke.

He waited until her sobbing subsided before he said, "Maybe you'd better explain it to me from the beginning."

At last she rested quietly against him, her hand lightly on his chest. "After I left you and reached Fort Vancouver, Dr. McLoughlin and I were going through the money Father had left with him. It wasn't until then that I discovered how much Father had paid you to keep me safe and that Dr. McLoughlin wasn't to give you the money unless he had my approval. In other words, you weren't to have the money if I felt you had not done your job well. If I had any doubts about you or about your part in what happened to us on that journey, the money was to be a reward for your life!"

He was silent as he remembered the first time he had seen her in McLoughlin's office more than half a continent away, in the wilderness known as Oregon. They had hired him to guide them across the vast Indian-inhabited country to the Whitman Mission and back to Fort Vancouver over the mountains in search of passes through which wagons could come into the Willamette Valley. They had been attacked by Indians on the way back to Fort Vancouver, and only he and Marlette had survived. "Yes, I agreed to those conditions with your father. What does it have to do with us?"

"Don't you see? I didn't know and you didn't tell me! It was such a shock. I couldn't imagine why you hadn't told me, unless you had wanted to deceive me all along and had only used me as a means to get the money."

It was Ross's turn to feel agony. So that had been the other reason she had mentioned. The money! It was the last thing he had been concerned with.

She went on. "When I got on that ship for home, I was never coming back to you. Then Captain McNeal brought me the silver, and I realized what a dreadful mistake I'd made."

He closed his hand over hers and felt the ring on her finger—his ring. He had almost lost her, and he hadn't even known it. "I

16

never guessed it was the money that kept you from coming back to me." He sighed and held her closer. "What a fool I was to let you go by yourself."

She touched his lips with her fingers. "Don't say it. I was the bigger fool for doubting you, and I will regret it always."

He kissed her fingers and then raised her head and kissed her lips. "Think of it no more. It's over, and I'll never let you leave me again. All that kept me in the valley—building our home and starting a business—was the hope that you would be back, but my hope was like autumn; it only brought winter, and my winter has lasted much too long." He kissed her again, but she had questions to ask and resisted his ardor.

"Oh, Ross, how unthinking I've been! Tell me about our place. And Jacques! How is Jacques? And you?" Guiltily, she remembered how he had looked the day she had left him, still suffering from a brain concussion and broken ribs, so weak he had hardly been able to stand long enough to marry her. "Are you all right now? I mean completely all right—no pain or headaches?"

"Jacques is fine. I couldn't have made it without him. I did have pain and headaches for a while, at first, but I'm not bothered much now. Jacques and I, with Nathaniel's help, got a house built, and we've been living in it and logging for McLoughlin's mill at the falls and anyone else who wants to buy logs. We've done well; we have two wagons now and haul freight besides. Cam will be a welcome partner—we needed another man to help."

She hugged him and said with excitement, "Oh, I'm so anxious to get there. I love you so much!"

He kissed her and enjoyed the sensation of her questing lips and body that moved to receive his. Now he could savor the kisses and caresses, and say the things selfish urgency had neglected before. He didn't hear the rain until much later and fell asleep, too content to worry about the problems the rain brought with it.

Ross awoke to a gray half light. There was a pervasive dampness in the air. Even his clothes were damp. He ducked out of the tent where a bleak dawn was lighting the eastern sky. Ross built up the fire, ignoring the drizzle of rain, and Liz, her clothes damp and her hair plastered wetly around her face, looked at him, stolidly squatting before the fire, and laughed.

"I believe everything Marlette told me about you now. You *are* more Indian than white!"

17

He smiled up at her and stood up. "I don't regret it, and I hope you won't either."

After a breakfast of biscuits, bacon, and eggs from Marlette's coop of chickens, John and Ross went over every piece of equipment they had, discussing changes and additions and making lists of things they would need.

The animals were given the same scrutiny as their supplies. They would be relying on them for the long, arduous journey across a continent none of them, except Ross, had traveled. Their teams especially needed to be sound and strong, with a good supply of shoes, nails, and tar. With lists in hand, the two men took John's buckboard, drove into Independence, and didn't return until almost dark.

The next few days, they spent hours working on the equipment. Word spread quickly through the camp that there was a man from Oregon among them, and their camp was mobbed with men seeking information on the trip, the trail, provisions, forts, Indians, and conditions in Oregon.

Ross watched with growing impatience as the wagons around them departed in increasing numbers. If John felt the tension, he didn't show it and worked steadily and uncomplainingly as Ross grew grimmer with each delay. But the two men worked well together, and Ross appreciated and respected his quiet, pipe-smoking, competent partner more with each passing day.

At last they had their wagons and equipment ready and after an early lunch, Ross helped his little company take down their tents and pack their wagons. They would start off by themselves, as others had been doing for days, hoping to join with a train they heard was forming out on the trail, a few miles from Independence.

Cam came up with a whip and goad in his hands and said, "We're ready to move. I wish I could be riding ahead with you."

Ross smiled at him and promised, "You will be—as much as possible—as soon as we get this outfit trail broke."

Cam's pleasure at Ross's promise was unconcealed as he said anxiously, "Then let's get movin'."

They helped the women into the wagon seat. John started off with his wagon, and Liz was behind him in the buckboard, pulled by a pair of matched mules, Jenny at her side. Marlette's wagon was last, and the three Jessup boys herded the stock behind. Ross

18

led the way, threading through the rutted and muddy camp ground toward the trail.

The sky was clearing and the sun came out, but there were more clouds forming in the west. The trail, already deeply rutted from many years' use as the main trade route to Santa Fe and the Rocky Mountains, was muddy and chewed up by the parties already gone in the days before. He turned back to see how his little caravan was coming and heard the bawls of the balky and rebelling oxen as they were forced into a new routine after several days' rest. The process of retraining them looked almost as difficult as it must have been on the first day they were yoked and hitched to the wagons.

Ross turned his horse away from the slow-moving wagons and loped along beside the trail, enjoying the temporary freedom from those lumbering along behind. There was no need to hurry. The cloying Missouri clay would hold them back, and no doubt every creek was bank-full from the rains. He shut out the thoughts of what flooded fords would mean to his small crew and galloped on, exhilarated by air heavy with the scent of freshly washed oak leaves from the scattered groves and the burgeoning blossoms of spring flowers in the emerald green grass.

Ahead of him, other wagons swayed along, creaking and rattling in the ruts. Coming toward him were mule-drawn wagons from the Sante Fe Trail, harnesses jingling with bells as the trail-weary animals lifted their feet faster in expectation of a few days' rest.

Ross turned back after another mile or two, satisfied the road was no worse ahead. If anything, it was somewhat drier. He loped his horse back to his own wallowing wagons. Marlette and Jenny were walking in the damp grass with the dog, Curly, romping beside them. Their skirts were dampened and stained with mud, but their spirits were undampened as they filled Jenny's apron full of bright spring flowers. John and Cam kept their oxen moving with urging voices and snapping whips, having let Liz and her lighter buckboard go ahead. She smiled gaily at Ross as he passed her on his way to the rear of the wagons to see how the boys were coming with the reluctant stock. He watched as they passed him and smiled. They had gone their first mile on the trail to Oregon.

2. *The Oregon Trail*

ROSS STAYED WITH his companions, satisfied that the trail ahead held no problems. He rode beside Cam when John's boys didn't need help with a recalcitrant cow, and admired the boy's skill as he kept the oxen moving. Ross regretted he hadn't had more time so far to spend with him or with John's boys. He had barely gotten acquainted with any of them, but vowed to spend more time with all of them, especially Cam. His admiration for Cam easily turned to affection as he watched the boy, who looked so much like himself that it became a fascination in itself.

Before long they passed some heavily loaded mule-drawn wagons, bells ajingle, outbound for Santa Fe. The teamster freely shouted advice to them, advice that was all too true, but warnings that Ross would just as soon had been left unsaid. No one but himself seemed too seriously affected by the teamster's warning. Marlette was thoroughly enjoying the mild spring day and threw back her sunbonnet and raised her face to the sun. Ross got down and walked with her, holding her hand, sharing this delightful spring day while bees zipped by and huge flies droned lazily after the oxen.

Jenny didn't miss this opportunity to be close to Cam and came purposely to walk beside him, showing him her apronful of spring flowers. He reacted with typical big-brother attitude.

"Jenny, can't you see I'm busy? Now go play somewhere else."

Jenny glared at him. "Cam Galligher, I am not playing, and I can walk anywhere I want to."

Cam's ears reddened with embarrassment, and Jenny's brothers, who had not missed the exchange, began to whistle and call teasing phrases to the embarrassed Cam.

Finally, he was reduced to total humiliation and begged, "Go away, Jenny, *please!*"

Jenny turned woeful eyes on the object of her affection and saw his utter distress. Hurting as much for herself as for him, she released her apronful of flowers and went running blindly toward the buckboard leading the wagons.

"Poor Jenny," Marlette said. "She wears her heart on her sleeve, and Cam breaks it for her every time she tries to get close to him."

"Give them both a couple of years, and I'll bet it'll be a different story."

Marlette smiled up at him. "Are those words of wisdom?"

He smiled back. "They should be. I did the very same thing to Spotted Fawn, only she was the one who was older and so much wiser than I."

She stopped and looked up at him with eyes so full of love his heart missed a beat. "And you, my love, were so much wiser than I," she whispered.

They camped early that evening on a flower-crowded prairie of new grass, within sight of a blacksmith shop and two farm houses. Other wagons were already encamped, and they set up their camp a short distance away. Jennifer discovered wild strawberries amidst the flowers, and the three older women soon joined her to pick the succulent fruit. Ross and John left them to their happy task and walked to their neighboring wagons.

A large man with thinning blond hair and ready smile offered his hand to John. "Hello, friend. I'm Daniel Heely. I think I remember seeing you back in Independence."

John took the hand and smiled. "I think you're right. I'm John Jessup, and this is Ross Chesnut. He's come from Oregon and is taking his wife back there."

Heely's friendly smile grew. "Glad to meet you. I'm traveling with Jacob Yetter, here, and Mr. Alfred just joined us this morning. We're headed out to Indian Creek. We heard there's a company forming out there. Be glad to have you join us."

Heely's sincerity and friendliness put Ross at ease, and he would have readily accepted the invitation, but Heely's companion, Yetter, his dour face never once smiling, greeted him with only a short handshake and a curt nod. Alfred's disposition was somewhere between the other two and seemed agreeable enough. As they talked, Ross observed their equipment and families. Yetter and Heely each had two wagons, and Ross counted more than enough oxen, cattle, and horses to see them through to the end of the trip. Yetter had a son old enough to help, and two younger children. Heely had a daughter about Joseph's age, a son a year or so younger, and four still younger children. Alfred, with one wagon, had four youngsters and was not quite as well outfitted as the other two men, but among these three families there were an additional number of hired men to help move the stock and drive the wagons.

Their women called them for supper, and Ross and John returned to their own camp, where their women were busy preparing the evening meal. Supper was served as the sun set, and the men from the adjoining camp arrived with what Ross knew would be the inevitable questions about Oregon and the trail.

The abrupt and unpersonable Yetter asked, without waiting for Ross to finish eating, "How many times you been over the trail to Oregon?"

Ross answered between mouthfuls. "Twice."

"That hardly makes you an authority on the trail, does it?"

Ross's feeling of uneasiness about Yetter became dislike. He answered just as curtly, "I didn't say I was an authority, did I?"

Heely laughed and asserted himself good-naturedly. "Come now, Jacob, I'm sure Mr. Chesnut knows more about the trail than we do, no matter how few times he's been on it. We need assurances on whether we can get there or not with all our equipment and stock, and what we can expect when we get to the Willamette Valley. Is it really a paradise? Can the soil grow anything that's planted in it? Is it true the Indians won't be a problem there? And how about the Hudson's Bay Company? Will they sell to us or try to make it hard on us?"

"You look like you're well enough equipped and have enough teams and stock. Mr. Yetter's wagons might be a problem on the trail, more so than the others because they're heavier, and a heavier wagon is harder to move through sand, mud, and streams. Whether you'll make it or not, I can't say. A lot depends on conditions—weather, game, water, how much food you've got, or whether you can afford to reprovision at the forts. And whether

22

you can afford the rafting of your equipment down the Columbia from the Dalles.

"You'll be arriving in Oregon at the beginning of the rainy season. If you've got money, you can buy from either the Methodist Mission or Hudson's Bay. The first thing you'll need is shelter. The weather doesn't get as cold as it gets in the mountains or on the plains, but because it rains so much, you can't work the ground or travel much until spring. The soil is fertile and will grow most things without too much trouble. The Indians are not as hostile as some along the trail, and there aren't many left in the valley, but they will steal anything they can. They won't be much of a problem."

Heely stood up. "Thank you, Mr. Chesnut. You have given us more than adequate assurance that it is possible to get to Oregon." He pulled out his pocket watch with deliberation and peered at it in the flickering light. "Well, it's time we got turned in. How about it, friends? Tomorrow is another day."

Alfred rose without hesitation, and Yetter followed more slowly. Alfred said, "Appreciate your talking to us, Chesnut. Good night."

Heely said, "See you tomorrow. Good night."

Yetter stalked off into the darkness without a word, and his companions followed. Silence reigned for several long moments as John and Ross filled their pipes. Marlette, finished storing away their cooking pots and tinware, came to sit beside Ross. He put his arm around her and held her close, feeling content. Yetter was forgotten as Ross listened to the muffled thud and crunch of their stock grazing a little ways away and the other night sounds of insects and birds. In the darkness along the road, he heard another sound, separate and distinct from the normal night sounds. A wagon approached.

John heard it, too, and remarked, "Sounds like a late traveler coming in."

Ross tapped out his pipe and rose, moving away from the light of the fire by instinct as he heard the wagon leave the road and move toward their fire. John lit the lantern and came after him just as the wagon stopped a few yards away and a man's voice called, "Hello, the fire. Is it all right if we join you?"

John answered, "Come on up."

The wagon rolled closer, and John held the lantern high. Even

23

in the poor light, Ross could see these people weren't outfitted as most of the emigrants were. Their wagon was even lighter than John's converted farm wagon and pulled by a team of mules. A slender, bearded man swung down from the seat. His wife remained seated and pulled her shawl around her, looking small and frightened.

"Thank you. My name's James—Adam James—and this is my wife, Sarah. Our daughter's asleep in the wagon. Are you sure we aren't imposing on you?"

John answered, "Not at all, Mr. James. This is Ross Chesnut and his wife Marlette, and I'm John Jessup, and this is my wife, Liz. We're bound for Oregon."

James stuck out his hand with a ready smile. Ross liked his honest, open manner and the sincerity of his handshake, but the impression that James was too poorly equipped and supplied to make it to Oregon without a great deal of help made him want to discourage their association, sensing the additional responsibility these people would cause him.

James smiled at Ross and said, "You don't look like an emigrant. Are you a guide?"

"No. At least not for a wagon train, but I am from Oregon."

"Then I feel fortunate in being in your company. Where can I put my mules, and what would you like us to do to help out?"

John offered, "We can put your mules with our stock or stake 'em out, whichever you want. Outside of that, there's nothin' to do but get you set up for the night. You got a tent that needs put up?"

"No. We're sleeping in the wagon. Now I don't want to be a bother. It's late and you were on your way to bed. We'll get along just fine."

He turned to unhitch his team, and Ross and John moved to help him. Marlette walked to the side of the wagon and said, "Why not come join us at the fire, Mrs. James? The air's so damp from all the rain."

Sarah James shyly left the safety of the wagon seat, and as she walked toward the fire with Marlette she asked, "Are you from Oregon, too, Mrs. Chesnut?"

"No. I did meet my husband there when I went west with my father several years ago. I had to return east, but now I'm going to Oregon to live with my husband."

24

"Then you know what it is like there. I have so many questions. We know so little about Oregon."

John chuckled, and Ross smiled. He knew what John was thinking.

Adam apparently realized it, too, and said, "I bet you've already been pestered to death with questions."

Ross nodded. "I can answer a few more."

He saw the flash of teeth in the dark beard. "Then I guess my main question would be, can we make it?"

"I'll have to be honest with you, Mr. James. From what I see of your outfit, I wouldn't advise you to attempt it. You should have another team, unless you've got money to buy animals ahead."

Adam shook his head sadly. "I'm afraid not."

"How are you fixed with supplies?"

"Not much better than animals. I planned on living off the land as much as possible."

"The best thing you could do is go back home and wait until you can outfit better. It's a rough trip, even when you've got everything you need."

"That's not possible. Our place burned and we lost everything. We've got to go ahead. There's nothing left behind."

Ross sighed inwardly as the mantle of responsibility settled on his shoulders a little heavier. He wanted to deny it, even refuse it, but he could not. He looked at John and saw John's eyes narrow with expectancy. Ross said, "We're pretty well provisioned, and I plan on bringing in enough meat so we should be able to stretch what we've got to get you through."

John added sincerely, "That includes me, too, Mr. James."

Adam James smiled again with relief and warmth, and his voice had the vibrancy of tears in it as he said, "You are true Samaritans. I'll be beholden to you and try not to be a burden."

Everyone was up early the next morning and eager to get on the trail. While the rest took down the tents and packed, Ross cut and loaded wood into Marlette's wagon.

Marlette watched him as she packed and asked, "Do you think we'll need that?"

"Yes. We'll soon be on the prairie, and wood is sometimes hard to find."

She shrugged as if she didn't quite believe him and went back to

25

her packing, leaving him to his wood-cutting. Heely, Yetter, and Alfred came up.

"Good morning," the jovial Heely called. "Do you think we'll need that wood, Mr. Chesnut?"

Ross straightened and smiled. "I'd count on it."

Daniel Heely laughed, and a skeptical smile crossed Alfred's face.

John came to join them, and Heely said, "Look's like you've added a wagon since last night."

John answered, "We sure enough did." He turned and called to Adam James, who was bringing in his team, "Adam, I'd like you to meet some other people travelin' west."

Adam tied his mules and came forward with a ready smile. John introduced him, and Ross saw Yetter appraise James with narrowed eyes, just as he had appraised Ross and John.

As they shook hands, Yetter asked, "Is that your wagon there, James?" He pointed to the James wagon.

James answered, "Yes."

"You're travelin' kind of light for such a long trip. Where you from anyway?"

The smile left Adam's face. He answered quietly, "Illinois."

Yetter's eyes narrowed even more, and his voice was tinged with malice from the silent and insidious conclusion he had already drawn as he asked, "From around Nauvoo, maybe?"

Before James could answer, Ross interjected, "Just what are you getting at, Mr. Yetter?"

"What I'm getting at is that these people could be Mormons by the look of 'em. If you've ever been in the same county with 'em like I have, you'd know they're a scourge, and I don't aim to let 'em travel in my company."

Ross saw Adam's mouth grow tight. Mrs. James was standing within hearing, and Ross could see the look of distress come into her eyes. Their little girl ran to her mother with a look of stark terror on her face.

Ross quickly cautioned before James could speak. "You don't have to answer him. We weren't traveling with you, Yetter, and we're still not."

Yetter turned on his heel, leaving Heely and Alfred in embarrassed silence. With an apologetic smile, Heely said, "I'm sorry about that, Mr. James. If you want me to say something to him, I will.''

James shook his head with a thin smile. "No. Thank you, Mr. Heely.''

Still embarrassed, Heely and a perplexed Alfred turned away.

When they were out of hearing, James said, "Thank you for defending me, Mr. Chesnut. I'm sorry this happened. If you want me to stay here while you go on with them, it's all right. I don't want to cause you any trouble.''

John spoke up. "You won't cause trouble with us, Adam. Can't you tell you're with a couple of rebels already?''

James smiled, and the white tightness around his mouth disappeared. "Thanks for that. I wouldn't give Yetter the satisfaction of knowing this, but I'm not a Mormon. I had a store in their area and traded with them. The 'good Christians' around there didn't like it and burned me out. What you see here is all I had left and all I could afford.''

John and Ross looked at each other, then at the Yetter wagons, which were just pulling out alone. John shrugged and returned to his wagon, and Ross finished loading his sizable stack of wood before fastening Marlette's coop of chickens precariously on top.

At last they were ready to pull out, and as they moved so did the Heely and Alfred wagons. In a matter of minutes the women were all walking and talking together. The younger children and dogs scampered over the flower-filled prairie, stooping to pick the ripe berries hiding in the green grass that seemed to grow before their eyes.

Ross was alone with Cam, and it pleased him, but the oxen were still being difficult in their new routine and Cam had his hands full for the first mile, keeping them working together. When Ross thought they had settled down and he had observed Cam's technique enough so he felt he could handle the job, he asked, "How about teaching me how to drive them?''

Cam grinned enthusiastically and handed Ross the whip and goad. It was the first time he had had time alone with Cam, and once he felt in complete control of the oxen, he wanted to ask Cam the questions that had been foremost in his mind since they had met.

Before he could speak, Cam exclaimed, "Hey! I think you've

got the hang of it. Do you want me to stay with you, or is there something else you want me to do?''

"I've been wanting to ask you about my mother and father, and this is the first chance we've had to be alone. Can you tell me about them?''

Cam's face lit in a smile. "Yes. But I don't know very much, really, just what I overheard. My grandmother was married to your father's oldest brother, Sean. Your father's name was Ross, too. Did you know that?''

"Yes, my mother told me.''

"Your mother's name was Abigail and she was a Whitteker, daughter of the richest man in our town. He owned the bank and the biggest, fanciest house in town. I don't know how they met, but they eloped and married against both the families' wishes. Your mother's father kept your mother locked up for months when they got back after being married, and your father wasn't allowed to go into town or the constable would put him in jail. My family is Catholic, and your mother wasn't. Uncle Ross wouldn't give her up, and finally they were able to escape and run away. I heard there was a reward out for them for a while, and the church excommunicated him because he wasn't married in the church and was living in sin. The family wouldn't talk about him, and I didn't know about him until I was old enough to understand what I had overheard at different times.

"When Marlette came to visit my father and grandmother, she told me about you. I couldn't understand why you should be blamed for something you had nothing to do with. That's when I began to ask a lot of questions and was forbidden to speak of your father and mother, or you. I felt that was wrong. I wanted to find you, to let you know someone cared that you were part of our family.'' He gave Ross a shy look. "I'm glad I did.''

Ross smiled at him. "I'm glad you did, too. Now tell me about your family. What are they like? Where do they come from?''

Cam grinned and went on. "They told me my great-grandfather came to America from Ireland as a bondsman and worked for several years until he could send for his wife and my grandfather and your father. When they got here, they lived in New York at first where my great-grandfather worked on the docks. Grandfather used to say that his mother insisted they get educated and that she sent him to school. He didn't go too long before he was old enough to work, but your father was younger and must have gone to school longer. Then the government stopped shipping, and they had no more work and moved to upstate New York and bought the farm where I grew up.''

"Then my father was a farmer?"

"As far as I know, he farmed until he ran away with your mother.''

"What about my mother? Did she have sisters or brothers?"

"I don't think so. There isn't anyone living around Riverwood with that name anyway. I never heard anyone else mentioned but your mother and Mr. and Mrs. Whitteker.''

Ross was silent, trying to absorb all he was learning.

"What was your mother like?" Cam asked. "Do you remember much about her?"

"Yes. She lived until I was almost as old as you. I remember one time when I was old enough to ask her why she was teaching me the ways of her people and she told me about my father. I wanted to know what she had looked like before she had taken the Indian dress, and she said she would show me. I remember how beautiful she was when all the paint and grease was washed from her skin and hair. She was very fair, with hair the color of the sun. I think she must have been a teacher. Do you know?"

"No. I never heard.''

"Now I'm sorry I didn't get to Philadelphia. I would've liked to have seen your family and my father's home.''

Cam was silent now; Ross tried to read what was in his eyes and saw a fleeting sadness. With a visible effort, Cam threw off the pang of homesickness and said, with a return of enthusiasm, "Do you think I can learn all the things you know about hunting and shooting and everything?"

Ross smiled at him and answered, "You can try. I'll help you all I can.''

The brilliant grin told Ross more than words that the boy wanted nothing more in the world. "Cam, I want to try to explain something to you. I think I can understand why you came with Marlette. My life seems to be everything that your own was not, and you find it exciting to think of doing what you have never had the chance to do. But understand this. My life has been harsh and lonely. I saw my mother suffer and wanted to take her back to her people, but I wasn't old enough to do so before she died. I married

29

an Indian woman when I was your age, and she died in childbirth within a year. I have killed and it has sickened me, and I've come close to being killed. My body is scarred and my head sometimes hurts from the last time I was almost beaten to death. I've suffered cold and hunger and fear. I am not a hero, and I don't want you to make me out to be one. I have not survived because I was better than anyone else. Call it luck or call it the will of the Great Spirit, if you will, but it's not because I am someone special. I was taught all the skills to survive. I can give you the same knowledge, but there are times you have to have something more. I have always had that something more, and I have not yet found the answer why. I was given a vision and my life seems to be lived to fulfill it, but I have no explanation beyond that. Do you understand what I'm trying to say?''

"I think so. In other words,'' he paused and smiled at Ross, "if you turn out to be only a man, you don't want me to be disappointed.''

Ross looked at the boy with pride. He had struggled to find the right words, but Cam had said it so much better than he had. "That's right!'' He had to laugh, and Cam joined him. They looked at each other with new understanding, and Ross reached out to put an approving hand on the younger man's shoulder.

Marlette was finally tired of walking and came back to the wagon. It was time for Cam to take a turn at driving the herd of stock straggling along behind, and Ross helped Marlette into the wagon and climbed in beside her. Martha was already riding with Liz in the buckboard, so they were alone.

"Are you enjoying yourself?'' Ross asked.

"Yes. I can't see what you are so worried about. The prairie is beautiful. Is it like this where you lived?''

"Yes. What do you think of our traveling companions?''

"They seem like nice people, but I feel so sorry for Mrs. James. She is so quiet and they have so little to get by on. I doubt they can afford to buy anything extra. I'm worried they won't make it on what they have.''

"You're right. They don't have enough. They'll be out of food before they reach Fort Laramie.''

"Is there anything we can do?''

"If they stay with us, I'll make sure they don't go hungry.'' The pressure of her hand on his told him she approved. He continued, "And what about the Jessups? You've traveled with them long enough to know what they have."

"Yes. I've had to help them. We were so late getting started and were afraid we'd get to Independence too late to make it to Oregon this year. We talked of going overland part of the way, but instead I helped pay for their passage on a steamboat so we would be sure to make it in time to leave this year. They have money left to help them get established once we get to Oregon and for supplies along the way, but they wouldn't have without my help."

"What else do you know about them? How did you meet them?"

"Didn't you find out anything all the time you've been with John?"

He smiled as he realized he hadn't. "No. We were too busy working and talking about the trip."

She shook her head at him in mock forbearance. "How is it possible for two men to spend days together and learn so little?"

He grinned and shrugged. "We had more important things to talk about."

She sighed and shook her head again. "I met them in Pittsburgh. They arrived about the same time we did, and they were looking to hire a flat boat to bring them down the Ohio like we were. I liked them and decided to travel with them and share expenses. They are from Virginia and had quite a large farm there."

"And what made them leave and want to come west?"

"John is against slavery and had no slaves on his land, and it became difficult for him to compete with the slave owners, who produced so much more at so much less than he could. It was a choice of moving out or losing everything. He chose to move to Oregon."

They rode in silence for a while, the oxen plodding along, needing only a few flicks of the whip now and then to keep them moving. Marlette seemed to be drinking in the limitless expanse of prairie, turned white with a blizzard of daisies that completely overwhelmed the rich green and softer pastels of the other spring flowers. At last she asked, "Did you get to talk to Cam this morning?"

"Yes."

"Did he fill in a lot of missing links to your past?"

31

"A few, but there is still so much more I'd like to know. Now I'm sorry I didn't get back to where you lived."

"I'm sorry, too. But what do you think of Cam?"

He smiled at her. "Every day I am prouder of him. I have to keep reminding myself he is not my son, but it is difficult not to want him to be my son. The same blood is in our veins, and looking at him is to see myself—and yet, I know another man is his father and I can't ever take his father's place."

"Don't be too sure of that. You will be much more to him than his father because you will try to understand him and be his friend. I doubt his father ever would have."

"I hope you are right."

She smiled, and her eyes flashed with that peculiar woman's wisdom he would never understand. "I know I am."

It was time for the noon stop, and Heely was turning his team off the road. They all followed and made a small circle in the luxuriant grass, then released the oxen from the wagons to graze. Ahead of them, a quarter of a mile away, they saw the Yetter wagons.

John came back to Marlette's wagon and said with a smile, "This morning I thought you were makin' unnecessary work, but now I'm glad you did. There's not a stick of wood in miles."

Ross scraped a small area clear of grass, and they soon had a fire going. Heely brought his coffeepot and set it close to the fire.

"Say, Chesnut, I'm beginning to think you ought to be the brains of this outfit. None of the rest of us was smart enough to think of packin' our own wood."

John agreed. "I think you're right, Dan'l. I'll nominate him if you'll second the motion."

Heely chuckled jovially. "You bet."

"Not so fast. I'm not sure I want the responsibility of leading all of you."

Heely laughed and said, "I don't think I blame you for that. But I still think it's a good idea. Most likely, though, anyone we join will already have a captain all picked out and you'll be safe."

The women came with their bread and meat, and all conversation ended as hungry movers made quick work of what was set out for them.

They were just preparing to move on when a small party of Indians came into view and stopped by the Yetter wagons. Ross, with mixed emotions about the Yetters, urged them to hurry their departure, feeling a prickle of warning as he rode ahead to make sure Yetter didn't do something foolish and jeopardize his family.

A shot rang out, and Ross spurred his horse forward. He pulled his rifle as the Indians scattered, and the Yetter wagons lurched forward with one Indian still clinging precariously to the provision barrel fastened to the side of one of the wagons. The Indian fell and screamed in agony as the wagon wheel rolled over his leg. The rest of the Indians immediately ran whooping after the wagons. Ross raised his rifle and fired a shot over their heads. They paused in their murderous intent and turned toward him, suddenly docile once they knew help was coming for the object of their harassment.

Ross rode by the Indian writhing on the ground, seeing a dark face twisted with pain, before he caught up with the wagons. Yetter stopped lashing his oxen when he saw Ross, and stood glaring at the handful of Indians looking back with hostile eyes.

"What happened, Yetter?"

"You need to ask? You got eyes! They were trying to rob me!"

Ross looked back at the Indians who still stood uncertain and were apparently oblivious to the moans of their injured companion. "You have anything we can use to set his leg? It's broken."

"To hell with him. I'm movin' on." Yetter turned back to his team and, with whip and goad, urged them quickly forward.

Ross watched him go, keeping his rifle pointed casually toward the Indians. They stood without movement, waiting—dirty, pitifully clothed, and underfed. He was at once disgusted and sorry for them, but showed nothing as he waited for his own party to come up.

John rode up first and asked, "What happened? What can I do?"

"Keep our wagons back and tell the women not to get down, and have the boys stand guard. Get Heely and Alfred up here with their guns to watch the Indians, and have James bring two of the straightest limbs he can find out of that wood in Marlette's wagon. I'll need your help and his to set his leg."

Without further questions, John went hurriedly to do as Ross asked, and Ross's estimation of the man doubled. Heely and Alfred came shortly with their guns and appraised the scene quietly. John and Adam came in another minute or so with the sticks Ross needed, and Ross joined them beside the profusely sweating Indian, who looked with unguarded terror at them through pained eyes.

John shook his head. "I don't know. Do you think we can help him?"

"He'll die if we don't."

Alfred spoke up. "What's the use? He was trying to rob Yetter, wasn't he?"

"For good will. Not only for us, but for anyone following us. Adam, I'll need something to tie these on with. Have Marlette give you some cloth."

James turned back to the wagon, and Ross tried to speak to the injured Indian and his companions, but they didn't understand any of the dialects he knew. He then used sign language, and this brought anxious consultation among them. The man on the ground understood them and, like a caged animal, tried to drag himself away, but the pain was too much for him and he groaned and fainted. Ross was beside him immediately, his job made easier by the man's unconsciousness.

John squatted beside him and asked, "What do you want me to do?"

"Help me turn him on his back, and then hold him down while I pull his leg straight."

James came back with rags and immediately went down on his knees beside the Indian, helping to hold him as Ross made sure the bone in his leg was lined up. Using his knife, he quickly shaped the sticks to fit the thin leg and bound the sticks tightly to hold it rigid.

Ross stood and signed to the watching Indians to remove their companion from the road, but they were afraid and made no move toward him, believing he was dead. Ross gave up and motioned the wagons forward, waiting for them to pass before he abandoned the unconscious Indian and his silent friends. He had done all he could.

By late afternoon they reached the large encampment of wagons at Indian Creek. It was a cheerfully noisy camp scattered along the timbered creek bank, with the smoke of many campfires rising through the trees. The shouts of children and barking of dogs were distinct over the bawl of cattle on the surrounding prairie. The laughter of men and women gave the gathering the air of a Sunday camp meeting. Ross and John followed the Heelys and the Alfreds along the wood's edge until they found an uninhabited area close to the creek. Yetter's wagons were there, and they were setting up camp. Alfred and Heely pulled within a few yards of them, and Heely greeted Yetter as if nothing had happened. John urged his oxen farther away from Heely and Alfred, and Ross went beyond where John stopped as Adam tactfully pulled in on the other side of Ross, leaving a wide space between the two camps.

Before camp was set up, a group of men came to visit the newcomers. Their leader, a tall, large man, expansive of gesture and voice, greeted them.

"Welcome, gentlemen and ladies. William Henry Russell at your service. Where you bound for?"

John held out his hand and answered, "John Jessup and my wife, Liz, and this is Ross Chesnut and his wife and Mrs. Yates, Mr. and Mrs. James, and our children. We're bound for Oregon."

John's hand was well shaken, and then Ross's was gripped powerfully and pumped with enthusiasm. "Glad to know you, gentlemen"—he finished shaking Adam's hand and made a sweeping bow to the women—"and ladies. Meet here the honorable Lilliburn Boggs, ex-governor of Missouri, and Edwin Bryant, late of Louisville, Kentucky. Mr. Chesnut, I notice by your outfit you appear to be from the mountains. Am I correct, sir?"

"I'm from the Oregon country."

The affable grin grew broader. "This is indeed fortunate for us. You're just in time, if you are wishing to join us. Tomorrow we start voting for a captain and the few trail laws for those who wish to travel with us. You are most certainly invited to attend, and I'm sure we can benefit from your knowledge of the trail ahead."

Ross offered, with a feeling of reservation, "I'd be glad to help in any way I can."

"Excellent, excellent! There are quite a number here going on to Oregon, and your services would be invaluable."

Boggs added, with a smile, "Colonel Russell is right, Mr. Chesnut. We're glad to have you. I'm going on to Oregon myself."

Bryant, who had been silent until now, said, "Perhaps we could get Mr. Chesnut to scout for us?"

Russell approved heartily. "Excellent idea, Mr. Bryant, but perhaps we are imposing on Mr. Chesnut too much."

"No," answered Ross. "If you need a scout, I am available."

"But what about your wagon, sir? Do you have someone to drive it?"

"Yes."

John added, "No worry there, Colonel Russell. I have three nearly grown boys, and Ross has a cousin's boy with him."

Russell grabbed Ross's hand and held it fiercely. "Your help will be most appreciated, sir. Now I will leave you to your camp makin'. We will look forward to seeing you in the morning."

John looked overwhelmed. "Well, what do you make of that?"

Martha answered, "A lot of wind."

John smiled and said, "I bet anything he's got his name in the hat to be elected tomorrow."

Adam agreed, "You're probably right. He and Boggs are both politicians."

Ross questioned, "But none of these men know what is ahead. How can they lead the train?"

John laughed. "You've hit the nail on the head exactly! That is what politicking is all about. And that is why they asked you to be scout—because they know nothing about it."

Adam laughed, too. "I agree with John. The men who know what they're doing are too smart to want the job."

John placed a friendly hand on Ross's shoulder. "You've got a lot to learn, Ross, and tomorrow you'll likely learn more than you want to know."

Early the next morning, the men gathered to choose their leader. The chairman asked for order, and the voting proceeded between Russell and Boggs. Russell was elected by a large majority and pushed through the cheering crowd to the front.

Stretching to his full and imposing height, he accepted the office of captain with a flourish. "Thank you, my friends. I deem it an honor to be allowed to be your leader. I will do all in my power to see you safely through to Oregon and California, and I will vow before God that the laws enacted by you will be carried out promptly and fairly."

Cheers went up again, and Bryant waved them down as Russell stood basking in the glory of his election. The next order of business was to form a committee to draft laws for the company; ex-Governor Boggs was made chairman. As soon as a committee was approved, the meeting was adjourned until after noon.

At two o'clock the meeting resumed to hear the laws drafted by the committee. Discussions were held, and motions and counter-motions made, until the majority of men agreed with the bylaws. Ross had remained silent throughout the noisy proceedings, his dismay at what was important to these people almost moving him to speak out. He could barely control his laughter when they included indecent language in the list of minor offenses that were punishable by fines, along with falling asleep on guard duty or leaving an assigned post without permission, which would have brought a good deal more than a fine if they had been traveling with the trappers' caravans. Their laws were adequate as far as they went, but they completely neglected to incorporate the disciplined travel he felt necessary to keep them from falling far behind on what he felt should have been a mandatory traveling schedule.

After noon the next day, they circled close to seventy wagons a few miles farther along the creek to make a corral for a portion of the nearly thousand head of stock owned by about three hundred men, women, and children. Another meeting was held, and the company was divided into four divisions, with a leader and assistants appointed for each section. Ross felt that they were at least beginning to act organized. Guard shifts were established, and they were all assigned herd duty and guard duty.

The next day travel was resumed over the undulating prairie. They reached the junction of the Santa Fe and Oregon Trails, and the carefree travelers stopped to rejoice at finally reaching this weathered board with its cryptic lettering, ROAD TO ORE-GON. It made no difference that many of them had traveled hundreds of miles already to get here. Here was where the real journey began. From now on they would be venturing into the West—that vast unknown and almost unmapped wilderness. Bottles were brought out and toasts made, everyone's faces full of the wonder and excitement of the adventure ahead.

Ross thought it was even more prophetic that in the midst of the celebration a sudden rain shower hit them. The deluge brought a quick end to the celebration, and the wagons continued on the Santa Fe Trail for a few miles before turning northwest.

As quickly as the rain had come, it stopped, but the traveling was considerably slower, and when they reached a creek with steep, high banks, enthusiasm seemed to wane. As soon as the wagons were crossed, they camped in a small grove of trees, wet and tired, with another shower hitting them before all the tents were up.

It was Ross's turn for guard duty. He mounted his horse when he finished eating, just escaping more visitors with their guidebooks to Oregon, asking him their interminable questions.

By the time his shift was over, the steadily falling rain had soaked him to the skin and chilled him to the bone. He unsaddled and tethered his horse before seeking the shelter of Marlette's tent, where he quietly and quickly peeled off his wet buckskins and dried himself as best he could before crawling under the blankets. Marlette stirred and turned to curl against him. The touch of his cold body brought her instantly awake, and she gasped. He wrapped his arms around her, laughing, and held her while she squirmed to move away from his chilling flesh.

"Ross," she cried, "you're cold and wet!"

He pulled her closer and buried his face in her soft, struggling warmth. "Now I know what I needed to keep me warm last winter." He kissed her, and slowly warmth returned.

She lay still and was silent for a moment before she asked, "Where did you spend the winter? You didn't come across the mountains in winter, did you?"

He kissed her shoulder and answered, "No. I started east last summer. I spent the winter with my brother."

She turned in his arms. "You mean with the Indians?"

"Yes."

"How were your brother and sister?"

"Well. They both have families now."

"Did your brother become chief?"

"Yes. And my bitterest rival is war chief."

"Your rival? You never told me about him."

"He was called Big Tree and was the tallest and strongest of the young men. He was also in love with Spotted Fawn and felt he should be chief of our band. If it hadn't been for him, I wouldn't be here now."

"Then he couldn't have been too bitter a rival. I'd like to thank him for whatever it was he did."

Ross smiled at the memory. "He wasn't trying to help me. He'd have killed me if he'd thought I wasn't going to suffer worse alive."

"Because of Spotted Fawn?"

"Yes. After she died, I purposely went with Big Tree on a hunt and tried to get him to kill me. He refused, but if I ever become a threat to him again, he would kill me without thinking twice."

She shuddered. "How awful." Burying her face against his neck, she whispered, "How little I know about your life. The more you tell me, the more frightened I am by it."

He stroked her smooth, silken hair. "Then I won't tell you any more."

"No. I want to know, but it is so violent—so tragic that it is hard to believe it's your life. I have seen you handle violence and death, and yet you are so gentle, so full of compassion. I don't understand it, but I love what it has made you."

Their lips touched. Their bodies touched, clung and melded together. Ross was cold no longer.

3. The Prairie

THEIR FIFTH MORNING on the trail dawned pleasantly, and the movers were up early, anxious to get to the Kansas River and cross it before dark. Captain Russell sent several men upriver to see if there was a ford within easy reach of the train. Leaving instructions with the company to get the wagons across the creek, Russell left the train to ride to the ferry crossing a few miles away and ascertain if it could transport them, should it be necessary.

By eight o'clock clouds had covered the sky, and rain began to fall. Thunder was heard in the distance. The banks of the creek were steep. Sweating and cursing men labored in the downpour to get the wagons across, breaking one wagon's axletree in the process.

Captain Russell arrived as the last wagons were crossing and was immediately engaged in discussion with the Reverend Mr. Dunleavy. After a lengthy conversation, it was decided that those who wished to remain with Captain Russell would move on to the ferry on the Kansas River. Those who didn't could stay with Dunleavy's group. There was no hesitation on Ross's part in determining to go on. John agreed that to delay was not in their best interests, so they joined the wagons rolling toward the Kansas River.

They arrived at the ferry crossing on the Kansas River near noon. Their arrival attracted the Kansas Indians, whose villages were not far from the river. They were just as impoverished as the other Indians they had encountered thus far, and Ross despaired at their poor and vermin-infested appearance. Once they had been a proud nation, but their pride had prevented them from adopting the white man's proclivity for work. The white man had encroached upon their lands and corrupted their culture, and now indolence made it easier to beg and steal than to hunt.

The sight of the ferry distressed the movers even more. It was nothing more than two waterlogged flatboats fastened together with planks and operated by two half-breed Indians. But the ferrying went smoothly, and before the afternoon was over another group of emigrants caught up with them. A vote was taken by the company to allow these new people to join; nine wagons belonging to three large families were added to the company. The families were the Reeds, the brothers Jacob and George Donner, and the Patrick Breen family and Breen's friend Patrick Dolan. The Donner men were older than most of the men moving west but seemed far more able to stand the trip than the Thorntons, who had joined the train with Governor Boggs's family and spent a good deal of time languishing in the wagon with some strange and debilitating illness.

By evening everyone was feeling in a festive mood, and the weather was clear and mild. It was time for music and dancing. This was the first time Ross had danced since Marlette had danced with him in Jacques's cabin so many winters ago. He quickly remembered the steps, and her eyes were just as bright as he remembered them being then.

Morning brought another leisurely start, prolonged as usual by the search for strayed stock. They traveled all day over the rolling prairie avoiding the low spots that were still boggy from the rain.

The next day they traveled only a short distance before they had to ford a steep-banked creek. The wagons had to be unhitched here and lowered with ropes, then double-teamed to get them through the creek and up the opposite bank. Clouds, like vast palls of smoke green-edged with dark, murky bodies, rolled in before the chore was finished, and distant thunder was heard. A strong wind rose suddenly, flattening the grass and hurling leaves and twigs everywhere. Flash after flash of lightning rent the sky in rapid succession as torrential rain fell, soaking men and beasts as the men struggled to get wagons up the muddy and slippery bank.

At last the thunder receded into the east, and a watery sun created a fragmented rainbow in the sky, delighting the children and relieving the men. They camped on the creek bank after all the wagons were over. No sooner had camp been set up than new wagons arrived on the opposite bank and the weary men had to repeat the exhausting chore of helping them cross.

* * *

41

The weary group pushed on the next day and camped again in the evening, this time not far from two Shawnee Indian villages near Sandy Creek. There were plenty of large oaks to be used for firewood but, except for those along the stream, few other trees grew here. Indians came from the villages, some better dressed and still possessing dignity, but others nothing more than dirty beggars. All had the common desire to trade for food, whiskey, or whatever caught their eye in fascination. One Indian offered the frail Mrs. Thornton all his money for the parasol she carried to protect her fair skin from the burning sun.

The principal chief was a much older man, but still a commanding figure, wearing a turban and what had once been a vividly colored dressing gown over his buckskin leggings and moccasins. This chief promised Russell there would be no stealing, but Russell wisely doubled the guard that night.

Long after dark, when most of the travelers were in bed, gunshots were heard from one of the villages, and the cry of, "Pawnee! Pawnee!" brought everyone out of their tents. Apparently, some of the younger men had gone into the village, and it was finally concluded the Indians had been trying to scare them. Later still, the guards brought in two Indians who were trying to sneak into camp for a rendezvous to trade a horse for four gallons of whiskey. Nothing more occurred before morning, and the camp was once again thronging with Indians, who were now bribing the emigrants with promises not to steal if they were given food.

The train finally got underway and moved a few miles to a place on the creek where a ford could be made. Once across, they traveled through a high fertile valley bounded on the east by a chain of mound-shaped hills and on the west by groves of trees. The smell of wild roses made the air fragrant, and other wild flowers still bloomed in brilliance in the grass.

At noon they had to cross another creek and lost two more hours getting the large company across. Ross was becoming increasingly dissatisfied as slow miles were made across a prairie broken with sharp gullies that had been water channels in the wet season. When Russell called a halt at a spring early in the afternoon, Ross knew he had to make a decision. Now was the time to separate if they ever hoped to make Oregon before winter set in.

He ate his evening meal in tense silence, knowing what he

should do, but knowing, too, the responsibility it would involve. John sat smoking his pipe and tapping an impatient finger on the arm of his rocker as he watched Ross.

Finally John couldn't stand Ross's silence and said, "Out with it, man. You've had that doomsday look all day. Don't you think it's about time you told the rest of us what's gallin' you?"

Ross set his half-eaten dinner aside and answered, "The same thing that's bothered me since we joined this train is still bothering me. I think it's time to separate. I'm even more sure I don't want the responsibility than I was in Independence, but if we don't separate, I'm afraid we're going to have trouble getting into the valley if they continue to travel this slowly."

"Well, you know I'd gladly do anything you think is best, but I'm even gladder I don't have to make the decision."

"Yes, you do have to make a decision. When we discussed this before, I decided then the only way we could do it was if I did the scouting and you were captain and they followed the orders I'd give you. Do you think you can do that?"

John sat with the pipe clenched between his teeth, his rocking and tapping momentarily still as he pondered Ross's question. After a moment he pulled the pipe from his mouth and said, "But what if no one wants to come with us? And if some do, what if they don't agree to me being captain?"

"I'm not worried about that. Either they agree to you being captain or they don't come with us."

John grinned. "As simple as that, you think?"

Ross smiled. "Yes."

"Of course you can do it, John," said Liz, coming forward eagerly. "I know you can."

John shook his head. "Now, how do you know? I've never done anything that would qualify me for it."

"I know you can do it. You're patient and calm, and with Ross's knowledge of how to do what you need to do, you can handle it. I know you can!"

John chuckled, but Ross saw the desperation in Liz's eyes and wondered why she was so eager to push him into something he wasn't sure he wanted. Finally John acquiesced. "All right, but I'm going to need a lot of help."

Ross rose to his feet. "Do you want to come help me recruit a party?"

They started around the circle of wagons and told each family they intended to separate. Anyone wanting to could join them in the morning at six, but they must be willing to obey the orders of the captain and the rules Ross would present to them when they gathered in the morning. He warned them they would have to all work together under strict discipline or they wouldn't make it before the snow fell in Oregon.

They reached Russell's campfire and, as usual, he had his friends Bryant and Boggs in attendance, as well as James Reed and the Donner brothers. Russell greeted them in the usual hearty manner. "Ah, good evening, gentlemen. How can I be of service to you tonight?"

"We wanted to speak to you about proposing another division of the train. We have almost added as many wagons in the past few days as separated from this company at the Kansas River. We are traveling too slowly and, with so many to cross at the fords, it is taking too long. We are losing an hour or two every morning looking for stray stock. Every mile and every hour we lose makes the chances of all of us getting to Oregon before the snow just that much less. I think it will be to everyone's advantage if I take whoever wants to come with me and separate, provided you will release me from my word to help you."

"Well now, I don't see any problem about releasing you from your word, but I do want to caution you against doing something rash. Unless you can take enough wagons with you, I'm afraid you'll jeopardize those who are willing to go with you."

"If I can take fifteen to twenty wagons, we will be strong enough."

"You have my blessings then, sir, and good luck to you."

Ross took the offered hand and turned to leave with Russell's wishes for good luck ringing in his ears. He would need all the luck he could get now.

At six in the morning, Cam and John pulled their wagons out of the circle. Ross and the boys drove their loose stock behind. The James wagon, along with the Heely, Alfred, and Yetter wagons, pulled out at the same time and followed them. Ross could see others leaving the circle and trailing up behind them.

Ross was soon able to go to the front of the growing caravan as the herd was joined, and he was no longer needed to help drive the stock. He led them for about five miles across rolling prairie dotted with clumps of trees until they came to a clear stream flowing by a spring that gushed from limestone rocks. Here Ross halted his followers and waited for them to gather.

When the last wagon came to a halt and everyone stood waiting, he stepped up on a wagon tongue and addressed his gathering. "I wanted you all to hear what I have to say before we go too far. It is important that we all agree on a plan that will be fair to everyone and will provide all of us with the quickest and safest trip to Oregon. I want it understood from the beginning what is expected of all of you. Any of you who do not wish to do what is required can wait here for Russell. I will be your guide from here to Oregon, and in order to do my job I will have to be ahead of the wagons most of the time. Since Mr. Jessup agrees to what must be done, he will be in charge with me, and we will both need your complete cooperation. First of all, we will need all the men and older boys to take their turn in keeping the stock together. We will need guards all night every night, and the shifts will be divided equally. At night the wagons will be circled close together, and all horses and teams to be used the next day will be tethered in that circle for the night so we don't have to waste time rounding up teams in the morning. The loose stock will not be allowed to wander out of sight of the camp at night.

"Every evening your wagons and equipment are to be inspected and repairs and maintenance taken care of before morning. We will get up before dawn and have breakfast over and teams hitched so we can be ready to roll when it is light, and we will travel until dark, if at all possible. In most places, until we reach Fort Laramie, we will be able to travel in a double line and will rotate the lead position every day.

"Everyone will have a job to do, and those jobs will be changed as the country changes. Getting to Oregon won't be easy, but it'll be less difficult if everyone is willing to do what he is told and do it without question."

There was silence in the gloomy crowd of faces as they weighed Ross's words. The choice would have to be theirs now. He stepped down. The little group scattered to their wagons, and he turned to John. "Well, how many do you think we'll have left?"

"Most of them, I think. A few might leave, but I think Yetter and Daniels will stay and be thorns in your side."

"I was afraid of that."

John laughed, "That's what you get for provin' you knew more about the trail than the rest of 'em."

Ross smiled wryly and said, "Well, while we're waiting, let's get some sort of duty schedule figured out for what we think we'll have."

The hour passed quickly, and when Ross looked up from his laboriously drawn schedule, not one wagon had departed. He gave a half smile to John and said, "Are you ready to lead your train, Captain?"

John's sober face forced a grin. "God, I hope so. I hope I can handle the job you've given me."

Ross smiled back. "You will."

They looked at each other with complete understanding. John stuck out his hand. "Good luck to us both, but especially to you."

Ross took the hand, covering it with both of his in complete respect and trust of the man he had chosen to be captain. "We'll need it."

John turned away and helped Liz into the buckboard. Jenny scrambled up beside her as Ross helped Martha and Marlette into their wagon. She held onto his hand, and he felt the tremble of excitement in her grip.

He kissed the trembling hand and put his other hand on top of it and squeezed it reassuringly. "Don't worry. I'll be back in a little while."

He rode down the line of wagons, getting them into position to cross the creek and giving instructions to the herders. He was now responsible for twenty wagons. Some of these people he knew and some he didn't, but by the time they reached Oregon he would know them all. And they would know him. But first of all, they would know the prairie.

When everyone was across the creek, Ross galloped ahead. He rode to the top of the first undulation and saw nothing ahead of him but a green, rolling, flower-dotted vastness. He felt a strange excitement as he viewed this limitless, windswept, rain-washed prairie he knew all too well. This was the land of his birth and with all the difficulties and hardships they would encounter here, the people he now led would never see it as he did or appreciate it for what it was.

On his way back to the train, he made wide sweeps to either side of the trail looking for any sign of Indians, but found nothing fresh. He met John and the train a few miles from the spring. He pulled up beside him and asked, "How are things going?"

John smiled wryly. "Well, if it's all going to be this easy, I'm going to be sorry we didn't do it sooner. What's up ahead?"

"A good spring for nooning in a few miles. I'd better go back and see if there are any complaints yet."

John chuckled. "You're askin' for it."

The wagons moved on after an hour's rest at the spring. By mid-afternoon a dry, warm wind began to blow and the drying trail grew dusty. Men and animals sweated as the prairie rose imperceptibly higher, and the sun beat down with only a few white clouds crossing the sky. Far off, low knolls lined each side of the horizon and occasional trees marked a water course or gulley.

Late in the afternoon, Ross saw horsemen on one of the distant knolls. These horsemen kept reappearing as the wagons traveled on. They camped an hour before dusk on the Vermillion River, and while camp was being set up, Ross took the opportunity to scout the area in the last light. Finding nothing that would indicate a large party of Indians in the area, he returned to camp after dark. Campfires were lit and he could smell food cooking. The guards were out and the herd was grazing contentedly. Women were busy over their kettles, and he could see men bending over wagon wheels as dogs and children played hide-and-seek around the wagons and between the legs of the grazing oxen in the center of the wagon corral. Somewhere in the circle, a harmonica began a dancing tune and a woman's laughter was heard.

John was smoking his pipe as Ross came up and sat in his chair, cocking his feet up on a log close to the fire. Martha gave him a grudging smile as he sat down, and handed him a plate full of tantalizing food.

"Tried to keep it from burnin' for you."

Ross smiled his appreciation, feeling a small victory gained. "Thank you."

"Fair day, wouldn't you say?" said John, removing the pipe.

Between bites, Ross answered, "Yes. Tomorrow should be just as good, if it doesn't get too warm."

Liz came from her tent and stood behind John, rubbing the aching muscles of her husband's neck and shoulders. Jonathan and Jeremy came in with water and more wood for the fire. Jenny came from somewhere around the circle of wagons, having found a friend her own age to share her dearest secrets with. The boys were ready to leave again when Liz told them, "You boys get washed and to bed. Your shift comes at midnight. And Jenny, I want you to get to bed, too."

John looked up at his wife and asked, "Does that go for me, too?"

She laughed seductively and rumpled his thinning hair. "Yes, that goes for you, too."

Ross, not aching but no less tired, stood with his empty plate and said, "That sounds like a good idea, but has anyone checked our wheels?"

John smiled. "All done, Captain."

Ross handed his plate to Martha with a smile and said, "See you at two, John."

A shot brought the good-humored complacency of the camp to sudden silence. Ross grabbed up his rifle as more shots rang out. Cam came riding in from the herd and pulled to a stop. "The Indians are stealing horses!" he yelled.

There was a frantic scramble of men for their saddle horses tethered inside the wagon circle, and they rode breakneck out to the herd. But it was too late. The first shot had scattered the thieves, and it was too dark to tell if anyone's stock was missing.

In the morning the herd was brought close to the wagons and the stock counted. Two horses and several oxen were missing. A dozen men volunteered to ride into the nearest Indian camp to look for the stolen animals. Ross headed the well-armed group of men toward the Indian camp, seeing the unmistakable signs that the animals they sought had passed ahead of them.

When they arrived at the shabby and nearly deserted village, Ross asked in sign language to see the head man and was taken to an old, half-blind Indian. The old man denied that any horses or oxen had been taken by his people, and Ross knew they would find no sign of the animals. They would have butchered the oxen and disposed of everything they couldn't eat, even if they had to haul it off. But he had to impress the few Indians left in camp that they would not tolerate stealing. Ross forcefully signed that they were going to search the village and they did so, ignoring the old chief's threats, fearing little physical obstruction from these apprehensive Indians.

After a few minutes, Ross gathered his search party together and asked them, "Did any of you find anything?"

There was a shake of heads and frustrated voices answering in the negative.

"I say we kill a few of them off to show them we won't take stealing lightly," said Yetter angrily.

Ross shook his head. "No. There's nothing more to be done. We're losing precious time. We could hunt for days and not find the horses. I wouldn't doubt the oxen have already been killed and eaten. Now let's get back to the wagons and get moving. We'll have to share our stock if it comes to that."

Stubborn faces looked at him, but the sparks of anger did not erupt. He turned his horse away, and they grudgingly followed him back to the wagons.

John had most of the wagons across the Vermillion River, but not without a great deal of effort. This was the biggest stream they had had to cross since the Kansas River. The east bank was very steep and brushy. It took all available men to lower the wagons by ropes into the water and even more effort to get them across the deep and swift current. The extra manpower Ross had with him was badly needed to finish the job. Once across, they were wet and tired, but the sun was shining and dried them. By noon dust was more of an annoyance than the water had been.

Ross made a thorough scout of the area while the last of the wagons were being forded, but he found no fresh sign of Indians on the west side of the river, and the hilltops were empty of observers. He felt confident the Indians would not be back. It would be too dangerous for them and, for a while, they would be satisfied with the meat they had. He rode back to the train with the intention of taking Cam with him for the rest of the day. He was sure there were deer in the thickets along the river, and some catfish had been caught the evening before. It was time Cam's wilderness training started.

Cam was with the herd this morning, riding close to Jeremy as they and the other herders guided the stock after the wagons. When Jeremy heard what Ross had planned for Cam, his initial excitement turned to disappointment as he realized he wasn't being asked to join them. Ross quickly changed his plans to include Jeremy, but they needed two replacements for herd duty. He saw Jenny and the Cadie girl walking together and had an

49

idea. He rode up to them and said, "Jenny, I need to take Cam and Jeremy hunting. Would you and your friend like to herd for them while we're gone?"

Jenny brightened and answered, "Oh, yes! That'd be fun. Don't you think so, Prissy?"

Priscilla Cadie's freckled face smiled with delight at the idea. "Oh, do you think we could?"

Ross smiled back. "I said everyone would have to do their share."

They looked at each other and giggled. Ross said, "I'll have the boys bring you some horses."

In record time, Cam and Jeremy had some horses for the girls to ride and followed Ross away from the train feeling more important, if possible, than the two girls who had replaced them on herd duty.

They rode northward, paralleling the stream's winding course, while Ross kept eyes and ears alert for Indian sign and deer sign. Finally he crossed what looked like a game trail going toward the river and they rode into the belt of trees lining the wide bottom of the river. Before they reached the trees, Ross readied his bow. Motioning the boys to lay along their horses' necks as he was, he led them silently into the trees. Not far from the river they jumped a deer out of a thicket, and Ross shot it with his arrow while the boys looked on in awe.

Then they received their first lesson in preparing a deer. The two boys were eager and learned quickly. In just a few minutes they had the carcass ready to put on a horse and take back to the train. But Ross was enjoying his opportunity to be with Cam and took time to teach them how to catch fish with makeshift lines, just as he had had to do many times. In less than an hour, they had a number of big catfish to take back to the wagons with the deer.

They caught up with the train just before the noon rest, and Ross soon found himself popular among the young men of the train. He realized he would have to take turns taking all the boys with him, and he was pleased they wanted him to share his wilderness expertise with them.

He decided to take Cam alone with him as he scouted that afternoon, and by the time they came to the crossing on the Blue River, where they would make camp for the night, his respect and affection for the boy had doubled. During their ride he had been

50

teacher, friend, and father to Cam and had enjoyed every minute of it. There was so much he wanted to share with the boy.

They reached the river with the wagons at just about the time Ross had thought they would. He ordered the stock kept close until he could make a double check of the area. Taking Jonathan and Joseph with him, he set out in ever-widening circles to check for any Indian sign in the area. They were just returning to the circled wagons, standing out ghostly white against the dark and turbulent sky, when the storm broke, blasting them with wind strong enough to rock the wagons, deafening and blinding them with thunder and lightning. It was a frightening few minutes as women screamed and children cried in terror. Everyone abandoned the wagons, only to be drenched by a downpour of rain. As quickly as it had come, the storm swept past them, leaving a distinctly beautiful rainbow, arched over the trail the wagons had just traveled.

Ross rode out to the herd to be on duty until the rest of the guard finished their half-cooked dinners and changed into dry clothing—if they had any left. There was nothing to indicate that a violent storm had just passed. The night was clear and star-filled, and the air was pure and sweet from the rain. Ross felt more at home than he had at any time since they had left Independence. If he rode straight north, he would be in the land of his birth, the home of his Indian family. He listened to the bark of the coyote and the howl of the wolf over the more immediate sounds of the night-chirping birds and insects. The pleasant memories of his recent visit with his half brother brought on a powerful longing for the less restricted life of his Indian brother. He pulled his eyes away from the invisible vastness of the northern prairie and looked toward the camp, seeing the feeble campfires and ghostly tents. The thought of Marlette waiting for him freed him of the tugging memories.

The herders were coming now from the circle of wagons, so he rode into camp. Marlette huddled over the spitting fire and saw that his supper was warm and ready for him. She was shivering and he told her, "Go on to bed. I'll take care of this."

After eating, he went to sleep but was up again in a few short hours to do his double shift of guard duty. It was getting more difficult to leave the warmth of his bed and pull on the damp buckskins as anxiety and the long hours were beginning to wear on

51

him. Yet the hours spent under the stars, watching the herd, were some of the most enjoyable he spent, except for those with Marlette and Cam. There was little difference in what he did now from what he had done as a youth guarding the horse herds of his Indian band as he strove to become a man and warrior. The prairie was the same: vast and starlit, moving like a sea under the force of the wind, bringing the heavy fragrance of flowers and grass in the freshening hours before dawn.

Suddenly the harsh banging of the fry pan broke into the natural night music of insects and coyotes, and Ross moved with the rest of the herders to gather in the grazing herd. Their reliefs were waiting as they brought the herd close to the wagons, and the smell of coffee and frying bacon made their stomachs churn in hunger. Here and there a whining child's voice could be heard, along with the sharper voices of impatient mothers. Ross had to smile. This, after all, was not much different from the life he remembered.

In the first grim light of dawn, it was all too apparent that the river was rising from the rain of the evening before. With breakfasts half-eaten, Ross ordered everyone to pack up as quickly as possible. While the women hurried to get the wagons packed, the men yoked oxen and herded the loose stock into the river to get them across. There was no time to waterproof wagon boxes. Every minute lost would mean more water to fight in the rapidly rising stream.

No sooner were they across, stationed on high ground to make repairs, than another column of wagons came to the ford. They recognized them as the wagons belonging to the Gordons and the Dickensons, who had separated the day before they had but had been staying close to Russell because of Indians. When they had helped get these wagons safely across, there was a general reunion as the emigrants exchanged hellos, asking news of former trailmates. Some even received letters from those behind and answered those letters with notes of their own left in split sticks beside the trail. Ross didn't let them linger long and moved his wagons out first amid the unhappy glances of the women who had hoped to have a big party.

They traveled onward between the branches of the Blue River. Ross, along with Cam and Jeremy, scouted the brushy river bottoms for game and brought in fresh elk meat for the train to feast on. A thunderstorm during the night rudely awakened the movers, drenching them to the skin. By morning many in the company were coughing and sneezing. Disgruntled, they rolled on over the deceptively smooth-looking prairie, experiencing breakdowns as wagon tongues and wheels broke from lurching across sharp ditches and gullies.

The camp was strangely silent that evening as tired movers went to still-damp beds without the usual evening activities. Ross felt their need to rest and dry out, but he couldn't let them. Not while the trail was good and they were still strong. He knew well enough that this was the first sign of trail weariness setting in. It would get worse.

4. The Pawnee

BEFORE MORNING TWO men on the guard shift with Ross were sick with diarrhea. He knew more would be afflicted in camp, and one of the men didn't come out to replace the night guard. When Ross finally came in for breakfast, John was already facing a distressed group of people. John looked relieved when he came to the fire and took the cup Marlette handed him.

"Several of the people are sick, Ross. They don't want to move on today until they're better."

"We have to keep moving, John. Make them as comfortable as possible and get ready to move out."

Mrs. Grady pleaded, "I can't move. My husband and my boy are both sick, and the baby is awful fussy, too."

"I'll send someone to drive for you."

Daniels was standing nearby and came up to join the group. "Look, Chesnut, what's so damned important about moving today? I say we stay here until our people are feeling better."

"We can't afford to lose any time when the weather and the trail are good. As long as we've got enough people to keep us moving, we have got to move."

Mrs. Grady burst out, "You are a hateful man! You won't let us wash, and you keep our men tired with your double guards. Will you be as eager to move when you're sick?"

"For your sake and everyone else's, I hope I don't get sick. Now go back to your wagons and get ready to leave. We're losing time."

The group broke up with resentful looks, but Ross was not done answering questions.

Marlette handed him his plate with angry eyes. "I think I'm beginning to agree with Mrs. Grady. Why can't we stay a day to let them recover?"

He looked at the accusing faces around him. Even John was looking at him anxiously. "Because it won't do any good to wait," said Ross. "The water gets worse, and when the food runs out and you have to eat mainly fresh meat, every one of you will probably suffer from what they have, sooner or later. We have to go on as long as we can."

They looked at him in despair, not wanting to believe what he told them. He wasn't hungry anymore and set down the plate Marlette had handed him. "Cam, take charge of the Grady wagon and make sure everyone has someone to move their wagon." Silence greeted his orders and he turned away. He hoped he hadn't made a mistake in telling them what was in store, but he didn't intend to lie or pamper them.

He rode ahead while the train sluggishly pulled itself into line. They would follow the river with its wooded bottom, which would afford some cover for the sick among them. When they got to open country, they would have to think of some other way to have privacy or simply disregard modesty.

The road ahead was clear, with no signs of Indians. He rode back to the wagon train. It would be a long night for him if some of them didn't recover by night guard. The men with their bigger appetites and bigger thirsts were struck harder than the women, but he could not expect the women to take their places.

Not only were they sick, but they still had the rough spots in the trail taking toll on wagons and animals as they began to throw shoes and strain legs. Stops were frequent and mileage far short of what they had been making.

One or two of the men were feeling better by night, but the rigorous day had exhausted the healthy ones and everyone turned in early despite the pleasant night. Ross took a turn at the herd until dark. The mosquitoes came into camp at the same time Ross did and drove those still awake into the sanctuary of tents and protective blankets. Ross ate alone from the Dutch oven left over the fire, picking out the mosquitoes and feeling quite cheerless. He washed his plate in the cooling water, scrubbing it with a bar of Martha's hard lye soap before stepping into the insect-free tent.

Marlette was silent and he sensed her restraint in the oppressively warm tent. He stripped off his buckskins and lay on top of the blanket to sleep for what time he could before he needed to be out to the herd again. He lay silent with eyes closed, not wanting to ignore Marlette, but not wanting her anger either.

She broke the silence. "I'm sorry, Ross. You didn't prepare us for this kind of trouble."

"I know. You wouldn't have wanted to believe it then any more than now."

"You think we'll all be sick?"

"If not here, then when we get to the mountains. Most everyone is who isn't conditioned to it."

She was silent for a long moment, then said, "Good night."

At midnight he arose and quietly left the tent. His horse was tied nearby and he mounted and rode out to the herd. He circled it and talked with each man on duty. He reached Cam, whose place he was to take. "Everything all right?"

"Yes," Cam answered.

"Better get in and get some sleep. I might need you."

"Some more sick?"

"Not yet, but there might be by morning."

Cam turned his horse away, and Ross was left alone feeling the loneliness of a man at odds with his followers.

When the morning wake up sounded, the herd was brought in close to the wagon circle. Only half the morning shift of herders came to replace those on duty. John came out to meet Ross as he came in, his face solemn. Ross dismounted.

"How many this morning?"

"At least as many more as yesterday. I'm not sure we have enough to move."

"Let's get everyone lined up and we'll see what we've got. Just remember one thing," he said, swinging up into his saddle. John looked at him questioningly, his pipe suspended next to his parted lips. "It'll get worse before it gets better."

The pipe was clamped between John's teeth with a snap and his look was grim. Ross pulled his horse around and went to help hold the herd while the wagons were prepared for travel. He chewed on his store of jerky and tried to keep tired men alert with a constant rotation of their positions around the herd. He watched the wagons pull slowly into their double line as men tried their best to yoke oxen and hitch up. The women were packing, but entirely too slowly as they had to run frequently for the woods, many of them pale and trembling from the constant evacuation of their bowels.

At last they were in some semblance of order, though more than half of the party was suffering now from bad colds or dysentery. Ross rode down one row of wagons and up the other, assessing his manpower. It was then that an idea struck him. He galloped to John's wagon, near the end of the double row in the rotation that day.

"If we put the stock between the wagons, we will need fewer men to watch them and have enough to move the wagons."

A smile lit John's face. "By God! That'll sure work. Jon, you take over here until we get this outfit moving."

Jon swung down off his horse and John took over with enthusiasm. Ross moved to help him rearrange the wagons. Marlette's voice stopped him. "Ross."

He stopped his horse and turned to face her. She looked at him with worried eyes and held a wrapped parcel out to him. "Your breakfast—and I've made a bed for you in the wagon. Try to come back for some sleep if you can."

He nudged his horse closer to the wagon, their hands touched, and he smiled. "Thank you. I will if I can." He turned to stow the food in his saddlebag and lifted the reins to move on but saw the hurt in her eyes. He stood in the stirrups, encircling her and drawing her to him with his free arm, and kissed her reassuringly. Then he moved his horse forward to inform the wagons ahead what his plan was.

As soon as the wagons were moving and the stock going along quietly between them, Ross had John take the lead, and he began the search in the area of their camp for Indian sign. He expected to find it, but when he did his feeling of dread deepened. The Pawnees would now keep an eye on them and wait for the opportune moment, when they were off guard, to steal whatever they could. He rode back to the trail and joined John at the head of the slow-moving wagons, the wheels beginning to pick up dust now as the trail dried out.

"The Pawnees have found us. Keep your eyes open. I'll warn the rest." He turned his horse away and rode down one side of the column and up the other, alerting his charges. Sick men propped themselves up against tailgates, their rifle barrels showing, trying to look alert. Ross rode along the woods side of their trail, making sure it was safe for those still able to make it to the trees for privacy. He made one more scouting circle along their route and came back to John. "I'm going to get some sleep. I'll have Daniels ride point for you. Twist is well enough to drive their team."

John nodded, and Ross went back to the Daniels wagon. Daniels was asleep and Pauly sat on the dropped tailgate, looking pale and weak from the illness.

"Wake him up."

Pauly reached an uncertain hand and shook the snoring man. He came awake slowly, cursing as he realized his sleep was being interrupted.

"What the hell'd you wake me for, Pauly?"

"I had him wake you," said Ross. "Get your horse and ride point for Jessup while I get some sleep. Watch the woods closely. I don't want any of our people caught in the woods."

Daniels scowled, but he moved. Ross rode back to his wagon. He stepped from the saddle and wrapped the reins around a stave. Marlette turned to see him through the front opening and gave him a pleased smile. He stretched out on the narrow bed she had made on top of the flour and sugar sacks and reached to take her hand, remembering nothing else as he relaxed into immediate sleep.

As long as the wagon jolted along, he slept. When the wagon stopped, he awoke instantly. He raised his head to see what was happening and saw Marlette move from the wagon seat. He was on hands and knees and reaching for his rifle as he scrambled from the wagon. He pulled his horse close and was in the saddle and moving before he realized they were stopping for their noon break. He rode forward and met John coming back.

"Anything?"

"No. Have a good nap?"

"Good enough. I'll scout around while you rest. I've got lunch with me."

John nodded and moved on down the line.

Late in the afternoon, Ross sighted a small group of Indians riding toward them and halted the train, passing a warning down the line. Women and children clambered into wagons, and men, some of them pale and weak, leaned heavily on their rifles or sat on wagon seats with rifles resting across trembling legs.

He rode ahead and stopped, waiting for the advancing warriors. He raised his hand in salutation and the Indians stopped a few yards from him, returning his salute. They were meticulously painted, their closely shaved heads adorned with colorful bird plummage and crests of deer hair. Grizzly bear-teeth necklaces gleamed dully under shoulder robes of buffalo and wolf skin. Weapons were prominently displayed in their attempt to show their strength. But it was only a guise. Their real intent was to peruse the wagon train and determine its strengths and weaknesses.

The leader asked if they had anything they wanted to trade. Ross answered that they had nothing of value. They were movers, not traders, and had nothing that would be worthy of esteem in the Pawnee eyes. They replied that they would like to decide that for themselves, as Ross knew they would. He then signed back that there were sick among them and that if they came close they would also be sick. They looked with concern at one another and conversed in rapid tongue, stopping when someone from the wagons went running for the grove of trees along the stream. That was enough to convince the Indians, and they pulled their horses around and galloped away.

Night found them camping at a smaller creek intersecting the larger stream. The afternoon had brought antelope sightings and Ross had taken some of the men to hunt. He had no fear of firing a rifle now. The Indians knew where they were. They brought back fresh antelope. Those who had been sick the longest were feeling a little better and looked forward to the fresh meat hungrily. Martha and Marlette were trying to make bread in the Dutch oven but were having difficulty keeping the mosquitoes out. Jennifer was using a broom to swish them away from the cooking meat while Liz turned the stick to keep the steaks from burning.

They ate as hurriedly as possible, doing their best to keep the mosquitoes out of their food, then washing the plates as quickly as possible. Bitten to the limit, they retired to the protection of their tents. When all the men had eaten, Ross allowed himself to come back to camp for a few hours' sleep. He would have to be up at twelve.

Marlette was awake and waiting for him. He lay down beside her and found her hand. He felt the effects the trail was having on her once-soft skin. He brought her hand to his lips and kissed the chapped skin.

"Would you rather sleep?" whispered Ross.

"No, but shouldn't you? You've gotten so little sleep. I don't see how you keep going."

"I keep going because I have to. Just to lie down and be with you helps, whether I sleep or not." She moved against him. He felt her warmth, sighed, and slept.

He was sleeping soundly and didn't waken until he heard John call him. Instantly awake, he dressed and stepped out into the starlit night.

"Wish I could let you sleep."

Ross smiled at him. "What I had will do."

John chuckled. "I bet it will. Well, good night." He rambled off to his tent, while Ross went to his horse and rode out to the herd. He saw no signs of anything out of the ordinary on the vast emptiness surrounding the wagons. The night was alive with crickets, and the voracious mosquitoes and coyotes yipped out in the silvered sea of grass.

When there was a subtle change in the crickets' voices, he was immediately aware of it. Slowly he began to move his horse around the herd, pausing to whisper a warning to each of the guards. Without any apparent alarm, he had them slowly bunch the grazing animals closer together. He was sure it was the Pawnee, and he knew exactly what they were doing. They had moved into the trees along the river and, leaving the horses with two or three young men, had crawled out to the vicinity of the herd.

He waited, scanning the featureless prairie for anything making a shape against its smooth background. Then he saw them rising to their feet, hunched over and running toward the herd. The stock moved as a horse snorted in warning.

Ross raised his gun and fired at the nearest running Indian and saw him somersault. More shots were fired, and the Indians answered with whoops and shots of their own. More Indians rushed from the trees, leading empty horses, knowing their braves were in trouble. The Indians saw their ponies coming and ran. Two more of the would-be horse thieves fell before they reached their mounts. He couldn't go after them now. The herd was spooked and milling. They had to be calmed and it would take all of them to hold them.

Men were coming from the wagons, now, and John rode around the herd to him. "Pawnee?"

"Yes. Should be able to find two or three of them out there when it's light."

"Should we double the guard again?"

"No need to. They won't be back tonight."

John peered at his watch, trying to see the time. "Don't think it's too long to wake-up time anyhow. I'll stay with the herd if you want to hunt Indians."

"Wouldn't be a bad idea." He reined his horse around toward where he had seen his Indian fall. He found the man dead, as he knew he would. The others were harder to find, but they, too, had been fatally wounded. The eastern sky was lightening perceptibly and it was time to get the camp up. He returned to the wagons and whacked the fry pan. There was little noise as women stepped, already awake and dressed, from their tents. Marlette was standing by their tent.

He bent to the remains of the previous night's fire and rekindled it. He smiled at her and the worry left her face. Jenny came from the tent with eyes wide and curious.

"Was it Indians?"

"Yes."

"Was anyone hurt?"

"No." He smiled at her. "Cam is all right and nothing was taken."

She blushed prettily and ducked back into the tent.

Liz laughed at her daughter's embarrassment and looked at Ross teasingly. "Can't say as I blame her. He's a handsome young man. If I were twenty years younger, I would be swept off my feet, too."

Her words may have been about Cam, but the violet eyes looking at Ross provocatively implied she wasn't talking about Cam.

Marlette added, unaware of Liz's double entendre, "It must be that Irish charm." She looked up from her work and smiled at Ross.

They moved on beneath an ominous sky brooding over the west. Ross knew worse weather was coming. At noon they were stopped on highlands along the river, the stream's bottoms soggy from the showers. The slate blue sky grew darker by the minute as lunch was prepared and oxen were loosed to graze for an hour. A rift appeared in the solid gloomy mass of deep violet clouds and the sun blazed through briefly, brilliantly haloing everything in a vividness brighter than any palette was capable of reproducing.

Everything was still for a moment. No cow bellowed; not even a man's voice intruded for that instant. Then, in terrifying fierceness, the sky was rent with crystal fire as sheet lightning surged across the darkened plain. Quickly the storm advanced across the prairie toward them, but they had little time to protect themselves as animals milled in terror before the oncoming thunder and lightning.

Sheets of rain driven by the wind blinded the eyes, and hailstones pelted them with bruising force, breaking limbs from the groves along the stream and shredding vibrant petals from the wild flowers. Praying men prayed and less religious men cursed the advancing lightning and earth-rattling thunder, as horses reared and cattle bellowed, white-eyed and ready to stampede.

Just as suddenly the storm passed, leaving them soaked to the skin. Ross gave the order to make camp.

As they began to set up tents and resurrect wagon canvases and stretch lines to dry clothes and blankets, Mr. and Mrs. James came to Ross, disaster written on their faces. "Mr. Chesnut, we can't find Amy."

"Where was she last seen?"

"She and some of the other girls went to the river for wash water just before the storm hit. The other girls came back, but Amy wasn't with them."

A dread settled over Ross. "You stay with your wife and get your camp set up. I'll take some men and look for her."

He went to his horse and rode down the line and gathered five of the best gun hands for the search.

"What do you think happened to her?" asked Daniels.

"I won't know until I've looked around, but my first guess is Pawnee."

"Damn! We'll get our horses."

They rode to the rising river, and while the men sat in glum silence, Ross dismounted and made a thorough search through the trees along the bank. In the grove he found tracks of Indians, but out in the open where the rain and hail had pelted the ground, everything had been obliterated. They rode to the nearest crests to see if they could determine where a camp might be but found nothing.

They returned to the circled wagons, unwillingly. Ross alone knew they could do nothing but wait for the Pawnee to approach them with their demands, if they did have the girl. He warned everyone to stay near the wagons and doubled the guard. It was to be a long, anxious night.

5. Owl Song

MORNING BROUGHT EVEN more anxiety. Ross spent the morning seeing that equipment got repaired. Before noon the herders spotted Indians coming. Ross rode out to meet them and knew immediately they were in a murderous mood. He lifted his hand in salutation and let them approach. They stopped a few yards distant, and a little girl's shoes were flung at his horse's feet. They wanted retribution for their dead warriors. Ross signed them to wait while he discussed their demands with his company.

"The Pawnee have your daughter, Mr. James."

"Oh, no! My baby, my baby!" cried Mrs. James. "What can we do? What do they want? Give it to them! Get my baby back!" She began crying hysterically, and men moved restlessly as Mr. James tried to calm the overwrought woman.

Ross went to Mrs. James and took her from her husband's arms. "Mrs. James, listen to me. They haven't harmed her. Now try to pull yourself together. I need your help in making this decision. It affects all of us." The harsh command of his voice broke through her grief, and her sobbing subsided.

"Now listen to me, all of you. We have killed three Pawnee warriors. They have taken the girl as hostage. They will kill her if we don't meet their demands. They demand the men responsible for killing their men or all our horses, guns, ammunition, and food." He paused, letting the enormity of the ransom soak in.

Yetter was the first to speak up, his voice adamant. "What the hell kind of choice is that? We can't turn over our men any more than we can our stock or guns."

Christopher, who had apparently had some ministerial training and had assumed that capacity for Ross's train, asked gently, but no less pointedly, "Are you suggesting we let them keep the girl?"

Yetter's face darkened perceptibly. "What other choice do we have? One child for three men or everything we have. What choice would you make, Christopher?"

"I'm not Solomon, Mr. Yetter. But couldn't we take her back by force, Mr. Chesnut?"

"No. They would kill her the moment they saw us coming."

Mrs. James pleaded, "You can't let my child die. What kind of men are you?" She looked at Ross in agony. He looked at Marlette and saw the fear in her eyes as her hand came to within inches of her mouth and stopped. She knew—perhaps before he had known or admitted to himself there was only one chance of recovering the child and escaping the wrath of the Pawnee. He looked away from her and said, with Indian impassiveness, "There is one way we can get the girl back. The Pawnee want revenge for their dead warriors. I think they'll take me in trade for the girl—" Marlette's cry was muffled, but as loud as a thunderclap in the quiet crowd before Ross continued—"if I can convince them I was responsible for their dead braves."

John protested, "You can't do it. I won't let you. We can't make it to Oregon without you."

"The Russell train is behind us. They can take you on if I don't come back. You have plenty of wood and water and game here, but you also have the Pawnee. Wait a day or two if you want to, but if no train comes, I would advise you to go on to the Platte River. You can follow the river all the way to the forks and cross it past the forks. If you head due north, it'll lead you to Fort Laramie. You can wait more safely there for another party to join or hire someone to lead you to Oregon."

Yetter was the first to approve the idea. Ross knew he would be. "Who else could do it, Jessup? He has a chance. None of the rest of us would."

Ross looked at the strained faces of the Jameses. He went to them and offered Mr. James his hand. "I'll get her back for you if I can."

James nodded, and Mrs. James sobbed and embraced him, her voice almost incoherent as she whispered, "God be with you."

He turned away and went to Marlette's tent, leaving the people, even John and Liz, standing in stricken silence. Inside the tent Martha was trying to comfort Marlette. When she saw him, she looked indecisive, not quite knowing whether to condemn him or praise him. She got to her feet heavily and left Ross alone with

Marlette. He kneeled down and touched her shoulder. "Marlette."

She turned her tear-streaked face to him and clutched at him, crying against him, "Why, Ross? Why does it have to be you?"

He held her and stroked her hair. "You know why. I'm the only one who can do this."

"No! You feel responsible to the people on this train because you have assumed the responsibility. But what about me, Ross?" she pleaded in anguish. "What about your responsibility to me?"

"What do you want me to do, Marlette? Do you want me to refuse to save the child? What if it was our child?"

Her tears abated and terrible, trembling anger raged in her. "Don't try to make me feel selfish or guilty! Not now! Not after having just found you after three years of wondering if I would ever see you again. If you leave me now, I won't see you again, because you won't come back! Then what am I to do, Ross? Where am I to go?"

"Marlette, listen to me. I have every chance of getting out of this alive, but it may take some time."

"Don't tell me that! Don't try to make me believe something I know isn't true. We killed three of their men and they will kill you!"

"No. I wish I had time to tell you how the Indian mind reasons. They could keep me as a slave if the families of the dead men don't ask for my death or, even if they do, I could survive for other reasons."

"I don't believe you. I can't believe you!"

"Then believe this. My vision does not show me dying."

"Your vision! Do you know how ridiculous that sounds, Ross?"

"Would it sound less ridiculous if I called it by the name of your God?"

Tears glistened in her eyes again. "Don't ridicule what I believe. Not now!"

"I wasn't. I'm only trying to make you see that whether I call it a vision or the Great Spirit, or God, it is what I believe. If you believe, you will not fear for me. I love you, Marlette, and I'm not going to let myself be killed if I can help it."

She turned a twisted face up to him, and he kissed her as she moaned in agony, clinging to him, not wanting to release him. At last he pulled himself free and left the tent. He walked quickly to his horse. While he had been consoling Marlette, a group of men had mounted and waited for him. Cam was among them, his young face bleak. Ross handed him his rifle. "Keep it for me."

"Keep it! I'm going with you and I'm going to use it!"

Mr. James pushed his horse through to the front. "I am, too. If they want three men, then I should be one of them. Only a coward would let another man die for his child."

Ross smiled at his two volunteers. "You can wait with me while they bring your daughter, Mr. James. But none of you can go with me if they take me. It would be suicide. Your families need you—and Marlette needs you, Cam." He put his hand on the boy's shoulder. "Now, we've kept them waiting long enough."

They rode out to the tight cluster of Indians and Ross signed his proposition to them. They pulled away to discuss his validity as a substitute hostage and then came back, asking for proof that he could have killed all three men. He consented to a test of his marksmanship. A limb was cut into small wooden targets, and he was told in sign that they would be launched one at a time into the river. Ross was to fire at each, and if he didn't blow all three out of the water, his proposal would not be accepted.

They didn't make it easy, throwing the blocks far out into the rapid water. He aimed and fired at the first block, and it leaped from the water in proof that he had hit it. The second block was thrown and he fired, skipping the block sideways. The third was even more difficult, and he only grazed it, but enough so that visible splinters flew from it. The Pawnee were convinced, and grunts of satisfaction echoed his shots. They signed they would take him.

He signed back he would go with them only when the girl was handed over to her father. They agreed to bring the girl, but the men with Ross would have to retire out of shooting distance and leave Ross between them, unarmed and without his horse. Mounting their horses, they rode out of the fringe of timber along the stream and onto the prairie. Ross glanced back at the wagons and saw a group of kneeling people with heads bowed, and their voices drifted to him as they prayed and sang. He saw Marlette kneeling with them and hoped her prayer for him would be answered.

The Indians stopped when they had gone out of sight of the wagons and signaled that this was the place where they wanted

Ross to wait. He dismounted and gave Cam his hatchet and knife, taking only his robe. Ross walked after the Indians, estimating how far he could outrun them if they planned on double-crossing him. He stopped a hundred feet away from his protectors and crossed his arms over his chest. The Pawnee turned their horses and rode away at a gallop.

Four hours passed before they returned. He searched with narrowed eyes against the lowering sun for the girl and saw her riding in front of one of the warriors. They stopped a good distance away and motioned him forward. He walked halfway toward the Indians and stopped. They lowered the girl from in front of her captor and she came running as fast as her thin legs could carry her, her dress torn, her face streaked from dirt and tears—hungry, tired, and frightened. He bent one knee to the ground and she came flying into his outstretched arms, shaking as she hugged him.

"Everything's going to be all right now, Amy. Your father is waiting for you behind me. You go to him, and I want you to keep this until I return." He picked up the folded buffalo robe from his knee and offered it to her.

Small hands touched the softness. "Where are you going?"

"I am going to visit the Indians for a while." He tried to smile encouragingly.

Her face paled under the streaks of dirt. "No! Don't go! They will hurt you. I know they will hurt you!"

"I have to. It is the bargain I made with them."

"For me?"

"Yes."

She flung small arms around him again and whispered, "I will pray for you."

He smiled and said, "I will need all you have. Now, Amy, I want you to run as fast as you can to your father and not look back."

She pulled away from him, clutched the robe tightly, and nodded solemnly, her eyes wide and fearful. Then she sprinted away from him, and with deliberate slowness he walked toward the restless Pawnee. Just before he reached them, he glanced over his shoulder and saw that Amy was safely in her father's arms. He stood motionless as the Pawnee surged around him, administering vicious blows as they bound him and put a lasso around his

68

neck. They goaded him into a run and kept him running all the way to their camp.

His lungs were aching, his body wet with sweat, and his head dully throbbing from the exertion as they entered the village. He was grateful when they stopped in the center of the village, knowing worse was ahead as the warriors turned him over to the women, whose cruelty could surpass the men's. They surrounded him with screaming taunts and began clubbing him, the children pelting him with stones. The buckskin shirt and pants saved him from bleeding wounds, but the bruises would be just as painful.

They herded him brutally around the village, everyone getting in all the blows they could possibly administer. One of them finally realized they weren't drawing enough blood and halted the proceedings long enough to use a knife to cut away his clothes. Then they beat him with renewed violence. At last he went to the ground, too battered and exhausted to be herded.

Then, as suddenly as it began, the beating stopped. A woman's voice was commanding them, and he was dragged into one of the earth-covered lodges and laid on a mat. His tormentors were ordered out, and he was left alone with one of the women. His eyes cleared and he gazed at his benefactor. She was a young woman and, by Indian standards, handsome.

She spoke to him in her language and he shook his head painfully, unable to understand what she was asking. She spoke again, and this time he recognized the dialect. It was the tongue of the Nakota, a dialect similar to his own Indian family. When she paused, he answered in the Yanktonaii dialect, "I understand you. Can you understand me?"

She nodded, her face softening. "Yes. I can understand, but it is not quite the same. Who are you? Where do you come from? Why do you wear this?" She bent over him and lifted the medallion that still hung around his neck.

"I am the adopted son of Snow Cloud of the Nakota."

She sucked in her breath. "Ay-ee! My mother was of the Nakota. It is her language I speak to you. But yours is not the same. Where are you from?"

"North of the people who speak your tongue."

"Are you a chief?"

"No. My father, Snow Cloud, was chief."

"Then why do you wear this?"

69

"I was given this when I left to follow my vision."

"Ah!" She paused and looked at him thoughtfully. Then, as if noticing for the first time that he was bleeding from dozens of cuts, she said, "But you are hurt. We will talk, but first I must make you comfortable."

She brought the water bowl near and began to bathe his wounds. Just then the leader of the men who had brought him in came through the doorway. His voice was harsh, but she didn't flinch, showing him the medallion and telling him what she had learned of their captive. The Indian listened, arms crossed over his well-muscled chest, his face intent. After a few moments he spoke, his voice less harsh. The girl looked down and nodded. She turned to Ross and said, "This is Strong Horse, my father, the chief of this village. He says you have been brave and worthy of respect and honor. He wishes to show you his respect by letting you die as a warrior in an honorable way."

"Tell your father I respect him as a worthy adversary, but I do not wish to die. I wish to live, and it is my desire to settle the death of his warriors in an honorable way, but I do not find honor in death."

She repeated his words to the stern-faced chief, and his face took on an incredulous look. It was an unheard-of request. The audacity of it might just be the stroke of boldness that would save him. But the chief was infuriated and his hands expressed his refusal, as well as his harsh voice.

"My father says you have killed three of his warriors and only death can repay their loss. The people will not accept any other solution."

"Remind your father that his warriors came to steal our horses and were killed in a brave and honorable way in a fight to protect our horses. Our hearts were good and we allowed them to join the spirit trail, but your father took a child in revenge. Is this honorable among the Pawnee? I cannot believe so. Honor is among men who are willing to prove themselves. I am willing to prove, in a contest of skill without bloodshed, that I am better than he or his mightiest warriors. If I lose, I deserve to die. If I win, I deserve freedom."

She repeated the offer to her father, but he remained adamant. She turned to Ross with the refusal, and he offered what he felt was his last resort. "Then I will propose a fight to the death with any warrior, and if I win I will go free and pass from the land of the Pawnee without further retribution to me or my people."

Strong Horse received this with a more thoughtful attitude. He gave a short answer to his daughter and left the hut. Ross breathed a little more easily even before the girl told him her father would consider his proposal and present it before the council. Then she busied herself with the fire and prepared food for him. After she fed him, he lay perfectly still on the couch she offered him, feeling the ache of every bruise and cut on his body. He heard the harangue going on in the council house and asked, "Can you tell what they are saying?"

She listened in silence for a short while and answered, "They have come to no decision yet. You will live through the night. What do they call you?"

"My warrior name was White Eagle."

"I am called Owl Song. Have you a woman?"

"Yes. My wife travels with the wagons."

"Those are white men's wagons. Is your wife white?"

"Yes."

She frowned. "Why? You are a warrior."

"No. I am a white man. Snow Cloud adopted me because he took my white mother as his wife, but she was already with child by her white husband. My vision showed the death of my mother and the Indian woman I was to marry, and of my search for the white eagle's nest. What was to happen to me when I found the white eagle's nest was not shown me—only that I would someday leave it again."

"And you have found the white eagle's nest?"

"Yes. I live there now, across the mountains near the big water of the west. The man who rules that land is called White-headed Eagle by the Indians there."

She was silent and he was tired. His eyes closed and he heard her say quietly, "Sleep now, man with the strange vision." And he slept.

He awoke at dawn and sat up with difficulty from the pain of every bruise on his battered body. Owl Song heard him and stirred. He heard no sound from the council lodge and wondered if his fate had been decided.

Owl Song looked at him intently and a faint smile touched her lips. "Did you sleep well, man of the strange vision?"

71

Before he could reply, Strong Horse appeared in the doorway. Ross stood bruised and naked before his captor, while his fate was related to him through Owl Song.

"The council has agreed to let you fight for your life." She paused meaningfully and his heart beat faster. Then she continued, "But you must fight three men. If you live, you will be allowed to live and go free."

His heart stopped altogether for a moment, then thudded heavily. He hardly felt up to one man, let alone three, but he did have a chance. The winter with his brother had hardened him and acutely sharpened his instincts. He nodded his acceptance of the sentence. Then Strong Horse said something to Owl Song and left.

She looked at Ross, starting from his moccasined feet and slowly traveling up his naked body to meet his eyes. "My father has instructed me to prepare you as a warrior is prepared for battle. If you are hungry, I will feed you."

"No. I am not hungry, but I would drink water."

After he had drained a horn of water, he asked, "Will I fight all three men at once or separately?"

"One by one."

He sighed inwardly and sat in waiting silence.

"I know how to save you," she said quietly.

He looked at her and saw a softness in her black eyes and face. "How?"

"I could take you as my husband."

In total surprise, he asked, "Why?"

"I have not yet married. No man here pleases me, but I watched you last night while you slept. You could please me very much, I think, man with the strange vision."

"I am grateful for your offer, Owl Song, but I already have a wife."

"It makes no difference. I would gladly be your second wife and follow you to the white eagle's nest. You are a man of my mother's people, and you have shown wisdom and courage."

"How much would you value my courage if I accepted your offer to save my life?"

She looked in confusion at him, meeting his eyes and then looking away. "I would not think less of you."

72

"Yes, you would, and I would not feel honor in taking you for such a purpose when I love another."

"You do not find me attractive enough to love?"

"You speak words I have not even thought. You are beautiful and worthy of much better than a man who would use you for the purpose of saving his life and return to a white wife. I would not shame you in such a way. You could not respect a man who would do such a thing."

She nodded and her eyes were liquid, but she rose and gathered the necessary articles to prepare him. She wrung pieces of tattered trade blankets in cool water and bathed his blood-crusted body. He sat stiffly passive as she washed him gently. When her hands touched him below the waist, he could not control the response of his body as she caressed him. He twisted away from her, and she cut the bonds that kept his hands securely behind his back and sat back on her heels, her eyes lowered, her lips parted expectantly.

Ross brought himself under control and said, "If you would help me, Owl Song, then help me to live. Tell me who I fight."

Without looking at him, she continued to wash his legs. "Father did not tell me, but I suppose it would be Snake for one. He is quick and clever, his knife darts as quick as the viper's tongue. Surely Echo of Thunder will be chosen. He is large, as powerful as the bull buffalo and as ponderous, but he can break your arm or your leg as easily as breaking a dry twig. Then it could be he would choose Painted Hand, who is nearer your equal in size and very brave—or he could fight you himself. He is very strong and very brave and has as much wisdom as I think you do."

She took in her hands a palm of grease and began working it into his sore body. He relaxed under her beneficial massage and stretched out on the couch while she worked over him. Then, following with infinite care the instructions he gave her, she painted him as he had painted himself so many years ago.

Done, she gave him a leather breechclout and he tied it around himself. She stood looking at her feet and he put his hands to her shoulders. "Thank you, Owl Song. I will not forget you."

She raised her eyes and looked at him. "And I shall not forget you. Now I had better tie your hands before Father comes for you."

Soon Strong Horse came into the lodge. Ross stood. Owl

73

Song placed a hand on his arm and said, "I will pray to the Great Spirit for your safety."

"Thank you. I will be unafraid. My medicine is strong, and the power of the Thunder God flows in my veins."

She gasped and jerked her hand from his arm. Strong Horse, watching their exchange with frowning curiosity, was quick to question her, and his eyes widened with surprise as she answered him in a shaking voice. Then he directed a question at Ross.

Owl Song asked, tremulously, "My father wishes to know if you are the man who was touched by thunder."

In equal surprise, Ross asked, "Have you heard of this?"

With a curious reverence, she answered, "Yes. A story comes from the north country about a man who was touched by thunder and lived. You are that man, aren't you?"

"Yes."

Her eyes raised to his in awe and she translated for Strong Horse. There was indecision written in the black eyes for a second, but he quickly masked it. With a gesture of contempt, he refuted Ross's claim, but the glance he gave Ross was one of doubt. He motioned Ross to go before him, and Ross stepped from the lodge into a crowd of Indians whose faces mirrored their hatred of him. Their taunts, as he walked between them, called for his blood. It was a literal threat, for the Pawnee were rumored to make human sacrifices.

At the end of the corridor of people stood his first combatant. From Owl Song's description, this would have to be the warrior Snake. He was a slender, wiry man, shorter than Ross, with the cold unblinking eyes of his namesake. Ross stopped where the people spread to make a circle in front of the council house. Strong Horse gave him a knife and axe and moved toward the council house. Ross waited for Snake to make the first move. He would save himself as long as possible.

Snake began stalking his prey in a slow, deliberate circle. Ross turned to follow the man as he circled and feinted, trying to draw Ross out, but Ross stood firm, deafened by the jeers from the crowd. A stone struck him with force from behind, but he didn't flinch, keeping his eyes on Snake.

The man darted in swiftly slashing, and Ross ducked the attack and whirled to cleave a little flesh with the axe, but Snake was too quick and his swing struck nothing but air. Taking advantage of

74

Ross's momentary imbalance, Snake drew first blood in the instant that Ross's swing carried him into Snake's range. This man was exceedingly quick; Ross would have to be much quicker to score against him.

He shut out the taunts and cries of blood lust and waited as Snake tried to lure him off balance again. The brave darted in and slashed at him while Ross waited for him to make a mistake—a slip of overconfidence—waiting patiently while the man wore himself out trying to find a way to get at Ross's already tender body.

As Snake's energy flagged, Ross began to move, baiting him to continue his aggressive attack. Snake's cunning was replaced with blind fury at this passive adversary. More surely, Ross began giving attack for attack and Snake became the defender. At last Ross's knife was finding flesh and sweat glistened on both men, shining more than the grease covering them. Snake lunged at him in desperation, and Ross caught him and held him, hand to wrist and ankle to ankle. He forced the man back until he could trip him, and his heavier body forced the smaller man to the ground.

Silence fell on the crowd as Ross held their champion in a stranglehold with the hard wood of the axe across his throat. He flipped the man and held him from behind, imprisoning his legs with his own and holding a knife to his ribs as he addressed Strong Horse. "I do not wish to kill this man. If you will honor my win, I will release him."

Strong Horse looked at Owl Song and she translated. A murmur ran through the crowd. Strong Horse nodded his consent, and Ross stepped quickly away from the man. As Ross pressed his hand firmly over the slash in his leg, Strong Horse called for the next warrior.

Echo of Thunder came through the crowd, fresh from the medicine lodge and reminding Ross of his fiercest adversary of old, Big Tree. This man was heavier and not as quick of movement, but undoubtedly he was as strong. They circled each other warily, the big man lunging with swinging tomahawk and driving Ross into the resisting crowd, who threw him gleefully forward into the larger man's path.

He could not let that happen again or the deadly axe would cripple him disastrously. He was the one now who had to depend on quickness to get behind the big man and carry on a rear attack. Using all the wisdom he had from his battles with Big Tree, he quickened his feints. It was the other man now who played the waiting game. And played it just as doggedly as Ross had such a short time ago. His breathing was heavy, and he felt a warning throb in his head. He was wearing himself out as he had worn out Snake. He stopped his attack and recovered his stamina by circling slowly. He saw the man waiting to meet him and, as if by slow motion, the arms came for him. Swinging the hatchet and stabbing with the knife, he ducked and dodged, but the man seemed impervious to his slashing knife and kept coming. Ross sidestepped his lunge, but a long strong arm clutched his leg and he was yanked from his feet. He fell heavily on his chest and his breath was knocked from him. The man released the leg the instant he felt his enemy was stunned and rose to fall spread-eagle on top of him, knife upraised. Ross saw it all through a blur and tried to roll away from the weight descending on him, holding his knife straight up.

Echo of Thunder fell on the upraised knife, roared like a wounded buffalo, and went limp as blood streamed from his wound. Ross pulled himself free and stood on shaking legs while the crowd converged on their downed warrior. Ross didn't think he had killed him but knew he would die if he wasn't tended to immediately. He turned to Owl Song and told her, "Bind him to stop the blood and he will live."

She bent over her father and repeated Ross's instructions. Strong Horse rose and went to the wounded man, urgently commanding his medicine men to care for Echo of Thunder. They carried him away still bleeding, and Ross looked with dismay after them. "The bleeding must be stopped quickly," he told Owl Song. "Sear it with a knife heated in the fire and close it with sinew, but do it now or it will be too late."

She ran after the men carrying Echo of Thunder and was lost from his sight as the crowd formed a ring around him again and stood in sullen, deadly silence while Strong Horse returned to his place and called for the next man.

The man who came through the crowd was more nearly Ross's size, his eyes full of deadly determination; this man would rely on skill rather than quickness or size. Ross wished he weren't so tired and tried to ignore the dull ache in his head.

The slow circling began as they measured each other. Ross had to avoid contact as long as he could, to renew his strength, but the other man was wise enough to see through this ploy and moved in to attack almost immediately. Ross dodged away, his reflexes slowed, and the Indian's knife cut his arm. He came back swinging his own knife and drew blood as Painted Hand met him bodily. His bleeding arm was weak and the knife fell from his grasp as Painted Hand twisted his wrist. Ross lunged, and they fell to the ground and rolled in heated struggle for an advantage. Ross knew he couldn't free his imprisoned hand unless he released his opponent's knife-holding arm. He didn't know if he had the speed left in his exhausted body to do it, but he had to try soon or die. He braced his feet in one last desperate effort and forced his adversary's arms to the ground just long enough to propel himself over Painted Hand's head in a forward roll. Painted Hand twisted after him, his free arm wielding his knife painfully across Ross's shoulders. Ross whipped the imprisoned arm under and behind Painted Hand until he heard the bone snap. Ross straddled his opponent. The man ceased to struggle and lay limp and sweating in pain. Ross took the knife and rose wearily to his feet. He faced Strong Horse, bruised and dripping blood, his legs shaking and sweat pouring from his exhausted body His tongue was thick from thirst.

A coolness brushed him and he dazedly looked up. The sky had clouded over and the sun disappeared behind dark clouds. No one but he was concerned about it as Strong Horse stood and looked at him with a face as dark as the clouds blotting out the sun. This was no cheerful loser he was facing. There was death written in Strong Horse's eyes, and he signaled his men to take Ross prisoner. As they bound him and dragged him closer to Strong Horse, Ross's thoughts were of Marlette.

Owl Song came pushing through the crowd and placed herself between Ross and the murderous Strong Horse. She was pleading for his life, and she pointed to the sky. Automatically, all faces turned to the sky. With perfect timing, lightning blinded them as it blazed not more than a mile or two away; they stood directly in its path. Thunder jarred the earth with earsplitting intensity and the terror-stricken crowd fell away from him. Strong Horse went from flushed rage to ashen awe. Here was power he could not dispute. Even the warriors were afraid to touch him now. Owl Song took the knife from her father and turned to him. Lightning flashed, lighting everything brighter than noon sun with blinding whiteness. She cowered before him as the thunder broke directly overhead, sending the last of them running for their lodges.

Owl Song hesitated, frightened and afraid to touch him. Quickly he said, "It's all right. I will not hurt you."

She caught her breath and slashed the thongs loose that bound him. She stood looking at him, convinced he had brought the Thunder God against them. The air was charged with electricity. He felt it crackle as he moved. He touched her in a final gesture of appreciation, and the sparks danced away from his fingers and she fled as he picked up the knife she had dropped. Summoning a reserve he wasn't sure he still had, he ran as fast as his leaden legs would carry him out of the village and along the river. He dove under an overhanging bank as lightning tore the sky and rain and thunder bounced off the earth. He got up and ran again, and the rain pounded down on him, washing away his blood, his sweat, and his tracks.

6. On to the Platte River

THE RAIN WAS still falling at dark, and it was too difficult for Ross to go on. He found a thicket in a grove of stunted oak and hacked brush with his knife. Placing his back against a tree, he covered himself with the leafy branches to await daybreak, sleeping fitfully in spite of his pain and anxiety. He arose at daybreak, stiff and sore, but alive, and went on.

Near noon he left the river bottom and the protection of the groves as he approached the area where he had left the wagon train. He sighted the wagons and heard the rifle report as the herders saw him. Ross stood where he was, exhaustion and relief overcoming him, knowing they would ride out to meet him. They stopped their horses a few yards from him as they viewed the apparition that stood before them.

John finally recovered enough to ask, "Ross, is that you? What in God's name did they do to you?"

"Just a little Pawnee welcoming ceremony." He glanced at the circle of wagons and saw a figure approaching. "Cam, Marlette is coming. I don't want her to see me like this. Take her back to the wagons and tell her I'm all right. Have her get me some clothes and some of Martha's soap, and better bring something for bandages. When I start scrubbing away this dirt and paint, I'll probably start bleeding. Bring them to the river."

Cam turned his horse away and galloped toward Marlette.

John recovered enough to ask, "Here, get up behind me and I'll take you to the river."

When they reached the river, Ross dismounted and waded into the cool water. He untied the breechclout and let it drift away from him. Cam came with his clothes and soap.

"I'll be all right. You can go back to camp and start getting things packed. I want to be moving as soon as possible. Cam, you can stay and help me. How are you at scrubbing backs?'' He smiled at the boy, but Cam's face paled. He was neither prepared nor conditioned to accept the brutality he was viewing, and he hesitated in revulsion.

John said quickly, ''I'll stay. You go on back, Cam.''

Relieved, Cam turned and rode away with the other horsemen. James was about to follow but turned back, rode his horse into the water, and held out his hand. ''I'll never forget what you've done for us, Chesnut. Whatever we have—whatever you need, just ask for it.''

Ross took the hand with a smile and felt the sincerity of the man in the strength of his grip. ''Thank you.''

James shook his head. ''No. Thank you.'' He released Ross's hand and turned away, but not before Ross saw the tears brimming in his eyes.

Ross began scrubbing with the harsh soap, cleaning away the dirt, grease, paint, and festering scabs, which oozed blood as he opened them.

John watched grimly. ''What did they use on you anyway?''

''Sticks, clubs, stones. Anything that was handy.''

''The longer I live, the less I believe man was made in the image of God. We're more like animals.''

Ross stopped long enough to look at him and said, ''Most of this wasn't done by the men.''

John paled. ''God! You mean the women did this?''

''Yes. And the children.''

''That's even harder to believe.''

''It is custom among most Indians to give captives to the women and children first.''

John looked at him in amazement. ''You mean you knew this would happen to you?''

''Yes. But I also knew what they would do to that little girl.'' He held out the soap to John. ''I could use some help with my back.''

John took the soap and scrubbed his shoulders and back. ''You know, I'm beginning to think you lead a charmed life.''

Ross rinsed and stepped out of the river. Marlette had thoughtfully included towels, and Ross began drying. The towel became blotched with red from his bleeding wounds. ''If you believe in Indian religion and superstition, then you would know I do.''

80

They bound the bleeding wounds, and John helped him dress. It was a painful chore that brought sweat to Ross's forehead as they worked the close-fitting buckskin pants over his bandaged legs, which were swollen by a solid mass of bruises. Whether it was by chance or by intuition, she had sent the shirt she had made him. He had worn it the day they were married, and he had kept it as a remembrance of her. Using the damp towel, he wiped the perspiration away and smiled a little wanly.

"How do I look?"

"Not too bad with clothes on."

"Then I'm ready."

John helped him mount and swung up behind him. Then they rode out of the river bottom and up onto the prairie where the wagons stood.

With aching slowness, he dismounted and turned, taking a step or two toward Marlette. She ran into his arms, holding him fiercely. He winced and she felt it. She looked into his face, asking anxiously, "What is it? What's wrong?"

He smiled reassuringly. "I'm all right—just a little bruised."

She looked at John. "Don't spare me, John. How is he, really?"

John looked at Ross and answered in total seriousness, "Pretty good for a man that's nigh been beat to death."

The tears spilled over and she cried, "Oh, Ross."

He held her gently and said softly, "It's all over now. I'll be all right."

Marlette tried to smile but failed. Ross kissed her forehead and turned her back toward the wagons. The crowd separated to let them through and smiles and words of welcome greeted him and he acknowledged them with a nod and a grave smile, glad to finally sit at his own campfire while a hasty lunch was prepared. Sitting helped ease the dull ache of his body, but not the hunger that gnawed at him. It had been over forty-eight hours since he had eaten. He felt stronger after eating and could put off the sleep he needed so urgently for a little while longer.

Jonathan saddled his horse for him, and he mounted with only a little less effort than before. As he turned away to do his job, he heard his name called. He stopped and saw Adam James coming with Amy. The girl carried his buffalo robe tightly rolled and hugged against her. He moved his horse toward them.

"Amy had to see you. I didn't think you'd mind."

He smiled at the child studying him with pensive eyes as she took in the signs of his torture—the bruised cheeks and cut eye. "I don't mind. How are you, Amy?"

"I feel lots better now you're back. Did they hurt you bad?"

"I've been hurt worse."

"I brought your robe back. Do you need it?"

"No. I don't need it now. You can keep it for me."

For the first time she smiled and said, "Are you sure?"

"I'm sure."

"Thank you, Mr. Chesnut. I'm so glad they didn't hurt you bad and you came back."

Mr. James broke in. "We'd better get back to our wagon now, Amy. Mr. Chesnut has work to do."

James turned away, and Amy waved as she looked back at him. He returned her wave and moved off again. Cam and Jeremy came riding in from the herd to drive wagons. Cam stopped his horse as he saw Ross. With confusion in his eyes and a catch in his voice, he said, "I'd like to ride with you."

"Can one of John's boys take Marlette's wagon?"

"Yes. Jeremy will see to it."

"All right. Let's go." He wheeled his horse away and Cam fell in beside him. He rode first to where the herders held the stock and went up to Daniel Heely.

Heely smiled at him happily. "Say, Chesnut! I sure am glad you made it back. You look like you had one helluva time."

Ross smiled back, "I did."

Heely held out his hand to Ross and said again, "I'm glad you made it."

Ross nodded as he took the offered hand, then pulled his horse away. He rode forward of the forming wagons, Cam following still, silently. He heard John's voice shout the order to move and heard the crack of whips and creak of wheels and boxes as the train moved forward.

They rode in silence for another few miles, Ross's concentration wandering away from the task at hand. It was even a chore to ride, and he could think of little else than the relief of sleep. The road ahead was good. Enough rain had fallen to dampen down the dust but not turn it muddy. Nothing suspicious stirred in the vivid green and blue vastness. Antelope, white rumps bobbing like balloons on short strings, loped away as they crested another little rise. Ross stopped to weigh the advisability of trying to shoot some for evening camp. He asked Cam, "How's the meat supply in camp?"

"Daniels, Twist, and Pauly caught some deer in the woods yesterday morning. We've got plenty of meat to last today."

"Good. Did everyone fill up on water?"

"I think so. Mr. Jessup did a good job keeping everyone going."

"I knew I could count on him."

Cam turned his face away, and Ross knew his words had struck the sensitive subject of Cam's guilt feelings. Ross put his hand on the boy's arm and said, "Cam. I understand what happened to you today. You don't have to be ashamed."

Cam looked back at him with agony on his face. "But I am ashamed. I let you down and I'm sorry, but I just have never seen anything like that before."

"I know. And I hope you never have to again, but if you do, you don't need to feel ashamed if it sickens you."

With eyes averted, he answered, "That is easy for you to say. It wasn't you who acted like a gutless coward."

"Do you think I have never felt like a coward? You're wrong. The first time I had to fight, I felt just as you do. I was so sick afterwards I lost consciousness for a while. When I woke up, my Indian father, Snow Cloud, was sitting with me and I didn't want to look at him, I was so ashamed. He talked to me about what had happened and told me he would have been disappointed in me if I had not been sickened by what had happened. It was a sign to him that I had the compassion he felt was necessary to be a chief."

Cam looked back at him and his eyes and voice registered surprise and anger. "How could he know anything about compassion after what he did to your mother and father? How can you still respect his words after what has just been done to you?"

"Cam, you must realize Snow Cloud was the only father I ever knew. For a good many years I didn't know what he had done to my mother or my father. I only knew how he treated me and my mother when I was in his lodge. It's true he killed my father and showed little compassion for my mother at first. But he changed. We all change. What you are now, you will not always be. The younger we are, the more we are ruled by passion—the passion to

83

love, hate, and to kill. As we add years, we usually add wisdom, and if we are unusually fortunate, our passion is tempered with compassion. Snow Cloud knew it took more to be a man than bravery; it takes compassion as well. I know this to be true, and I want you to know it.

"As for the Pawnee, you must understand I am still more Indian than white. I lived with Indians for twenty years. When I moved to the Oregon country, I was following my vision. I sought to learn the white man's language and customs because my mother was white and she wanted me to have this knowledge, but I did not necessarily desire to be a white man. I still lived more like an Indian. I didn't desire to become a white man until I knew I wanted Marlette as my wife. I knew what to expect from the Pawnee and hold no bitterness toward them. In fact, if it hadn't been for the Pawnee chief's daughter, I would not be alive now."

"But how will I know if it is compassion I have or if I am just gutless? How long does it take to know?"

Ross smiled at him. "I think we should have a pretty good idea by the time we get to Oregon."

The worried frown left Cam's face. "I hope so."

Ross turned his horse around and said, "I'm going back to the wagons now. Do you want to come with me or stay here?"

Cam turned his horse and followed Ross back the way they came. John rode out to meet them. "How does it look ahead?"

"The road is good, and nothing but antelope out there that I can see. I don't think we'll be bothered by this band of Pawnee again, but keep on eye open. Wake me if you need to."

John nodded and pulled the ever-present pipe from his mouth. "I will, but I hope I don't need to. Rest easy."

The ritual of setting up camp that night was only impeded by the insects that insisted on chewing on the road-weary company. Tempers shortened as the women tried to make supper amidst clouds of mosquitoes and gnats, and water had to be transported some distance as the river had curved away from the trail. But the next day they would reach the Platte.

7. *A Seed Is Planted*

IN THE MORNING they crossed the arid, sandy distance between widely separated, low, steep-footed hills to the Platte and felt the exhilaration of knowing they had reached another milestone in their trek. But the exhilaration quickly ebbed as they discovered the valley of the Platte was a more destitute country than what they had just come through. The first level next to the river extended back a half mile and was a marshy area of grass, rushes, and brush, with few trees. The next level, the one they would travel on, was a dusty wasteland; there was little grass, but it was plentiful in cactus. Most of the trees grew on the islands cluttering the shallow, mile-wide river, moving with the thickness and color of old and darkened honey.

It was even less a joy when they took their first taste of the only drinkable water they would have—except for an occasional spring—until they reached the clear mountain streams of the Rockies. Ross dashed their spirits even more when he gathered them together at the noon rest and informed them that from now on they would have to gather the sun-dried disks of buffalo droppings for their evening fires. Women protested not only at the thought of the odious task, but also at the thought of having to use their pillowcases or some equally precious container for the job.

Evening brought no solace for the hot and tired travelers. The wind still blew sand, and the insects plagued them. Thirst remained unquenched by the silty water tainted with mineral salts, and the sparse grass had already been cropped close by the wagon trains that had passed them while they'd waited for Ross. Martha bridled at using the offensive buffalo chips for the evening fire, but Marlette grimly carried on with the preparation of the evening meal and cooked it over the buffalo-chip fire. Ross was the only one who eagerly consumed his meal. The rest questioned his truthfulness when he denied that his meat tasted like fresh buffalo dung. Unconvinced, the bulk of the movers went to bed not only tired, but hungry, too.

They camped the following evening close to the Platte River and, in spite of the mosquitoes, the grit-encrusted movers bathed in the river. The night was mild and the moon shined benevolently. After a good meal—one day of hunger had been enough to cure their aversion to buffalo-chip fires—they felt revived enough to play a little music and dance. The German watchmaker, Weis, got out his violin, and Pauly played his harmonica. Mrs. Yetter joined them on her water-soaked organ and made it sound almost in tune. Ross didn't try to discourage the dancing and singing. They needed the few festive moments to bolster morale and spirits.

They made very few miles over the next two days as dysentery began claiming them again. This time none of them escaped the debilitating illness. Cam, Martha, and Marlette, along with all the Jessups, were stricken in turn. Along the barren Platte, the sickness was even more of a problem than it had been along the tree-lined Blue River. There was nowhere to hide, and blankets were used in desperation when the cramps struck them. Ross kept them moving as long as he could, knowing they would overcome their incapacity in time, but finally they came to a stop. Too many were stricken to keep the wagons and stock moving.

By the third day, the illness had started to taper off, and most who had been stricken at first were feeling better. All except Marlette. An unexplained complication had afflicted her. She was sick to her stomach and vomiting.

Another day passed without any improvement in Marlette's condition and Ross was becoming increasingly concerned, particularly when Yetter made it a point to hint that she could have something a lot more serious than just trail sickness.

By noon the next day Marlette was too hungry to refuse food, but she was still suffering from diarrhea and had to leave the wagon more than once during the afternoon. She was terribly thirsty and drank water without seeming to worsen. By late afternoon she'd had enough of lying inside the hot wagon and sat on the seat. By evening camp she was hungry, but supper only made her ill again.

The next morning she was still nauseous, but at their noon stop she ate with renewed interest and during the long afternoon she had to leave the wagon only once. At supper she was ravenous and ate without any ill effects. Their spirits soared, and when Ross entered the tent at midnight, she was awake and waiting for him. He took her in his arms and felt a deep relief at knowing she was going to be all right.

In the morning Marlette had to dash from camp during breakfast and Ross went after her and found her retching and weeping.

"I just don't understand! What is happening to me? I really feel better. I can eat lunch and supper. But what is wrong with breakfast? Why can't I eat breakfast!"

Ross's heart began to pound as he realized what the answer was. He knelt on the ground beside her dejected body and took her in his arms, his heart swelling to bursting as he lifted her dismayed face to his. "I know, Marlette! I *know!*"

She looked at him incredulously. "How? What? Tell me!"

Laughing, he asked, "How long have we been on the trail?"

She shook her head, mystified. "I don't know for sure. Almost four weeks—or more. I've lost track."

"And how long since we met in Independence?"

"Another four or five days. What are you trying to tell me? What are you so happy about? I don't understand."

"We have been together for over a month. How many days have you not been able to receive me?"

Her eyes widened and her mouth opened as she realized what he meant. "Oh, Ross," she cried, "I'm *pregnant!*"

"I'd bet on it." He grinned back at her.

She looked frightened and ecstatic all at once. "What'll I do? I can't have a baby now!" She stopped, and then counting to herself, whispered, "May, June . . .," her voice trailing off, and then she burst out, "January! I'll have a baby in January. Oh, Ross! Is it all right?"

He took her in his arms and pulled her to her feet and swung her around like a child. "All right!" he shouted, "All right!" He brought her back to the ground and looked at her in pure joy. "Nothing was ever *more* all right."

His joy enveloped her, and all doubt vanished from her face as she came into his arms and he hugged her. She laughed, caught up in his joy. Then, with undimmed happiness showing on his face, Ross walked arm in arm with her back to the camp, where his exuberance had not gone unnoticed. Even Marlette had a radiance that gave pause to the morning bustle of cooking and packing.

Martha looked at her with a curious frown and asked, "Mind telling the rest of us what's happened to make you both act so happy?"

All heads turned to hear the answer, and Ross looked at Marlette. She returned his gaze with a touch of color staining her cheeks. Ross answered simply, "Marlette carries my child."

Silence reigned for a long moment, and then smiles blossomed. John stepped forward with a broad grin and stuck out his hand. "That's good news! Congratulations!"

Liz smiled, but Martha looked dumbfounded. "Now why didn't I figure that one out?" Then her stiff reserve cracked and tears streamed down her smooth cheeks. Marlette pulled away from Ross and went to hold the older woman.

Soon the Jameses and Heelys came to congratulate them and the word quickly spread around the circle and everyone came to see for themselves that Marlette was indeed better. Ross accepted the congratulations, but already the happiness he felt was beginning to fade as he realized Marlette's pregnancy could be complicated by what still lay ahead of them. The smile that had so seldom lit his handsome face faded altogether as he heard Martha's tones of worry, magnifying his own concern. He was not unaware that part of the worry stemmed from the memory still disturbing him of his first wife's pregnancy and her death in childbirth. If his feeling of urgency had been great before, it was now doubled in intensity.

Daniels and Yetter came on the heels of their well wishers and whatever afterglow of happiness Ross had left disappeared as he looked into Yetter's dour face. He expected no congratulations from Yetter and got none.

Daniels spoke first. "When do we go after meat, Chesnut? Most of us are out. We been seein' buffalo and we need some fresh meat."

Yetter added, "And I got an ox that won't get up. If we go off and leave him, he'll die. Now how about layin' over for the rest of the day and getting some meat and resting the stock?"

Ross looked at them and beyond, observing not only the people, but their stock and equipment as well. He would have to let them stay. The day was already hot and the insects vicious in spite of the stiff wind blowing the dust in swirls about the wagons. Lips that had held up under sun and wind this far were now cracking and bleeding. They had grown weary of trying to keep off the hordes of biting and stinging insects, and eyes were beginning to swell shut from the attacks. No fair, soft cheek could be seen among the women now. All were burnt so deeply by the unrelenting sun and wind that layer after layer peeled and bled and burned again, leaving all their skins looking like very old buffalo-hide tepee covers, creased and darkened from long use and the smoke of many fires.

The stock and equipment were faring no better. The water was bad and the grass scarce. Many animals were lame from festering cactus spines in their hooves. The hot, dry days were shrinking the wagons until wide cracks separated the boards, and wheels were beginning to loosen in their rims. Bouncing over the deep, narrow tracks left by the buffalo was loosening bolts and splitting boards.

"All right," Ross answered. "Make camp here and"—he looked at Daniels—"I'll need you and Twist and Pauly to hunt buffalo." He paused and saw some of the men look at him expectantly. He would have liked to take more, but the buffalo were too far back along the trail to risk taking many men from camp. What he needed were the men without families and the younger boys who would ride along as helpers to carry extra guns and load for the men doing the shooting. "John," he continued, "I'd like to take Joseph; and Daniel," he turned his eyes on Heely, "I'll need your boy Nelson. Yetter, I could use Sam, too." He wanted to take Cam, too, but he decided against it; he needed no other backup than his bow. He finished, "Each of them will need a gun."

He saw the eyes of the boys he mentioned widen with anticipation, but Yetter protested, "Now, look, Chesnut, you can't take these boys out without some men along, too."

Grady interjected, "Yeah, when are the rest of us going to get a chance to hunt buffalo?"

Heads nodded in agreement as contemptuous eyes glared at Ross. They thought they had won a victory by getting him to agree to stop, and now they were trying to push their authority farther. It was time they knew he was still in charge.

"I agreed to stop because I know we need meat and the animals need a rest. I also know we are still in Pawnee country, and the buffalo I saw are miles behind us and we may not get back tonight. That is why I want every man who has a family to stay with his family and protect them, if it comes to that. Also, there are repairs to be made on your wagons and feet on the animals to be doctored. By the time we get back, I want this train ready to roll again. Now the quicker we can leave, the quicker we can get back. You're wasting time."

The fire went out of several pairs of eyes, and without further words the gathering broke up to set up camp.

John looked at him with a gleam in his eyes. "You're one hell of a man to try to get the best of."

Ross smiled bleakly and asked, "Did you think I was weakening?"

The respect in John's eyes belied the chuckle as he answered, "Well, I was beginning to think so for about five words, but I should've known better."

"Unless we find buffalo closer than those I saw, we'll be gone all night. Take extra precautions to keep everyone close, armed, and watchful."

In an hour they were riding back along their trail, watching the bluffs and prepared to spend the night away from the wagons if they didn't find any buffalo early enough to get back by dark.

Late in the afternoon Ross's keen ears heard the familiar pounding of hooves and located the cloud of dust raised beyond the opposite bluffs by running buffalo. In a few minutes the buffalo began to crest the bluffs, and Ross deployed his men into two groups along the river near where the buffalo would cross. The animals were already plowing into the river on the far side as the men parted and took positions in the rushes and willows along the bank.

Soon the foremost buffalo were out of the water and came trotting toward the bluffs. From their positions on each side of the herd, the men mounted their horses and fired into the bewildered herd as the great shaggy beasts plunged on up the bluffs, leaving some down and some valiantly trying to follow the herd, running a few hundred feet before losing their speed and balance. Ross quickly dispatched these animals with his well-aimed arrows, and they were all soon engaged in skinning and butchering buffalo, stripped to the waist and covered with blood and sweat.

During the long afternoon other wagon trains came into view and passed them as they worked. When they bedded down near their kill, the clear night revealed a string of campfires at intervals ahead and behind them along the Platte. It depressed Ross to realize he was not making any better time than the other trains. In spite of his every effort to keep moving, there had been delays. His resolve deepened, even though he knew there would still be unforeseen delays he couldn't anticipate or avoid.

They arrived back at their camp at noon the next day. Everyone was in much better spirits. Marlette looked less tired and greeted him with a kiss. The women cooked fresh buffalo meat for lunch while the men got teams ready to move.

They moved out immediately after lunch. The heat and the insects were oppressive between the bleached and barren sand bluffs. Heat waves and mirages danced ahead of them and the animals' tongues hung out of their mouths as the sun burned down relentlessly.

Late in the afternoon the wind died down and the heat and dust became stifling. An hour later they reached one of the few good springs they would pass for the remainder of the trip over the Rocky Mountains. They were now within a mile or so of the forks of the Platte River, and soon another leg of their journey would begin—the leg that would take them to Fort Laramie.

8. Hawk

DURING THE NIGHT another thunderstorm passed to the north of the movers. Though the storm had missed them, it had affected the river. At the first ford of the South Platte, the trains ahead of them were already waiting to cross the rising river. Ross moved his train on up the South Fork, the heat and the dust taking its toll on man and beast, the rutted buffalo trails equally punishing to the wagons. Frequent stops were made to repair broken wheels and cracked tongues. Ross, his patience worn thin by the delays, took one last look at the river at dusk and decided if it still was rising in the morning they would lay over and he would personally see that every wheel was bolted to its rim before they moved again.

In the first light of morning he rode to the river and the stick he had driven in at the water's edge the night before was whipping in the current several feet from the new shoreline. He returned to the wagons and announced to his weary movers that they would lay-over and repair their wagons. With dogged determination, they turned to their task.

The sun was well above the bluffs across the river when a shot rang out from one of the herd guards. Ross was on his feet with his rifle in his hand and scanning the skyline by the time John reached his side. Together they saw the small group of horsemen, marked by a cloud of dust, traveling down the sandy bluff across the river.

John said, "Looks like Indians. What do you make of 'em?"

"Can't tell from this distance. We're in the hunting area of the Lakota, but they could be any one of several tribes that pass through this range hunting buffalo."

"Do you think there's more of 'em over the bluffs?"

"Hard to tell. If not, there's not enough of them to cause us trouble. If we're lucky, they're just a curious bunch of hunters. I'll ride out and meet them.''

He mounted his horse and left the group of armed men standing near the wagons just as the Indians rode their horses into the turbid river of roiling sand, more than a mile across. As the horses and riders floundered, Ross began to detect details of dress and horses which looked familiar. As they drew closer, he was sure he recognized the figure on the lead horse. He galloped toward the Indians who were plunging through the shallows near shore, whooping as they recognized him.

He was grinning broadly as the Indians surrounded him and his half brother embraced him. ''Hawk!'' Ross exclaimed. ''What brings you here, my brother?''

The darker skinned man, almost as handsome as Ross but with the more prominent features of his Indian father, Snow Cloud, answered, ''Our brothers, the Lakota, wish to war against the Crow and Snake and called us to council. We were returning home but,'' his face split into a broad smile, ''I had to see what manner of woman could cloud my brother's mind so darkly he would give up the freedom and the promise of his youth to become a white man.''

Ross grinned, ''You'll be disappointed, brother. You won't see in her what I see in her.''

Hawk shrugged, ''I will decide that.''

Ross looked at the circle of grinning faces. He knew all of these men. Most of them he had grown up with and those who had not been a part of his childhood he had met during his stay with his half brother the past winter. ''I will take you to meet her and the rest of the people with me, but I must warn you they will be frightened and suspicious of you. We have had trouble with the Pawnee and they fear all Indians now. Take nothing which is not given to you and act with good will and you are welcome to come among us.''

Affirmative grunts issued from the ring of carefully ornamented and painted warriors and Hawk declared, ''I will see that your request is honored, brother. If any of my men cause trouble, I will personally be responsible and he will answer to me.''

Heads nodded in agreement and Ross nodded in return, ''I trust your word. Now come, and make me proud of you, my brothers.''

They separated to let Ross and Hawk lead the way. Ross was well aware of what kind of an impression these men wanted to make and he kicked his horse into a gallop and let them rush at the wagon train with all the fierce savagery they delighted in, showing off their horsemanship and elaborately painted and bedecked bodies.

They pulled their horses to rearing stops a few yards from the group of gathered men with stoic regalness.

John stepped from the group with his rifle casually over his arm and asked, "Friends of yours?"

Ross nodded and said, "John, this is my half brother, Hawk."

Hawk touched his horse and came forward with his hand held out in white man fashion. John took it and said, "Glad to meet you, Hawk." Then he looked at Ross and asked, embarrassed, "Does he understand English?"

Hawk answered with studied slowness, "I speak some. White Eagle teach me." He smiled proudly at Ross.

Ross saw Martha and Marlette coming from the other side of the wagon circle and motioned them forward. Marlette looked hesitant, yet curious. As she came forward, he dismounted and put his arm around her. "Marlette, this is my half brother, Hawk. He came to meet you."

Marlette looked up at Ross and then at Hawk and smiled uncertainly. Hawk dismounted and offered Marlette his hand, peering at her intently. Marlette took the offered hand somewhat reluctantly. Hawk nodded and smiled at her, saying something in his own language. Ross grinned and the onlooking Indians laughed.

Marlette looked puzzled and the color rose to her cheeks. She asked, "What did he say?"

Ross translated, "He said I was right. He does not understand what I see in you."

The smile left Marlette's face and she pulled her hand free from Hawk's. Ross felt her stiffen and held her tighter, his eyes teasing her as he admonished, "Don't be too hard on him. Have you seen yourself in a mirror lately?"

She nodded and relaxed, recognizing the truth of his words.

Marlette asked, "Will he understand me if I apologize for taking offense at his remarks?"

Hawk answered in English, "It is I who have offended my

brother's wife.'' He turned away, strode to his horse and brought a bundle back and held it out to Marlette. "For you.''

Marlette took the skin and carefully unrolled it. The bleached and softened hide was intricately painted with small figures. Marlette could not understand them, but Ross did. It was the story of his life portrayed year by year and deed by deed—the only type of permanent record kept by his Indian people.

Marlette finally said, "It's beautiful, Hawk. Thank you.''

Hawk asked Ross in his own tongue, "Does she understand what it is, brother?''

Ross answered, "No. But I will teach her to read it.'' Marlette looked at him for an explanation and he said, "Hawk wants to make sure you know what he has given you. It is the history of my life up until the time I left them to find the meaning of my vision.''

She looked at the unwinding circle of figures again and touched them tentatively. "You will have to explain each one to me.''

An excited exclamation from the Indians behind Hawk took their attention away from the skin. Hawk raised his eyes and they widened as he gasped, "My brother! There is another one of you here.''

Ross turned and saw Cam and motioned the boy forward. He came and stood beside Ross and the Indians commented on the resemblance. Ross told them in their language, "This is a son of the man who was nephew to my white father. My wife found my white father's family in the East and this boy has come with her.'' Hawk smiled and extended his hand as Ross said in English, "Cam, this is my half brother, Hawk.''

Cam's hand eagerly took Hawk's and he asked, "What relation is he to me?''

"None. He is my mother's child.''

Cam looked disappointed, but Hawk, understanding English better than he spoke it, said, "White Eagle brother, you brother, too.''

Cam grinned with delight as Hawk took the necklace of claws he wore and placed it over Cam's head.

Ross turned to the group of people standing curiously behind him and said, "This man is my half brother, Hawk. I have invited him and his men to be our guests for as long as they wish. They are my friends and you do not need to be afraid of them. They know you are in my protection and they will also protect you. If

95

you treat them as friends, they will be your friends. Now let's get back to work. We have to move out in the morning and I want every wagon ready to roll."

The group of people dispersed slowly and Marlette went with them, carrying the painted skin.

When she was out of hearing, Hawk said, "Your people look bad, my brother. Your wife is sickly. I fear she will not make it to your Oregon."

"They are not used to the prairie as you are. Buffalo tallow and paint offends them after it turns sour and the meat spoils quickly in this heat and the water sickens them."

Hawk grunted, and offered, "Then we will get buffalo and make fresh tallow and meat."

Ross hesitated a moment. He didn't want to take time to go hunting now, but he almost had to. They could use the meat and maybe he could get the emigrants to use the tallow on their skins if it was fresh. "How far away are the buffalo?"

Hawk smiled, "Only over the bluffs. Not far. But will this be enough to help your wife?"

Ross answered, appreciating Hawk's concern, "She is strong in spite of how she looks. She is thin now, but she will not be long. She carries my child."

Hawk let out an exuberant whoop and gripped Ross's shoulder affectionately. "I am happy for you, my brother. At last you will have the son you want."

Ross looked at him with mixed emotions and Hawk sensed his anxiety. "You worry, and rightly so, but you should not. Your vision showed no tragedy for you now."

"No. But neither did it show me anything else during this time of my life. I go, but I go blindly. It is almost as frightening as knowing what to expect. I wish I could take her and ride swiftly to where she will be safe and comfortable."

Hawk laughed, "My brother should have been wiser and saved his seed for when he reached his home."

Ross grinned with him and agreed, "You're right. My will power has been no stronger than that of an untried youth."

There was answering laughter and hoots of derision from the Indians still sitting their horses and Ross laughed good-naturedly with them.

Hawk finally said, "Come. Gather your hunters and we will get you meat."

Ross turned to John who still stood by him and said, "Hawk says there are buffalo just over the bluff across the river. I'll take what men we can spare and be back by dark. Do you want to come with us?"

John smiled, but shook his head, "I'd like to, but I'd better stay and see that the wagons get done. You can take one of my boys, and, no doubt, Cam will want to go."

"All right. You tell them to get ready and I'll get whoever else can be spared."

Ross went around the circle of working men and took any man or boy who could be spared and while they went to gather up guns and get horses, Ross went to where Marlette was hanging clothes between the wagons to dry. She looked hot and miserable and he wished he could help her, but that too, would have to wait.

"I'm going with Hawk to hunt buffalo. I'll be back by dark. John'll stay with the wagons."

"Oh?" Her voice had a touch of question and resentment.

He knew what she was thinking but he couldn't take time to explain things to her now. He said, "We do need meat and it makes sense to get it while we're stopped."

She nodded and turned back to her laundry and he left, feeling a little guilty that she must work so hard while it appeared he could change his priorities at the least excuse. What she didn't understand was no matter how much he wanted to help her, or repair the wagons, he couldn't with Hawk and his men in camp. Hawk and his men had to see Ross as their leader or their respect for him would turn to contempt, just as it had so many years ago when he had helped Spotted Fawn, his first wife. There was too much involved to risk that just now.

Ross mounted his horse and rode to where Hawk waited with his men and the men Ross had gathered. They crossed the river and rode up the bluff. They pulled their horses to a stop as they topped the bluff and saw the buffalo herd like a vast brown blanket thrown over the lighter golden grassed prairie.

Hawk asked, "What you think, White Eagle?"

Ross answered, "I'll deploy my men along the cut in the bluff while you take your men and drive the herd this way."

Hawk nodded in agreement. The buffalo would head down the

draw to the river and be closer to the wagons. He looked at Cam and Jeremy and said, "But what about these two? Are they good with those rifles?"

Ross shook his head and said, "None of them are as good as you with your bows, but their horses aren't used to buffalo. It is better if they are with me at the trap, especially the boys."

"But you can't watch them both. I'll take your cousin's son and you take the other boy."

Ross told the boys of Hawk's offer and Cam grinned with excitement. Hawk, seeing the boy's enthusiasm, said, with a malicious gleam in his eyes, "And how about a bet that we can kill more buffalo than you, my brother?"

Ross shook his head and said, "Oh no you don't, Hawk. I'm not betting."

Hawk spat contemptuously. "Has my brother become an old woman?"

Ross looked at Hawk without expression. It was a challenge he couldn't refuse or he would lose face. With a guarded smile, he asked, "And what is the bet to be?"

Hawk's dark eyes twinkled as he said, "If I win you will dance with us tonight around the coup pole and recount all your deeds for your white people to see."

"You can't be serious, Hawk!" But Ross could see he was. He stared back into those cunning eyes, knowing exactly what his brother was up to. "All right. But what if I win?"

Hawk laughed, "I do not worry. You won't win."

Hawk signaled his men toward the buffalo and Ross told the rest of the men what they were to do as they rode toward the pass between the bluffs. When they reached the draw the men took up positions along each side, with Hawk and Ross closest to the bottom of the draw. Here they would have the best chance to turn the running animals back into the draw, giving them all a better chance to kill a buffalo.

They waited with tense excitement as they heard the thunder of hooves draw near, and then the buffalo were pouring down through the pass and the men on the slopes above were mounting their horses and galloping along the curve of the bluffs toward the running herd, their rifle shots almost lost in the crescendo of noise. Ross and Jeremy mounted and saw Hawk and Cam already running toward the herd. Ross saw Hawk's bow come up and the arrow fly before dust enveloped them.

A big cow and a calf were running close to the outside edge of the herd and Ross yelled at Jeremy to shoot. The shot went wild and the cow swerved away. Ross handed the boy his rifle just as a big bull came thundering past them. Jeremy raced after the buffalo and Ross followed him, his bow ready. As Jeremy came alongside the running bull, he fired. The ball smacked into the animal's shoulder. The bull faltered and swung his massive head toward his assailant, one wicked horn catching Jeremy's horse on the shoulder. The horse stumbled and Jeremy went sprawling into the cloud of dust left by the charging buffalo. Ross lashed his horse toward the downed boy as the buffalo turned to come back. Ross hauled his horse to a stop between the boy and the buffalo, his hatchet in his hand as the buffalo charged. He threw the hatchet with all his strength and it struck the animal between the eyes, cleaving the thick skull. The great shaggy beast bellowed, staggered, and sank to its knees, and slowly rolled on its side in a swirl of dust.

Ross made sure the animal was dead before turning to the stunned boy. "Are you all right?"

"I think so. Just knocked the wind out of me."

"You want to try for another one?"

Jeremy paled and shook his head. "I don't think so. That was too close. I'm shaking so bad I don't think I could hit another one."

Ross gave him an understanding smile and helped him up. "There'll be another day. Come on, I'll show you how to skin him out."

It was well after noon when the successful hunters returned to camp. Cam and Jeremy eagerly relived their hunting stories to anyone who would listen and Ross wondered wearily how Marlette was going to take the news that he had lost a bet with his brother and would have to dance with Hawk and his warriors.

Wood was gathered and the cook fires replenished to start roasting the fresh meat for the evening meal. The Indians gathered more wood and cleared a flat area near camp and built their pyres and planted poles in preparation for the dance. As they returned to their own campfire, Hawk came to where Ross and

John sat smoking and asked, "Does your wife have something I can use to catch tallow for her?"

Ross rose and went to where Marlette was making biscuits for the Dutch oven and said, "Hawk wants to borrow one of your cups if you can spare it."

She looked at him questioningly but answered, "I suppose so, if he brings it back. I'll need it again in the morning."

Hawk returned to his own fire and held the cup on the end of a stick under the fat buffalo hump as it dripped into the fire.

Marlette asked, "What's he doing?"

"He's catching buffalo tallow for you."

"For me!" she gasped. "What on earth for?"

"He's worried about you. He's going to bring you some tallow to put on your face to protect your skin."

She grimaced and said, "How awful. You know I can't stand to use that terrible stuff."

"This will be fresh. It won't smell for a few days if we can keep it cool enough until he leaves. He'll be offended if you don't."

Martha heard them talking and commented, "My mother used to save bear grease in the winter time to use but it stayed cold enough it didn't sour till spring. I'll try some if it'll help this burn and keep these awful bugs from chewin' on me."

Ross smiled at her, "That would please Hawk and it will help as long as you can stand to use it."

Marlette frowned, but agreed reluctantly, "All right, but the moment it starts to smell—out it goes."

Ross returned to the fire as Yetter came into the circle and stood before him with his usual sour expression.

Yetter's chin jutted, as he demanded, "How long will these Injuns stay with us?"

"Until they want to leave."

"Well, I don't like havin' them around. Are you sure we can trust them?"

"You have my word, Yetter."

"You better know what you're talkin' about, Chesnut, or there's some of us'll make sure you do."

Ross's face lost its impassive expression and his dark eyes flashed dangerously. "Don't threaten me, Yetter. If you don't like my friends, you can join another train. There's one ahead of us; one behind us and one across the river."

100

Yetter looked even more adamant. "I knew there was something about you I didn't like the first time I saw you. Now I know you're one of them, I know what it was. I think we ought to fire you and leave you with your redskin friends."

John exploded. "Fire him! Now just how in the hell do you think you're going to do that? If I remember right, it was you who was given the choice of coming with us or stayin' with Russell. No one twisted your arm, and no one is chargin' you any money."

Yetter turned away, his jaw set stubbornly. John looked after the man in disgust, his teeth clamped hard on his pipe. "That son-of-a-bitch! You've saved his bacon so damn many times and he wants to fire you!" John shook his head in dismay. "I just don't understand him."

Ross laughed as he pulled his knife to test the ribs and said, "I wouldn't waste the effort to try." He separated the sizzling ribs and called, "Martha, bring on the plates. These ribs are ready."

They sat down to eat the sumptuous ribs and the Indians squatted around their fire a few yards away and sliced fat chunks of hump, jesting and insulting each other and Ross as they ate. Ross joined in the good humored repartee, knowing it was part of the mental preparation for the dance ahead.

No one else around his fire said anything as their expressions ranged from curious interest to disgust. Marlette finally asked, "What are they saying?"

"I can't tell you because most of it would make you blush."

Liz laughed throatily, a strange excitement lighting her eyes, but Marlette only gave him a dark look and walked away, to the delight of the Indians who insulted him more raucously. His blood pounded in his veins and he wanted to answer their taunts with a gesture of his own, but didn't, knowing all too well what his limits as a white man were.

Hawk stood up and said, "It is time to prepare for the dance."

Ross sighed and arose. It was time to tell Marlette what he had to do. She was washing dishes on the end of the wagon with Martha. "I need to talk to you. Will you walk with me?"

She looked puzzled, but dried her hands and took his offered arm. He led her out of hearing and explained what he was going to do.

Her voice revealed her dismay as she said, "Oh, Ross! Don't do it. I'll be so embarrassed."

101

"I have to. It was a bet and I lost. Everyone on the hunt knows of it. Can you understand how it would look to Hawk, and to the rest of them, if I didn't go through with it?"

Stubbornly, she said, "All right. Do it if you must, but I will stay in the tent and not watch."

"There was a time you wanted to know these things about me."

"I still do, but not in front of other people."

"Will you be ashamed?"

"Yes, I'm afraid I will be." Then in desperation, she pleaded, "Please don't do it."

He looked at her and didn't know what to answer. He knew she felt threatened by Hawk's presence, but hadn't realized just how afraid she was that he might revert to his Indian life. "I can't back out now. I will have to do it. You can stay in the tent, if you wish, but it would look better if you didn't."

He turned to leave her but her voice stopped him. "Ross."

He spun and faced her. "Yes?"

"It was a mistake, wasn't it?"

The pain in her eyes hurt him. "What?"

"Marrying me and trying to become a white man."

"At this moment I can't answer that. I have not yet thought so, but now I find you don't accept me as I am. This is what Hawk wants to prove to me. This is the whole purpose of his visit and this dance. I don't want to do it, Marlette, but I have no choice but to prove to him, as well as to myself, that I can be both the man he wants me to be and the man you want me to be. But if you don't support me, Hawk has made his point, whether I dance or not."

She stood, silent and unrelenting. He sighed inwardly and turned away again.

"Ross."

He stopped, but didn't turn around, a touch of impatience in his voice as he answered, "Yes."

"Don't leave me like this."

He turned around, anger rising into his voice as he admonished, "Marlette . . ." but he didn't finish the reproof as he saw her anguished face.

"I'm sorry, Ross. Please forgive me. I didn't understand. I'll come watch you. I'll do whatever you want me to do to help."

His anger fled and he took her in his arms. "All I want is for you not to be ashamed of what I do. Blush and be embarrassed, but not ashamed. I won't lie and tell you it won't shock you. It will, but that, too, is a part of me and you must understand it or you will never understand me."

"I'll try very hard."

"Good." A brief smile touched his lips and he kissed her. "Now I must start my preparations. You can shut your eyes if you wish during the dance, but don't leave, whatever you do."

Ross took her arm and walked back toward the camp. He told Marlette to go on to the wagons and he went to where Rabbit Legs and Jumps Bull were testing their makeshift drums, and said, "As soon as your drums are ready, begin playing. I want to attract as many white people as possible."

Born conspirators, both men grinned and nodded. Hawk heard him and came toward him, his visage fearsome in his warrior's paint. Ross told him what he planned to do.

Hawk protested, "No, my brother, it is a sacred ritual."

"I know, and that is why it will work so well to help the white people understand that the difference between themselves and the Indian is not one of intelligence, but of culture and religion."

Hawk appraised him thoughtfully, and finally nodded, "All right. I will help you."

Ross smiled, "Good. Let's get your things. The drummers are ready."

Rabbit Legs and Jumps Bull were beating their drums and singing in unison, their voices attracting people from the circle of wagons. The crowd closed in as Ross stripped off his shirt and tied the breechclout Hawk had fashioned for him around his waist, and removed his buckskin pants, feeling self-consciously naked for the first time in his life. He would have to work fast, darkness was setting in. An attentive audience watched as Ross transformed himself into an Indian warrior. First, fresh buffalo tallow was rubbed over his body. The movers were just beginning to appreciate its soothing effect, but now a new use was learned as Ross explained how the grease highlighted the body during the dance by firelight.

Next came the paint in the most fearsome colors of black and vermillion, not because the Indian thought it was beautiful, or protective, but the ludicrous lines and designs were intentionally used to frighten the enemy, as well as denote the wearer's own power. Then he explained exactly what the dance would be about and the significance of the performance of the dance to each Indian warrior in terms of tribal history, religion, and just as important, to keep the warrior's confidence at a high level.

He was finished and stood before them. The children were wide-eyed and full of questions. He answered them, enjoying the feeling that he had favorably impressed their young, curious minds, and the knowledge that his answers were providing information to the adults as well. When all the questions were answered, Ross signaled the drummers, and the drumming began in earnest, a throbbing accompaniment to their vibrant voices that grew stronger as they warmed to their task.

At the right moment, Hawk led a gleaming, lithe and fearsome line of dancers around the blazing fires. It took Ross only a few moments to rid himself of his self-imposed inhibitions and for his feet to become confident in the long unused, but still remembered patterns and rhythms of his boyhood. Forgotten was his weariness and reluctance to perform. His blood raced in his veins, as he became White Eagle, the warrior touched by thunder.

The drummers increased the tempo and the dancers moved faster. Voices shrilled the chants higher and the first warrior counted coup on one of the posts and Ross's blood flowed hot and wild. He glanced at Marlette seated near the front of the gathered emigrants and her eyes were wide with disbelief. Martha, next to her, scowled in disapproval. But it was Liz's reaction which bothered him most. She was enjoying the performance, leaning forward to see, excitement showing in her eyes, her lips parted expectantly.

It was his turn to strike a post and he did so with what had been his customary flourish of old and personal trademark. His brother wanted him to be the man he remembered and Ross gave it everything he had, frequently glancing at Marlette to catch her reaction. There were times he looked at her and her eyes would be closed, and when they were open, they would be wide with shock, her hands clasped tightly to keep from covering her face. Martha got up and left, her back rigid as she walked away.

He saw the boys and caught the expressions on their faces and then on Jennifer's the next time he turned. They appeared neither shocked, nor disgusted, but intensely interested and excited, almost as much as the younger children, who were still uninhibited enough not to try repressing the feelings the drums and the dancing caused in their freer, more fanciful souls. Their bodies swayed and hands clapped to the rhythm.

It was then Ross realized something he had not comprehended before. A child was born free of prejudices and inhibitions. It was the child's environment which created what the child would eventually be. He realized for the first time he was what he was because of both his white mother's influence and his Indian environment, and he would always be both and neither—he was the half light and half dark horse of his vision and the knowledge frightened him and he shut it from his mind.

The dance went on until after the guard changed and all the men could see them perform. It could have gone on all night, but Ross knew he couldn't last that long. The trail had been taking its toll on him, too. He was in no condition to dance this hard and his head was throbbing from more than just the beat of the drums. He stopped before the drummers and signaled an end to the dance.

Trying hard not to sound as winded as he felt, he said to the audience, "The warriors of the Nakota thank you for attending their dance, but now it is late and we leave at six in the morning. Good night."

He ignored his brother's puzzled look and went to the wagon to get a bar of Martha's strong soap and proceeded on to the river. He waded into the water carefully and began scouring away the grease and paint, as his heart slowed and his legs ceased their trembling. Hawk's disgusted voice cut through his weariness.

"Why did you stop the dance, my brother?"

"Because I am old, and tired, and in less than three hours I have guard duty and two hours after that we will be packing to continue our journey. I said I would dance, and I have, but I didn't say for how long."

Hawk laughed, "My brother grows fat and soft in the arms of the white woman."

Ross grinned back at him, "I don't deny it, my brother."

"And no doubt there is another reason my brother wishes to go to bed so early." He raised a finger, making an obscene gesture.

Ross laughed and answered, "That, too."

He turned away from Hawk and waded into deeper water to rinse himself off. Hawk watched him silently and when Ross

105

waded out of the water, he walked beside him to the wagons. They parted at Marlette's tent without a word and Ross knew his brother was feeling defeated.

Inside the tent he cast aside the dripping breechclout and dried before laying down beside Marlette. He felt her indecision and asked softly, "Am I still welcome?"

She turned her head toward him and asked, "Which one of you comes to bed with me? The savage, wild Indian warrior, or the gentle and tender husband?"

"Both."

"No. I can't accept that. The man I saw out there tonight has nothing to do with my husband. I have seen that man before, but I don't know him."

"Then I am your husband."

She turned to face him and her voice had a faint breathless excitement, as she whispered, "I can't believe that man is you, Ross. It was terrible to see you like that. I doubt if I'll be able to face anyone tomorrow without blushing." After a long pause, she added, "But you were magnificent."

He took her in his arms and kissed her, relieved that she wasn't ashamed. "Then I don't have to pack my things?"

"Only if Hawk has won."

He pulled her closer. "No, Hawk hasn't won. I won't leave you—not now, not ever. But one thing you must realize is how difficult it is for me to be with your people. Hawk is my family and his warriors are my friends. With them I don't have to try to be what I am not. All the time I am with you and your people, I have to think before I can react as a white man should. It will be easier someday, I hope, and I can be what you think I am."

She touched his cheek and caressed his aching head, and said, "You are already what I want you to be. The things I sometimes think I would change are the very things that made me love you in the first place—like offering yourself for a child's life, and leading this train. So you see, I really would not want you to be less than you are, but I do wish you could smile more and laugh more like you did tonight, because you are beautiful when you do."

He smiled and whispered, "Don't let anyone else hear you say that. Now go to sleep before you succeed in completely wearing me out."

She giggled and turned away from him and he let his hand slide lovingly down her arm and across the barely swelling abdomen where his child was growing, and whispered against her hair, "I am happy, Marlette. Even if you can't see it, I am very happy."

When his relief guard came out at dawn, Ross didn't go to his own fire for breakfast, but went instead to Hawk's camp. He felt it would be easier for Marlette to face Martha and Liz without his presence.

He ate with Hawk and his warriors and they bantered lightly, insultingly, about his performance, but he couldn't stay long with Hawk. He sensed a restrained sadness in Hawk as he rose to make sure everything was in order with the wagons. When he was assured everything was in order, he rode to the front of the train and gave the signal to move out.

Hawk and his men were mounting their horses and Hawk came riding up to him alone. He was freshly painted and the sadness Ross had felt earlier was clearly evident in his brother's eyes.

In their own language, Hawk said, "I have decided it is time for us to return to our people."

"You know you are welcome to stay with us as long as you wish, Hawk."

"No. You have much to do here. Your responsibilities are many. I am satisfied that, for now, this is to be your life."

"It is as my vision guides me."

"I do not wish it so, but I must accept the fact it is so. My heart is heavy to leave without you, knowing I may never see you again."

"No less heavy than mine, my brother."

Hawk released the reins he held and, with arms outstretched, leaned toward Ross and Ross reached out to hold his brother in a farewell embrace. They released each other silently and Hawk grasped his older brother's forearms strongly. "My brother is still a man worthy to be chief. You did well last night. I am still proud to say you are my brother."

"And I am prouder still to say you are my brother. May the Great Spirit grant you a safe journey home. And tell my sister I will think of her often."

Hawk nodded, too close to tears to speak. With a last fierce pressure on Ross's arms he released his grip and whirled his horse away and rode swiftly toward the rising sun. His warriors lashed their horses after him and soon they were obscured by dust. He felt the urge to follow them, knowing what his day would be like and envying their swift, uninhibited travel.

John came up and pulled his horse in beside Ross. "Your brother leavin'?"

Still watching the cloud of dust, Ross answered, "Yes."

"He's a fine man."

Ross forced his eyes away from the Indians, only half hearing John, and murmured, "Yes."

John continued, "That was some performance you two gave last night. You know I really didn't understand about you until last night. I couldn't quite associate you—I mean the man beside me right now—with the man you had to be to go to the Pawnee and come back alive. I think I can now."

"Marlette is having the same problem."

John chuckled, and said, "I can see where she would."

Ross nodded and glanced back toward the Indians and saw nothing but a receding cloud of dust. He felt again the strong pull of freedom tugging at his heart. He could be with them, riding wild and free, except for one thing—a woman with ash-blond hair who carried his child. With an effort he turned his horse away and loped toward the front of the train, keeping his face westward.

9. *Fort Laramie*

THE NEXT DAY they were able to cross the South Platte and continue along the north side of the river beneath the bluffs, camping that night where the trail left the river to cross the barren tableland to the North Platte.

In the morning they filled their water kegs and followed the ascending trail over the top of the diminishing bluffs. They found themselves on a high, hot, waterless plain, dotted with showy clumps of yellow and pink cactus and alive with lizards. Incongruous with the heat and dust surrounding the wagons, a black cloud obliterated the sky to the northwest. Lightning could be seen forking against the blueblack cloud, but it continued drifting eastward to the north, and eventually a beautiful rainbow appeared in the storm's wake.

The train nooned in the midst of the barren prairie. Overcome with heat, dust, and insects, they saw water where none existed. As they neared the North Platte, the air became worse as the wagons wound among sand hills where no wind stirred and oxen began to fail from heat, thirst and cactus spine inbedded hooves.

Late in the afternoon the sand hills steepened and the landscape sharpened into ravines. The trail led them to the brink of a valley. With weary determination, the movers prepared to lower the wagons down the steep hill into Ash Hollow.

Ash Hollow seemed an oasis compared to what they had just been through. Laurel and dwarf cedar grew along the hillsides and currants, cherries and gooseberries grew along the dry stream bed and were quickly snatched to slack the emigrants' thirst. The stock found water in the few stagnant pools left amidst the groves of ash trees, but the grass had already been eaten short by the trains ahead of them. They moved down the widening hollow toward the North Platte and camped at the mouth of Ash Hollow near the spring.

The cabin standing near the mouth of Ash Creek was an immediate curiosity to the movers. It had been built a few years before by wintering trappers and was now a prairie post office. Most evident here, as at no other place along the trail, was the need of the emigrants to communicate with families left behind in the east or with fellow travelers separated for unknown reasons. Letters waited to be taken east a few miles or clear to the states. Ross, usually ahead of the train, always stopped to read the messages left along the trail, except those with specific names on the outside. Some of the messages were poignant, telling of death or stolen stock, and some were informative, warning of bad water or hidden springs away from the trail, but all dramatized the spirit of oneness the emigrants felt as they experienced what would be the most memorable event in most of their lives. The concern for one another Ross perceived in these notes was perhaps the most admirable quality he could find in the emigrants as a whole.

The cabin was not only a place to leave letters, but also a place to advertise for lost stock, and a place to lighten loads. Inside and outside of the cabin were the abandoned possessions of other trains, possessions that had suddenly become less important as the strength of animals and men deteriorated. Some of them had notes attached with the history of the article and a plea for someone to bring it on if they could, or use it if it happened to be food.

Beyond Ash Hollow, game was plentiful again and the main staple of their diet was buffalo meat. They plodded along through violent thunderstorms and stifling dust and heat, ever in need of urging on as the weather and country taxed their strength and tried their patience, wearying them to exhaustion.

Imperceptibly, the scenery changed from subtle sand hills to more spectacular bluffs, which were broken and tortured in appearance and streaked with hot desert colors. For days they traveled through the fortresses of rock, passing the spectacular spire of Chimney Rock and starting to climb upward as they circumvented the formidable barrier of Scotts Bluff.

Late one afternoon, after traveling over increasingly rough and desolate country where the only green to be seen was on the islands of the Platte, they came within sight of Fort Bernard. This fort was several miles away from Fort Laramie, and the first sight of habitation they had seen for weeks. There were cries of joy among the women and cheers from the younger men as Ross ordered them to circle the wagons within sight of the fort, still some distance away across a grassy plain populated by a herd of mules and a large camp of Indian lodges belonging to the Lakota. Once the noise of the wagons was stilled, Ross could hear the distinct sound of war drums and knew the Lakota were working themselves into a frenzy in preparation for war against the Crow and Snake Indians.

With more energy than they'd had for days, the camp was set up in hopes of going to the fort, but Ross ordered them not to leave camp. He doubled the guard and prepared to ride to the fort himself to talk to Richard and Bissonette, who operated the establishment. Then he would visit the Indians.

It was midnight before Ross returned to his own camp. He took a turn at guard duty before he finally was able to retire to his tent. Marlette was sleeping soundly and Ross, too exhausted to undress, lay down on top of the blankets and slept immediately.

He slept through all the busy sounds of morning as if drugged, and would have slept longer if Marlette hadn't come into the tent and bent over him, speaking his name. Slowly he opened his eyes and blinked away sleep. "What's wrong?" he asked, almost incoherently.

"Nothing. Everyone's ready to go but us."

"Did you go to the fort?"

"No. I thought I should stay and help you get the wagon loaded."

He sighed and pushed himself up to a sitting position, fully awake at last. "I'll take you after we get things loaded."

"I thought you wanted to move on to Fort Laramie."

"I do, but John can take the wagons, and you and I can visit the fort here and catch up with them later."

Her smile was radiant. "Oh, Ross. I'd really like that. Do you know how little we've seen of each other, except when I was sick and couldn't have cared less?"

He reached out and tangled his fingers in her straight, fine hair. "I know."

She leaned toward him, and he took her face in his hands and brought her lips to his. All else was forgotten as his body warmed to hers. He kissed the smooth, pale skin of her throat, kept soft

111

and protected from sun and dust by high collars and large bandanas she used to pull over her face in the dust. All else was forgotten in their need for each other. Quickly they shed encumbering clothing and came together beneath the blanket on their bed. In a few moments Marlette was struggling to push away from his embrace, and he released her, alarmed by the distress in her eyes.

"What is it? Is there something wrong?"

"I don't know. You were hurting me. Not a sharp pain, but something like pressure. Do you suppose I'm going to miscarry?"

"I don't know." He couldn't say more as the memory of what had happened to Spotted Fawn sent his thoughts into panic. He sat up, fighting to remain calm and not let her see his fear. He couldn't believe this was happening. He had lost his first wife and baby in childbirth, and now something was happening to Marlette.

He felt her hand on his arm, and her voice had a reassuring calm as she said, "Ross. I'm all right now. Please don't worry. I'll be fine."

His hand covered hers as it rested lightly on his arm. "If you're not, I'll never forgive myself." His voice was steady but husky with emotion. He pulled away and rose to his feet and dressed, trying to fight the feeling of dread heavy in his stomach. Once dressed, he turned to her with a composed face and asked, "Do you think you can still go with me to the fort?"

Matching his forced calm, she answered, "I won't know until I try."

He nodded and left the tent. John was bringing Martha, Liz, and the rest of the family back from the fort in the buckboard. Ross squatted before the coffeepot and poured himself a cup with unsteady hands. John joined him at the fire, took one look at his ashen face, and asked, "What's wrong, man? You look like you've just seen a ghost."

Ross saw the deep concern in John's eyes, but he couldn't talk about what had happened until he had himself under control. He took a long swallow of the hot coffee and threw the rest on the fire, answering, "Maybe I have." He turned away and continued into the corral to get his horse before John could question him further. He brought in Marlette's horse, and the action helped calm him. He tied it to the wagon where Marlette was loading blankets.

Placing his hand gently on her shoulder, he asked, "Are you still all right?"

She nodded gravely in answer, and he walked over to John and said, "I want to take Marlette into the fort. You'll have no trouble keeping on the trail between here and Fort Laramie until we can catch up with you."

"Fine with me. This hasn't been much of a honeymoon for you two. Are you sure everything's all right?"

"As far as I know, everything is fine."

The train was moving away as Marlette and Ross walked with their horses into the stockaded fort. He paid particular attention to everything she did, but there was no sign of any kind that she was not all right. In fact, she seemed to have completely forgotten the incident as she priced goods in the trade store and bought a small quantity of staples, remarking at the inflated prices.

Ross packed her purchases into the saddlebags and helped her mount, but as soon as they left the security of the fort Ross felt his anxiety return. He purposely kept his horse at a walk to make it easier on her, but was too full of concern for her to realize he wasn't using this time to talk to her.

Finally Marlette broke the silence. "Ross, you're not talking to me. Are you still worried about what happened this morning?"

Without looking at her, he replied, "Yes."

Her hand reached out and covered his for a moment before their horses swayed apart. "Please don't worry. I feel fine now. Besides, I've been thinking about those mountains ahead of us. We have to cross them, don't we?"

"Yes."

"And it's going to be a lot worse traveling than what we've had, isn't it?"

"Yes."

"All right, then, let's be practical. Maybe I will miscarry if it is not meant for me to keep this pregnancy. If not now, surely when it gets rougher. Maybe it is for the best, Ross. Later on it could be a lot harder on me than now. When we get to Oregon and this is all behind us, we can have another child. You have to believe that, Ross."

He moved his horse closer to hers and took her hand and smiled at her. "I hope you are right. But it is not losing the child I worry about as much as losing you, if things are not right. For that I could not forgive myself."

"I know, my darling, I know, and I won't give up my life without a terrible battle. I have wasted too many years alone and unloved. I need your love and I need your touch. Can you understand? I never want you to stop holding me. This is the bond that exists between us. Not the church, or the minister and his words, or the paper we signed. Not even God. Those three years away from you made me realize it. I thought of your touch more than anything else. I need you to hold me and to touch me. Every time you touch me I feel your love, and my heart is at peace in the security of your love. Do you feel it, too?"

"Yes. I feel it. I have always felt it."

She shook her head, smiling, and exclaimed, "Oh, you! I could hate you for being so wise." But she didn't pull her hand away from his. Instead she looked around her, seeing the wild flowers just coming into bloom and smelling the crisp air fresh from the mountains scented with the fragrances of earth and flowers. "What a strange, frightening country, ever changing and each change with a distinct beauty all its own. Imagine having all of this to roam, unfettered by any other man or woman. Are you sure you want to give it up?"

"If I didn't, I wouldn't be here. I have had it all, but it was not enough. To be free is usually to be lonely. I knew what it was like not to be lonely, and it was more gratifying than being free." He looked into her eyes and saw the love there and smiled tenderly, but the moment was soon gone as they caught up to the train and the dust of the wagons enveloped them.

Ross saw Marlette safely to her wagon and rode on to join John at the head of the train. He kept the wagons rolling through the noon rest, knowing they were almost to Fort Laramie. And then it came into view as they passed out of a belt of timber. The sun was full on the large white adobe structure standing on a vast grassy plain rising away from the smaller river, a mile upstream from its junction with the Platte. In the distance beyond the fort rose the jagged ridges of the Black Hills and the flattened top of Laramie Peak. Moving toward that peak was a line of white-topped wagons pulling westward. On the point of land between the fort and the meeting of the two rivers, were as many Indian lodges as there had been at Fort Bernard, most of them belonging to the Lakota. Contending with that many Indians was going to be a problem.

John felt the same way and said with a sigh, "God! They'll empty every barrel and sack of food we have. What can we do?"

"I'm not sure, but I'd better think of something. I'll ride ahead and see what the fort has to say."

He left John and sent his horse at a lope across the plain, then waded belly deep through Laramie Creek. He rode through the double-gated entrance that opened at his approach and dismounted in front of the two-storied building and climbed the steps to the trader's office. Bordeaux, in charge with Papin gone downriver, greeted him. "Hallo. I remember you from last fall— Monsieur Chesnut, is it not?"

"Yes." Their hands met. "I'm bringing in a bunch of wagons headed for Oregon. Have any particular place you want us?"

"Wherever you can find grass. Been helluva time here with all these damn Sioux. They prepare for war against the Crow and Snake."

"Any danger from them?"

"The usual. Theft and bribery. They want tribute for the wagons passing through their land, and they make it rough on the train ahead of you. Keep your guards doubled or you'll be missing anything that's not too heavy to carry off or lead."

"Thanks for the warning. I half-suspected that was the way it was. Do you have enough supplies for my wagons to stock up on?"

"Stock is running low. So many have passed ahead of you. But we will do what we can."

"As soon as we get set up and can safely leave camp, I'll send a few in at a time for supplies."

Bordeaux held out his hand. "You will be taken care of, Monsieur."

Ross left the office and rode out of the fort. The wagons were just crossing the deep little creek, blocked up as high as possible. Ross sent his horse along the creek toward the line of cottonwood trees and found an area still showing some graze. The wagons swung after him, and soon they were making a circle where he indicated.

The wagons were hardly unhitched before the Indians descended like locusts, overrunning the camp, peering and prying.

Fires were quickly built and buffalo meat, already on the verge of spoiling, was hastily thrown into cooking pots and set to boil. Ross, ever the able diplomat, was even more effective now among people whose language and customs he understood, and the toll from the emigrants' diminishing supplies was minimal. By dusk the last of the Indians were straggling back to their own camp.

After supper, Ross and John made the rounds of their wagon train, making sure every man knew they were doubling the guard and that nothing was left where it could be easily taken. The dogs were tied to wagon wheels with extra admonitions to bark if anything came near.

When they were sure everything was as secure as it could be, they returned to camp. Ross said his good night and retreated to Marlette's tent, feeling anxiety rise in him again as he wondered how she really felt.

She straightened up when he entered the tent and came into his arms. She felt his tenseness, and asked, "What's wrong?"

"You know what's wrong."

She kissed him and whispered, "Yes. But I'm not worried. I've felt perfectly normal all day."

As if to prove her point, she finished undressing and beckoned him down beside her, but the pain came again and she lay there, crying in his arms. Ross held her until she was asleep, and for a long while after he lay unable to sleep himself, tormented by doubts and fears and anger. Restless, he finally rose and dressed and left the tent. He looked up at the clear, star-filled sky and silently issued a fierce and desperate plea to the deity he knew as the Great Spirit. He stood a long time staring skyward but felt no solace. He went to his horse, rode out to where the herd grazed, and began a check of the area.

John saw him coming and rode to meet him. "Why aren't you in bed? It's another hour before you're supposed to be out here."

"I couldn't sleep."

John grunted in disbelief. "If you couldn't sleep, you've got something bothering you. I saw it this morning. You asked me to help you and now I'm askin' you to let me. If you've got a problem, I want to know it."

"I'm worried about Marlette. Something is not quite right with her pregnancy."

"Oh God, no! You don't think she's going to lose it, do you?"

"I don't know. Tell Liz and Martha to keep an eye on her for me. Tell them not to let her overdo or lift more than she should."

"I'll tell Liz. They won't let anything happen to her if they can help it."

"Good. She won't want me to know if she has trouble, so I'll have to depend on you to let me know."

John chuckled grimly. "You won't be too popular in Martha's book if anything happens to Marlette."

"I'm not anyway, but I'm glad Marlette has her, especially now. I'm going to look around for a while. I'll be back in time to replace you."

Ross turned his horse and rode toward the trees along the creek. If anything was hiding, it would most likely be in the trees. He worked his way through the fringe of cottonwoods without finding any lurking man or beast and made a methodical search of the grassy plain. He returned to the herd to relieve John and began a lonely vigil with the other men and boys coming out to watch the herd.

When his duty was over, he returned to the tent and lay down on top of the blankets and slept, not waking until the noise of the camp aroused him long after sunup. He lay watching Marlette for a long time, taking in every detail of her face as he prepared himself to tell her the decision he had made. She finally stirred and opened her eyes. His face was bleak as she looked at him, and his heart squeezed with hard-knotted determination.

"Ross, what is it? You look so strange."

"How do you feel this morning?"

"All right, I think."

He reached out to touch her cheek and brush the silvered golden hair from her face. "I have decided that it is better if we do not try to be together until after the baby is born. I don't want to hurt you and I don't want you to lose our baby. You said yesterday it is being able to touch and to hold me that binds us together, but it will be hard for me to touch you and hold you and remember I shouldn't have you. You must understand this when I do not share our bed. You will have to remember that I love you more than anything on this earth, and it is because I love you I must stay away from you. Will you be able to understand and accept this without being hurt when I have to stay away from you?"

She held his hand to her face and barely nodded. He leaned

over to kiss her and said, "Now get dressed. I want to take you up to the fort." She nodded again, but the anguish in her eyes made his heart twist. He got up and quickly went outside. Liz and Martha were already cooking breakfast, but he wasn't hungry. John was sitting in his chair, rocking and smoking.

"I'm going around to make sure everyone gets their supplies today. I want to pull out tomorrow. When all the boys are able to stay with the wagons, I would like to take the rest of you up to the fort for supplies, so get lists made out and I'll be back."

"You better have something to eat first. You look like you could use a good meal."

"I'm not hungry. Do you mind if we take your light wagon up?"

"Nope. I'll get the team ready and we can go when you get back."

Ross nodded and turned away from the fire, ignoring the curious looks following him. The gloomy response to his order that they would be moving out the next day only added to his distressed mood.

He approached the Yetter wagon with dread. Yetter was there dutifully tarring his wagon wheels. He was not the easiest person to get along with, but he did take good care of his wagons and stock. It was about the only admirable trait Ross found in the man.

"Mr. Yetter, I want to leave first thing in the morning. Find time to get your supplies today."

"What the hell's your hurry, Chesnut? What's wrong with staying one more day to let the stock get fed up and rested?"

"Nothing is wrong with letting the stock get into shape, except we just don't have that much time. If you want to wait for the next company and go on with them while your stock rests, that will be fine with me, but I'm leaving tomorrow."

With stiff dismissal, Yetter said, "I'll consider it."

When Ross returned to his own camp, the Jessups' buckboard was unloaded and the team hitched in readiness. Jennifer saw him coming and was the first one to scramble into the back of the light wagon. Ross helped Marlette and Martha to get in, while John helped Liz into the back of the wagon, and they all set off for the fort.

They renewed their dwindling supplies for considerably more

118

money than ever before and traveled silently back to the wagons. The Jessups were especially dismayed. They had bought nothing at Fort Bernard because of the high prices there, only to find the prices here even higher. None of them had extra money now to save for later necessities and John was feeling depressed at the thought of arriving in Oregon broke.

Ross, overcoming his own downheartedness, told John as they unloaded the flour and sugar, "Don't worry about things in Oregon. Just worry about getting there. I'll take care of you once we're there. With me gone so long, we'll probably be able to use you for a while to get the logs rolling again, but before we do we'll get a cabin up for you."

John looked at him with a slow smile. "I wish I could ease your mind as much as you've just eased mine."

The evening meal was quiet, but only for their immediate campfire. While they had been gone to the fort, the Rice Dunbar train, which included their earlier companions, the Thorntons, had circled not too far from them. Visiting between the two camps had lifted everyone's spirits except theirs. Liz tried to be cheerful, but no one responded. She perched on the arm of John's chair in silence, alternately staring at Ross and Marlette. Ross held Marlette close with his arm around her, but there was no comfort in doing so because it was merely a pretense to make everything seem normal.

From the Dunbar circle they could hear a fiddle being tuned up, and Liz jumped to her feet with hands on her hips and gave them all a fiery look. "Well! I declare! You all can sit here like a bunch of undertakers if you want, but I'm going to go join the dance. If you don't want to come with me, John, I'll find someone who does." With a swish of her skirts, she went determinedly into the darkness.

John got up and tapped out his pipe. "By golly, I think she's right. Here we are on a lovely night with everybody fed and well, and we're wasting it."

Martha looked at them and said, "Might be a good idea. We could use a little cheerin' up around here, I'd say."

Cam looked at Jeremy, and the two of them slowly stood up and started to leave as unobtrusively as possible. Jennifer saw them and raced after them with skirts flying, grabbing Cam by the arm.

119

"No you don't, Cam Galligher. You promised me you'd teach me how to dance."

Jeremy snickered and Cam stood awkwardly, trapped.

Ross, smiling at the boy's embarrassment, commented, "I think she's got you, Cam."

Cam mumbled, "Aw, Jenny. I don't like to dance."

"You'd dance quick enough if Suzannah Heely was doing the asking. Now you promised!"

More instruments joined the violin tuning up in the Dunbar circle and Ross asked Marlette, "Do you feel like dancing with me?"

"I'd like that very much."

"Come on then." He rose to his feet and lifted her up easily. She was so terribly thin again. His heart ached with concern for her. "Martha, I'll need someone to dance with while Marlette rests. Will you come with us?"

"Who's going to stay with the wagons if I leave?"

Jeremy eagerly volunteered, "I will."

Ross smiled at him, "You're too willing, but you've got the job if Martha wants to come."

"Well," said Martha grudgingly, "I guess it won't hurt me none."

It didn't take long for the bright music, and Liz's wholehearted enthusiasm as she led the first few dances, to get the whole company into a happier mood. Even Ross was enjoying himself as he was able to be close to Marlette and see her smile and, for the moment, forget about what might be ahead.

He let Marlette rest and pulled Martha into the lively round dance with him and found she was as light on her feet as Marlette. Before the dance was over, she was laughing and fanning herself but still keeping up with him.

When it was time for the guard to change, Ross told Marlette, "We'd better go back to the wagons. The boys have to go on guard duty."

"Martha and I'll go. You stay and dance with Jenny. She looks so unhappy. She's so crazy about Cam and he thinks she's still a child."

"He's the one that's crazy. Are you sure you want to leave me with her?"

120

She looked at him and the sadness returned to her eyes. "There isn't much choice."

He stopped dancing and took her to the side of the waltzing circle. "I'm sorry, Marlette. Don't make it difficult."

She nodded and he kissed her briefly. "Good night. I love you."

She didn't say anything, but the misery in her eyes told him more than enough. She joined Martha and Cam, and he watched them disappear into the darkness before he walked to where Jenny watched the resuming dancers.

"Would you mind dancing with me, Jenny?"

Her eyes brightened and she held up her arms. "Oh, would you!"

He took her in his arms and led her back into the waltzing circle. She was concentrating so hard on her feet she was frowning, and he finally said, "You're doing just fine, Jenny; now relax and enjoy it."

She pulled her eyes away from her feet and looked up into his face and, with a determined smile, forced herself to dance like she supposed a woman would do. He laughed at her, and she giggled and stumbled. They had to stop and start again, and she said, "I wish Cam would treat me like you do."

"He just hasn't realized that you're not a little girl. When he does, he'll act differently."

She was delighted. "Do you really think I'm a woman?"

"Not quite yet, but I can see what you will be in a couple of years and I like what I see—and he will, too."

"Oh, I hope so. I like him so much and he doesn't even care."

"Be patient, Jenny. When someone else starts noticing you, he will, too."

The waltz was over and he released Jenny, who was escorted away a few moments later by one of the hired herdsmen. He watched the dancers for a few minutes longer, then, feeling tired, he returned to camp. He didn't go inside Marlette's tent but crawled under the wagon where Joseph already slept. He had seen Jonathan dancing with the Heely girl and wondered if Cam really felt anything for the fairer-haired Suzannah. But he was too tired to wonder long, and slept an exhausted, troubled sleep until he was aroused by John for his guard duty.

Ross came in at four and hammered on the frying pan. He

watched the dark heads under the wagon shift, stretching, yawning, and recurling in an attempt to ignore the rude interruption of their sleep. Ross squatted to build the fire and then carried the water bucket to the creek and came back to fill the coffeepot. Marlette came from her tent and joined him at the fire. He could tell she hadn't slept well.

"How do you feel this morning?"

"Just fine," she answered without looking at him.

He turned her face up and looked into sad eyes. "Don't do this to yourself, Marlette. It's not your fault."

She turned her head away, and he took her in his arms and held her. She clung to him in despair. Martha came over to the coffeepot, eying Ross. Marlette relaxed her embrace and he let her go.

Martha took one look at her and scowled. "Don't you feel well this morning?"

Marlette forced a smile and said, "I feel just fine. Now please stop treating me like a piece of glass. I won't break." She turned away from them and attacked the morning bread-making with a vengeance. Martha gave Ross a look that clearly held him to blame for everything.

Other fires were going now around the circle, and the camp came alive with voices and clanging kettles as people began their morning chores. By six the wagons were loaded and rolling past the white, bastioned fort, avoiding the Indian lodges still wrapped in early morning gloom. The rising sun was just lighting the top of the brutal-looking butte behind the cottonwoods and touching fire to the vibrant red, yellow, and orange hues on the twisted hills and ridges to the west.

For the first few miles they traveled near the Platte, climbing sand hills covered with sunflowers, prickly pear, and sage before they entered a rough, volcanic area. They nooned at a small creek on what appeared to be the last nearly level area they would see for some time. The hills ahead were getting bigger, rougher, and rockier. Beyond the hills they could see the jagged, swiftly rising buttresses of the cedar-covered Black Hills, where Ross had spent some of his happiest boyhood hours, and where he had taken Spotted Fawn as his wife.

Here Ross had to regroup his wagons. He called them together and told them what was ahead, and faces of those already dubious of the trail behind them became grim as he told them the easy part of the trip was over. From now on they would have to travel single file. They would be double-teaming, roping wagons into ravines and over ridges, and smoothing trail with picks and shovels where necessary. The women, who would have to walk to lighten the load, would have to be especially careful not to stray off the trail into the rattlesnake-infested rocks and to be on the lookout for bears, as well as Indians. They were entering an area used by several tribes, some of them more hostile than those they had yet encountered. He hoped silently they would not meet any of the Indians he referred to. Not even he would have a chance against the Blackfoot, and perhaps not the Crow.

The next day was even more grueling than the day before. Up before dawn and on the trail at six, they traveled over increasingly desolate country of sand hills, furrowed by rock chasms and populated by swarms of grasshoppers, which rose in clouds as they walked. Water and grass were to be had only in ravines or along creek courses—poor reward for hours of toil under the hot sun. They camped that night with formidable Laramie Peak in full view and dreaded to think what tomorrow might bring.

The highest hill they had yet had to climb was conquered the next day, but not without a great deal of effort and many broken wheels. Men sweated and cursed while animals strained to pull wagons up the incline. Here Mrs. Yetter had to leave behind an old and treasured bureau when not even double-teaming would pull their heavy wagon up the steep grade.

Late in the afternoon Ross discovered a small herd of buffalo in one of the deep ravines along a creek. It was an ideal situation in which to block both ends of the ravine and keep the buffalo corralled until they had what they needed for food. It was dark before Ross and his hunters had all the meat packed in, but the exhausted men had plenty of fresh meat to revive their strength on.

10. To the Sweetwater and South Pass

Ross's train celebrated the Fourth of July at noon, with singing and cheering in honor of Independence Day. Then Ross had the wagons on the move. The trail was less dusty and the travelers could see glimpses of wild sunflowers, daisies, and other flowers among the sage and greasewood. They passed outcroppings of coal and were plagued with clouds of flies. By evening they were camping on the Platte River again. Mosquitoes were plentiful, and so were ground toads, which caused much excitement among the women and girls, who were startled by them leaping out from nearly underneath them. The boys, needing a diversion and hearing the startled screams of the girls, were soon catching the hopping toads to terrorize the girls and improvise races along the riverbank with them. There were currants to be had along the river and fruit-hungry movers picked as many as they could before dark, adding them to the evening meal.

The travel was somewhat easier as they neared the ford of the Platte, though now the trail was extremely dusty. They would not have to double-team or rope their wagons, which required every man to give his strength to the point of exhaustion and took its toll in possessions jettisoned when men and animals could no longer move heavy wagons upward. They were silently grateful for the respite and afraid to ask how long it would last.

Deer and antelope were seen, so Ross took a few of the men hunting for fresh meat and was back in the early afternoon with meat for the whole camp. They camped within sight of another group of wagons that night and there was some visiting back and forth, since these wagons had once been a part of the original group camping at Indian Creek.

They reached the lower ford on the Platte, where much work had to be done to ready the wagons for crossing the deep and swift river. The buffalo hides Ross had advised they keep were now brought into use. The wagon boxes, now so dry that boards no longer met, would quickly fill with water and sink. The buffalo hides were used to wrap around the wagons so that, with the wheels removed, they could be floated across the river—though not without difficulty.

They traveled for two days through a parched and desolate landscape, barren except for brackish ponds, sagebrush, and broken hills of granite blocks rising from prairies of dried grass where buffalo fed. On the evening of the second day, they camped between the Sweetwater and the gray mound of Independence Rock, whose smooth bowl-shaped hulk had been in sight for most of the day.

In the morning they prepared for a long climb over a ridge into the next valley. On top of the ridge, Ross let the teams rest and taking Marlette and anyone else who wished to ride with him, he led a little party of sightseers to the brink of the gorge the Sweetwater had carved through the granite ridge.

He led the wagons down the long slope into the next valley, and the travelers could see now more clearly the beginnings of the chasm from the west side where the Sweetwater wandered through a fertile meadow along an abruptly rising granite ridge. At the foot of this high precipice, the Sweetwater flowed amidst piles of rock, lush green grass, and a profusion of flowers before pouring through the gorge into the valley beyond.

Ross helped set up camp, aiding those who needed help with maintenance on deteriorating equipment. Some of the men were too sick with mountain fever to do the necessary repairs. John, in a little better shape than the rest of them, somehow managed to keep their own equipment together with the help of the boys.

Ross returned to his own camp at dark and ate in exhausted silence. John sat equally exhausted in his chair, drinking coffee and smoking his pipe and looking like he was enjoying neither.

John finally sighed and commented, "I don't know how you do it."

"I've had better conditioning than the rest of you. Why don't you go to bed? You don't look like you can last much longer."

"You're right. Never quite felt so tired and sick. I'm beginning to wonder if it's worth it."

"It depends on what you expect when you get there."

John waved a weak hand. "Never mind. I don't think I want to know just now." He rose and walked shakily to his tent, leaving Ross alone.

He wondered how Marlette was. He hadn't even had time to talk with her that evening. He cleaned his plate and looked with longing at her tent, needing her as much as he wanted to comfort her. He turned away and crawled into some blankets to get a few hours' sleep before his herd duty. He had no doubt he would be awakened before two because someone else would be unable to take their turn.

The next day they made their noon stop where the trail swung away from the river over an arid plain of sage and greasewood. A shout from one of the herders alerted the circle of wagons that a rider was approaching. Ross and John rose from their places and walked out of the circle to see who was coming. A few other men who still had strength enough to stand joined them.

The rider pulled his horse to a halt a few yards away, and Ross thought there was something vaguely familiar in the man's appearance.

"Hallo, friends. Do you have a cup to spare? I'm William Bonney of Oregon."

The name refreshed Ross's memory. Bonney was from Oregon, but everything he knew about the man was less than favorable. Nevertheless he answered, "We can spare a cup. Come on in."

Bonney dismounted with a smile and walked toward them.

Ross asked, "Are you traveling alone?"

"I am now, but I been with Lansford Hastings at Bridger's fort. Any of you got one of Hastings' books?"

Someone behind Ross answered, "Yep. Is there any truth in it, Mr. Bonney?"

He smiled again and chuckled. "I ain't read it so I can't say to that, but I do have a letter from Mr. Hastings for all you emigrants thinkin' of headin' for California. Mr. Hastings has opened a new trail." He pulled a letter out of his pocket and

126

handed it to Ross. It was worse for wear, indicating a good many people had read it. Ross glanced over it, with John peering over his shoulder.

Yetter asked, "What does it say?"

Ross looked up. "Hastings has opened a new trail from Fort Bridger into California by way of Salt Lake. He is urging all California-bound trains to use it instead of going to Fort Hall first."

John asked, "Is it possible?"

Ross answered, "It's possible, but not with wagons. I've heard stories of that crossing on horseback. I don't think wagons could make it."

Bonney interjected, "But Hastings just come that way."

"Did he come by wagon?"

"Well, no, he didn't, but he says it's possible and all wagons headed for California would save lots of time and miles usin' his trail."

"None of us are going to California, and if we were, I wouldn't take Mr. Hastings' advice."

Bonney shrugged and took back the letter, stuffing it in his pocket, and appeared reluctant to stay now that he had found no emigrants bound for California. Gathering up his reins, he said, "Well, maybe I'll just head on down the trail since I can't be any help to you folks. Good luck to you."

Ross nodded, and Bonney swung onto his horse. They watched him ride past their wagons and out of sight.

John wondered out loud, "I wonder how many of them California-bound wagons ahead of us have taken his advice."

"I hope none of them have."

Yetter's small eyes squinted even smaller. "How can you be so damn sure they haven't got a better trail, Chesnut?"

"For the simple reason I've seen the country. But I'm not opposed to you finding out for yourself if you don't want to take my advice."

Daniels asked, "Then why would Hastings send this man with a letter telling us about this new trail?"

"I don't know what Hastings has to gain," Ross answered, ".but I know Bonney well enough to know he'd do anything for money."

Yetter blinked but said nothing more, and Ross turned away,

thinking of the wagons before him that could now be making a fatal decision to use a new and unexplored trail. He wondered if he went ahead to warn them whether it would do any good. A terrible dread added weight to his already overburdening weariness and worry.

By mid-afternoon of the following day, they started the climb out of the canyon up a steep sandy ridge. Once on top of the ridge, the emigrants could see the purple snowcapped peaks of the Wind River Mountains. A wind blowing from those permanent snowfields did more than Ross ever could to warn them of what lay ahead.

They camped that night on a small stream barely affording the stock enough water to drink. A cold wind howled and dust swirled through camp, whipping tents and filling cooking pots with sand. Women cried and men swore and during the night tired men, with eyes blinded by dust and fingers numbed with cold, didn't see oxen seek shelter and separate from the herd.

Several days' climb through the Sweetwater Valley brought them at last to the base of a broad plateau with a cold crisp wind in their faces. To the north and south, the mountains seemed to butt up against the plateau that stretched to the horizon, and they traveled ever upward through a desert of sand and tall gray rocks. After nooning in a pleasant grassy basin for an unusually long rest period, the caravan left the sheltered bowl over what seemed the highest elevation on the broad plateau, with a strong west wind blowing against them. But the summit was yet two miles away.

Ross pulled his horse to a stop when the horizon became a succession of descending ridges with nothing obstructing his view. They had reached the South Pass. He waited for the wagons traveling in a staggered column on the broad plateau. They came almost as one to the crest of the Rockies. Tired as they were, and suffering from altitude, poor diet, poor water, and diarrhea, they cheered and shook hands and laughed with relief. Mr. Tannelow brought out a jug of Kentucky corn whiskey he had been saving for this moment. Every man with a cup got a half ration of the potent home brew.

Ross stood aside and watched, feeling, as he somehow always did, apart and alone. Marlette edged her way out of the happy crowd and came to join him. He held her wordlessly. He could offer no word of encouragement. They had come not quite halfway. The worse half—the longer half—was yet to come.

John broke out of the happy throng and came toward Ross with a cup and offered it to him. He tried to decline, but John insisted, as the rest of the men raised their cups and toasted the West. Ross took a sip of the burning liquid. But John was not done with him yet. He called to the men and motioned them around where he and Ross stood, calling out in a loud voice, "And how about a toast to the man who got us this far?" He turned to Ross and raised his cup in salute, his eyes misty with emotion.

A chorus of "Here, here" echoed around Ross, who smiled and turned slowly with his cup upraised, feeling honored and wanting to salute them in return. They deserved it. It had taken more than just guts to get this far and he knew that, somehow or other, they would make it the rest of the way. They tossed off the last of their ration of whiskey and returned to their wagons. Ross escorted Marlette back to her wagon and once again they were underway, downhill.

After a layover at Pacific Springs the wagons moved on, crossing the gully of Dry Sandy where what water there was lay in stagnant pools. They rolled on toward Little Sandy, fighting dust and shortness of breath, crunching through hordes of crickets, spurred on by the sight of fresh snow on the mountains on either side. At Little Sandy the crickets took wing and attacked them in droves like mosquitoes. Sage fires were built in self-defense, but they gave little protection; the only salve was buffalo grease, which was becoming quite aromatic after days in the heat. Women, who a few weeks ago wouldn't have considered using the rancid grease, overcame their disdain and spread grease on smarting faces and cracked lips that bled at the slightest smile.

There was little grass here, but a dense growth of willow brush along the stream provided some forage. Fish caught from the stream made a welcome change for supper, after which Ross called his emigrants together and told them just what was ahead.

"We have reached the junction of the trail to Fort Bridger and the cutoff to Fort Hall. If there are any of you wanting to go by way of Fort Bridger, you can make that choice now. Tomorrow we have a short drive to Big Sandy, where we will camp and rest the oxen and repair equipment and shoe any animals needing it. At midnight I want everyone ready to roll with water kegs filled.

We'll have a good two-day run to make in one day. There will be no water and no grass for the animals until we reach the Green River, except what we can spare from our water kegs, so those kegs must be full and used sparingly." He stepped down from the wagon tongue without asking for questions. But, as he expected, Yetter was not quite satisfied.

"I planned on going to Fort Bridger. Most of us did. Now why are you changing plans?"

"I'm not changing plans. I never intended to go to Fort Bridger. There is nothing there in the way of supplies, and it would cost time and a lot of miles, which none of us can afford to waste if we are going to make it to the Willamette Valley before it snows. If you want to go to Bridger, you can wait here until another party comes and go with them, but I'm not going to Bridger."

He turned on his heel, and John fell in beside him with a wry smile on his face, squinting at him through swollen eyes. "You think he'll go to Bridger?"

"I doubt it. He has an uncanny way of doing the right thing just when I wish he wouldn't."

John chuckled. "You really cut him kinda short. I think you're losin' your sense of humor."

A fleeting smile touched Ross's lips. "How do you know I ever had one?"

"I don't. But I've seen glimpses of one a couple of times. I'm looking forward to knowing you when you aren't dog tired and carrying a load of worry big enough to make a mountain as tall as any we've climbed."

Ross stopped and put a hand on John's shoulder, a smile lighting his face and his eyes filling with genuine warmth. "Thank you, John. I've appreciated you and your help more than I will ever be able to tell you. I couldn't have done this without you."

John shrugged with a happy smile. "I don't figure you owe me any, but I sure feel like I been collectin' every inch of the way and probably will collect a whole lot more the rest of the way."

Ross let his hand drop, the momentary interlude ending with the reminder of what was ahead. The smile was gone and the stoicism returned as he nodded. "I won't deny that. Well, we'd better take a look at the wagons and then get some sleep. Tomorrow night will be a short night."

Their own camp was quiet. The mosquitoes had driven the

130

women inside their tents, and the boys were rolled in their blankets with heads covered. John stepped quickly inside his tent, and Ross paused with weary eyes on Marlette's tent. The flap opened and Marlette looked at him with the same longing he felt. "Ross," she called softly.

The flap dropped and Ross stood looking at it with indecision. But he couldn't deny his desire to be with her, nor the compassion he felt for her need of him—the need he had tried desperately to ignore. He stepped to the tent and ducked in. She looked at him, her face burned; lips cracked; eyes swollen and red with dust, sand, and insect bites. She looked more miserable than he ever remembered her, and they had been through some rough times together. He took her in his arms and just held her and knew she was crying. He didn't try to soothe away her tears. They would wash the grit from her eyes.

Finally he released her, stepped back, and asked, "How have you been feeling?"

"No better, no worse, I guess. I didn't realize how awful this was going to be. I thought I could stand anything rather than another trip by sea to be with you. Now I am with you and it is worse than not having found you at all. It is bad enough I don't see you during the day, but not to have the comfort of your arms at night is more than I can endure. I want to miscarry, Ross. I can't stand not having you."

He took her in his arms and ran his hand over her dust-dulled hair. "I'm sorry, Marlette. I didn't want things to be like this for you, but now the only other choice we have is to go back. I'll take you back as far as you want to go—to Independence, or to Philadelphia, if that is what you want. It would be easier for you than going ahead. I'd be lying if I told you anything else. Don't answer me now. I want you to sleep on it. You can tell me in the morning. Now, I'd better get some sleep and you had, too. Good night." He released her with a brush of his lips on her rough forehead.

But she wasn't willing to let him go just yet. She held him by the arms and said, "Do you have to leave so quickly? You haven't even really kissed me. I know you're tired, but can't you just please kiss me?"

He gently touched his lips to hers. Her arms slid up around his neck and her hands held his head as she pressed her lips fiercely against his until he tasted blood and pulled away.

131

He looked at her in dismay, softly reprimanding, "Marlette! Don't do this to yourself." He reached for her towel and gently pressed it against the oozing cracks. "That's why I didn't want to kiss you on the lips. I didn't want them to bleed."

He motioned her down onto the bed and followed her. It was getting dark and his head was aching. He pulled a blanket over them and took her in his arms and held her, keeping the towel pressed firmly against her lips with his shoulder, and they slept.

Ross didn't awaken until John stuck his head into the tent with a lantern and said, "Hey, what's wrong? I didn't know where to find you."

Ross sat up sleepily, his mind only half-awake. He remembered dimly why he was here and asked, "Bring the lamp closer. I want to see her lips." He gently pulled the towel away, revealing the bloody and swollen lips. Marlette stirred but didn't awaken.

"Good lord, man! What happened?"

"Just a bad lip. See if you can find the tallow."

John rummaged through the cook box while Ross sat looking at the exhausted and deeply sleeping woman, realizing she hadn't slept well since he had left her bed. John found the tin of rancid tallow. Ross gently daubed it on the severely cracked lips and, with one last anxious look, left the tent behind John.

John turned to him and said, "Maybe you should stay with her. Neither one of you look like you can take much more of what you're doin'. I'll take your watch."

"No. I'll be all right, but I don't know about Marlette. I told her I'd take her back if she decides she can't go on. You may have to go on without us."

John's face twisted in disbelief. "God, no! I can't go on without you!"

"You may have to. Maybe you can join up with one of the other trains."

"Well, I guess you have to do what you have to do. I'm sorry, Ross. What will you do if you go back?"

"I don't know. I'm hoping a good night's sleep will change her mind. It's been rough on her."

John gripped his shoulder in understanding. "It's been rough on you both. Well, we'll see what comes in the morning. Good night."

He turned away, and Ross went to get his horse. It was going to be a long night with nothing to think about but the possibility of having to go east. He tried to push the thought from his mind and doggedly refused to think of it. But it lurked there, tearing at him, wearing on him until he welcomed banging the fry pan, if for no other reason than to hear what his fate would be.

He went to start the fire and get water as the camp came sluggishly to life. When he heard Marlette call his name, he stood and slowly turned to face her, dreading what she might say.

She stood holding her hands with her eyes down. "Ross, forgive me for putting you through what I did last night. I'm sorry. I was only thinking of myself. We have to go on. There is nothing to go back to. Less for you than for me. I realize that now."

He stood in silent relief, the realization of what going back would have meant to him hitting with full impact now that he didn't have to face it. He felt weak and took her in his arms as much to hold her as to get a hold of himself.

"You're not to blame. I'll try to be with you more and sleep with you, too, if I can. I want more than anything to share what you are going through, but you know why I can't. Just remember I do love you and get through each day the best you can, and if you need me, I'll come. It will end, Marlette. I promise."

He felt her nod and sigh and released her. Gently he tipped up her face and kissed the rancid-tasting tallow of her lips as she stood impassively.

Martha came unannounced into the tent and scolded, "Just like a man! Comin' and goin' at your pleasure, while she cries her heart out. And look what you've done now! You've hurt her!"

Marlette reacted swiftly and harshly to Martha's attack and said with a sharpness of her own, "Oh, Martha! You can protect me from everyone else, but don't try to protect me from Ross. I need him more than I need anything, or anyone on this earth— even you—and I don't want you ever to speak to him like that again."

The fire went out in Martha's eyes and she turned heavily and left the tent. Ross stared at Marlette, disapproving of the haughtiness she had just displayed. He suddenly felt he understood Martha better. He had resented her constant disapproval and intrusion into the intimate moments and feelings of their life together, but now he realized they were so alike in their feelings for Marlette that it was jealousy which kept Martha from accepting him.

133

Gently, he chided Marlette, "You were too hard on her. She loves you as much as I do and needs you as much as you need me, and you're going to need her much more than me in the days to come. Don't destroy her loyalty to you because of me."

The imperious look left her face. "Oh, Ross. Of course, you're right. I'm so upset and I'm taking it out on you and Martha, too. I'll apologize to her immediately."

She moved toward him and he stepped aside, but not before he held her to him for another fleeting moment and kissed the back of her neck. The pressure of her hand on his arm told him she was all right. She went out of the tent and put her arm around the older woman. He couldn't hear their whispered words as Marlette led Martha away from the fire to talk with her. The sun was lighting the mountains from behind, framing them in a golden glow, and he breathed deeply of the sage-freshened air. He was still tired but somehow felt more able to go on than he had for some days.

11. *Tragedy on the Greenwood Cutoff*

AT BIG SANDY they soaked wagon tongues and wheels in preparation to cross fifty miles of waterless desert. At midnight Ross woke them, and they started out in darkness made darker by the dust-laden air. They were only able to see their guide by the glimmer of a sagebrush torch Ross carried. It was noon the next day before he let them stop.

At midnight they went on, not because they wanted to, but because they had to, finally reaching the valley of the Green River, where they rested. But they needed more rest than they were allowed, and the climb out of the valley saw more precious tools and trunks jettisoned to help the straining oxen.

For three more days they struggled up rocky slopes and down steep ridges from one stream valley to the next, the nights freezing and the wind cold during the day as they passed among aspen groves and pines.

They nooned in another valley bottom, where there was grass for the stock, and followed it until they could climb to the next plateau over an exceedingly long but gradual ascent. Complacently, they gained the ridge until they realized the only way down off this high elevation was down a steep, naked mountain.

Ropes were brought out, chains locked around the wheels, and all but the wheel oxen were unyoked as one after another the wagons were eased down the ridge into the canyon below. Marlette's wagon made the perilous descent safely and joined those already down. Ross and John took over the leads on each side of John's wagon while the teams of men set callused hands to the ropes behind. They reached the steepest drop without difficulty and took

135

an extra twist on the leads, as the oxen began to slide and dug in their heels. A rope broke with an ominous popping of strands. The wagon slid forward faster, gathering momentum, dragging the other team of rope holders off their feet, pulling them harshly across the rocks. Ross yelled at John, but the lurching thrust of the wagon had frightened the oxen and they lunged forward, dragging John off his feet. The oxen swerved toward Ross, who yelled in panic at John as he tried desperately to control the oxen and stop the downhill movement of the wagon. The wheels lurched forward, bouncing uncontrolled over boulders, the left front wheel rolling with horrible, crushing slowness over John.

A scream came cascading down the hill and echoed back and forth along the canyon. There was no stopping the wagon now as it gathered speed and the back wheel bounced over John's broken body. Ross heaved on the oxen with all his strength in an effort to stop the wagon. The oxen turned sharply toward him and the wagon overturned with the crash of splintering wood and tearing canvas, the tongue snapping and releasing the oxen. Ross dropped his rope and scrambled up the slope to where John lay. The men were recovering themselves and coming down the hill, white-faced and grim from what they had witnessed.

Ross kneeled over John with his heart in his throat. John moaned in pain, blood streaming from his mouth. His face was twisted in agony, his eyes shut tight against the overwhelming pain of his crushed body.

"John! John! Can you hear me?"

The eyes opened but didn't focus, and closed again. He groaned and shuddered and groaned no more as his mouth slackened and blood flowed freely, staining the rocks.

Ross heard Liz crying hysterically. He stood up and pushed through the stunned men, hearing John's boys, who had helped hold the ropes with the other men, begin to cry as they realized their father was dead. Ross caught Liz before she got to the huddle of men and held her from going farther.

"Let me see him," she screamed, struggling fiercely, trying to break Ross's grip on her arms.

"No, Liz, it's too late."

She collapsed against him, crying, "Oh no! Oh, dear God, NO!"

Jonathan, Jeremy, and Joseph came up the slope with Cam and

136

stopped. Jonathan said, in a shaking voice, "Come on, Mother. Come with us."

She looked at them wildly, "I want to see him. *Please* let me see him."

Ross relinquished his hold on her as Jonathan and Jeremy took her.

Jonathan, tears streaming down his face, said, "No, Mother. You don't want to see him like he is now."

Ross said, his own voice husky with unshed tears, "Take her to the bottom of the hill and keep her there. We'll do what we can to get the wagon down and—" but he couldn't finish as tears choked him, blurring his eyes. He went to the overturned wagon, found a blanket, and brought it up to cover John, while the men looked on in disbelieving silence.

He got to his feet and, choking back his emotions, said, "Let's get the wagon upright and down the hill. Cam, get some more rope and tell the herders to go on down to the herd for now. We'll get the rest of the wagons down later."

Cam started up the hill and Ross saw the women approaching. Marlette looked at him with frightened eyes, her lip caught between her teeth. It could have been he instead of John. He waved her on and went to help the men unload the wrecked wagon and see what they could do about righting and repairing it.

At dusk they buried John. The widower Christopher, who had undertaken the ministerial duties of the train, gave a stirring service in his hypnotic voice. Liz stood with her dark hair wild and uncovered, wracked with tears streaming down her tortured face. The boys stood in silence, shedding silent tears, while Jennifer cried openly, clinging to the only person who could possibly give her comfort—Cam—suddenly transformed by her loss into her protector and comforter.

For Ross, John's death was more than the loss of a good friend and traveling companion. He had lost a faithful partner—a captain whom he had trusted implicitly and who had done his job quietly and efficiently. There wasn't another man among them who was respected as much as John.

The camp was subdued with the silence death brings, and Ross felt the grief and uncertainty in the aimless and confused glances of John's boys. He had felt the same devastation too many times not to know it and feel it with them. He knew they needed to be

137

given hope—an assurance that their world had not ended here, with the death of their father. He could at least give them that.

He sat down his plate with an intentional noise, bringing their attention to him, and said, quietly, earnestly, "Jonathan, I have something I want to say to you, Jeremy and Joseph. I don't want you to worry about what is ahead. We will go on together and I will do everything I can to help you. I told your father I would help him settle in Oregon and I intend to keep that promise to you and your mother and sister. Now I want you all to get some sleep. We'll have to move on in the morning."

Slowly the boys got to their feet and stood uncertainly for a moment before turning away, but Jonathan turned back and reached out his hand. Ross took it firmly, reassuringly.

"Thank you, Ross."

Ross nodded and watched the oldest of John's sons, no longer a boy but a young man, and now the head of his father's house, walk with a weary heaviness to his bed. Ross stood and went to his tent. Marlette was with Liz and Jenny, and the tent seemed lonely and confining without her presence. He went out again after picking up his robe to throw over his shoulders in the chill night air.

Adam James came out of the shadows and squatted beside him. "Anything I can do?"

"No. Marlette and Martha are taking care of Liz, and Jenny and the boys have gone to bed."

"There's more to worry about now than just the family."

Ross looked at Adam intently. "You want the job?"

He shook his head slowly. "No. But I thought if you needed an opinion, I could give you one."

"All right."

"Heely. Next to John, he's about the best-liked man among us."

"You don't think I should let them vote on it?"

"Why? We all know who's the real captain. The man you need is one who can get this bunch to do what you want with the least amount of resentment. That man is Heely."

"You're right."

They walked to the Heely tents, and Daniel stood to greet them with a subdued smile and handshake. "How's the family doing?"

"The boys are taking it pretty well. I don't know about Liz."

"You tell them we'll help in any way we can."

138

"Does that go for me, too?"

Surprise flashed through Heely's eyes and he grinned. "It depends on what you want and whether I have a choice."

Ross smiled. "You have a choice, but I want you to consider the choices I've got."

"There might be a few to disagree with you."

"There always are, but I don't let them bother me when I know I'm right."

Heely chuckled softly. "You know, a few hundred miles ago I might have considered this an honor, but I know a hell of a lot better now. John was a damn good man."

"So are you, Daniel."

"All right, Chesnut, you got yourself a new captain, but I can't guarantee for how long. Fair enough?"

Ross stuck out his hand. "Fair enough. Tomorrow we should be into the Bear River Valley fairly early in the day. We'll have a chance to rework schedules then. For tonight I'll take John's shift."

He and Adam said their good nights and went back to their own camps. Ross felt somewhat relieved that the decision had been made so easily. Marlette was in the tent and she came into his arms, clinging to him in silence and sadness.

Finally he asked, "How is Liz doing?"

She released him and turned away, wringing her hands in anxiety. "She's very distraught. I don't know. . . ." Her voice trailed off and she stood in abject silence.

He put his arms around her and held her, brushing her neck with his lips and tasting the sweat and dust of the day still lingering there. "What don't you know?"

"Whether she'll be able to handle it."

"She's a strong woman."

"I'm not talking about strength, Ross, at least not the physical kind. I'm talking about emotional strength and stability."

"I don't know what you mean."

"She's emotionally unstable. I thought it was just her nature to react to things more than other people, but it's more than that. John stabilized her moods. Without him, I'm not sure anyone can."

Ross rested his cheek against her hair and sighed deeply, inwardly. What she was telling him only reinforced the misgivings he already had about Liz. This was trouble he didn't need; none of them needed it, but he could not discount Marlette's apprehension.

Marlette turned in his arms and held him fiercely, and he knew what she was thinking before she spoke. "Thank God it wasn't you, Ross. I feel so sorry for Liz and the children and so guilty for thinking it, but thank God it wasn't you!"

He brushed her hair with his hand and kissed her, and at last she released him. "I'm sorry. It's late and you need to rest. Maybe you should sleep outside tonight. I'll just keep you awake if you stay here."

"It's all right. I'm taking John's shift. I won't sleep. I'll stay with you until midnight."

They sank onto the blankets and pulled the covers over them, and he took her in his arms and held her. At last she asked, "What will you do now without John?"

"I've asked Heely to be captain. He said he'd try it."

"He would've been my choice, too." She was silent again for a long moment, and he was almost dozing when she said, "They'll need a lot of help when we reach the valley. Do we have enough help to give them?"

"Yes. Don't worry about it. I told John I would help him and that holds true for his family, too. We may have to share the house with them for a while, but it's roomy enough if we need to, until we can put up a place for them. The boys will be a big help. It won't be all that bad for them except. . . ." He didn't finish. It was too difficult to explain that "except." Marlette knew. They had had to be without each other long enough to understand what separation meant. Only Liz's separation was final. Just as his separation from Spotted Fawn had been. How well he remembered the loss his first wife's death had meant, but he had loved again and perhaps Liz would, too.

Marlette was relaxing against him and he knew she would soon be asleep. He kissed her again and quietly left her. Soon it would be time for his duty. He picked up his rifle and walked out to the fresh mound of earth a little way from the tents and wagons. He gently placed his hand on the crumbling earth. Tomorrow by the time they were gone, there would be nothing left to mark this place, and those who would pass this way in the future would not know the place where John lay. His grave would be lost forever, as would be hundreds—perhaps thousands of others, but it had to be if his last resting place were to remain undisturbed. The tears Ross had kept controlled until now fell upon the loose earth and he regretted he could not bury John in the manner of warriors, so all who passed would know that here lay a man of honor and courage.

He stood and said softly, in a tear-choked and husky voice, "I salute you, friend, and wish you a quick journey to the place of your God."

He mounted his horse and rode slowly out to take John's shift with the herd, giving himself time to control his grief.

Dawn came crisp and cold, and the morning fires were welcome as the emigrants prepared for another day on the trail. Ross ate his breakfast quickly and went around the circle of wagons to give Daniel Heely his first instructions as captain of the train.

Heely greeted him jovially. "Good morning, Chesnut. What can I do for you?"

"I'm going to take the Jessup wagons on ahead. I want you to make sure nothing can be seen of John's grave when the last wagon has passed. That's all, for now. We'll move out as usual."

"I'll see to it."

"I'll count on that." He wheeled away and strode back to his own camp in time to see Liz emerge from her tent looking as distraught as she had the day before and even more haggard from sleepless suffering. She looked up the hill where John had been killed and Ross followed her gaze. Joseph was climbing toward the broken rocking chair Ross had purposely left behind. She gave Joseph no more than a glance and went along the creek, gathering the blue wild flowers growing there.

Joseph brought the chair into camp and Ross confronted him. "Did your mother ask you to bring the chair down?"

"Yes. She wants me to carve his name on it. It was his favorite chair and she thinks it should be left to mark his grave."

"We can leave it here with his name on it but not on his grave. We don't want his grave disturbed."

Joseph dropped his eyes. "Yes, sir. I won't put it on his grave. I'll carve his name and put it back up there where he died. Will that be all right?"

Ross put a gentle hand on the boy's shoulder. "Yes. I think that will be fine."

Ross did most of the camp chores with the boys helping. Liz stayed at John's grave, and Joseph painstakingly carved John's name and the date of his birth and death on the smooth wood of the rocker back. He reverently carried it back up the hill to place it where traces of his father's blood still showed. When he got back, they were ready to leave.

"Jonathan, go get your mother."

He watched the boy walk out to the grave and saw him plead helplessly with Liz. He came back after his futile attempt and said, "She says she won't leave."

Marlette was beside him now and offered, "Do you want me to try to bring her back to the wagons?"

"No. I'll do it. You get ready to roll as soon as we can get her away."

He walked out to the grave and looked down on the wretched, defiant face. "Liz, we have to go now."

"I'll not leave here!"

"You have to leave. We have to go on."

"To what?" she shrilled. "Everything that means anything to me is right here."

"What about your children?"

"You can take them with you. They'll get by."

"Not Jenny. She needs you."

"No! Now where is John's rocker? I want it here!"

"Liz, if you don't come willingly, I'll have to use force."

"Force! *Force!* Do you think it matters to me what you do to me now! Why don't you shoot me and leave me here with my husband! Yes! Yes!" she cried. "Kill me! Leave me here with my John!" The tears came with renewed torrents down her face and she threw herself across the mound.

Ross bent down and lifted the shaking body away from the earth while she cried hysterically and screamed, "No! No! No!"

He picked her up and carried her toward the buckboard. She was too exhausted from her grief to struggle effectively. He placed her in the buckboard beside Jonathan and said, "You're going to lead today. Follow me."

Ross mounted his horse and turned away as the onlookers hurried back to their wagons. He rode past the grave and turned to see Liz's reaction as the buckboard rolled by, but she only buried her head deeper in her hands and cried harder.

The rebuilt Jessup wagon followed and went around the grave, as did Marlette's wagon, but Adam James guided his team over the top of the mound and the rest followed in his path. Ross looked away but was brought back abruptly as Jonathan called his name. He yanked his horse around as he saw Liz leap from the buck-board and run back to the grave, throwing herself across it in the path of the next wagon. Jenny ran after her crying, "Mother! Mother!"

The oxen stopped short of stepping on her, and she screamed at them to stay off the grave. Ross dismounted beside her and tried to pull her from the grave, but she struggled and fought him with the strength of a wild animal. Jenny stood crying and calling her mother in despair, reaching for her in agony until Cam came and she let him lead her away, while Liz screamed, "You can't do this to my John! You let me go!"

Ross finally had both flailing arms pinned and said, "Liz, you know why we have to do this. Do you want his grave discovered by wolves, or worse?"

She collapsed against him in another torrent of tears, and he led her back to the buckboard and helped Jon lift her in. He retrieved his horse and signaled the wagons to start rolling again, hearing Liz's sobs above the jolt and bounce of the buckboard.

They reached the valley of the Bear River early in the afternoon. This valley was wide and much greener than any they had been in for many days. Here there were willows along the river, an occasional grove of quaking aspen, and a scattering of cedar trees. The hills were beautifully banded in shades of yellow, red, black, and white. Grass, though dry, was abundant, and trout were raising for insects in the river.

Ross circled the wagons. He helped the boys set up camp as quickly as possible in order to have time to spend with Heely reorganizing the duty schedule. Then there were repairs to be made, sore feet to tend on the stock, and shoeing to be done. He invited Adam James to come with him, thereby bestowing upon Adam a vestige of leadership and trust of which Ross felt he was worthy.

They were just finishing the new duty roster when Marlette came to the Heely fire. "Ross, Liz left camp a few minutes ago and hasn't returned. I'm afraid something has happened to her."

Adam stood up. "I'll help you look for her."

"No. You stay here and help get this finished up. No need for more than one of us to get lost. Did she say anything to you?"

Marlette answered, "No. She left after supper and I thought she would be right back."

Ross picked up his rifle and said, "Show me which way she went."

Ross followed Marlette until she stopped between their tents and said, "I think she went out that way." She pointed toward the sagebrush valley away from the river and Ross bent to see if he could find a footprint in the dust, but the light from the stars, as bright as it seemed, was not bright enough to track by. He went to get his horse. He could cover a lot more ground with a horse, and the increased elevation would enable him to see better.

He started off for the nearest trees but found no one there, then went on methodically to check each tree scattered on the plain beyond the camp. He finally saw Liz walking swiftly back along their trail, a ghostly figure among the silvered sage and dark bushy trees. She glanced over her shoulder, saw him, and began to run. He urged his horse into a gallop after her and saw her stumble and fall. She rose and ran again as he closed in on her. She looked back and went sprawling once more. He leaped from his saddle and caught her before she could run again.

·"Where do you think you're going?" he demanded harshly.

"You let go of me, you hear!" She started struggling, and he had to force her down and imprison her wrists against the ground.

"I'm not going to let you go. You're coming back to the wagons with me. Now quit struggling."

She spat at him, "I hate you! Do you hear? I hate you and I'm not going back with you. I'm going to John and you can't stop me!"

"Liz! Be reasonable. There is nothing to go back to. John isn't back there. He's dead. There's nothing left but your memory of him, and that's all there is ever going to be."

"How do you know?" she screamed. "How could you possibly know? It's easy for you tell me how I feel. You've still got Marlette!"

"Listen to me, Liz. I know. I understand. Before Marlette, I lost my first wife in childbirth. I suffered then as you do now, but it doesn't have to be the end of everything. I thought so then, too, but it isn't. You can go on. Time will heal the wound if you will let it. It isn't easy, but it is possible."

Her voice broke and she sobbed, "I don't have anything to live for without John."

"Yes, you do. Jenny needs you and so do the boys, no matter what you think."

She began to shake and the fight went out of her. He pulled her to her feet, and she stumbled against him blindly and clung to him, and he held her and let her cry.

At last she had exhausted her tears and he released her. She looked at him, wiping her wet face, and choked, "But how will I get along? What am I to do without John? It's different for a woman."

"I told John I would help him, and I told Jonathan I intend to keep that promise to you and your children. I can use the boys in the business I have started. You can stay with us until we get you a cabin built. You should have no trouble." He wanted to say more, but thought better of it. This wasn't the time to tell her women were in short supply in Oregon, especially beautiful ones.

She dropped her head in acceptance, and he took her arm and led her to where his horse stood and helped her up behind him. She sagged against him, and he felt the fullness of her breasts warm against his back and her head against his shoulder. It was a night to be in the arms of a woman. The stars were brilliant overhead and the sage fragrant as his horse brushed it in passing. He felt an intense longing in the arms of this woman who was not his, a longing that couldn't be satisfied by his own woman. He hoped Marlette would understand and forgive him if he didn't sleep with her this night.

12. Along the Bear River to Fort Hall

TRAVELING ALONG THE Bear River was a reprieve from the hardships of the past few days. The valley floor was level, so they could spread out and avoid some of the dust generated by the wagons. The desolation of the higher mountains was relieved by trees and grass and flowers along the riverbank. Within a few miles of their night camp, they passed an Indian village and continued up the valley until Ross found a good campsite.

The women were busy cleaning up the utensils after the evening meal. The boys were either already in bed or on duty, and Ross was helping Adam grease wheels when Christopher approached them. Ross straightened up as Christopher stopped before him and said, "Good evening. How is Mrs. Jessup? She seemed less distraught today."

Ross answered, "I think she's better," and waited for Christopher to come to the point of his visit.

"I thought I might talk with her, if you think she is in need of comfort and will benefit from whatever help I can give her. I was a minister, and I understand her grief and can comfort her."

Ross looked at Christopher intently for a moment. He had the most compelling eyes of any man Ross had met—not compelling with power as he spoke now, but with tenderness, compassion, and beauty. And the rest of his appearance, too, exuded gentleness. No sharp feature distracted the observer from the spellbinding beauty of his eyes. Not even his well-modulated conversational voice matched the power of his eyes until he was speaking as an instrument of his faith and convictions.

"All right, Christopher, if she is willing to listen, you can talk with her, but not out of my hearing."

"As you wish."

Christopher walked on to where the women were finishing the preparations for the morning and said, "Good evening, ladies." Their voices returned his pleasant salutation and asked about his children, exchanging politenesses with him until he said, "Mrs. Jessup, I don't want to dwell on or remind you of your recent tragedy, but I know how deeply your husband's loss must be felt. I wanted you to know I understand and share your grief, and since I have the comfort and strength of God's word in my possession, I want you to feel free to come to me anytime you feel the need to be comforted by the holy word."

"Why, thank you, Mr. Christopher. You are more than kind. I—I think I would like you to help me pray." Her voice took on a distraught tone once more as she added, "I need to understand why this terrible, terrible thing happened to me and my children. Please help me to understand!"

"Of course. Would you like to go into your tent?"

Ross straightened up and watched with thoughtful eyes while Christopher followed Liz into the sanctuary of her tent.

Adam said quietly, "Bewareth the wolf in sheep's clothing."

"Don't worry, Adam. I'll keep an eye on him."

They finished their job on the wagon wheels, and Ross moved to his own fire to hear what went on in Liz's tent. Marlette came to sit beside him, and he put his arm around her and held her close.

"I missed you last night."

"I'm sorry."

"Well, at least you found Liz. What happened? She was much better today."

"Not much. I just told her she didn't need to worry about what was ahead—that we would help her."

Christopher and Liz came out of the tent, interrupting their quiet conversation. Christopher held Liz's hands and said, "Anytime you need me, just call."

"I surely will, Mr. Christopher. You've eased my mind a great deal and I truly thank you."

"It is what I am here for. Good night and sleep well, now."

Christopher hurried away from the tent, and Liz watched him until he disappeared, then dropped the tent flap and was lost from sight herself.

Ross said, "Well, we'd better turn in." He helped Marlette to her feet and followed her into the tent but knew he couldn't stay with her as she began to undress. "Marlette, I'd better stay outside again tonight."

"Why?"

"Do you need to ask? I'm not tired enough not to want you." He took her in his arms, kissed her on the lips, and released her quickly. "I'm sorry. Good night."

He left the tent before she could protest more and crawled into a bedroll under the wagon. He watched the stars, finding little comfort in their twinkling beauty.

The next few days they traveled along the pleasant Bear River in relative ease. There was grass here for the stock, and the river was abundant in fish. The effects of altitude sickness were all but gone and the cool, clear water helped restore the emigrants' health. Still weary, still aching, but feeling better than they had for a long time, they moved on to Soda Springs, where mineral springs of hot water erupted between the river and the cedar-covered hills.

When Ross broke the news they would spend the next day in this delightful area while he took a party of men hunting, the whole company brightened considerably. He expected them to think he was becoming lax, but they would soon know his reason for letting them have an extra day of respite at this place of relative abundance. Ahead the Snake Plains would make them wish for a day such as he was giving them, and he hoped they would remember it when he once more had to become their whip and goad.

A festive air pervaded the camp by nightfall. Good spirits couldn't resist an interlude of music and dancing. Ross danced with Marlette, but it only made them more aware of the desire they tried to restrain. It was with relief that Ross turned Marlette over to Cam and took his turn with Jenny. He saw the light in her eyes as she watched Cam dance away with Marlette.

Liz and Martha came to watch and seated themselves on the log hauled in for firewood. But Liz wasn't seated long. Christopher came up to her and she accepted his invitation to dance. Ross noticed Jenny's frown. The dance ended, partners changed, and Cam returned Marlette but ignored Jenny's expectant look and went to claim Suzannah Heely. The fiddle began a waltz and Ross took Marlette in his arms again, but neither one of them could concentrate on the music.

Finally Marlette stopped and dropped her arms. "I think I'd better go to bed."

"Do you want me to send Cam with you?"

"No. Martha will go. She doesn't look like she'd mind leaving."

"All right. I'll see you in the morning."

He turned his eyes back to the dancers and watched Liz and Christopher. There was a difference in Liz tonight, but it was hardly one that worried Ross. She was acting very subdued. No coy looks or gay laughter; just a sweet, haunting smile that was somehow more appealing to Ross than her usual vivaciousness. As he watched, Daniels joined Liz and Christopher and, to Ross's surprise, Liz accepted his invitation to dance.

At the end of the waltz, another widowed man, Hiram Powell, came to dance with Liz, and Ross became aware of a number of eager looks cast her way as the other men noticed her willingness to dance with everyone who asked her. Pauly stuffed his harmonica into his pocket and took his turn with the serenely smiling and beautiful Liz. She finally begged for a rest and came to sit on the log a few feet from Ross as the dance went on without her.

The next man who came to ask for a dance was told with a hint of her old coyness, "I'm sorry, but Mr. Chesnut has already asked for the next dance." She flashed bright eyes on Ross and he nodded his agreement, not knowing what she was trying to do now.

When the music started up again, she turned to Ross with expectant eyes, and he took her in his arms. "What are you up to, Liz? I thought I was the last man you would want to dance with."

"Why, Ross, you do surprise me. Can't you see I'm trying to let you know I'm sorry for that? I just didn't know how to do it and not feel foolish. I don't want that and all the other foolish things I've done to stand in the way of my gratitude for what you have tried to do to help us. Do you understand now?"

"Yes. But you didn't need to do this just to tell me that."

"Oh, but I did. I'm ready to go to my tent now, and I wanted you to take me." She stopped dancing and Ross released her. He followed her away from the dancers and walked her to her tent.

149

She turned and smiled sweetly, saying, "Thank you, Ross, and good night."

He turned away and had the strange feeling he was being used. It appeared innocent enough, wanting him to escort her back to her tent, but was it? What could Liz possibly be trying to do? He would have to wait and see. But now he was tired, and his guard duty would come all too soon. He crawled into the empty blankets under the wagon and listened to the music and laughter, wondering if Marlette slept. He turned restlessly for long minutes before finally dozing.

After the day of rest and hunting, they were back on the trail as usual. They crossed over a ridge out of the pleasant Bear River Valley into a desolate, forbidding landscape of black volcanic rock. The black dust quickly turned their freshly washed clothes, hair, and faces black. It was like traveling through hell. By evening they had crossed another ridge and were glad to see sage and sand plains again.

They reached the Portneuf River the next day and followed it northward, realizing they were finally in the drainage of the Columbia River. Even the rain in the afternoon and the hard going through rocky and broken country and deep, dragging sand could not dampen their spirits.

Before noon on the following day, they could see Fort Hall ahead of them sticking up boldly on a flat plain bordering the Snake River. The adobe fort walls were twenty feet high, with a heavy wooden door at the entrance. Behind the fort, grazing on the green bottoms along the Snake, was a large herd of emigrant stock left or traded here by other caravans. Ross moved them on past the fort to find a good area to camp in. They would be here one or two days while he hunted more meat to see them through the barren country ahead, and they would have plenty of time to explore the fort once camp was set up.

When they found a campsite affording grass and water, Ross took his own little group of women into the fort to shop before supplies were depleted. Captain Richard Grant and his assistant, Archibald McDonald, treated them with the greatest of courtesy, but the bill for the provisions was much too high. Marlette could still afford to pay forty dollars for a barrel of flour and fifty cents a pound for brown sugar, but not many others would be able to, nor would they be able to pay the difference between their trail-worn stock and fresh oxen to take them into the Willamette Valley.

That evening Christopher came to speak to Liz, and Ross watched them go arm in arm toward the river. Martha frowned and sniffed with disapproval. Marlette snuggled against Ross, drawing her shawl closer about her in the chill evening air.

"Do I need to ask you if you would like to walk by the river, too?"

"Well, it is one way of being alone with you."

He pulled her up with him as he rose and, keeping his arm around her, took an unhurried pace following Christopher and Liz. They were almost to the river when Marlette stopped. He looked down at her, realizing he had been so deep in thought he hadn't said a word to her.

"Ross, I wanted us to be alone together, but I'm still alone even with you beside me. What are you thinking about?"

"I'm sorry. Nothing and everything."

"Well, share it with me. We've had so little to share for so many weeks, I might as well be traveling by myself."

"I was thinking about Liz."

"Liz! Why on earth for?"

"I have the feeling things aren't what they appear to be with her."

Her look was thoughtful. "It's not easy for a woman to get by on her own. I hope she's not misinterpreting Christopher's offer of help."

"Then you don't think she just wants attention?"

"That, too. Most of us do."

He smiled at her, feeling guilty. "I'm sorry about that."

She smiled back at him. "I understand, Ross, and I can't blame you. I'm just feeling sorry for myself."

He touched her hair and she came into his arms, her lips parted expectantly, and he kissed her, long and gently, then released her. "I better take you back before the mosquitoes carry you away."

She laughed, and they walked slowly back toward the campfires around their circle of wagons. He left her at her tent and went out to the herd to make sure all the herders were back from the fort before he crawled under Marlette's wagon for a few hours' sleep.

By morning his train was ready to pull out. Several hours later they caught up with the Boggs train and Ross let them stop nearby so they could visit with friends from their early days on the trail. The Boggs train was going to lay over for a day. Ross hoped to move on, and if things went well, they would not see each other again until the Willamette Valley. He talked with Boggs and Thornton, who said they had last seen the California section of the train, with the Reeds and Donners, on the Little Sandy. That group, who were California-bound, had decided to go to Fort Bridger and take the trail Lansford Hastings had recommended, by way of Great Salt Lake.

Ross was about to express his opinion of the supposed new trail to California when a small party of riders came up to the circled wagons. The men looked trail-weary and hungry, and Boggs was the first to invite the newcomers to eat with them. Ross thought he recognized one of the men as Moses Harris, a mountain man. The others he didn't know.

The haggard face of the leader split into a grin, and a bony hand came forward. "Be much obliged, sir. My name's Applegate, Jesse Applegate, and these men with me are Colonel Ford, Major Harris, Major Goff, and Captain Scott," he said in a southern drawl.

Boggs responded, "It's our pleasure, Mr. Applegate. You look like you've come a far piece. Meet Colonel Thornton, Mr. Boone, Mr. Chesnut, Mr. Heely, and Mr. James."

Grimy hands met dusty hands and shook briefly. When Ross and Moses Harris stood face to face, the old mountain man asked, "Ain't I seen you before?"

Ross smiled at the sun-blackened, darkly bearded man known to all as "Black" Harris, and answered, "You have, but I didn't think you'd remember. I saw you at the rendezvous about sixteen years ago."

"Well, I'll be damned. What you doin' here with these movers?"

"I was taking my wife back to Oregon and ended up guiding a train."

Applegate heard them and interrupted. "Oregon! Did I hear you say you were going to Oregon?"

Boggs answered for them, "Yes, sir. All of us here are bound for Oregon."

The grin on Applegate's face grew even broader. "Well, I'm rightly glad to meet up with you gentlemen, then. We've just

152

come from Oregon by a new route, and we'd be mighty proud to take you back there by it."

Incredulous looks passed among them, and Thornton, with his quick lawyer's mind, asked, "And by what route would that be, sir?"

"We come by the way of the Umpqua and Rogue Rivers through the south end of the Willamette Valley. There's more water available, with only one dry drive of about thirty miles over a much better road. Save you folks about two hundred miles, at least, and a lot of hardships. You won't have to ferry down the Columbia and take a chance on bein' caught in the rapids and losin' everything you've struggled so hard to get this far with."

Boggs said, incredulously, "Why, that almost sounds too good to be true. But what guarantee do we have that it is a better road?"

"Only my word, and the word of these men with me. But I might add that the party just ahead of you has decided to take the trail."

Boggs and Thornton turned to Ross, and Thornton asked, "What do you say about it, Mr. Chesnut? You're from Oregon. Is such a route feasible?"

"I've been down the southern route with the Hudson's Bay men and I wouldn't advise trying to get wagons through."

Applegate railed righteously, "Are you calling me a liar, sir?"

Softly, Ross answered, "No. I'm not calling you a liar. What I'm saying is the trail I went over was passable for horses, but not for wagons."

"Well, I don't know what trail you took, but the one we have blazed can be taken by wagons. Now, if you are willing to listen to me, I will tell you every step of the way and let you judge for yourselves whether you think this trail is what I say it is or not."

Boggs, a little flustered, answered, "By all means, we're willing to listen. None of us relish the thought of shooting the rapids on the Columbia. How about you, Chesnut?"

Ross shook his head. "I'm sorry, but I'm going to take the road I know best. You will have to make your own decision. I hope you make the right one."

Ross turned away, and a clearly hesitant Heely and James followed him. He heard Applegate start his description with, "From here we go on to Raft River and take the California trail. . . ."

153

Heely said, "Maybe we should stay and listen to him. I wouldn't mind cutting off a few miles and days."

Ross stopped and faced the two men. "And neither would I, but I don't think Applegate's route will be any shorter or easier than the old trail. I'm going to take the trail I know and leave nothing to chance. You can go with him if you wish."

Heely and James eyed each other, but neither said anything. Ross turned away and went to bang the fry pan to gather his group and continue the journey.

13. *The Snake River Trail*

THE TRAIN MOVED on along the wide, rock-littered valley of the Snake River with dust blowing and the sun blazing down. To the south a low range of snowcapped mountains could be seen when the dust was blown away. To the north, much farther away, the higher Salmon River Range was visible. Between these mountains and the river, the plain was broken only by three prominent, isolated buttes.

At noon the next day, after encountering some of the worst travel conditions yet, they arrived at Raft River, the old junction of the California Trail—the trail that would also become the southern route into the Willamette Valley if Jesse Applegate succeeded in convincing the wagon trains to follow him.

Ross sat with Heely and James, preparing them for the afternoon's travel, when Christopher approached them.

"Something I can help you with, Christopher?" Ross asked.

He came over a little hesitantly. "I'd like to talk to you, Mr. Chesnut. Do you think you could spare a private moment?"

Ross glanced at the puzzled faces of his companions, answering, "Yes. We can talk while Adam and Daniel get the teams hitched up."

He moved away and Christopher followed him. "What is it, Christopher?"

"I was interested in what you had to say about the trail south. I have been thinking of maybe waiting here for the Boggs train and taking the southern trail with them."

Ross already had an idea what Christopher's reason might be but asked, "Why?"

He smiled at Ross's seeming naiveté. "I think you know why. I feel it is best for me to leave before there is trouble with Mrs. Jessup. I fear she has misinterpreted my interest in her."

155

Ross nodded. "I don't like leaving you by yourself, but I can't delay without jeopardizing the rest of the train either. If you want to wait until Boggs catches up, I guess that will have to be your decision. They should be here by this time tomorrow."

A smile of relief crossed his face and he held out his hand. "Thank you, Mr. Chesnut. I appreciate all you have done for me and my family. I'll pray for your safety."

Ross shook the proffered hand with a feeling of regret and sincerity. Nevertheless, he had a feeling that Christopher was not what he appeared to be. "Thank you, and good luck to you, too."

They walked back to the readied wagons, and Ross mounted his horse and led the wagons westward, leaving one wagon behind, looking very small and vulnerable as they drew away.

For several more days they struggled across bleak sagebrush plains rippled by ravines along the Snake River. They were tortured by heat, dust, and thirst—and tortured even more by the knowledge that there was a river of fresh, cool water nearby in a deep, inaccessible gorge. When they stopped, they could hear it, which only added to the misery and exhaustion. At last, they reached the river crossing, but the respite was brief. Once again, their road became a tortuous trail of sharp stones, mercilessly cutting the feet of animals and humans alike.

Ross drove the caravan as hard as he could until the oxen began to fall and cut their knees. It was time to take emergency measures or they would have no teams at all. Buffalo hides, which he had not let them abandon no matter what else they had to discard, were fashioned into boots for the sore oxen feet, and for anyone whose shoes no longer had soles.

Late the next day they camped beside hot running springs, finding the water near enough to boiling that it would cook the fish they had caught at the Snake River crossing. It helped to cheer the otherwise grim group of dispirited and footsore emigrants. They made few complaints now, knowing it was a waste of energy. Mistakes had been few at the crossing. They were all competent now in what it took to keep the wagons moving. It should have made Ross's job easier, but it didn't. He had no outlet for the growing apprehension that they would never make it to the valley before the first snow. The only one he could be angry with for not having made better time was himself. His mind relived every step of their journey, magnifying each delay until his burden of guilt for their slow progress was crucifying him. The only talking he did was to brief Heely and Adam for the next day's travel. He avoided Marlette's anxious looks and purposely chose not to eat when he knew the rest of them would be eating.

He watched with interest as Daniels courted Liz, but was aware that his partners, Twist and Pauly, were not denied her company either, which eased Ross's mind a little. She seemed to have taken Christopher's departure calmly. But he still felt Liz was not herself—still felt a deep undercurrent of grief and bitterness waiting to spring to the surface in some violent, perhaps self-destructive climax, and he dreaded it. He missed John, too, though Daniel Heely and Adam James were both good men.

The journey resumed in the morning through a desert of jagged rocks. Often they saw the grim evidence of the trains ahead of them—blood-stained rocks and carcasses of dead stock. Adam's remaining mule fell and refused to get up. Ross ordered him shot and butchered, knowing that if they didn't use the animal themselves, there would be Indians there to take the animal apart like wolves.

The next several days they traveled along the river on a much better trail than they had since leaving the Platte River. Grass was available at every camp, and nearly naked Indians converged on the train in numbers with food and horses to trade with those still having anything left to trade. The others went hunting with Ross, and no one went hungry now. By the time the train reached the Hudson's Bay post near the mouth of the Boise River, the emigrants and animals were in the best shape they'd been in since leaving Fort Hall, and spirits were high. They had come a long way and could begin to visualize the end of the trail. They were at the last crossing of the Snake River. The country beyond looked no different from what they had been seeing for the last two weeks, but somehow it seemed magical because their goal was in sight.

They circled their wagons some distance upriver from the post. This area was occupied by the company herds of livestock and Indians. Ross rode into the post—more of a dwelling structure than a real fort like Laramie or Fort Hall—and talked with the clerk in charge. The report wasn't encouraging. Prices were high, and warnings of Indian trouble with the Cayuse and Walla Walla disturbed him. He talked well into the night and rode back to camp in time to assume his guard duty with the herd.

The camp slept in that morning except for those on guard duty, and Ross remained with them until after dawn. There were too many Indians for him to feel the wagons and stock were safe. When the sun was streaming over the snow-peaked mountains towering to the east, Ross finally went in to start the cook fire.

Marlette was the first out of her tent and came hesitantly toward him, her face drawn with anxiety.

"Do you need to get supplies here?" Ross asked her.

"I intended to. Can I afford them?"

"They'll be high. Flour is twenty dollars a hundred pounds. How much do you need to get us to the valley?"

"At least a hundred pounds, and more for emergency. Some of the women are very short on supplies and a lot of them won't be able to afford those prices. What else did you learn?"

"Not too much that will affect us, but they have been getting reports of trouble with the Cayuse and Walla Walla Indians."

Alarm creased her forehead. "What about the Whitmans?"

"They're still at the mission, but it doesn't sound good for them. The Indians are resentful of all the white people coming and the help the Whitmans have given them."

"Will we be in danger?"

He shrugged. "I don't know. We won't go as far north as the mission. It will take too much time and we don't have any time to spare."

She nodded and continued to look at him intently. "Did you get any sleep last night?"

"No. I thought I would sleep today while you are at the post, if you don't mind going with one of the boys."

She looked disappointed but said, "No. I don't mind. You need to rest. You look very tired, Ross."

He smiled halfheartedly. "Just haven't shaved is all."

Ross joined Adam and Heely to visit among the wagons and take inventory of the supplies. Most were dangerously low, clearly not enough to see them through to the valley, even with good luck, and only a few of the people had any amount of money to spend. Still, everyone wanted to go to the post and see for themselves what was to be had. They divided the company into groups so only part of them would be gone from camp at a time.

158

Ross, long overdue for some time to himself, mounted his horse and rode away from the camp, heading southward toward the mouth of the Boise River where it joined the Snake. When he found a stretch of river uninhabited by Indians and screened by brush, he dismounted and stripped off his trail-grimed buckskins. Leading his horse into the water to protect his weapons and clothes, he luxuriated in a bath, cleaned the blackened buckskins, and finished his ritual by shaving.

Refreshed but tired, he returned to camp. Marlette, Martha, Liz, Jenny, and the boys were all gone, and he ducked into Marlette's tent. Warmed by the sun, he removed his buckskins once more and crawled into her blankets, sleep almost beating him to her pillow.

He heard nothing, sleeping the sound sleep of total exhaustion, and was aware of nothing until he dreamed. The dream was of Marlette and she was beside him. He didn't want to waken, knowing she would be gone, and he wanted to hold her, needed to hold her, if only in a dream. The fantasy touched him and caressed him, arousing his desire. A moan brought him suddenly to consciousness. He remembered that Marlette could not receive his body. Lips and hands were bruising and demanding as he came completely awake and gazed with shocked eyes into Liz's flushed and impassioned face. He tried to pull away from her, not believing he wasn't dreaming, but she held him, her mouth coming to his hotly as he struggled and broke free.

"What are you doing here?" he gasped.

A shaft of light streamed into the tent as the flap was raised, and Ross's eyes darted to the opening to see Marlette, her hand going to her mouth to stifle her shocked gasp. The flap was dropped as quickly as it had been raised.

Liz's arms pulled at him and he roughly pushed her away, too angry to be concerned about hurting her. "Just what are you trying to do? Get dressed and get out of here!"

She looked at him with wild eyes and laughed, her drawl exaggerated as she said, "Why, darlin', there's no need to leave. We have nothin' to hide now."

He lurched out of the bed and pulled on his clothes, only concerned by what Marlette was thinking and had every right to think. He yanked up the tent flap and saw Martha's puzzled face first. Jenny was there, too, along with Joseph and the Yetter boy.

He saw Marlette heading for the river with the water bucket. He strode after her, wondering how he would explain what really happened and knowing no one but a fool could possibly believe what he was going to tell her. He didn't believe it himself.

Marlette stopped by the river and knelt down, but instead of dipping the bucket into the water she leaned across it, burying her head in her arms, her body convulsing.

He stopped behind her, wanting to take her in his arms but not daring to, remembering another time he had tried to do so when she had cried like this and she had fought him until she exhausted herself. He didn't want her to do that now.

Apologetically, he said, "Marlette."

She straightened as if by command, stiffly, facing away from him. Her hands gripped the edge of the wooden bucket until he saw her knuckles whiten.

"Marlette, I can understand what you are feeling now and I can't blame you, but try to listen to me and believe what I am going to tell you. What you saw isn't really what was happening." He paused, already knowing he had lost her. How could she believe him when her eyes had seen him? His voice shook with desperation as he continued. "I know what you saw, Marlette, and it was happening. I can't deny it, but I didn't want it to happen. Believe me! I was asleep and I dreamed you were in my arms. I didn't want to wake up. Then I realized it wasn't a dream and it was Liz in my arms instead of you. That is when you saw us. Marlette, I don't expect you to believe me. I wouldn't believe it either, but it is the truth. I love you and I want no one but you. I don't know how I am going to prove that to you now, but I would if I could. There is no way I can justify what happened, even to myself, and I won't speak of it again, nor will I bother you in any other way, but I will be close by if you need me."

He waited for a long moment, but she offered no response. He turned and walked with heavy footsteps to his horse. Liz was just emerging from Marlette's tent, and she saw him and laughed, blowing him a kiss. Martha, Jenny, and the boys saw Liz, and the looks they gave Ross, especially Martha's, eloquently conveyed all the shock and disgust they felt. It was no less than Ross felt for himself. He mounted his horse, yanked the animal around, and galloped toward the fort, only wanting to escape.

Halfway to the post he began to realize the full implication of what had just happened. It went far beyond just Marlette, Liz, and himself. Not only had Liz succeeded in destroying Marlette's hard-won trust in him, and possibly her love—which was bad enough—but Sam Yetter had witnessed the scene, and Jacob Yetter would soon hear what happened. It would be a weapon Yetter could use most effectively against him to have him deposed as leader of the train. He had lived among white people long enough to know infidelity was condoned only as long as it could be kept secret. Once discovered, the pious teachings of their religion demanded punishment.

And Liz. What would happen to her? She was so full of grief and bitterness that he doubted she even comprehended the rashness of her act. It would do little good to talk to her, and even if she was rational, he couldn't and wouldn't ask her to take the blame for what had happened. He was just as guilty. He had been so consciously needing just what she offered that he had let it happen.

With growing realization of what could happen if Yetter succeeded in turning the company against him, he urged his horse even faster toward the fort. He had to find Adam and Daniel and tell them first before they heard it from someone else.

He saw Adam, Sarah, and Amy coming on foot and rode up to them, wondering what would happen to them if Yetter succeeded in deposing him. Adam carried a small sack of staples purchased at the fort. It was all he could afford, Ross knew, and not nearly enough to last until they reached the valley. They had lived mostly on what Ross and his hunters provided and were just one step from starvation.

Too distressed to pretend graciousness, he pulled up before Adam and said in a strained voice, "I've got to talk to you, Adam."

The smile left Adam's face. "What's wrong?"

Ross ignored the question and commanded, "Come with me. We've got to find Daniel. Is he at the fort yet?"

"Yes, but what's this about, Ross? What has happened?" Alarm tinged his voice.

"I'll tell you as soon as we find Daniel." He urged his horse on past Adam, never questioning that Adam would follow, and saw the Heely wagon coming away from the post. He waited between the two men.

When Heely was abreast of him he said, "I would like to talk to you and Adam. Can your wife take the wagon?"

Daniel smiled in his usual affable way and answered, "She can if you need me."

Ross nodded and said, "I need you," pulling his horse away from the wagon and dismounting.

Adam and Daniel approached him with puzzled looks. He braced himself mentally and physically, his expressionless face masking the depth of his emotions, and began, "Something has happened that will affect us all. I wanted to tell you about it myself before anyone else did. You know I stayed in camp this morning to sleep. I went to the river and wasn't there when everyone left for the fort. When I returned from the river, I went to my wife's tent. I didn't know Mrs. Jessup didn't go with them. When I woke up, Liz was in bed with me. Before I fully realized what she was doing there and could get myself, or her, out of the tent, Marlette and the rest of them returned and Marlette came to the tent and saw us together. Martha, Jenny, Joseph, and Sam Yetter all witnessed me leaving the tent and Liz leaving the same tent after I did. I'm not asking you to believe whether I'm innocent or not of what they think went on in that tent, but you can bet Yetter is probably hearing about it right now and he won't let it go. If he can possibly do it, he'll see that I'm relieved of my duties—and you may be, too, since you are my friends. I wanted you to know what to expect so you can be ready for it."

They both looked at him in stunned silence. Heely exclaimed, "My God! You're right! Not one of them's goin' to believe a man's innocent with a woman like that involved. Does your wife believe you're innocent?"

"Would your wife believe you if she found you in bed with another woman?"

Heely grinned grimly. "Not on your life. That means if it comes to a trial, none of them would be on your side, except Mrs. Jessup."

"I don't even know about her. She hasn't been herself since John's death. I didn't realize how distraught she was or I would have done things differently. I can't ask her to take the blame for what happened. I don't think she realizes what it might mean to all of you. If it comes to me having to leave the train, I won't even be able to help you."

Adam broke his silence, saying, "You didn't abandon me when I needed help, and I owe you a lot more than just my vote of confidence. If it comes to a split, I will go on with you because I know you're the only man capable of getting us where we're going."

"And that is just what we can't let happen. If there is a split, Marlette and the Jessups would be the last ones to want to go on with me the way things are right now."

Heely swore again. "Good God, man, do you realize what you are asking? I'd rather try to convince your wife you were innocent of what she saw than try to work with Yetter!"

A hint of a smile quirked Ross's mouth. "I know. That's why I'm telling you this. Your decisions are going to be harder than mine."

Adam asked, "Have you talked to Liz's boys yet?"

"No. I hadn't thought of it, but I suppose I'd better talk to Jonathan before he hears of it through someone else." He turned to mount his horse.

Adam stopped him with, "You'd better let us go with you. You shouldn't try to reason with him alone."

"You're probably right, but I don't think there's much time. I don't want Yetter to talk to him first."

"Yetter won't get to him first. He's still at the fort. And it's probably already too late to beat Joseph. Now give us some time to get some horses. I don't want you meeting Jonathan by yourself."

Ross nodded. Adam was probably right on all counts and he grudgingly agreed, "All right. Let's go."

They walked back to the circle of wagons, Ross stoically restraining his urge to leave them. He waited outside while Adam and Daniel got their horses, then led them in a hard gallop to where the herd was grazing close to the river. He slowed his horse when he saw a familiar cluster of horses and men. He was too late. Joseph was already with Jonathan. And Jeremy and Cam were with them. They saw him coming and the huddled group separated; Jonathan came forward, his rifle across his thighs. A prickle of apprehension ran up Ross's neck. Their faces told him more than he wanted to know. He didn't have to worry about being on a pedestal any longer. Cam's face showed as much contempt as the Jessup boys.

Silently, they waited for him to approach until he was just a few yards away. Suddenly Jonathan jerked up the rifle and cried, "You dirty son of a bitch!"

Instinctively, Ross catapulted out of the saddle as the rifle fired almost point-blank, and he felt a hot searing pain in his left side. Heely grabbed at the rifle and pulled the boy to the ground. Adam was on the ground beside Ross, trying to stop the blood flowing from his wound with a handkerchief. Cam, Jeremy, and Joseph dismounted and stood in hostile silence around Jonathan.

Ross struggled to his feet and stood on unsteady legs to face the angry boy, more his mother's child than his father's. "Jonathan, I don't blame you for feeling I deserved that, but please just listen to me. Don't make any judgments just yet. There is more to consider than what happened between your mother and me."

"Listen to you! You bastard! You ask me not to make any judgments after what you did to my mother!"

"Jon! Just listen! I am not trying to hide anything from you and I'm not going to lie to you. I need your help." He paused. The other herders were riding up, more than curious about the scene they were witnessing. Ross turned to them and ordered, "You men get back to your positions."

Daniels wasn't about to leave without an explanation. He demanded, "What the hell's going on here, Chesnut?"

"You'll find out about it later, Daniels. Now do as you're told!"

Jonathan countermanded, "No! You men stay. I want you to hear this."

Ross looked at the distraught young man and said quietly, "No, Jon. Don't do this. It can only make things worse."

Adam agreed. "He's right, Jon. Don't jump to conclusions until you hear what Ross has to say. It could do irreparable harm at this point."

Heely advised, "You better think about it, son. This affects us all and could bring worse hurt where you don't want it."

Jonathan didn't reply and Ross gave his order again. "That's it, men. Get back to your positions." Grudgingly, the herdsmen turned their horses away with wondering looks.

Ross waited, and Adam asked, "Are you going to be all right? Maybe we should take you into camp."

Ross shook his head and turned back to Jonathan. "Jon, I'm sorry this happened—sorrier than you'll ever realize, but it has

164

happened, and we've got to face the fact that your mother hasn't been herself since your father died.''

"Don't you mention my father! After what you did, you're not good enough to clean his boots!"

Heely stated loudly, "And you ain't listenin', son! Now you're not too old for me to tan your hide like your daddy'd do if he heard the way you were talking right now."

Jonathan's eyes blazed, but he asked with less heat, "Just what are you getting at, Chesnut?"

"Two things, Jon. The first is your mother needs help until she realizes what she is doing. The second thing is when Sam tells his father what Joseph told you, he's not going to overlook it. He's going to try to get me removed from this train. We can't let that happen, Jon. No matter what, I've got to stay where I can help your mother and you and my wife, whether any of you want it or not."

"Do you think I'm going to agree to that? The sooner you leave the better! The next time I won't miss."

"You're not listening, Jon. Your mother needs help. If I'm not here, she may go to someone else. The next man she goes to isn't going to realize what she's really suffering from and will take full advantage of what she's offering."

Jonathan's face blanched whiter as he comprehended what Ross was saying. He lunged at Ross, every vile name he knew spitting from his curled lips. Cam and Jeremy caught and held him before he could hit Ross.

They stood face to face and Jonathan was livid with hate. "I wish I would've killed you, you foul-mouthed liar!"

Ross's heart wrenched with compassion for what the boy was feeling, and he didn't know how to make the boy understand. He placed his hands on Jon's shaking shoulders, feeling the blood run faster from his side as he stretched the wound. "Jon, if I am lying to you, then I deserve your hate, and whatever else you have for me, but I asked you not to make judgments. Your mother needs help. It is not her fault. She is sick with grief and she feels lost and alone. She wants desperately to feel secure again, and she is trying to find that security with anyone who will give her attention. I know that now and I can deal with it. Yes, I made a mistake—a mistake I am already paying dearly for. I don't intend on letting it happen again. When we are in Oregon—when she has a home, and feels secure once more—she is going to realize what happened here. I don't want her to remember it happened with every man willing to take advantage of her, and I don't think you do either.''

The boy looked into his eyes and Ross could see the war of emotions being waged. Slowly the fire went out of his eyes. His trembling increased, tears welling in his eyes. Ross took the boy in his arms and held him until he felt control returning. Then he released him, and Jonathan backed up to look at him, a far different expression in his eyes.

"I'm sorry, Ross. Mother hasn't been right since Father's death. It's hard to admit she may be guilty of what happened today but—" He didn't finish, and Ross saw unspoken pain in the boy's eyes. He continued, "I don't want her to do this to herself. I'll help you to try to keep us together.''

Ross smiled. "Good. I hope time will prove me wrong.''

Adam, in a relieved voice, said, "Now will you come back to the wagons so we can get that wound taken care of?''

Ross nodded and reached for the rifle Heely still held. He gave it back to Jonathan. "You'd better keep this.''

The boy smiled faintly and said, "Thanks.''

Adam stood ready to help him onto his horse, but first he had to make peace with the three other boys. "Jeremy—Joseph, do I have your help, too?''

Faint smiles slowly replaced uncertainty as both boys held out their hands to him and he took them with relief. He faced Cam and said, "I told you that someday you would discover I was only a man, and today I have kept my word. I'm sorry I disappointed you, Cam, but I would ask one thing of you now. Will you take care of Marlette for me? She will need you now, more than ever.''

Cam nodded his head abruptly and turned away. Ross stood looking at the stiff back and knew he had not been forgiven. He couldn't blame Cam, but it hurt, and hurt deeply, to be rejected by the two people he loved the most.

Adam took hold of him and forcibly helped him into the saddle. He felt very tired and drained of every incentive to continue to lead this group.

Adam took him to his wagon and Sarah, without question or hesitation, used the last of her sheets to make a bandage for him. The camp quickly became aware of the fact that he had come in wounded, and there was soon a gathering of curious and questioning movers.

When Sarah finished, he stood and tried to smile reassuringly. "Everything's all right. Just a little accident. Now go on back to your wagons. We leave as usual in the morning." He turned back to his nurse and said, "Thank you, Sarah. I'll see that you have new sheets when we get to the valley."

She smiled and answered, "I'm not worried about that, but I am worried about you. You look a little pale. I think you should lie down."

"She's right, Ross. You'd better take it easy. I'll help you back to your tent."

With Adam's help, Ross walked to his own wagons. There appeared to be no one there, and Ross could see the women doing their washing along the riverbank.

Adam said, "Looks like you'll get to rest some before you have to face them."

With a grim smile, Ross agreed. "Yes. Thank you, Adam. I appreciate having your help and hope I can justify your trust in me."

Adam smiled back and said, "You already have."

Ross was about to crawl under the wagon into his bed when Liz came from her tent. Adam didn't know whether to stay or leave as Liz came hesitantly over to Ross.

"Ross, what is it? You don't look well, darlin'."

Ross stiffened at the word. "I'm all right, Liz."

She looked him over carefully and saw the bloody rent in his shirt. "Why, you've been hurt! How did it happen? You'd better sit down and let me take care of you."

"It was an accident and it's already been taken care of. Why aren't you down with the others, washing clothes?"

She smiled coyly and answered, "Why, you should know the answer to that, Ross, darlin'."

"Liz, I am not your darling and I don't want to hear you call me that again."

She looked offended and hurt. "Please don't be angry with me, Ross. You're the only one I have now. You know I'd do anything in the world for you, don't you?"

"All right, Liz. Do this for me. Explain to Marlette I had nothing to do with you being in bed with me."

She laughed. "You really don't think she would believe me, do you? After all, she did see what was happening."

Anger overwhelmed him and his voice became low and harsh. "Liz, do you realize what you did may split this train up or worse?"

Before she could answer, Adam added, "And Ross was lying about that wound being an accident, Mrs. Jessup. Your son shot him because he thought Ross seduced you. If the members of this train vote to remove Ross and refuse to let him stay with the train, do you realize what that will mean to the rest of us?"

Her eyes widened as Adam's words brought realization. Her face crumpled and tears spilled down her cheeks. "Oh, Ross! I'm so sorry. My own son! Can you forgive me? I'm so afraid and so alone and I needed someone. I needed you. I know you felt it, too."

His compassion for her overruled his anger, and he said gently, "I know, Liz, I know. Everything you're feeling I have felt, too. I said I'd take care of you and your family, and I will, but I can't be a husband to you. I love Marlette and I want only her love. If you have destroyed her love for me, Liz, by what you tried to do today, you have destroyed the only thing I value."

Adam interrupted his words with, "Marlette and Martha are coming."

He saw them with Jenny and knew they had seen him and Liz together. Liz turned away and ran quickly into her tent, leaving him to face three very hostile faces. He turned back to Adam and said, "Thank you, Adam. I'll see you later."

Adam nodded and left silently. Ross went to help Marlette carry her wet clothes, folded into a bundle and wrapped in a wet sheet. She yielded them to him without a word.

As he turned, he heard her gasp and knew she saw his bloodied shirt. Her anxious voice asked, "What happened? Are you hurt?"

"It's nothing. Just an accident."

She questioned him no more, and he set down her bundle on the end of the wagon. He took the rope from his saddle and reached with an effort to roll back the canvas far enough to secure a rope to the end bow. The effort was too much and he felt the wound bleeding again. Feeling shaky, he went to sit against a rock by the dead campfire, pressing his hand over the troublesome wound.

Jenny came out of Liz's tent and cried, "Mother!"

The urgency in her voice brought Liz to the opening and she came quickly to Ross. "Why, you're bleeding!" She turned to Jenny and ordered, "Get me some clean cloths. Quickly, now!"

Marlette watched with angry eyes while Liz replaced the bloodied bandage with a clean one.

"There," she said when she had finished knotting the cloth. "Now you sit still. The boys will be in shortly and they can take care of things. You hear?"

He nodded. "Thank you, Liz."

She smiled and turned away with the blood-soaked bandage in her hands, heading for the river. He looked at Marlette, but she ignored him and continued hanging up the wash. Jenny took her milk pail and went to look for one of her brothers to go with her to the herd For a brief interval, he was able to close his eyes and rest.

The boys came in noisily, and preparations for the evening meal began as Jonathan got the fire going again. To look at them with an unobserving eye, they would seem to have returned to normal, but Ross could feel the undercurrent of tension, magnified by his own dread of facing Yetter.

Jonathan was the first to see Yetter coming and warned Ross in a low voice, "Here comes Yetter."

Ross rose to his feet and was able to stand to face Yetter, but his legs were far from strong. Adam and Daniel followed in the mob of accusing faces and came to stand with him.

Yetter looked at him with the same antagonistic expression, but with a new and hopeful light in his eyes, as he saw a means of finally humiliating Ross. "Guess you know why we're here, Chesnut."

Ross, unwilling to admit any amount of guilt—especially to this man—calmly replied, "No, Yetter, I don't. What can I do to help you?"

The small eyes narrowed. He had expected something different—denials or offers of compromise, but not complete ignorance. Contempt tinged Yetter's voice. "Look at him! This is the man you are trusting with leadership of this whole train, and he won't even tell the truth. He knows damn good and well why we are here." He swung his eyes around the crowd and then back to Ross, continuing, "We are here to relieve you of your duties of leading this train."

"On what grounds?"

"On the grounds of adultery."

"What proof do you have of that charge, Yetter?"

Yetter looked startled. "Proof? Proof! We don't need proof. My boy told me what he saw."

"What did your boy see, Yetter?"

"He saw you come out of your tent followed by Mrs. Jessup."

"Is that your proof? That Sam saw me come out of my tent followed by Mrs. Jessup? That isn't proof."

Yetter was turning red in the face. "Damn you, Chesnut. You were in that tent with Mrs. Jessup and we all know what you were doing. You can't talk your way out of it. We all know her boy shot you because of what happened. Now try to deny that!"

"I won't deny Jonathan shot me, but it was an accident."

Yetter searched for Jonathan and said, "Are you going to say it was an accident, Jonathan?"

Jonathan stepped forward to stand beside Ross. "Yes, sir. It was an accident."

Yetter shouted angrily at them, "By God, Chesnut! You aren't going to get away with this. You're guilty, and this outfit can vote you out just like we've been seein' people voted out ever since we left Missouri. Now you'd better saddle your horse, because when I come back I'll have a tally of votes against you."

Ross countered, "You get that vote, Yetter, and it'll be the biggest mistake you and everyone on this train can make. You can't make it without me. You've still got a long way to go, and I know not many of you could buy supplies at the fort. The Cayuse and Walla Walla Indians are just waiting to plunder some outfit. If you split this train up, you won't have the strength or the knowledge to deal with the Indians you still have to meet. You don't know the trail and you don't know where the water is, and if you don't have someone who does, you are going to risk your life and the lives of your family. Then who is going to be guilty, Yetter? How are you going to justify relieving me of my job when you're attacked by Indians or thirsty, hungry, or stranded?"

Yetter wheeled around and plunged through the crowd. Daniels looked at Ross with a wry smile and said, "You better be careful, Chesnut. He's liable to finish what young Jessup started."

"I expect him to. How are you going to vote?"

"Oh, I'm going to stay with you. You are guilty as hell, but I wouldn't follow Yetter from here to the river."

Ross gave the man a half smile. He would have just as soon Daniels hadn't expressed his opinion; he saw too many onlookers who would take that statement into consideration. He said, "I thought the white man believed every man to be innocent until proven guilty."

"True, Chesnut. But I been watchin' your wife. One look at her tells me all I need to know to make my judgment."

Ross turned to look at Marlette and knew it was true. Her face was drawn, indignity and self-righteousness written in her aloof eyes. She dropped her eyes and turned away, stepping into her tent.

Daniels laughed and walked away, and the crowd broke up.

"I didn't come out too well, did I?"

"That man is too smart for his britches. I'd like to burn him one across the mouth."

"Easy, Daniel. He's carrying a grudge against me, too. Only difference is he realizes he can't make it without me. Yetter doesn't."

Liz came up to him and pleaded, "Ross, please come sit down. Let me get you your supper."

He was terribly tired and knew she meant well, even though any extra concern toward him now would be mistaken for a continuance of what had happened earlier. There was no way of knowing whether she was actually concerned or playing a role. He believed she was being sincere and answered, "Thank you, Liz."

Night came with a hush, except for the voices of a million night insects, mostly crickets. Ross waited and listened in tense silence for the verdict to be reached around the circle of campfires. There was no friendly companionship to encourage him. The women were in their tents, the boys on duty or finding company elsewhere, while Adam and Daniel were stumping the circle advising against a split. He knew it would be close if it came to a vote. The teamsters, who were, with few exceptions, older than the drovers, would be swayed by Daniels's opinion of him, since Daniels and his traveling companions seemed to be their leaders. But the

171

younger herdsmen, he felt, would remain loyal to him in spite of either Yetter or Daniels. He had tried to be fair with them, never asking them to do what he wasn't willing to do himself, and he had tried to give each one of them a chance to go hunting with him. He had considered them equal with the other boys and had treated them accordingly. They were no more than boys, most of them. Finally Ross could fight his heavy eyes no more and dozed.

Joseph awakened him some time later, his voice tinged with urgency. "Ross! Ross, wake up! Mother is missing!"

The distress in the boy's voice brought him immediately awake. "How long? Where did she go? Have you checked with the other women?"

"She told Jenny she was going out to, well, you know. But that was an hour ago. I've been clear around the circle and no one has seen her. Didn't you see her?"

"No. I fell asleep." He rose to his feet slowly, feeling weak and in pain.

"Do you want me to get Jon and Jeremy?"

"No. I'll take a look around first. No use alarming them until we know if there is something to alarm them about. You stay with the women."

He picked up his rifle and moved out into the darkness away from the glow of the fire. Slowly, his eyes adjusted until he could see the sweep of brightly moonlit sage, glinting silver in the cool night breeze. He saw no foreign shape as his eyes roamed over the desert from the hills to the fort and river. He headed toward the river.

The night guard came riding toward him and he raised his hand. It was one of the hired teamsters. "Did you see Mrs. Jessup come this way?"

"Yep. She went out about an hour ago, I reckon. Said she needed some water. Didn't she come back?"

"No. Why didn't you report to me? You know no one is supposed to go out alone, especially after dark."

"How the hell was I supposed to know? She said you told her it was all right."

Ross sighed, too tired even to get angry. "No one is supposed to leave, and if anyone tells you different you come see me. You understand?"

The man turned his head and spat contemptuously into the dust on the other side of his horse. "I understood you ain't goin' to be runnin' things anymore."

Now the anger came and Ross replied harshly, "Well you heard wrong. As long as I'm still here, I'm running things."

Ross walked on, his irritation giving him strength for the moment, but by the time he reached the river his strength was gone and he stood resting for a few moments. He walked along the riverbank for several hundred yards before he saw Liz sitting on a rock. He could tell she was aware of his approach, but she kept her face turned away. When he stopped beside her, she bolted from her perch and he had to leap after her to grab her and hold her.

"Why don't you leave me alone?" she cried angrily.

Just as angrily, he retorted, "I would if you'd stay where you belong. Just what do you think you're doing out here?"

She yanked her arm free and faced him defiantly. "It's none of your business. Now leave me alone!"

"Not until you come back to the wagons."

"I am waiting for someone and I am not going anywhere."

"The only thing you're waiting for is trouble. You've already caused enough of that today. Now come back to the wagons with me willingly or I'll have to drag you back."

"You wouldn't dare!"

"Wouldn't I?"

She glared at him for a moment, then turned to run again. He ran after her and yanked her around roughly, holding her to him, his temper matching hers as his patience with her games and the overwhelming exhaustion he felt wore on him. "What is it you want, Liz? Do you want the Indians to take you? You think that will be exciting? Do you want me to show you what they would do to you? Or is it just a man you want? Any man? Do you want me to finish what you started this morning? Shall I rip your clothes off so they will really have a reason for their accusations?"

She looked at him with wild eyes and parted lips, her breath coming in struggling gasps as he held her forcibly against him and felt the throb of her heart and fullness of her breasts. His mouth bruised hers, his arms crushing her with the violence he felt. He expected her to fight him, wanted her to react to his brutality with hate for him, but she wasn't even resisting him. Her body was pliant, her mouth open and seeking his. Anger turned to passion as desires too long restrained ruled them both, and he was consumed

173

as her kisses burned him and her body set fire to his. For a few moments he could think of nothing but fulfilling his desires, but her gasps and wild murmurings as she writhed against him were so different from Marlette that reason returned. The arms that had so strongly held her now pushed her away and his body shook.

She tried to come back into his arms, her voice pleading huskily, "Oh, Ross, Ross. I want you. Please don't stop now."

He pushed her away again and said, his anger returning, "No! Get back to the wagons."

She didn't move. Her eyes were deeply shadowed and her breasts still rose sharply as she whispered, "No, Ross. You want me. I know you want me. I've felt it from the first time we met. There is nothing to stop us now from having each other."

His own breath was still coming heavily. "I don't deny I want you, Liz. I wouldn't doubt that every man you've ever met has wanted you, but there is a difference between wanting you and loving you. You must understand that. I love Marlette."

"But she doesn't love you. Not now. Not after what happened today. She would give you a divorce."

His anger was mounting again. "No! Sooner or later she will realize I was telling her the truth, and I want to be with her when she does."

Fire flared in her eyes again and she cried, "Then leave me here! I don't care what happens to me! John is dead and you refuse me. What do I have to live for?" She turned away and stumbled blindly back to the rock, weeping.

He followed, feeling the anger wash out of him in response to her tears. "Liz, listen to me. You have everything to live for. First of all, you have your children. I'm sorry I have hurt you, but you will realize someday that what you are asking now is wrong. I told you I have felt everything you are feeling and it is true. You can't bring John back no matter what you do. Just as I will never be able to bring back my first wife. Thinking you can just by going to bed with me or with any other man is a mistake—a mistake I don't want you to make no matter how desperately you think you need what another man can give you. It just isn't going to be there now, Liz. You've got to realize that before you do something you will regret. You have to find the strength to go on within yourself, not in the arms of every man who would take advantage of you. I'm not saying it will be easy. It took me over ten years, but I did

and walked to Heely's fire. Adam was there and the two men were relaxing, as they well needed to do.

Heely smiled up at him from his comfortable chair and said, "Come join us. Adam and I were just wondering if the trail ahead is going to be as good as it has been the past two days?"

Ross squatted and pulled out his pipe. "It will be for a few miles yet, but after that we'll be going through some country that is rougher than any we've had to go through so far."

The air of relaxation slipped away, and Adam said, "That means we all need to make sure our wagons will not fall apart tomorrow. Right?"

Ross nodded, "Right. Do I have any volunteers?"

Heely groaned, "Just when I was beginning to think we had it made." He tapped out his pipe and sat looking at Ross with a quizzical expression. "You know, I'm wonderin' just how much more this outfit can take. Do you think we'll make it?"

Ross put away his pipe without lighting it and rose, looking down at the two men. "You have no choice now."

"You're such an optimist," said Heely with a sigh.

Ross smiled. "I have to be to do this job."

Heely laughed and got to his feet, shaking his head. "Hell, Chesnut, I bet you don't even know what that means."

"If it means I'm crazy, it's close enough."

"It's close enough," chuckled Adam. "Come on. We better get the grease on those wheels."

It was hard enough for Ross to face each family around the circle, knowing how they felt about him since the ordeal at Fort Boise. It was harder still to have to tell them what lay ahead and order tired men to go over their equipment. By the time he got back to his own fire, he was drained both physically and emotionally but still had his own equipment to look after.

"Can you give me a hand with the wagons?" he asked Jeremy. "Tomorrow we'll be entering some rough country."

Without rancor, the boy answered, "Sure. Do you want me to get Cam to help us?"

Ross hesitated. He didn't feel up to a confrontation with Cam. "No. I don't think he'd like helping me do anything right now."

Jeremy nodded and said, "I'm sorry, Ross. I wish there was something I could say to him, but he's taking your wife's side and I guess I can't blame him."

"I don't blame him either, Jeremy. If I could undo what happened that day, I would."

"I believe that, now. I wasn't so sure about it then, but I think Mother is better. I'd like to think whatever went on in that tent between you helped her."

"You've got it wrong, Jeremy. What helped her wasn't what happened in that tent. Come on. Let's get to work."

As they started working on the Jessup wagon, Cam came into camp. He watched them for a few moments in indecision. Ross kept working without acknowledging him, but when he came to help Ross gave him a smile of welcome. Cam took no notice of the acknowledgment, but when the work was finished Ross thanked him. The boy nodded, then said to Jeremy, "It's time for our shift."

In the morning Ross woke the camp as usual and started the fire, then went to the stream. The bandage was pulling and irritating him, and needed changing. He stripped off his clothes and lay in the chilling water until he could gently soak the cloth loose. Then he washed the rest of his body, rose from the stream, dried, and dressed, just as the first gray light of dawn began to creep over the eastern mountains.

He walked back along the stream with his shirt thrown over his shoulder, his rifle in one hand and holding the wet bandage against his side to catch the trickles of blood from where the bandage had pulled the scab loose. He would cover the area with tallow before putting the bandage back on.

He turned toward the wagon circle and saw Cam coming down the path with the bucket for water. Ross stopped and waited for the boy until they stood face to face. Ross nodded and acknowledged, "Cam."

Uncertain eyes traveled over his naked chest to the wound and then looked away as Cam moved forward to pass him. Ross, wanting desperately to have a chance to talk alone to Cam, asked, "How is Marlette?"

Cam stopped again, and the eyes that briefly met Ross's were still filled with indecision. They dropped quickly as Cam murmured, "She's fine." He started to move on again, then raised contempt-filled eyes to Ross and said, "No, that's not true. She's mad and she's hurt. Why did you do it?"

180

Accusing eyes bored into his and Ross said, "I'm sorry. If I'd had a choice, it wouldn't have happened."

Anger flared in the boy's eyes. "I don't believe you had no choice."

"I know you don't, but someday you will when something happens that you have no control over. I will regret what happened the rest of my life, but I can't change it. I have not changed, Cam. I love Marlette and I want her to be my wife, and I still want you to stay with me."

Cam said nothing, his jaw set stubbornly. Ross stepped aside and watched the boy until he reached the stream, then continued on to camp wondering if the boy believed him.

He walked into his own camp and went straight to the container of buffalo tallow they used to grease their pans and as shortening for their baking, in spite of its ripening flavor. Martha and Marlette both saw him. Martha ignored him, and Marlette, though her eyes were wide as she glanced at him, made no move to come help him as he daubed the tallow on his wound.

Liz looked at both women with a frown and came to help him. "Here, let me do that, Ross. Now you hold it where you want it and I'll tie it for you."

He gave her a pained look but stood still for her help.

She gave him a smile and said, "Now you put your shirt on and I'll get you a plate of breakfast."

She turned away and he pulled on his shirt, not unaware of the dark glances cast their way. He went to take the plate Liz held for him and ate in silence. He wanted more, but was too uncomfortable in the presence of such animosity, and went to bring the teams to the wagons.

Soon the whole train was ready, the lead wagons for that day broke the circle and followed his direction. The train crawled up a long hill viewing the Snake River where it made a huge bend and then was lost to their sight. The wagons crested the hill and were presented with an all-too-clear view of the terrain ahead where the country roughened considerably into steep ridges, worse than any they'd crossed yet.

The wagons made it into the Burnt River Canyon with no mishap, but they were soon to discover that that had been the easy part of the ordeal. The Burnt River was swift and rocky, with deep holes. The canyon walls were steep and covered in places with thick brush. Fresh animals and rested men would have had trouble hacking their way through the tangle of briars and underbrush, holding the wagons upright on nearly perpendicular slopes, but these men and animals were near the end of their stamina. Animals that had not succumbed in the desert heat fell down exhausted here. Men fared only a little better.

Ross led the way on foot, choosing the best trail through the brush more by instinct than sight, and wielding an axe alongside his hand-picked crew of trail clearers and builders. They rested precariously on the edge of a rock slide at noon, repairing wagons and bringing up fresh teams from what was left of their diminished reserve stock.

Late in the afternoon they were easing the wagons one at a time across another particularly bad rock slide. Men with ropes helped to hold the wagons upright as other men tried to keep the teams going. One of the Yetter wagons began to slide at the steepest incline, and exhausted men were straining to their limit to hold onto hand-burning ropes. The oxen bellowed as the wagon slid unchecked down the hill, Ross and Jacob Yetter fighting to drive the frightened team forward with maximum effort. Yetter, on the downhill side of the team, lost his footing and fell in the jumble of moving rocks and animals. The wagon lurched over and Ross was yanked along with the oxen and wagon into the river, his arm tangling in the rope they had needed to help hold the oxen. His left shoulder was wrenched with excruciating pain before he was able to free himself from the frantic, floundering oxen. Gritting his teeth against the pain, he struggled to release the animals being dragged in the current by the weight of the drifting wagon. His left arm was almost useless, and sweat mingled with tears of pain as he tried to unyoke the bawling animals. Jonathan came to his aid, but he hardly realized who it was until the animals were free and he had time to duck his head in the cool water.

"Ross, Ross! Are you all right?"

He heard Jonathan's anxious voice and looked at him with pain-blurred eyes. "Yes. Who's hurt up there? Yetter?" His breath came in gasps.

"We think he's got a broken arm. What can we do about the wagon?"

"Nothing. We'll have to leave it. Bring the oxen, if you can get them."

182

He started climbing up the rock bank and found that any movement of his arm brought a dizzying pain. He picked his way carefully, feeling faint. He looked back once for Jonathan and saw the boy struggling with the oxen on the unstable slide. He yelled, "Take them on upstream to better footing."

Some of the other men were coming back along the trail now to help them and Ross yelled again, "Help Jon get those oxen, and get what you can out of the wagon."

He watched and rested as the men waded into the water after the wrecked wagon and began to retrieve what they could from it and herd the oxen onto the right bank. Ross joined the group of men where Yetter lay moaning. Adam was setting the arm with the help of Heely, as they had seen him set the Indian's leg so many miles back. There was plenty of wood here to make splints, and someone found a cup of whiskey to help ease the pain.

Adam looked up briefly and asked, "Am I doing it right, Ross, or do you want to take over?"

"You're doing fine." He got down on his knees and gently felt the broken limb, causing Yetter to groan, "For God's sake, Chesnut, leave it alone."

"Just wanted to make sure it was straight, Yetter, which is more than you did for that Indian back along the Kansas."

Yetter closed his eyes and Adam finished securing the splint. "What about his wagon?"

"He'll have to get by with the one he's got left."

Yetter's eyes opened at that, and he glared at Ross, his voice rasping through clenched teeth. "I knew we should've fired you at Fort Boise. You did it on purpose! You'd like nothing better than to see me broken and bankrupt, you dirty half-breed!"

"You're wrong, Yetter. And you're lucky. If you didn't have a broken arm, I'd leave you here to get to the valley by yourself." Ross rose and swayed unsteadily, stumbling against Horace Kalber, who caught him. Adam stepped to his side and helped Kalber ease his shaking body back to the rocks.

"What is it, man?"

Ross tried to wave Adam away, saying, "It's nothing."

Heely exclaimed, "Nothing! Good God, Adam! Look at his arm!"

Ross blinked hard, focusing on his arm, and saw the grotesquely twisted limb.

Kalber asked, "Is it broken?"

Ross answered, "No. Just out of place, I think. It got twisted in the rope when the wagon dragged the oxen into the river."

Kalber reached for the knife at Ross's belt and said, "Let's cut his shirt away so we can see."

Heely interjected, "Good Lord, Horace, look at your arm!"

All eyes shifted to where Horace Kalber's arm supported Ross's left side. His shirt sleeve was staining dark red.

Adam choked, "Ross, you damn fool! Give me his knife, Horace."

Ross protested, "No. It'll be all right."

Adam overruled him. "You lay still and shut up." He looked up at the group of silent men and ordered, "Take Yetter forward to the wagons, and somebody bring back some cloth to make a sling and a blanket and a couple of the boys. We'll have to carry Ross in."

Adam took the knife and gingerly cut the buckskin up the side and along the shoulder until they could ease the sleeve away and see the blood-soaked bandage and the dislocated shoulder.

Sweat stood on Adam's forehead as he said, "I'm going to have to try and get that arm back into the socket, Ross. Are you willing to let me try?"

Ross turned his head as far as he could to see the deformed shoulder and nodded. "Somebody'll have to. I can't. Give me the knife."

Adam handed him the knife and Ross placed the handle between his teeth and nodded his readiness as Heely dropped down to hold his legs. Adam asked, "Ready?" Ross closed his eyes as Adam grasped his arm. There was a great flash of pain as Adam wrenched the arm back into place, and Ross moaned involuntarily, almost blacking out. Then it was over and Adam held the arm across Ross's chest while he made sure the arm was back in its socket. Ross opened his eyes and had to wipe the sweat from his face before he could see.

"How's that feel?"

"Better." Gingerly, he felt around the aching shoulder and was satisfied it was returned to the proper place.

"All right, Horace, hold him up a little straighter and Ross, you hang onto that arm. Don't let it move while I take care of this wound. How long has it been bleeding?"

"I could feel it pulling open when we started cutting brush."

Adam didn't comment as he removed the cloth and scrambled down to rinse the bandage in the river. He placed the cool dampness against the oozing wound and tied it tightly.

"Looks like we will have to lay over until you can move."

"No. I'll be able to move tomorrow."

"Ross, it isn't going to do any of us any good if you kill yourself. Now I say we'll lay over, and Daniel will agree with me."

Heely affirmed, "You're outnumbered, Chesnut. I say we lay over."

"And I say I can move tomorrow. Granted I won't be able to cut brush or much of anything else, but I'll be able to move. When we get to the Grand Ronde we'll lay over, and not until then."

Adam shrugged his shoulders. "All right. I'll compromise. We'll decide what you can do in the morning."

Ross agreed, "Fair enough."

They heard the men coming and saw Jonathan, his face drawn with concern as he dropped to his knees beside Ross. "Why didn't you tell me what was wrong instead of sending me off with those damn oxen?" He sounded just like his father and Ross had to smile wistfully, wishing at the same time it was Cam so concerned about him.

Ross answered, "Someone had to take them."

The rest of the men caught up with Jonathan.

"How bad is he, Adam?" Jonathan asked.

"Not good. He's been losing blood, and dislocated his shoulder when Yetter's wagon slid into the river. Let's ease him onto that blanket and see if we can't carry him on to camp. Did anyone bring something to make a sling out of?"

Jonathan unfolded the blanket and said, "Here. Mother sent this sheet to use."

Adam tore the sheet into smaller strips and literally bound his arm into place. Ross protested, "I thought you said a sling?"

"I think this will be even better. I'll know you can't move it at all this way."

"Adam!"

Adam looked at him with stern blue eyes. Necessity had put him in command and he wasn't going to back down. "You're in no condition to argue. Now let these men take you on to camp while Daniel and I get the rest of the wagons across this slide before dark."

Ross relented and let the men put the blanket underneath him. He watched Adam and Daniel walk back to where the few remaining wagons waited and said, "I'll send these men back to help you as soon as they get me into camp."

Adam turned to look at him with a smile and a wave. It was a concession to Ross's leadership and they both knew it.

They carried him to his own wagons, but he found little comfort there. Liz came immediately to help, but Marlette was out of sight, and Martha and Jenny watched with an air of aloofness.

As soon as the men were gone, Liz took warm water from the kettle by the fire and proceeded to sponge his dirt-streaked face. "What have you been doing?"

"Liz, please, I'm all right." Softer, he said, "You'll only make matters worse by doing this."

She whispered back, "I don't care. Someone has got to do for you, and it looks like I'm the only one who cares." Louder, she said, "Jenny, go fetch another shirt for Ross from Marlette. He can't wear this thing."

Jenny went to Marlette's tent. He could see Marlette follow Jenny to the tent opening and look at him while Jenny returned with the cloth shirt Marlette had made him.

"Just put it there, Jennifer." She indicated a place on the log, ignoring Marlette's icy look as she continued to wash Ross's uninjured arm and back. Done, she helped him on with the clean shirt and buttoned it over his trussed-up arm.

"There, now, doesn't that feel better?"

With little change of his pained expression, Ross answered, "Thank you, Liz."

She looked at him with a wicked gleam in her eyes and said, "Now why don't you come lay down in my tent and rest until I get supper ready for you?"

He lurched to his feet, giving her an angry look. "I can rest just fine in my own bed." On shaking legs, he walked to where the bedrolls were laid out under the wagon, seeing Marlette's white-lipped expression before she dropped the tent flap angrily. He eased himself down onto his robe and closed his eyes against the ache of his shoulder and the throb in his side.

All the wagons were in camp by dark. As the evening meal was being prepared, Ross crawled out from under his wagon, walked to the log by the fire, and settled himself to wait for supper. Liz made a great show of taking care of him by preparing a plate and buttering a biscuit and sitting down before him to feed him.

"Liz, I'm able to feed myself."

"You are not. How are you going to hang onto this plate and eat, too?"

He knew she had a point, but he would never win Marlette's sympathy or trust if Liz continued to make him her main concern.

"Liz, I've got to do this myself," he said pointedly.

Martha, overhearing the whole exchange, unintentionally became his ally by saying, "You heard him, Liz. Now I've stood by and watched you two carry on long enough, and it's time I spoke my piece even though I been told it ain't my business. Well, it is my business when you are hurtin' somebody who's been like my own to me. You two may deserve each other, but as long as he's married to Marlette, he ain't free to carry on with you, Liz Jessup, and you best let him be and let his wife do for him." There was fire in the older woman's eyes.

Liz stood up with a fire in her own eyes to match Martha's. "All right! I'd be glad to let his wife take care of him, but where is she? Is she out here taking care of her man when he needs her? No! She's off in her tent and doesn't even care that he's hurt. I don't call that bein' a wife. She doesn't deserve him any more than I do if you want to look at it that way. I know what it is to lose my man, and she'll soon find out if she doesn't start acting like a wife to him!"

"Liz!" Ross groaned.

Before he could say more, Marlette came from her tent and stood looking at Liz with her chin squared and haughty. "I'll take over now, Liz. You don't have to worry about him anymore."

Liz handed her the plate with a frosty smile and said, "As you please."

Marlette knelt before him with the plate, still not looking at him, and he said, "Marlette, you don't have to do this."

She looked at him with cold eyes and said, "I want to," and held a forkful of beans for him to eat.

He let her feed him without further protest, and finally she said, "I'm sorry you are hurt. Is there anything I can do?"

"Don't ask that question unless you are ready to hear my answer."

She dropped her eyes and he thought he saw the glimmer of tears. Finally she asked, as he finished, "Would you like some more?" in a voice vibrating with emotion.

"Please."

She stood up and turned to the bean kettle, ladling more into the plate. Seeing Jenny was done, she asked, "Jenny, would you mind finishing this for me? I don't feel well."

Marlette handed Jenny the plate and walked quickly to hide again in her tent. Jenny held the plate and looked at him with as much curiosity as doubt.

"Jenny, you don't have to do this."

She forked up a mouthful for him and held it to his lips. "I guess I can do it, only I'm not sure I like doing it after what you've done. I really thought you were someone we could trust."

"Jenny, how can I explain it to you so you will understand?"

"Do you love my mother?"

"Not in the way you mean. I care a great deal for your mother, and for all of you, and I want your mother to be happy again. I will do everything I can to see that all of you are safe and have a place to live when we get to the Willamette Valley."

"Then is that why you did what you did—to make my mother happy?" There was an edge of anger to her voice.

He felt sweat rising to his temples again. How was he going to answer her and be honest with her and keep her friendship? "It's hard to answer that question, Jenny. As far as I'm concerned, nothing happened. It could have, but I didn't want it to because I love Marlette and your mother still loves your father."

She finished feeding him the cold beans and left without speaking again. Ross slid carefully down off the log and sat staring into the fire, the lines in his face deepening with despondency.

The boys came in to eat, and Jonathan squatted down where Ross leaned against the log. "How are you doing?"

Ross replied, "I could be better."

"I told Adam I would take your shift tonight."

"You didn't need to do that, but I appreciate it."

Jonathan stood and walked over to fill his plate. Cam pretended not to notice Jonathan's concern, and Ross looked at him with torn emotions. He wanted so much to have the boy's respect, but

188

Cam was deliberately avoiding him, and Ross found it worse than the outright contempt of a few days before.

As soon as Cam and Jeremy were done eating, they went out to take their shift and Jon and Joseph went to bed under the wagon. There was a chill in the night air, hinting of things to come. Ross could see the stars winking coldly in the dark strip of sky visible above the canyon walls. The women had retired, and Ross could hear Martha's exhausted snoring over the rush of the stream. Except for the contented munching and stamping of the stock in the brush, the camp was quiet. Ross rose from before the fire and started toward the wagon and his own bed. Marlette's tent flap moved and caught his eye. Marlette just stood there, a darker shadow against the gray tent. He wondered if she'd been watching him and for what reason. Was she waiting to see what bed he went to? The thought angered him and he didn't pause to acknowledge her as he went to his own cold bedroll.

"Ross." Her voice came softly and stopped him. He didn't turn around immediately. A deep tiredness settled over him. He dreaded a confrontation with her at this time. He didn't know how much more he could take, but he decided now was as good a time as any to find out just what she did intend to do. Slowly, he turned and faced her.

She came to him a little hesitantly and he could see, even in the darkness, a luster about her eyes caused by tears. He waited for her to speak, steeling himself against her animosity.

"Ross," she began, softly, tremulously, "I'm sorry. Liz was right. I haven't acted like a wife at all. A wife would fight for the man she loved and all I've done is drive you into Liz's arms. Will you come to bed with me, Ross?"

His defense was shattered. He replied huskily, "Marlette, you don't have to do this. You know why I can't go to bed with you. It hasn't changed, the way I feel about you. I love you and I don't want to hurt you. Now go to bed and don't worry about me."

The tears so near the surface broke forth with a sob and she stepped closer, reaching for him. He held her with his one good arm and kissed the top of her head as she cried against him.

"You don't understand, Ross," she sobbed. "I *want* you to come to bed with me. I need you, Ross. Please don't refuse me."

He was too filled with the expectation of what she was offering to speak, wanting her desperately but still hesitant, unwilling to cause her pain, or worse. "Marlette, don't do this to us. There'll be plenty of time for us to be together once the baby is born."

She looked at him, her face contorted. "I want to be in your arms now. I can't go on like this. I'm not sure I want to go on if we have to spend one more night apart. I'm losing you and I don't want to. I love you and I need you."

With caught breath, he asked, "Are you sure?"

Her arms went around his neck and pulled his head down to hers. Trembling lips caressed his as she breathed into his mouth, "I'm sure, I'm sure." He felt the pounding of her heart against the arm bound to his chest between them, and then she pulled away from him and took his hand and led the way to her tent. He stood in the darkness and fumbled with the buttons on his shirt until she turned to help him.

"Unbind my arm."

"Are you sure we should?"

"It'll be all right. I can't hold you against me with an arm in the way."

She gently freed the arm, and he winced as he tried to move it away from his body, the weight bringing pain as well. He held the aching arm while she finished undressing him and raised the covers for him, covering him before she undressed. He waited with bated breath while she removed her clothes, and felt the rush of cold air as she came into bed with him and then the sudden electric heat where her body came against his.

"Oh, Marlette," he moaned as he drew her fiercely to him with his one good arm and found her questing lips with his. But her hand felt the damp bandage and her lips pulled away from his.

"Ross, your bandage is wet. Let me change it before it wets the bed."

He released her, and she found the candle and lit it. The glowing light fell on her body swelling with his child and he was overcome by the change. It had been gradual but seemed sudden to him after not being with her for so long. Her breasts, always small and high, seemed fuller, rounder, and tantalizingly near as she removed his bloody bandage. Sand-colored hair hid her face and touched his chest with feather softness, and the taut curve of her unborn child glowed in a corona of light. He was too awed to touch her, yet his body ached for her.

She found clean cloths and sacking to make a thick absorbent pad, and he sat up as she replaced the bandage and turned to extinguish the candle.

"Don't," he breathed.

"Ross! Everyone will see."

"I want to see you." He reach out with his hand and touched the dark aureole of her swelling breast.

"Oh, Ross," she quivered, taking the hand that caressed her breast and holding it to her lips. "What if someone should see us?"

He knew she was self-conscious of the silhouette they made on the walls of the tent and said, "All right. Blow it out." He eased himself back down on the bed while she turned to the candle and waited until she was beside him again, pain sharpening his every sense. She bent over him and kissed him, and he pulled her down to him and held her, filling his unquenched need for her.

Finally she pulled her lips away and shuddered, her breath warm against his cheek, her body trembling. "Oh, Ross, my darling, I want you, but how are we going to keep from hurting your arm?"

His hand combed through her hair and rested on her shoulder as he answered, "Don't worry about hurting me. Just worry about me not hurting you."

She bent to kiss him again and he let his hand slide slowly down the length of her body until it rested on her leg. Gently he slid his hand between her legs, lifting her until she rested over him. She needed no more guiding as their trembling, expectant bodies touched and the overwhelming sensation of her gently enclosed him in warmth and delight. He was afraid to move, afraid to breath. His hand trembled lightly on her back, consciously refraining from pulling her to him. She made a small sound and he immediately fell away from her, fearing he had caused her pain.

He asked, breathlessly, "Did I hurt you?"

"No," she breathed against his cheek. "Don't stop. Don't stop!"

His lips covered hers, and their bodies moved gently against each other until they were no longer aware of any pain, only a deep consuming need that was being fulfilled in ever-increasing intensity until the ultimate ectasy was reached.

It was then Ross felt a hard jab against his abdomen, and it startled Marlette as much as Ross. Marlette gasped, "Did you feel that?"

"Yes," he answered, an excitement growing in him as he drew his arm out from around her and placed his hand against the swelling curve of her belly, feeling the movement there.

"What is it? Do you think—" She didn't finish, unable to speak the frightening thought she had.

"Is this the first time you've felt it?"

"Yes."

He laughed softly, pushed himself to a sitting position, and bent over to kiss her. "Don't worry. It is just our child protesting my intrusion into his world."

Delighted awe filled her voice, "Oh, Ross. I was so frightened."

He bent to kiss the struggling life within her, and joy flowed through him as he felt the life he had given her move inside her. He reached to take her in his arms, forgetting everything but his love and need for her, but his arm couldn't be forgotten as he attempted to use it. Pain blurred his joy, and he knew it was useless to pretend the pain didn't exist now. It stabbed at him with relentless insistence, and he released her.

"I'm sorry, Marlette. You'd better bind up my arm like Adam had it."

"Never mind, my darling, you've made me happier than I have any right to be."

She found the candle and lit it so she could bind his arm. He was achingly tired and almost fell asleep before she tied the ends of the cloth together. She reached to blow out the candle, and he waited while darkness settled over them again and he felt her bump against him.

"Oh!" she breathed. "Why aren't you lying down?"

He encircled her with his good arm and clasped her to him. "Because I love you too much to go to sleep without telling you how much I love you and how important you are to me."

Her arms went around his neck and her lips touched his in a long, tender kiss.

15. The Grand Ronde

MARLETTE AWOKE AT the sound of the fry pan being banged in the cold darkness of morning. She started as she felt Ross's body and remembered with a happy flush that he was in bed with her. She turned so she lay against him and knew by the quietness of his breathing that he was awake, too. Her hand crept to hold the unbound fingers of his injured arm and he whispered, "Are you all right?"

"Yes," she sighed, smiling as she realized just how all right she was. She continued, "I feel wonderful. No pain. Nothing! I can't believe it. What happened? How could something like this happen and then disappear as suddenly as it began? I just don't understand it."

"Neither do I, but let's not worry about it now. It may never happen again. The only thing that matters is that you are all right."

A deep reverence for what she felt with him filled her, and she clung to him fiercely.

Ross winced, and she realized she was hurting him and slowly released her hold.

"What are you thinking?"

His question released a long sigh from her, and the intensity of feelings and emotion escaped as she answered, "Just how much I love you." She was silent for a moment and then she cried, "Oh, Ross, just now I never want to let you go. I only live, really live, when I am in your arms. Anything else is unbearable. Is that possible? Am I crazy?"

He was silent and she wondered if she really was crazy.

"Not crazy," he finally said, "just suffering like I am from too much strain. This isn't how I wanted it to be for you. It isn't what I wanted either, and I have wanted to put you on your horse and take you with me and leave this train and not look back."

193

"I know, and I'm so sorry. I have seen what it is doing to you—and just look what it almost caused between us. It isn't fair you should have to take the burden of all of us on your shoulders, Ross. Only what can you do?"

"Nothing. It's almost over. That's all I can look forward to now. Soon we'll be in our home and can forget about what happened on this trail."

"Yes," she sighed, "but I don't want to forget all of it. I don't want to ever forget the times I spend with you like this. They are too precious and too beautiful."

He kissed her and pushed himself up. "And all too short. I'd better get up and get the train moving or we'll never get out of this canyon."

"Can you? I mean, are you feeling up to it?"

"I don't even want to decide if I'm feeling up to it or not. I have to do it if we're to make the valley before it snows. Now light your candle and see if I'm going to hold together for the day."

Marlette lit the candle and turned to look at Ross. The sight of him wrenched her heart. Her mind's eye saw him as she remembered him—strong, virile, handsome, and smiling—but the man who sat before her wrapped in bandages looked expendable and thin, his face deeply lined by pain and anxiety, with no hint of the dimples she remembered.

She carefully unwrapped the bandage and loosened the thick padding she had used to cover the bleeding wound the night before. The wound had stopped bleeding and the pad was not soaked through. She daubed more grease over the healing scabs and found another thick sack to fold over the wound before retying the outer bandage.

"There. You should last the day if you don't do anything foolish."

"I'll try to remember that."

"Now do something for me."

"What?"

"Smile for me."

"What?" he asked again, giving her a surprised look.

"I want you to smile for me."

"Why?"

"I want to see if you still have dimples."

This brought a slight smile to his lips, and the suggestion of dimples deepened the lines in his face.

"Not good enough. Try a little harder."

He reached out and pulled her close with his good arm and kissed her, and she returned his kiss until she heard voices outside and realized everything they did was clearly visible with the candle lit. She pulled away from him, blushing. She saw him smile then, very nearly like he had smiled a dozen times at her embarrassment, and she blew out the candle and stood up to dress.

"I love you," he said.

She finished buttoning her dress and held out her hand to him, helping him up. She bent to find his pants, but he didn't let her go and pulled her back to him.

"I mean it."

She slipped her arms around his neck and said, "I know." Then she pulled away, reluctantly, and helped him dress. "Will you need something more? It's chilly out."

"I'll be all right. Cam's got the fire going."

He held up the flap for her, and she could see Cam did have the fire going and Martha was already putting the coffeepot next to it. Liz was just coming from her tent and saw them together, and there was a wistful smile on her face. Martha looked up and followed Cam's gaze, and Marlette was dismayed by their looks of disapproval. Cam got up and deliberately left the fire as Ross went to it. Marlette's heart ached. Ross hadn't said anything about Cam. They'd been too involved in rediscovering each other, but she knew how much Cam's disapproval must hurt him.

Martha moved to the end of the wagon to get the morning meal prepared, and Marlette followed her.

"Good morning, Martha."

Martha harrumphed disgustedly and said, "I don't see one good thing about it."

Cam came back with water from the stream and Marlette asked, "Cam, would you escort me to the necessary?"

"All right," he answered unenthusiastically.

Marlette walked along the row of wagons up the small stream until they were beyond the last wagons and well hidden by brush in the early gray light. Marlette found a dense bush and stepped behind it while Cam stood looking the other way.

"Cam, can I ask something of you?"

"Sure."

"I have forgiven Ross and I want you to, too." She came out of the brush in time to see his face twist with reproach.

"How could you after what he did?"

She put her hand on his arm and said, "Cam, I appreciate your loyalty, but Ross doesn't deserve your hate."

"How can you say that? You were the one who told me you never wanted to see him again."

"I know, and I was wrong, Cam. Every time I saw him I hated him, but I still loved him, too, and I finally realized he could have been telling me the truth. I went over that scene in the tent a million times, and I kept seeing the way he looked and remembering what I heard him say just before I opened the flap to the tent. Cam, he wasn't a man enjoying a tryst. He was angry and shocked and confused and on the defensive. I finally saw that and I believe him, now. Will it be so hard for you to believe him, and forgive him, too?"

"I didn't see what you saw or hear what you heard. I don't know."

"Cam, I remember when you came to Philadelphia and told me why you wanted to find Ross. Do you remember what you told me?"

"Yes. But this is different."

"No, it isn't, Cam. If you can't see that now, then you will someday. Just as someday you will know love overcomes many things, and each time it does that love is stronger. I can't explain it to you; you'll just have to experience it. I'm sure you can see how Ross has acted since that day and know he showed more compassion and understanding than any of us toward Liz. I know your respect and love mean a great deal to him. Try your best to care for him as much as I know he cares for you."

Cam nodded and looked away. "All right, I'll try."

Marlette put her arms around Cam and hugged him, seeing in him so much that was Ross and so much that was still to be discovered about himself and life.

Breakfast was well underway when they got back to camp, and the Jessup boys were waiting eagerly with plates in hand for Liz to start forking out the crispy fish they had caught. Marlette took Ross a plate and sat in front of him to feed him, feeling a tranquility she had not felt for weeks.

When he was finished, she stood with him and he bent to kiss her. She unashamedly returned his kiss, only feeling the flush rise to her cheeks as he left her.

Martha came to take the emptied plate from her and said gruffly, "I will never understand what it is about that man that makes you happy, but it appears you are only happy when you can be with him."

"Is it so obvious? I'm sorry. It isn't good breeding to show that much feeling about someone, but I was never good at hiding my feelings."

"Well, I guess it is better than having you so depressed, but I sure wish you'd've found a more suitable man to moon over."

"Martha!" There was an edge to her voice as anger rose in her. "All of us owe our lives to him. He is carrying a great burden of responsibility, and you are unfairly judging him against men who could never do what he has done."

Martha stated defensively, "Well that's right enough. Most men wouldn't do what he has done." She shot a meaningful glance at Liz, who was washing dishes on the end of her wagon. "Or are you going to overlook that?"

"No, I haven't overlooked it. And that's just the point, Martha. Most men wouldn't have allowed themselves to be found out, and Ross is far too intelligent for that, too. I was hurt and angered, but I realized there had to be some other explanation for what happened, and that explanation lies with someone else. I love Ross and I want to be his wife, and if you want to stay with me, then you will have to accept him or leave. I do not wish to hear you speak against him again."

Martha bit back a retort and lowered her eyes respectfully, acknowledging Marlette was still her mistress. Marlette felt a pang of guilt over her harsh words. Reaching out to touch the older woman's arm, she said, "I would be much happier if the two people I care about the most would get along. You are both dear to me and both of you have my interest at heart. Please try to see him as I do and you will be able to see that he is a good man."

Martha sniffed and said, "I just don't want you hurt."

"I know you don't, and you must realize Ross doesn't either, if you will give him half a chance."

"Well, we'll see."

Martha turned away, and Marlette wasn't sure whether she

197

had convinced the older woman or not. She was to the point of almost firing Martha. The last time Martha had spoken against Ross, Ross had made her apologize, but she was tiring of Martha's constant animosity toward Ross. More than once she had wished Martha had not come with her, yet knew how much she needed the older woman—how much they needed each other. Her gaze went to Liz, and their eyes met and locked. A frown creased Marlette's forehead and she turned to her own tent. The boys were ready to hitch up the teams and she needed to get her things packed. She would have to deal with her feelings toward Liz some other time. Now that she had been able to forgive Ross, she felt even more inclined to burden Liz with the blame, although she realized Liz was suffering a deep loss, both emotional and physical.

The next day saw them leave the difficult trail in Burnt River Canyon and follow a winding course over a range of hills into the pleasant Powder River Valley. Here grass was abundant, and they made camp early so the men could hunt and bring in fresh meat and the stock could fill themselves. The jagged snowcapped peaks rising abrubtly in the northeast filled Marlette's heart with excitement and expectation. She recognized these mountains, which marked the beginning of the end of this long and difficult trip. The sight of the majestic peaks also brought a flood of memories as she remembered the first time she had seen them four years earlier.

She walked to the river with her bucket to get water and to be alone to recall those days when she, along with her father and six other men, had come to the Oregon country. Ross Chesnut, the man who was now her husband, had been their guide on that cross-country trip on horseback from Fort Vancouver to the Whitman Mission and back. None of the memories were pleasant, except those that had culminated in her love for Ross. Her father and the rest of the men had been killed, and only she and Ross had survived. So vivid were the pictures flashing through her mind that she wasn't aware of someone coming up behind her until Cam's voice broke into her thoughts.

"Marlette, is there something wrong?"

She started and turned, the flood of memories vanishing. "No. I'm all right, Cam. Just thinking of things that happened long ago."

"Ross told us the Whitman Mission is not too far from those mountains. That's where you went, wasn't it?"

"Yes. I would like to see the Whitmans again."

"Ross sounded like we wouldn't be going there. It's too far out of the way."

She dropped her eyes and nodded with a sigh. "Yes, I know. He was worried about snow on that trip, too."

"That's when your father was killed, wasn't it?"

"Not here, but we were attacked by Indians after we left the mission. We escaped them, but they continued to follow us and set fire to the sagebrush one night while we slept, and we barely escaped again. It was several days later and farther west where they finally caught us in an ambush and killed Father and the men with us."

"Then you spent the winter in the mountains?"

"Yes." Marlette turned away and gazed at the mountains again, remembering the horrible ordeal of hunger and cold until they had finally reached Jacques's cabin and the snowbound winter she had spent hating and fighting Ross, and finally loving him.

Three days later they descended a long, steep hill into the Grand Ronde Valley, a great bowl-shaped valley ringed by tall forested mountains capped with snow. Here grass, water, and wood were abundant, and Indians brought fresh vegetables, meat, and fish to trade with the emigrants.

Ross allowed them to lay over here to rest and repair their wagons for the long, tough climb over the Blue Mountains. It would be the last great barrier to cross, and spirits were high and cooking pots full for the first time in weeks.

The next morning they headed west to begin their difficult ascent over the mountains, double- and triple-teaming up the steep rocky incline. At night they descended a mile-long hill to camp beside the Grand Ronde again.

There was another long hill to climb in the morning as the wagons left the river and drove along a high ridge climbing ever upward to the towering trees. The emigrants had never seen such tall trees and were awed by the giants as they entered a terrain totally different than any they had yet traversed.

Late in the third day, the wagons crawled upward almost to the summit between the trees, and Ross led them to a spring for the night camp. Marlette was busy getting her wagon unloaded while the boys set up the tent when Ross came and asked, "Can you leave that a few minutes?"

"Not if you want a bed to sleep in tonight."

He smiled and said, "I'll worry about that later. Come with me. I have something to show you."

She set the bundle of bedding down and grabbed a shawl. Already the chill air was sweeping through the shaded forest. He took her arm and walked with her until the trees opened up and she gasped with surprised delight, "Oh, Ross!"

Across a great expanse of darkening sagebrush plain, the sun was setting behind a range of familiar mountains. Here were the mountains that had become familiar to her during her first trip to this vast country and which she now viewed as belonging to home. It was a home she had not seen but nevertheless knew existed because the man who stood beside her said it did. Her home lay just beyond those mountains in the valley of the Willamette; now she could begin to feel that the end was in sight.

They watched the sun disappear behind the far peaks, lighting them in a brief rosy glow and then fading out altogether as the gray light of dusk grew steadily darker and the forest frogs began to sing. Silently she turned with him and walked back to the wagons, following the campfires as beacons.

Martha saw her coming and both hands went to her diminished hips in an air of reproach as she asked, "Well, you might tell a body what you been up to."

"Oh, Martha," she bubbled, "I can see home from here!" She turned to include everyone in the circle of their fire and said, "Listen, everybody. I saw where home is! We are almost there!"

Martha asked skeptically, "Now just how can you see home from here? I thought we had a long way to go yet."

"We do, but I saw the mountains that line the valley on the eastern side. And everyone will be able to see them tomorrow as we leave the timber."

She looked eagerly for some excitement to infect them but realized they would have to see the mountains, too, before they could comprehend the end of the trail was near. Tomorrow they could measure the distance; tomorrow they would know their goal was in sight.

That night when she unbound Ross's arm and he took her in his arms, she knew more than just the joy of being with him and being held by him. She knew the feeling of peace, the deep secure peace of finally going home.

It was cold when Marlette awoke in the morning to the ring of the fry pan. There was an eerie hush to the forest. She curled against Ross and he turned to hold her in the chill darkness, the wind in the trees sounding strange to ears so long used to only the sounds of the prairie.

"Feels like it got pretty cold last night."

"It reminds me of the night we spent in the mountains and it snowed. Do you remember?"

"How can I forget? You were the most unreasonable woman I'd ever gone to bed with."

She hugged him tighter, memories of that night seeming almost unreal. So much had happened since that night of grief and terror, making it seem like a nightmare more than reality. She had seen her father and the man she had thought she was going to marry, Gaylord Taylor, fall in the onslaught of ambushing Indians, and she had been carried away by a man she viewed as little better than the savages he had saved her from. She had been too frightened to cry and too shocked to even think when she saw him coldly kill the Indians that had come after them. She had had to go on with him—cold, hungry, and hunted until the Indians found them again and took their horses and guns and they started across the pass in those mountains, now the symbol of home, with snow falling. Vividly, she remembered fighting him in wild desperation, wanting him to kill her, wanting him to brutalize her. When her hysterical outburst was over, he had not hurt her but kept her warm with the same arms holding her now and had even kissed her. Or had she dreamed that kiss? It was so vague. She had been asleep in a sound deep sleep of pure exhaustion, and he had awakened her and her eyes had opened and looked into his eyes, and she remembered thinking how beautiful they were, so deep and so full of compassion. She had somehow known in that moment he would not hurt her, and then he had so gently kissed her as if to reassure and comfort her, and then he had been up and breaking through the shelter he had made them, and the terrible cold had come, just as it came now.

Cam's voice interrupted their thoughtful silence with, "Ross, there's snow out here and I can't get the fire going."

His arms left her and she felt the rush of cold as he sat up and answered, "I'll be right out."

Then he kissed her, dressed, and was gone in another cold blast as he lifted the tent flap. She cowered under the covers, trying to get enough courage to get dressed and hoped the rest of the trip wasn't going to be like this.

The covering of snow on the ground put the emigrants into a solemn, almost frightened mood as speculation became a fact. They knew now what Ross had known all along. Weather was a real and unavoidable threat and they could no longer ignore it. A feeling of urgency accompanied their preparations for the trail, and they were under way earlier than usual without Ross's urging. It was hard to believe that only two days before they had been suffering from heat.

The wagons rolled out, making tracks in the thin covering of snow that was already turning soft as daylight crept into the forest. They emerged from the forest and Marlette looked with renewed excitement for the mountains, but they were lost in the gray blanket of clouds that had brought the snow. Perhaps before the day was over they could see the mountains, but for now there was only the cold wind and gray skies and a treacherously long and steep hill to descend. Teams had to be broken and wheels locked, and for the first part of the descent they had trees to use as snubbing posts.

It was a hill they would never forget. All others they remembered paled in comparison to this hill, but surprisingly few mistakes were made and only one wagon was upset. The animals, not having to work in scorching heat, withstood stress better, as did their masters.

The wind came up before Marlette, Martha, and Liz had gone very far down the mountain following in the wake of their wagons, nearly the last to go down. The sun rose over the top of the tall pines behind them and helped dissipate the clouds until they blew away and Marlette, her eyes searching for the landmark mountain to the west, finally saw the lofty ridge materialize. "Look. Look!" she cried. "There! You can see the mountains. Beyond that mountain with the snow, straight to the west, lies your new home!"

The women coming behind them heard her, and all eyes turned and gazed with growing realization that what they saw was within reach and it would be theirs. Women lifted skirts and, crying excitedly to their preoccupied men, scrambled down the mountain. Everyone stopped to look to the west, and aching arms paused to rest as eyes turned westward and brightened. A shout went up, to be followed by more shouts until the air was filled with whoops of gladness.

Liz said wistfully, "I wish John were here. This was his dream."

Marlette turned to look at Liz, and her heart felt pity in spite of what this woman had put her through. Encouragingly, she said, "Don't forget, Liz, it was his dream for all of you and, even though he isn't with you, I'm sure he is happy knowing you are still going ahead."

"I suppose, but it seems to mean so little without John, and I'm so terribly frightened at what is still ahead for us."

Martha spoke up, "It means even less to me. I can just imagine what it's going to be like. Like campin' and livin' with the Indians on a permanent basis."

Marlette laughed. "Oh, Martha. You'll be surprised. You might even find you like it, and maybe one of those old mountain men will come courting and I'll lose my dearest friend and housekeeper."

Martha snorted in disbelief and started down the trail made by the wagons which were now moving again. Liz and Marlette followed her.

Liz asked, "Do you think some old mountain man will come courtin' me?"

Marlette looked at her and saw she was perfectly serious. Liz was suffering from the same discouragement they all suffered. Anyone with a piece of glass left to look into had long since given up hope of ever having soft, white skin again or hair that wasn't powdered with dust and smelled of sweat. Liz, the most beautiful of all the women on the train, must have felt even more disheartened.

"Liz, there is no doubt in my mind that you will be the most sought-after woman in the whole valley. And I know one man in particular who will fall madly and passionately in love with you the first time he sees you."

Listless eyes brightened and a hint of the southern belle returned to her voice, "Who? Oh, you must tell me who, so I can hide from him until my skin is the color of peach blossoms again."

Marlette laughed. "He is Ross's friend. He is a big, happy bear of a man. A Frenchman. Can you speak French?"

"French? Oh Lordy, no. What'll I do? What is his name?"

"Jacques. And don't worry, he speaks English, too."

"Tell me all about him."

"Oh, let's see. I believe he is not much older than Ross. Taller, heavier, with a huge thick curling head of hair and beard. He is sensitive like Ross but not nearly so quiet. He has charm and a devil-may-care attitude. He can cook and play the harmonica and sing, and yet, I have seen him very tender. Yes, I think he is very much like Ross in some ways."

Liz was silent for a moment as they made their way down the hillside. Then she said very quietly, "Thank you, Marlette, for being so understanding about Ross."

Marlette stopped and faced the woman who had almost ruined her marriage. "I'm not as understanding as you think, Liz. It would be very easy for me to hate you for what you tried to do, but I think I know what you were feeling and I did understand that feeling. I also understand Ross is vulnerable to women, and because he happens to be very attractive, women will also desire him. But now I know I must fight to keep him, and no other woman will have the chance you had—and I will especially watch you, Liz."

A smile quirked Liz's sunburned lips, but her beautiful blue-violet eyes were deeply serious as she replied, "Your honesty is appreciated and I will be honest with you. If I thought I could win him from you, I would. He loves you, but you can bet your life I won't turn him down if he ever comes to me."

"Then I will make sure he never has any reason to come to you."

"We understand each other perfectly. Can we still be friends?"

"That will depend on you, Liz. As long as I feel you do not threaten my marriage, I will be your friend."

Their eyes locked in an understanding that went deeper than words, and Liz nodded. Marlette turned away, and the two women continued down the hill toward another hot, sagebrush-covered plain.

16. Reunion at the Dalles

FOR THE NEXT several days, the trail followed the Umatilla River, then led them for several more days through deep sand over rolling sagebrush hills, in blinding dust and heat, into increasingly deeper canyons. At last they reached a high steep bluff overlooking a deep canyon where flowed the rapid John Day River, coursing north to the Columbia. The stream was named for one of the men of the overland Astor party who had passed this way more than thirty years before. John Day has lost his mind in this wilderness, and Marlette well understood how easily this harsh country could defeat the strongest of men. But from here there was only grandeur and beauty to awe even the tiredest of emigrants. The Cascade Mountains stood in all their glory with the sentinel of the valley they were headed for standing squarely in front of them. The river bottom, wide at this point, offered room for the stock to graze on dried grass, and the loose stock was herded ahead while the wagons were prepared to descend this long, steep hill. Since there were no trees to snub ropes on, the men, with the aid of the weary teams, had to hold back the gravity-drawn wagons. Ross, his arm still not recovered completely, had to rely on the strength left in the men with him.

As they neared the Columbia the next day, they followed a high ridge overlooking the forbidding bluffs. The trail dropped nearer to the river until they were between the barren bluffs, dwarfed by the gorge and its broad swift-flowing river moving more water than they had seen since the Missouri and Mississippi. Another canyon intersected the gorge, and they braked down a hill toward a clear river rushing noisily through basalt rapids and too treacherous-looking to cross. The Indians fished at these rapids and offered help with their canoes to ferry the wagons across, but the skeptical travelers doubted the safety of this and most could not pay the price the Indians asked. They decided to camp here until the men had time to determine the best method of crossing.

For Marlette this stream was more than just another river to cross. This was the Deschutes, and she looked at the swift stream with reverence, straining to see upriver as far as she could, but the river was lost shortly as it wound behind high bluffs.

A hand touched her shoulder and she started, so lost in her memory she hadn't been aware Ross was beside her. "How far is it to where we were attacked?" she asked.

"A few days ride upriver, without the wagons."

"I want to go."

"I know, but it isn't wise or even possible to go now. I promise I will take you there, but not now. The rains could come any time, and that means snow in the mountains. I want you home and safe before the bad weather comes."

She sighed deeply. "You're right. I couldn't do it now, but I want to. I have to someday, when I'm not pregnant and tired. We will come, won't we?"

He raised her face and looked with deep understanding into her eyes. "I promise you. We will come bury your father."

In the morning the wagons moved downstream and crossed the Deschutes River at its mouth, using the sandbar the river had built up where it met the Columbia. There was another steep hill to ascend out of the canyon of the Deschutes, taxing men and animals as they double- and triple-teamed to make the steep grade. From the top of the bluff, the view of the Columbia was spectacular. The snowcapped peaks of the mountains, seemingly close enough to touch in the clear air, sparkled cool and tantalizing to the hot and weary travelers.

The trail followed the high bluffs overlooking the rapids. Even from here they could see the Indians wielding their long spears and nets from flimsy platforms built among the huge channels of black rock. The trail wound away from the Columbia before long and dropped down into another hot, rocky, sage-choked canyon. They camped for the night at the edge of it, herding the stock down to the pools of water. Most of them believed it was their last night on the Oregon Trail. Only a few miles ahead was the Methodist Mission, with supplies and boats to carry them down the Columbia to the valley of their hopes and dreams.

They started early and eagerly in the morning, anxious to end this last hill. They crossed the canyon and choked in the dust churned up on another bluff, following a trail almost unseen as it wound and dipped nearer the Columbia. They followed a ravine toward the river and soon saw the mission buildings ahead, standing bleakly on the treeless bank above the river. Marlette's heart started pounding with excitement. Unable to contain her excitement, she bubbled, "There it is, Martha! The end of the trail for us! From here we won't have to walk or worry about whether the wagon will last another mile or not." Overcome with gladness, she threw her arms around the older woman and hugged her.

The excitement was contagious and Martha began to cry and laugh at the same time. All up and down the travel-worn train, shouts were echoing as the emigrants realized they had finally reached the end of the trail. Down on the flat in the shadow of the rimming bluffs, Ross directed them to make a circle amid shouts of joy, relief, and congratulation. Only Liz didn't share the excitement. Her look was wistful, and Marlette's own soaring spirits floundered a little to think of what still lay ahead for Liz in a strange land without her husband.

Ross was coming into camp and Marlette ran to meet him, wanting to share her joy with him. She held out her arms to him, crying, "Ross! Ross! You did it! You got us here!"

The smile on his face as he took her in his arms was one of genuine and total relief. Still, his voice cautioned, "We're not all the way home yet. You'd better not praise me too much."

"We're close enough. You won't have to worry any more about anyone else. All you have to keep track of now is me, Martha, and Cam—and, of course, the Jessups."

The light in his eyes dimmed. "That'll be enough. We still have some hard days ahead."

She knew he meant down the rapids and portaging around the falls. Others were coming now with Adam and Daniel. Kalber had managed to save a jug of whiskey for this moment, and everyone was bringing a cup to get his swallow. Ross held Marlette tightly with one arm while his right hand was being grabbed and pumped vigorously as voices rose in a confusing din of toasts and testimonials.

Another voice boomed above the merriment—a voice Marlette had not heard for years but remembered as well as she remembered Ross's. She looked up and saw coming through the crowd, a head taller than most of the men he was shoving aside, a black-bearded man whose white teeth flashed in a huge grin.

"Jacques!" she cried.

He took them in his arms together, laughing, weeping, cursing happily in French as he nearly crushed Marlette before finally releasing his bear grip on them and stepping back. "Mon Dieu, Chesnut, mon ami! Jacques wait long time to see you." His eyes turned to Marlette and looked her over intently and softened as he said, "And Madame Chesnut, you have come back to us. Jacques is very happy you have come home." He swept her into his arms for a fervent kiss on each cheek and said, "Mon Dieu! What do I feel? Mon ami, are you to be a father?"

Jacques was hugging Ross now, the impulsive Frenchman not waiting for an answer as his joy enveloped them. Ross winced as Jacques's enthusiasm pained his still-sore arm. Jacques released him, immediately concerned. "What is this? You are hurt. Of course! Jacques forget you have come a long way and have had a hard time, eh?"

Ross grinned at the big Frenchman. "Yes, Jacques. It's good to see you, my friend. What brings you here?"

"Why, you, of course!" he answered with a wider smile, as if there could be any doubt. "I have come to help you get over the mountain. I go to the valley now you are here and get teams and food and meet you by the time you get to the pass, mon ami. You need food and teams, oui?"

"Wait a minute, Jacques. You'd better start from the beginning. Are you telling us it is now possible to take these wagons over the mountain?"

"Oui. Last year a man came who decided not to go downriver. This man, Barlow, decided maybe he could go around the mountain, there." Jacques's arm swept toward the westward bluffs, behind which stood the mountain, now hidden. "He made it around the mountain, and now all summer long he has been building a road with money he get from the men in the valley. Now you can take your wagons into the valley—just like Mademoiselle's ," he paused and corrected himself, "Madame's father wished."

There was a long hush as the emigrants realized what Jacques was telling them. Most of them would have had to leave their wagons here because it cost too much money to raft the wagons. There would be some who could not even afford to pay the rafting fee for

208

their families and would have had to walk with what they could carry into their promised land, arriving at the coming of winter with almost nothing. To be able to take their wagons and what possessions they still had would mean the difference between total poverty and dependence on others, and surviving with dignity.

Ross held up his hand for quiet, and slowly the crowd quieted. "How long will it take to go over the pass?" asked Ross.

Jacques's smile dimmed as he thought and answered, "Should not take longer than two or three weeks at the most. Barlow did it in a month, but they had many troubles. I will go to the valley and bring help to you."

Everyone was talking at once again and Marlette saw indecision and concern cloud Ross's face. "Jacques," he said quietly, earnestly, "did you come by way of the trail?"

The smile left the big Frenchman's face completely as he answered, "No, Jacques come by river, but I have been assured you can make it."

Ross shook his head and said tiredly, "Jacques, you are my friend and I would not doubt your word, but the word of other men about the trail I have seriously doubted. Have you heard of Jesse Applegate?"

"Oui. He took men to make a trail into the valley from the south. Did he meet you?"

"Yes. Near Fort Hall. Some of the other wagons went with him. He said he had found a shorter and easier route. I didn't trust his judgment and would not follow him. Has he arrived in the valley yet?"

"No. Not before Jacques left anyway."

Adam spoke up. "Ross, it would mean a lot to us to be able to get our wagon over the mountain. I'm sure it would to several of us. I would like to try it."

"I know it would, Adam. I know you can't afford the cost of even your wife and child to boat downriver, but we are facing something I have no control over now. It is near the end of September, and we had snow already in the last mountains we crossed. We could have snow here, and soon."

"I think we all realize that, and those who don't want to take the chance don't have to, but if you will take us, I will follow you."

Yetter, who had been taking it all in without a word up to this point, spoke up. "Well, I for one don't plan on following you any farther. I have damn little left, thanks to you, and I don't plan on losing any more. I'm rafting the rest of the way."

Ross said, "That's your choice, Yetter." The two men looked at each other, and Marlette knew what Ross was thinking as the veins in his jaw pounded with anger. Yetter wheeled away and his family, showing the embarrassment they felt, slowly followed him.

Jacques's eyes narrowed as they followed the vindictive man, and he echoed the feeling most of them had about Yetter. "That man one big fool, Jacques think."

That brought a quick smile to Ross's face and a chuckle from Daniel Heely. Heely held his hand out to Jacques. "I don't care if you know what you're talking about or not, but if you're a friend of Ross's, you're a friend of mine. I'm Daniel Heely."

Jacques took the hand and shook it earnestly. "Oui, Monsieur. Jacques is proud to shake your hand."

In the excitement of seeing Jacques, they had forgotten to introduce him. Marlette now undertook to correct their social error by introducing him to everyone who crowded near to shake hands. Daniels, Twist, and Pauly came forward. Daniels held out his hand as Marlette introduced them, and asked, "Can we trust this man's word, Chesnut, if he says he'll bring us help to get over the mountain?"

"Yes, I'd bet my life on it."

"But not on his word about us being able to get the wagons over?"

"No."

Daniels directed another question to Jacques. "What about going down the river?"

Jacques laughed. "The river is not safe, Monsieur, unless you are like me—a *voyageur*." He said it proudly, with shoulders squared and head high, leaving no doubt he was confident in his skill.

"Then how about you taking us down the river?"

"You, oui, but not with the wagon."

"I thought you said you could do it."

Ross interrupted Daniels's baiting. "Look, Daniels, Jacques told you he can get you through if you want to go by river, but that does not include a wagon."

"Oui. No wagon on the river. Big trouble to get wagons down in one piece. I refuse to take wagon. Jacques do not want to die yet."

"Well, we'll think about it."

Ross said curtly, "You do that, Daniels."

The two men eyed each other and Jacques frowned, but more were there to question him and shake his hand until finally a face in the crowd made him exclaim, "Mon Dieu! Ross, it is you! Are there two of you?"

Cam came forward with a grin and held out his hand as Ross said, "Jacques, this is Cam Galligher, my cousin's son."

"Mother of God! You have found your family!" Tears blurred the black eyes as he embraced Cam in a bear hug.

Ross smiled wistfully and answered, "Not quite. Marlette found them, and Cam came with her."

Jacques held the boy away from him and looked him over closely. "Well, what you think of this man—this half-wild man of the mountains who is your relative?"

Cam looked at Ross, and Marlette could see a look of pain in Ross's eyes. Quickly, Ross said, "Jacques, don't make it hard on him. We've come a long way and have had some difficult times. He's had a lot to do and he's done it well, but I'm still a stranger to him."

Jacques looked intently at Ross, and Marlette knew the perceptive Frenchman caught the protectiveness in Ross's voice and understood there was something wrong. His eyes narrowed as he looked at Cam and patted his shoulder. "Oui. I remember when I left home I was no older than this one. It was hard. Once we are home, then you will know this man."

Cam nodded and said, his eyes fastened on Ross, "I hope so."

They finished the introductions and answered more questions. Then the three of them were alone.

Jacques asked, "The boy—things are not good between you?"

"No. I'm afraid I'm not all he expected in some ways, and more than he expected in others."

"That is too bad. How did it happen?"

Marlette answered, "It wasn't Ross's fault. It was. . . ." She paused, not knowing how to explain, then saw Liz standing by her wagon and blurted, "It was Liz's."

"Liz?" Jacques questioned.

"Yes. You haven't met Liz. Come, Jacques, you must meet her. It will explain a lot."

Ross said, "You'd better explain first that Liz lost her husband back on the Greenwood cutoff. Her grief's been pretty hard to handle."

"Ah, Jacques begin to see. You, mon ami, have had more than one trouble, eh?"

Marlette answered, "Yes. Fortunately, it has worked itself out. All except for Cam. He still thinks what happened was Ross's fault."

Jacques looked at her keenly. "Because of you?"

"Yes. I jumped to all the wrong conclusions, as usual, Jacques. You know me. Cam upheld my view of things."

"And now—you two, is there still trouble?" His face was solemn.

Marlette reached for Ross and shook her head. "No. I finally decided I couldn't live without him and made up my mind to fight for him."

Jacques looked at Ross and said, "You don't say much, mon ami."

Ross grinned. "With you two, I don't stand a chance, or I'd have said there was never any doubt in my mind."

Jacques laughed and said, "Good! Jacques glad. Now I must meet this woman. Oui?"

They turned toward the wagons; Liz was still standing at the end of her wagon making bread while the boys set up the tents. Marlette said, "That's Liz, Jacques." Then she called, "Liz!" As Liz looked at them, Jacques breathed, "Mon Dieu! Even from here Jacques can tell she is a woman of great beauty."

Liz wiped the flour from her hands and brushed back a wisp of dark hair with her wrist. As Jacques stared, spellbound, Marlette introduced them.

"Liz, this is Ross's friend, Jacques Broulette. Madame Jessup has traveled with me ever since leaving Pittsburgh, Jacques."

Liz smiled shyly and offered Jacques her hand as she curtsied in southern belle fashion and said, "It is a pleasure to meet you, Monsieur Broulette."

Jacques was momentarily speechless. He recovered with a definite darkening of his already dark skin, took her hand, and bowed deeply. His eyes never leaving her face, he said, "What a great pleasure to meet you, Madame Jessup." Then he impulsively lifted the still-floured hand to his lips and kissed it gallantly.

"Won't you stay and join us for dinner, Monsieur Broulette?"

He released her hand and stammered, "Oui, that is, if you are sure Jacques will not be imposing?"

Marlette laughed and said, "No, Jacques. You know better than that."

Liz's boys were edging closer, and Jacques's eyes tore themselves away from Liz long enough to recognize their similarity of appearance. "Madame! Are these your sons?"

Liz laughed and answered with introductions. "Yes, Monsieur. My oldest boy, Jonathan, followed by Jeremy and then my youngest son, Joseph. Meet Jacques Broulette, a friend of Ross's."

They shook hands and Jacques praised Liz on her boys with, "Ah, Madame, what fine young men. You must be very proud. You have done well."

Liz's eyes sparkled and she added, "I also have a daughter of fourteen." Then she paused and a pained look came into her eyes. "Oh, my goodness. What month is it? Is it September?"

"Oui, Madame, it is September."

Liz looked stricken. "Oh dear, Jenny is fifteen. We all forgot her birthday. What am I going to do?"

Jacques was not at a loss for words now and said, eagerly, "What do you need, Madame? Tell Jacques and he will get it for you."

Liz thought a moment and answered, "Fruit. Do you think the mission has any fresh fruit? I could make her a pie. She really would like that."

"Oui. Jacques think they have apples. We will go see, no?"

Ross chuckled and answered, "I think they can spare us long enough to do that."

Marlette saw Martha come out of her tent and look toward them with a curious frown. Marlette said, "Jacques, before you go, there is someone else I would like you to meet."

Jacques turned reluctantly away and followed Marlette to where Martha stood firmly resistant at the tent entrance. Her look was disapproving, but Marlette hardly expected anything different.

"Martha, I would like you to meet Jacques Broulette. He is

213

Ross's friend and the man we spent the winter with when Father was killed.'' She turned to Jacques and explained, ''Mrs. Yates has been with my family since my mother died.''

Jacques smiled broadly and bowed deeply and sweepingly. ''Madame Yates, Jacques is at your service.''

Martha said stiffly, ''Pleased to meet you.''

A twinkle was in Jacques's eyes as he said, ''Ah, Madame, I hope you will someday think so.''

He reached for her hand and she backed away, only to be stopped by the tent, saying, ''I doubt that.''

Jacques imprisoned her hand and kissed it quickly before Martha realized what he was doing. She yanked her hand away and growled, ''Ruffian!''

Jacques laughed and said to Marlette, ''This one takes a little winning, no?''

Marlette laughed and answered, ''No. Not a little, Jacques, a lot. She still doesn't approve of Ross.''

Jacques's eyebrows raised. ''Ahh,'' he sighed, ''I can see now why Ross does not smile with ease.''

Martha harrumphed and stepped sideways to dodge around Jacques and Marlette answered, ''It has been a very hard trip for him. I worry about him constantly. He has had so much responsibility, and he still has headaches from his beating three years ago. Did you know that?''

''Oui. He cannot hide much from Jacques, but he try, like I think he try with you, eh?''

''Yes. I didn't find out for quite some time or I would never have let him do this. Do you think we can get over the mountain without much trouble? So many of these people can't afford to hire the boats, and I know Ross will try to lead them if he thinks they might attempt it without him.''

''Oui. There have been some come over already. You can make it, Jacques thinks.''

''We will need all the help you can bring us.''

''Oui, Jacques sees that, too.''

Ross came up to them and said, ''I think you two are plotting against me.''

Jacques put a gentle arm around Ross and said, ''Oui. We don't want you to kill yourself before you get your wife home. We think you will take them over the mountain whether you trust the words of Jacques or not.''

Ross smiled and nodded. "I suppose you are right.''

"Jacques forget to tell you others have already come over. It helps to know this?''

Ross's face relaxed in a relieved smile. "Helps! It does more than help. Now, come on, my friend, we have work to do if we are to travel farther with these wagons.''

Jacques released him, and Marlette said, "You'd better get a cook fire lit or you won't have strength enough to do anything.''

He pulled her to him and kissed her, for a moment like the Ross she once knew, happy and almost carefree. "All right. A fire first before anything else.''

Jenny came bounding into camp from across the wagon circle and stopped when she saw an unfamiliar man in their midst. Jacques saw her almost as quickly, and his eyes sparkled with delight as he watched Jenny sidle toward her mother. Marlette caught her hand and said, "Jenny, I have someone special I want you to meet.''

She led the shy girl closer to where Jacques rose to his full towering height, making the girl stop in awe. "Jenny, this is Jacques Broulette. He is Ross's friend and has come from the valley to meet us.''

Jacques bowed another exaggerated bow, sweeping his grimy knitted cap from his head and releasing his unruly dark hair once more. "It is a pleasure to meet such a beautiful mademoiselle.''

Jenny dropped a quick curtsy and fled like a deer. Jacques chuckled and, looking toward Liz, said, "The daughter is as lovely as her mother.''

Liz smiled graciously and turned back to her work. Ross rose from his fire-making and the two men left the camp circle. Marlette raised an eyebrow at Liz and said, "Well, what do you think of him?''

Liz turned and looked at her with sparking eyes and snapped, "What should I think of him? He is a big, uncouth, unkempt, uneducated buffoon of a man. Is this the type of man you think I will want courting me?''

She turned away in disgust and Marlette was dismayed. Liz was affronted. Marlette could see now she had described Jacques as she knew him, forgetting all the uncivilized and uneducated

215

characteristics about him and remembering only those qualities which had made him dear.

"Liz, I'm truly sorry. I was remembering Jacques for what he is to me and not how he would appear to you, but believe me, under that unkempt exterior is a kind and gentle man."

She turned back with flashing eyes. "Well, kind and gentle just aren't enough."

Marlette sighed, "All right, Liz, let's not argue about it. I made a mistake thinking you could see what I see in Jacques. I'm sorry if you are insulted. I'll not mention it again." She walked away and saw Martha's equally disapproving stare.

The camp was alive with speculation and questions during the long afternoon. Jacques and Ross had been to the mission buildings along with other members of the company who needed supplies, and they had all come back unhappy with the exorbitant prices. Those who had felt as Yetter did about going on by boat changed their minds when they learned it would cost them thirty dollars for each wagon and five dollars for each person to be ferried down the Columbia. The stock would have to be driven over the Indian trail along the gorge that passed on the north side of the mountain they now proposed to cross. They all gathered in the late afternoon around Jacques and Ross to make final plans. Yetter, looking more sour than ever that he was again losing face because of his rash statements earlier, was in attendance, but silent.

Jacques was just finishing the details of the trail as he had heard it from men who had used it when Daniels asked, "When do you plan on leaving, Broulette?"

"Jacques think maybe he leave soon. The sooner to get back and get help to you."

Daniels frowned. "That don't give my men and me much time to get ready to go with you."

"Jacques think again about taking you and think maybe it better for you to go with my friend, Chesnut. He will need help, and I can get to the valley much quicker if only have Jacques to worry about."

"Now look, friend, you said you'd take us."

Ross interrupted. "Jacques has decided not to take you and I agree with him. We need you on the trail and he doesn't need you

216

on the river. Your weight and inexperience would only delay him."

"You stay out of this, Chesnut."

Ross stood and his voice lowered with tenseness. "I'm still captain of this outfit, Daniels, and I say you are staying with the train or you can go by regular boat, but you are not going with Jacques if he says he will not take you."

Daniels jumped up, his hands curling into fists. "You son of a bitch! I'm tired of you telling me what to do. I don't think you can make it stick."

Ross's hand rested on his knife and he invited, "Try me, Daniels."

Marlette stood with held breath. Surely Ross wouldn't be stupid enough to fight this man. But she was wrong. Daniels swung and Ross blocked the swing with his bad arm and smashed a fist against Daniels's chin, staggering the man but not knocking him down. Marlette, fearful for Ross's shoulder, immediately pushed through the crowd of men.

"Jacques!" she cried. "Stop them! Ross will hurt his arm again, and Daniels knows it or he wouldn't be doing this."

Jacques, cat-quick for his size, seized Daniels and held him, ending the fight.

Ross's eyes blazed at her. "You stay out of this, Marlette."

"No! I will not stay out of it. You know what he's doing and why he's doing it, and you're going along with it and risking your arm." She turned on the onlooking men and cried accusingly, "And you! All of you! How could you just stand there and let him be hurt after what he has done for you? He's suffered for every one of you and you would let him be beaten by this, this—" She couldn't finish. She charged blindly out of the circle, shame-faced men standing aside for her, and went to her tent. She stood wringing her hands, knowing Ross would be angry with her for interfering.

The tent flap raised and Ross came in. She turned to face him defiantly, ready to fend off his anger. Jacques stood behind him in the opening. They stared at each other for a long moment and Marlette couldn't tell what he was thinking. He had pulled the veil of stoicism over his emotions and she could not fight his indifference. Quietly he said, "Jacques is leaving and wanted to tell you good-bye."

217

He stepped aside and Marlette went into the big Frenchman's arms. "Thank you for coming, Jacques. Take care and come back to us quickly."

"Jacques will. You take care of this stubborn half-breed so he don't kill himself, eh?"

She only nodded against him. He released her and took Ross's hand. "It will be over soon, mon ami. Jacques will see to it."

"Merci, Jacques. Bon voyage."

The flap dropped and Jacques was gone. Marlette turned with an anguished face to Ross and said softly, "I'm sorry, Ross. I couldn't stand by and see you hurt again, not for that man. Will you forgive me?"

His arms went around her and she held him tightly. He kissed her long and gently and then looked at her, his eyes not veiled anymore. She saw so much pain, so much anxiety, so much weariness, and so much love, tenderness, and compassion in those deep, dark, beautiful eyes. "Did I ever tell you what I should do to you for disobeying orders like that?"

Tremulously, she said, "Yes."

He shook his head, a small smile touching his lips. "You don't frighten easily, do you?"

"If I did I wouldn't be here and I wouldn't love you."

"And I wouldn't love you."

17. The Barlow Road

By MID-MORNING the wagons were out of sight of the Methodist
Mission, headed south under a bright blue sky with only a few
wispy clouds trailing over the high ridge to the west. But the emigrants had little time to enjoy the fair day. A series of deep valleys
lay ahead of them, and it was late the next day before they crossed
the last one.

They had a day of fairly level going before they ascended another hill and found themselves on the brink of a large valley in-
habited by Indians and abundant in water and grass. There was
no question they had to go down and they prepared for the descent
with resignation, knowing they would face a difficult climb in the
morning up the almost perpendicular hill on the other side of the
valley.

It took a day and a half to get all the wagons out of the valley,
and then they were traveling over a pleasant, gently rising plain
through sage, juniper, and pine, crossing creeks and draws no
more difficult than a hundred others they had crossed on their
long journey, the mountain sentinel in full, glorious view straight
ahead.

At noon the next day they rounded the end of a low ridge,
thickly timbered with oak and pine, and entered an open meadow
with a stream wandering through between green-hummocked
grass banks. Under a tree close to the opposite side of the meadow
stood a tent, and across the road, where it turned up a slight grade
to leave the valley, was a gate. A man came out of the tent. Ross
stopped in front of him, and the wagons behind came to a halt.
Those on foot hopped the creek and came forward with curiosity,
Marlette joining them.

The lanky, slope-shouldered man with a unruly shock of dark
hair springing above his wide forehead held out his hand to Ross

and said, "Welcome to the Barlow Road, friend. I'm Sam Barlow."

Ross took the offered hand and Marlette, edging forward, heard him answer, "I'm Ross Chesnut. We didn't expect to find anyone on this side of the mountains."

The craggy face split for a short laugh and answered, "Well, it's a little hard to turn people back on the other side of the mountains."

"Turn people back? I don't understand."

"If they can't pay the toll. This here's a toll road. How many wagons you got, Mr. Chesnut?"

Ross answered, "Seventeen."

"That'll be eighty-five dollars for the wagons at five dollars apiece. How many head of stock you got, including your saddle horses and teams?"

"We'll have to count. What will they cost?"

"Ten cents each, to be paid before you go through."

Ross turned, and Marlette saw a frown crease his forehead. He had not counted on this. Neither had the rest of them and Ross was immediately surrounded by unhappy travelers. Marlette looked beyond the thin-lipped man still standing in the road. The trail looked no different beyond the gate than here as it climbed gently up out of the little creek valley through the pines.

Marlette could judge the depths of Ross's exhaustion by how silent he was as he listened to the angry complaints. Yetter's voice was the loudest, though he was probably the only man with the train who had any amount of money left. When Ross turned around after he had gotten a count of animals, Marlette's heart ached for him. He had a defeated look as he walked wearily back to Mr. Barlow.

"All right, Mr. Barlow, we have one hundred and fifty-seven animals. If you have some paper, I'll sign a note for them."

Barlow laughed condescendingly. "I'm sorry, Mr. Chesnut. I can't take a note. I've got a family to take care of, too, and winter is coming on. If you can't pay in cash, I'll take goods."

"That's what the note is for, Mr. Barlow. You can take my note to the Hudson's Bay Store in Oregon City and cash it in there for whatever you want."

Barlow looked at Ross with surprise. "Now wait a minute. What are you tryin' to do here?"

"You wait a minute. I own land and a business in the valley. I've been east to get my wife and am leading this train into the valley. These people don't have credit in the valley, but I do. Jacques Broulette is my partner. Have you heard of him?"

Barlow nodded, his face changing from one of sternness to acceptance. "I remember now. I've heard your name now that I think on it, and I've seen Broulette a time or two, too. A big Frenchman. Seen him rafting logs down the river."

Ross nodded. "That's Broulette. Now, if you'll give me some paper and a pencil, I'll give you a note of credit against my account with Hudson's Bay."

"What do you want to put up for collateral?"

"Collateral? Why do I need collateral? You'll have my word in writing."

"I never take a man's word I don't know. You back that note with something of value, like stock or wagons, or guns that I can use in case you don't have the credit you say you have, and I'll honor your note, Mister."

"All right." Marlette could see Ross's shoulders sag just a little bit more. "You can have my horse and saddle. I've got another."

Barlow shook his head. "It'll take more than one horse and saddle, friend. What else you got?"

Marlette was suddenly angry. Why should Ross be put through this for these people? She had money enough to pay their way. She had the impulse to get her money and pay for her wagon and the Jessups and Jameses, and let the rest do what they wanted. Instead, an even better idea occurred to her. She turned abruptly and went with quick steps back across the creek to where Yetter stood.

"Mr. Yetter, I want to ask something of you. You have money left and most of the rest of us don't. I'm asking you to let us use your money to pay for the rest of these wagons to get through. I have enough for us and the Jessups and Jameses. Jacques will be coming with supplies for us all, and Ross's note is good. If it isn't, you can have the stock we have left once we are in the valley. I give you my word."

"You expect me to help him out after what we've lost at his hands? No! It would take more than your stock to replace my wagon and furniture and everything his negligence has brought ruin to." Yetter wheeled away and walked stiffly to the back of his wagon.

"Mr. Yetter!" Marlette cried in desperation, but she didn't go after him. It would be useless. Her eyes looked frantically about for some answer and came to rest on Mrs. Yetter, looking so frail on the seat of the wagon, her mouth a thin, tired line in her pinched face. Marlette walked away in despair. She would offer Barlow her wagon and teams and walk the rest of the way with Ross if she had to.

"Mrs. Chesnut."

Marlette turned and saw Mrs. Yetter following her, holding out a sack with shaking hands.

"Here, you take the money. I'll take Mr. Chesnut's note. I believe he's an honest man."

"Mrs. Yetter! Are you sure? What about your husband?"

Her chin lifted stubbornly. "The money's half mine. Now you take it and pay the man." She turned around and walked quickly away before Marlette could even thank her.

Marlette hurried back across the creek. Ross was still trying to agree with Barlow on collateral.

"Ross, here's enough money to get us through. Give me your note."

"But how?"

"Never mind, now. I'll tell you later."

Ross took the money as Barlow asked, "Got any widows in your train?"

"Yes. One. Why?"

"Widows don't have to pay. You can subtract for her and her stock."

Marlette walked back to her wagon. She found paper and pencil and her own dwindling store of money and figured out how much to subtract for Liz. She added the coins to Mrs. Yetter's purse and wrote out the note for the remaining amount on Ross's account at the Hudson's Bay store at Oregon City and took it to Ross to sign. By the time Marlette was back to her wagon with the note and Mrs. Yetter's money, Ross had mounted his horse and Barlow was opening the gate.

Silently, the emigrants drove their wagons through, without looking at Barlow or at Ross, their pride hurting as they took one more step on the trail that had been degrading them for nearly two thousand miles. Marlette felt sorry for all of them, except Yetter, and even sorrier for Ross. He had given so much, and he would get so little in return. Some of these people would never pay him back. She could name those who would, as well as those who wouldn't. When it was her turn to go through the gate, she went with head held high and smiled and nodded graciously at Sam Barlow. The rest may not have had anything to be proud of, but she did.

The emigrants moved on, their trail winding ever upward through the scattering groves of oaks and pines into deeper, denser forests of fir and hemlock. Water from clear, cold springs and swift mountain streams fed by the glaciers of Mt. Hood refreshed the weary travelers as the ridges became steeper and the wagons had to be lowered with ropes.

On the third day, in the last burnished glow of the setting sun, they broke out of the timber and into a meadow where the view of the mountain was breathtakingly beautiful. It seemed awesomely close. Clouds, dark and ominous, reached up the troughs along the timberline, wisping in the stiff wind. Shivering and tired, they circled the wagons in the meadow and quickly went into the timber for firewood. They felt they were on top of the world, and the adventuresome young men scouted ahead and came back with news that the pass was just ahead. Tomorrow they would finally be on the west slope of the mountain.

The climb to the pass was difficult but had a special reward for the women walking along the trail. Ripe huckleberries grew abundantly along the steep slope. While the men fought to pull the wagons up the last steep grade to the pass, the women and children were filling buckets and aprons with the small sweet berries, envisioning cobblers and pies if they could find enough flour left to make a crust.

Across the pass they followed the trail into another high mountain meadow, and even though it was early in the day, Ross circled the wagons. The teams were exhausted and so were the men. Leaving Marlette to her baking, he disappeared into the forest at the edge of the meadow, as he used the afternoon daylight left to scout the road ahead. He had been gone almost two hours when Marlette thought she heard a familiar voice echoing against the mountain, bellowing out a French voyageur's song. Jacques! She walked with expectant steps along the dusty trail and saw Jacques

223

and Ross break through the timber into the open. Jacques was leading a string of pack mules laden with provisions, followed by a herd of loose oxen, horses, and mules driven by a half dozen men. She hurried forward to be swept up in Jacques's strong arms.

"Jacques, Jacques," she cried as he held her in a crushing hug.

And there were more familiar faces among the men with Jacques. Ezra Tucker and Nathaniel were waiting to shake her hand. Overcome at seeing these friends after three and a half years, she ignored Ezra's polite hand and hugged him, and Nathaniel, too, though the boy, much taller than he had been the last time she saw him, blushed with embarrassment.

In spite of the cold and fatigue, the emigrants were in a festive mood. They had coffee, tea, sugar, flour, salt, and bacon for the first time in weeks. Even more appreciated by the men were the several jugs of moonshine Jacques had brought along to celebrate with. Weis's fiddle, long silent, was brought out and Jacques joined in with his mouth organ, and happy music echoed across the gorges and meadows. Soon the young were dancing, and the older people, catching the spirit, were also swinging and reeling under the darkening sky, their breath a white vapor in the crisp mountain air.

Marlette wrapped a warm shawl around her shoulders and went to join Ross where he stood watching the happy dancers. She wanted to dance, but felt too awkward now with her conspicuous pregnancy. Ross's arm came tenderly around her and she leaned against him, feeling warm with love, her foot tapping uncontrollably in the grass.

"Do you want to dance?"

She looked up with a smile. "Oh, yes!" she said enthusiastically, "but I feel too awkward. I'd better not."

He nodded and she felt let down that he didn't insist, but knew his concern for her wouldn't allow him to. When the dancers began to drop out because of the thin air at the high altitude, the musicians slowed their tempo to a waltz. This Marlette could not let go by. She turned in Ross's arms and held up her hand, her eyes pleading with him. He took her upraised hand and danced the first few steps of the waltz a little wearily, his face stoic. It took only a few moments before he began to move more easily and guided her gracefully in a small circle at the edge of the dancers. Marlette was caught up in the memory of the music and dance.

She remembered when she had begun teaching Ross how to dance, to pass the time during their long enforced winter stay with Jacques so many years ago. She could feel Ross relaxing now. His eyes looked down at her and their smiles were only for each other as their hearts remembered the beginning of their love. One by one the other dancers stopped to watch their private waltz—a man in buckskin and moccasins, a woman in worn and faded linsey-woolsy with cracked and scuffed walking shoes, dancing on a floor of dried grass under a ceiling of brilliant stars as if they were in the most elegant of ballrooms.

The next day they wound slowly along the forest trail, following a high ridge. Suddenly they were stopped. When Marlette went to the front of the train, she wished she hadn't. The ridge ended abruptly in a vertical rock point. On the west side of the point, a narrow avenue led downward. Marlette didn't believe they were actually going to descend here, but the scarred earth showed that others had. Sharp, jagged rocks were torn out of the earth as if by a plow and she could see where the fragile layer of topsoil made of the forest humus had already started to wash away in brown rivulets from the first fall rains. The trees standing on either side were raw near the base where ropes had burned away the bark, leaving deep scars.

The men were already preparing the wagons. Most of the teams were taken back to the meadow to spend the rest of the day and night. Only two teams were used to move the wagons forward. Ross and the men from the valley uncoiled the new ropes Jacques had brought and tied them securely to the wagons, snubbing the loose ends around the stout trees near the top of the slide. Drag trees were being cut and attached to the rear axles to help brake the wagons. A chill wind brought the first drops of rain to patter on the wagon tops and a shiver, as much from fear as from the damp chill, ran through Marlette. She listened breathlessly as they started the first wagon down; the men shouted and the rocks, grating against the wheels, made an ominous echo through the woods.

Finally, darkness ended the treacherous lowering of wagons and they spent the night high on the cloud-shrouded ridge, with the rain beating against the tents. Ross feel asleep immediately, exhausted, but Marlette lay awake for long hours listening to the rain and the eerie soughing of the trees. It was a long and dreadful night for Marlette, and she only slept when the rain became a soft patter and finally stopped just before dawn.

Inevitably her wagon reached the brink of the ridge. Cam unhitched the oxen and led them through the timber down a steep, zigzag trail to the bottom of the ridge with the help of Jeremy and a couple of other men. Marlette and Martha started to follow, but Ross called to her and she waited for him to come to her. He looked so tired as he stood before her, her heart ached for him.

"Find a place to sit and wait for me. I don't want you trying to go down this mountain without me."

"I'm sure we can make it. You look too tired to have to come back up here after us. Let us try it."

"No. It's steep and slippery from the rain. You could fall. I don't want to take that chance. Now find a place to wait and I'll come back for you."

She nodded and he turned away, his shoulders rigid with tension and fatigue. Martha harrumphed and sat down on a log as the rocks began to rattle and the ropes grated against the trees. From where Marlette stood, she could smell the ropes burning against the trees as the friction made them hot enough to smoke. Soon Cam came puffing up through the timber and collapsed beside them with Ross's rifle across his knees.

Ross came up the trail and said, "Cam, go ahead with Martha. I'll take care of Marlette."

Cam handed the rifle to Ross and held out his hand to Martha, leaving Marlette and Ross alone in the stillness of the forest as they started down the trail. Marlette looked at Ross, feeling absolutely wretched, almost too tired to go on.

She held onto his hand and, step by slippery step, they climbed down off the terrible ridge, her legs aching and trembling from the strain when they finally reached the gentler slope that eased out into a canyon. The wagon was ready, and Ross helped Marlette into the seat beside Martha. He and Cam urged the team along the side hill through the trees after the other wagons, disappearing into the thickening rain clouds and rising fog.

Late in the afternoon of the next day they arrived at the camp where Jacques and some of the young men from the train were holding the spare teams. They had been busy while waiting, building fences to enclose the meadow. The smaller children of the train were fascinated with the large fortresslike rocks standing big as houses in the meadow, and made them the center of their activity from the moment the train circled between them. Jacques already had a fire against the back-slanting side of the westernmost rock, and the heat radiating from its broad surface warmed an area as big as a kitchen, providing room nearby for all of them to work and keep warm.

By morning the sky had cleared. The company moved out, following a gentle saddle to the top of another ridge, descending to the river late in the day, and crossing the receding stream the next day.

It was with unbelieving joy that most of them saw the first sign of habitation a few miles beyond the river crossing as they dropped down into a wide valley with a small stream coursing through it. This homestead, they learned, as soon as they could circle their wagons and meet the owners, belonged to Phillip Foster and his wife, Mary. They discovered that Phillip Foster was more than just a settler on the trail when he asked to see their toll receipt. The Foster place was the western toll gate of the Barlow Road, and Foster was Sam Barlow's partner. But that mattered little now to the emigrants as they saw the Foster garden still overflowing with fresh vegetables and vines still laden with berries. Those with money eagerly bought what the Fosters would sell them. Their livestock, already here for several days, was beginning to fatten on the first green grass sprouting in the dead and drying summer grasses.

Traveling was easy as they rolled westward to the brink of a wide, deep river valley. Marlette began to despair that these difficult descents would never end as they had to bring out the ropes once more to reach the river crossing. The road up the opposite hill was shorter and not as steep, but they were still in the hills. The road followed shoulders of forested hills and crossed valleys as it headed toward Oregon City, the place she had known as Willamette Falls—the place she had married Ross.

They all camped for their last night together a few miles away from the end of the trail, seeing lights of the cabins in the area as darkness fell. It was a sad but happy camp as friends of the trail promised to write or visit once they were settled in the valley. Amid tears and laughter, they looked forward to the morrow.

They were eager for the most memorable trip of their lives to end and yet regretted losing something that had bound them together and had tested them beyond believable endurance. They had proved more than equal to the test. The special bond this trail had forged was too precious, too strong to break easily.

The celebration and toasting began in small groups around the campfires but ended where Marlette thought it should—at Ross's campfire. She was only surprised at who were the first to come—Daniels, Twist, and Pauly. Ross saw them and rose. Marlette knew he half-expected trouble, but Daniels stepped forward and held out his hand, saying, "Chesnut, I never thought when we started this trip I'd want to shake your hand at the end of it, but I do. How about it?"

Ross smiled and held out his hand, replying, "No hard feelings, Daniels?"

Daniels smiled back and repeated, "No hard feelings."

Twist and Pauly eagerly stepped forward to follow Daniels's lead, and Ross shook each of their hands in turn.

Then Daniel Heely stood up and said with enthusiasm, "We got to do this right! Jacques, you got any of that firewater left? We need a proper toast to the man who got us through."

"Oui," Jacques said, and hurried to his packs. The rest of the men sitting near their fire tossed down their last swallows of coffee and had their cups ready when Jacques returned with two more jugs of whiskey. They stood and received their ration, and then Heely raised his voice so the whole camp could hear. "To Ross Chesnut, the best damn guide on the Oregon Trail!"

A cheer went up and the whiskey went down, and in a matter of minutes every man not on guard duty or herd duty came to their fire to toast Ross. Marlette's heart swelled with pride.

Martha said, "I feel just like that young ruffian Daniels. I never thought I'd be praisin' your man at the end of the trail either."

Marlette put her arms around the older woman and said, "Why, Martha, I do believe you finally like him."

She harrumphed characteristically but smiled and admitted, "Well, maybe, but I still don't think he's the man for you."

"Oh, Martha!" Marlette chided and kissed the older woman's cheek.

When they neared Oregon City, Ross came back down the line

of wagons to direct Marlette's wagon to take the road leading south along the bluffs instead of following the draw down into the settlement. Their stock and the stock belonging to the men coming to help them were cut from the herd, and the emigrants were on their own as Ross led them away from the main group.

"Chesnut!"

The voice stopped them, and Ross turned his horse around. Marlette saw surprise and then concern before he wiped every trace of expression from his face. Marlette peered around the edge of the wagon cover and saw Yetter ride up. The two men faced each other as they had done so many times before, and Marlette wondered what complaint Yetter would make now.

Yetter urged his horse forward until he was beside Ross. "I want to give you something, Chesnut." He held his clenched hand out to Ross and Ross hesitantly held his hand under Yetter's. Yetter opened his hand and a flutter of tiny pieces of paper drifted down, some landing on Ross's palm, the rest floating to the ground.

"I don't understand, Yetter. What is this?"

"Your note. I want no man saying Jacob Yetter didn't pay his way or was too small to help his fellow human beings in time of need. From here on out, you owe me nothin' and I owe you nothin'."

Yetter pulled his horse away before Ross had a chance to reply, and galloped back to his own wagon. Adam James, who watched from beside his wagon, said out loud, "I don't believe it!"

Ross dropped the rest of the torn pieces of paper and smiled. "I don't either. But I'll try." He turned his horse around and the wagons moved forward again.

18. Home

THEY TRAVELED MOST of the day, following the river for a few miles before the road swung away to cross the Molalla and Pudding Rivers, then angling back to hit the river again a few miles from Champoeg. A chill wind had blown black rain clouds over the Coast Range, threatening rain. Just after noon it started, and Martha and Marlette took refuge inside the wagon to avoid the miserable wind and spattering rain.

Jacques stuck his head into the back of the wagon and said, "We are almost there, Mademoiselle—ah, Madame. Look ahead and you will see your home."

Marlette cautiously worked her way past Martha and stood holding the back of the wagon seat. The sun came out from behind the clouds and a rainbow appeared vividly beautiful with one end drifting in the river and the other disappearing behind a forested hill. Under the arch of the rainbow stood her home, in a meadow of dark green grass sloping gently up to the forested hill behind the house. Beyond the house, where the meadow fell away toward a creek, stood the barn and corrals.

In that first brief moment with the sun striking it and the rainbow overhead, the setting seemed no less than perfect to Marlette, as if she had found the gold at the rainbow's end. Then the sun and the rainbow faded and she could see the home without its halo of gold for what it really was—more than a cabin, but less than the home she had once known in Philadelphia. It was rectangular and low like a cabin, with a high, steep roof of thick cedar shakes. In the front the roof flattened to make a veranda across the whole front wall of the house. The construction was of squared logs, expertly fitted and chinked with mortar. The same mortar was used in the massive stone chimneys rising from each end of the house and smokeless now.

The wagons stopped and Ross came over and dismounted as she excitedly climbed over the seat, her heart beating faster now as Ross raised his arms to help her down. Martha was following her, but she heard Jacques say, "One moment, Madame. Let them go first." Quietly, too filled with emotion to talk, Marlette took Ross's arm and walked toward her home, already visualizing how it would look once she and Martha had a chance to plant flowers and enclose a yard with a fence and perhaps plant an orchard between the house and the hill.

Ross helped her up the two steps onto the porch and she turned to look back at the wagons. Beyond them was the panoramic view she would be able to see every day from the two large windows on either side of the door and the smaller window at the other end of the front wall. It was breathtaking now as the sun glistened off the river where it curved around the hill and flowed through green meadows and dark-timbered hills.

She turned back, and Ross slid back the bar on the massive, tight-fitting door and swung it open. She closed her eyes and stood still, eager to see what was inside, but not until the ritual was performed.

Ross asked, "Aren't you going to come in?"

With trembling voice, she answered, "It is a custom of white people for the bridegroom to carry his bride over the threshold of their new home for luck."

She felt his arms cradle her at the knees and shoulders and had second thoughts as she thought of his arm. "Oh, Ross, I'm being silly. I'm too heavy for you; you'll hurt your arm again."

He didn't release her but swept her up, saying, "And it is an old Indian custom to never ignore a ritual and bring bad luck."

She laughed as he carried her inside and gently set her on her feet. She opened her eyes and faced a huge stone fireplace with the fire laid and ready to light. Grouped near the fireplace were rough-hewn chairs and a long couch, all covered with beautiful tanned hides and furs, with a huge bearskin rug on the floor. In the other half of the large room she could envision her lovely table, chairs, and buffet full of china. In the corner on the far wall was a door to another room. With growing delight and appreciation, she noted that the walls were not the inside of the logs but were finished with plained and fitted boards and hung with finely tanned furs and magnificent sets of antlers. The low ceiling was also of smooth and tightly fitted boards. Midway in the fireplace wall was an alcove with more doors and a stairway up to the attic.

She turned to Ross and threw her arms around his neck. "Oh, Ross! I love it! I feel like I have come home, really come home! It is everything I wanted it to be and so like you." She pulled away and said, "Show me the rest of it."

With his arm lovingly around her shoulder, he opened the door to the room directly behind the fireplace. The first thing that caught her eye was the large bed placed under a window on the end wall. Another window gave her a view of the timbered hill rising behind the house. The bed, like the other furniture, was luxuriant in pieced fur robes and Hudson's Bay blankets. Along the inside wall stood wardrobes and shelves, and fur rugs lay on the floor. A smaller fireplace opening would provide heat on the dampest, coldest nights.

"This is our bedroom," he said quietly.

She went to the window and looked out across the meadow. Midway between the hill and the barn turned a waterwheel, which dumped water into a trough running toward the house. She turned with widened eyes at the thought of water so near the house. "Ross! You've brought water right up to the house!"

"Closer than that." He smiled.

She came quickly to him and threw her arms around him, pulling his head down to kiss him. "I love you!" she breathed against his lips and for a brief instant didn't care whether she saw the rest of the house or not.

"Are you ready to see the rest?"

She leaned away from him and let her hands cup his face and caress his temple and cheek and mouth, giving him one last, quick kiss before she released him. He went past her to open the door into a smaller room, empty except for a bed, but with the rock of the second fireplace extending into the room from the corner and adjoined by another wardrobe. This she knew would be her child's room. Between the two rooms rose the staircase leading up to the attic, and Marlette climbed it. She was surprised by the amount of room under the high-peaked roof. Large windows lighted the room from each end, and the warming chimneys of the two fireplaces rose up through the center. She could tell Jacques had been using this room. His belongings were scattered helter-skelter over much of the floor and his lumped bed stood in disarray.

Downstairs again, Ross showed her through the door that led into the kitchen. She was delighted by the large roomy area with two windows and shelves, and cupboards enough to store all she would need. But it was the water coming into the corner of the kitchen by the outside door that delighted her most. It ran in a continuous stream to fall into a large wooden sink, which drained through the floor of the house. She hurried to the window and saw the covered trough leading away at an angle to rejoin the creek between the barn and the river. She could visualize her garden out there with a continuous water supply to irrigate it and imagined all the things she would grow.

Turning away from the window with bright eyes, she saw the fireplace in the inside corner of the room, with a raised hearth and iron arms for hanging pots, blackened already from use. She could put her stove, when it came, just on the other side of the inside door.

Ross opened the last door next to the fireplace into another room, and she knew this room would be Martha's. She turned with shining eyes to her husband and told him, "You have done a wonderful job. It is just perfect." She went into his arms and continued, "I'm so happy to be here. You have made everything we've come through worth the effort. You have done so much better than I could have dared hope. I don't want to change a thing." She paused and her eyes clouded. "Yes. Yes, I would change something. I wish we could change having all those people here. We won't have a moment alone to enjoy what you have done until we get the Jameses and Jessups into their own homes."

The smile of pleasure at her pleasure faded from his face. "I'm afraid you're right, but it will only make me work all the harder so I can be alone with you before the baby comes."

"We'll never really be alone. Not ever again—not like it was when we came down the river together—not even before the baby comes. Not with Cam and Martha. But we have our room and it is a lovely big room, and at least we can be alone there."

"I almost forgot about them. This then will be the last moment we will ever have in this house alone. What would you like to do with it before we have to invite the others in?"

"Love you," she whispered, and she raised her lips for his kiss and felt the surge of warmth go through her as he pulled her close and kissed her long and tenderly. She clung to him for a long silent moment, wanting to remember the quiet, wanting to remember the joy she felt, letting her mind capture forever the security and love just being here and in Ross's arms gave her. Finally she said, "I'm ready to invite them in now. Will you light the fire?"

He nodded and, holding her yet to his side, walked her back into the dimming front room. She looked into his eyes for a long moment, then turned toward the door as he moved to the fireplace. Marlette stepped to the edge of the porch and called, "Come in, everyone. Ross is lighting the fire to welcome you into my new home. Come in and make yourselves comfortable."

The motionless group of people came to life and started forward. Ross stood by the fire as it began to blaze and crackle, and she went to stand by him, their arms going around each other reassuringly as Martha came into her new home. She looked about the darkened room at the crude furniture draped in animal skins, and Marlette saw disapproval etched on her face.

"Well, guess it's better than a tent, but it could use some decent furniture."

Marlette released her tight grip around Ross's waist and said, "Come on, Martha, let me show you the kitchen and your room. I know you'll like them once we get the furniture here."

Martha, still skeptical, followed her into the kitchen. Marlette lit a candle and Martha looked around the room that would become her domain. Then Marlette led her into the bedroom, saying, "And I thought this would be your room, if you don't object."

"Well, can't object, now, can I? Guess it will do," she sniffed.

"Martha, you do not have to stay here. The bond holding you is the one you made. As much as I would like to have your help in the time to come, I am sure Ross is entirely capable of performing every service you could render me. I don't wish to hurt your feelings, but you force me to make choices continually between your affection and loyalty or that of my husband's and, though I love you deeply, I will not give up Ross. You are welcome to live with us for as long or as short a time as you wish, but while you are here, I will demand you respect him as you do me, and respect this home he has built for me. Do I make myself clear?"

Stiffly, Martha answered, "Yes, ma'am."

"Good. I will have Ross come get the fire lighted in the kitchen and show you where he has food stored so we can get something cooked.''

Marlette returned to the main room, leaving the candle for Martha in the kitchen. Liz was engaged in animated conversation with Ross until she saw Marlette and gushed, ''Oh, Marlette, this is a delightful place. I was just asking Ross if he could make our home like it, if you wouldn't mind?''

''Whatever would make you happy, Liz, I'm sure Ross would try to do for you. Ross, would you help Martha get the fire going in the kitchen and show her where you store things? I'm sure all of us could use something to eat.''

Liz offered, ''Oh, let me help. It won't seem normal not to.''

Marlette answered, ''Thank you, Liz. Would you and Jenny mind sharing Martha's room for the time being? We are going to have to be a little crowded for a while.''

Liz answered, ''If Martha doesn't mind, we won't either. Jenny, honey, go out and bring in our things.''

Jenny, with a silent glance at Cam, went back outside, and Marlette was suddenly aware of changes in Jenny. She had definitely lost the girlishness of a fourteen-year-old during the trip. Her swelling breasts strained against the tight confines of her child's dress, and the look she had given Cam was not a look of worshipping puppy love but one of quiet yearning—a look that was completely lost on Cam, who still did not see Jenny as anything but a child.

Marlette turned to the Jameses, who were standing quietly just inside the door, and smiled, wanting to make them feel welcome. ''Sarah, you and Adam and Amy can have the bedroom next to ours, if you don't mind, and Cam, I want you and the boys to carry all your beds upstairs and bring in the rest of our things to our bedroom. Jacques, would you help the boys get the animals taken care of, too?''

''Oui. You don't worry about a thing.''

Sarah found her voice as the men trooped back outside. ''Marlette, this is so good of you and Ross. How can we ever thank you?''

''Just by being my friend. Don't worry about a thing. You have stuck by us in difficult times. Now it is our turn to help you.''

Sarah held out her arms and Marlette went to her. They parted with understanding smiles, feeling reassured, and Sarah said, ''I think this is a beautiful place, Marlette. I feel like Liz. I want one just like it. Ross has done such a nice job. I am continually amazed at his skill to do the seemingly impossible. He's a remarkable man."

Marlette smiled. "I couldn't agree with you more. Now come, let me show you your room. I'm sorry he didn't build a hotel."

Just how remarkable Ross was became even more apparent as the days went by. The Boggs train, which had taken the shorter route opened by Jesse Applegate through southern Oregon, still had not reached the valley, and the rainy season had long since set in. A few of the ill-fated train finally made it to the settlements of the valley, and the story of the miserable conditions the rest of the emigrants were struggling under became known. Jesse Quinn Thornton was one of the first to make it through to the valley, and he began enlisting help to rescue those still forced to camp in the Umpqua Canyon, some of them without food, clothing, or animals to take them farther.

Ross had declined to involve himself with the parties headed south to help the unfortunate emigrants. There was too much he had to do for those he had taken the responsibility of, but he did help equip the rescuers with extra teams and their wagon and food.

Less than a month after their arrival in the valley, Ross was able to help Adam secure a building in Champoeg. It was with both relief and regret that Marlette watched them load what few things they had into their wagon and leave for their own place. It did ease the room shortage at Marlette's home, providing Jenny and Liz a room of their own while Liz's home was being built on a land claim next to theirs. With the building of her home begun, Liz was often gone from Marlette's home, and Marlette relished these relatively quiet times, needing them to regain her strength for what lay ahead. She spent hours working on her baby's wardrobe as her body became awkward and heavy with the child she carried.

In December Marlette's furniture arrived, and the arrival of some of the comforts of polite society also brought a change in Martha's attitude. She had been restrained and distant, keeping to her room and kitchen, but having a real cook stove, real furniture to polish, and an array of treasured mementoes from the past restored her pride. She could be at ease in Ross's presence and would join them before the fire after dinner, trading good-natured insults with Jacques over cooking and cleaning.

By the first of the year, the Jessup home was finished and Liz, as relieved as Marlette to get into her own home at last, packed her things. Jenny was the only one who appeared sad to be leaving, and Marlette knew it was because she would no longer be seeing Cam every day.

Ross returned to business under the worst of conditions. The sawmill at Oregon City was desperately in need of logs to provide lumber for the emigrant needs in the valley and to fill the Hudson's Bay Company's export contracts. He was able to put the Jessup boys and Cam to work and, along with Jacques and himself, they worked during the daylight hours to prepare logs for rafting to Oregon City. It was a trying time for Ross, and Marlette worried about him. He had never had time to rest and heal after their trip had ended. He was exhausted and she knew it. He came in at dark to eat and would fall asleep before the fire without hearing about what she had been doing for the day. Fortunately, Jacques, Cam, and Martha kept her company or she would have been more unhappy than she was. She knew it was more than just orders to fill that kept him involved so totally. He was afraid of hurting her now with the baby so close to being born, añd it was his way of resolving his desire for her. But it didn't help Marlette's need, particularly at this time when she felt awkward, uncomfortable, and grossly undesirable. Even though she knew why he couldn't be as attentive as she desired, it caused only depression and resentment in her.

The resentment turned to anger one night when Jacques and Cam left early to ride to the Jessups for supper and Martha was in the kitchen taking care of washing the dishes. Ross stretched out before the fire on the bearskin rug, and Marlette sank heavily into her chair. Almost immediately, Ross slept.

She nudged him vindictively with her toe, and his eyes opened slowly, sleepily. He mumbled, "What's wrong?"

"Everything. How long before you will be able to take some time off to be with me?"

He shook off sleep with an effort and answered, "I plan to be caught up by the time the baby comes."

"And what am I supposed to do in the meantime?"

A slow smile pulled at the corners of his mouth and he put his hand on hers, answering, "I'm sorry. I haven't been much of a husband since we got home."

She smiled back at him. "Oh no, on the contrary, you've been a wonderful husband, thinking only of me and not wanting to hurt me. I know you too well not to know what you've been doing. But you've been a very poor lover."

He rose wearily to his feet, saying, "You're right." And he pulled her to her feet and lifted her in his arms.

"Ross, put me down. I—we're too heavy."

"Not as heavy as those trees I lift all day long. Now be still and let me pack you off to bed."

She laughed as he carried her into their bedroom and gently placed her on the bed. He lit the lamp, then came back to the bed, leaned over her, and kissed her, and then proceeded to undress her, caressing and kissing her as he removed her clothing. He stood back and looked at her and she felt her cheeks flush under his intent scrutiny. She reached self-consciously for a blanket, but he knelt beside the bed and captured her hand.

A soft smile lit his face. "Would you believe me if I told you you never looked more beautiful?"

"Hardly. But tell me anyway. I feel so awkward and ugly, I need to be lied to."

"I'm not lying to you and I won't ever lie to you, but I do want to lie with you."

She sat up and pulled his head against her heavy breasts. "Oh Ross, I love you so much, and it seems something is always keeping us from enjoying our love to the fullest. After the baby comes, I want you to stay with me for as long as you can, until spring if possible. Can you do that?"

He raised his head and gazed into her eyes. "I will try. I want to promise I will be able to, because I should be able to. Jacques and Cam can take care of things, but if I can't, I don't want you to be disappointed."

She stroked his dark, waving hair, seeing the subtle gleam of silver strands invading the deep chestnut. She nodded and said, "It's all right. Now come to bed. I know you're tired and I've been selfish to keep you awake."

He kissed her, and she let her hands slide reluctantly back to the bed. Then he covered her before he undressed and blew out the light. He climbed under the covers and came to her side to hold her, his lips against her neck, until they both slept.

19. *The Fruit of the Seed*

ROSS CAME TO the house at dark and washed in the cold water running into the house, glad to be getting in out of the cold, drizzling rain that had fallen all day. Jacques and Cam had taken the wagon loaded with wood to the Jessups, where they would stay for dinner, their usual pay for bringing Liz wood. He stepped into the warm kitchen and was surprised to find Martha was not here and cooking something for supper.

It took him only a moment to realize what had disrupted the usual schedule, and he walked quickly through the empty front room into the alcove where his bedroom door was barely ajar. He pushed it open and stood with his heart in his throat as he saw Marlette's pale face and pale hair against the pillow. Martha straightened officiously and glared at him, ready to send him out of her domain, but he ignored her look and asked, "How long has she been in labor?" He strode to the bedside, took Marlette's damp hand in his, and pressed his fingers over her pulse until he was satisfied it was strong and regular.

"Just after noon."

"Why didn't you have Cam come after me?" His voice had an angry edge to it.

Marlette spoke up in defense. "I wouldn't let her, Ross. There is nothing you can do, and if Cam had gone, he wouldn't have gotten the wood cut for Liz. Besides, the pains are still quite far apart."

He bent to kiss her damp forehead and looked into her uncertain eyes. "What do you want me to do?"

Martha answered, "There's nothing you can do, except wait outside like men are supposed to do."

He looked at Marlette and waited for her answer, but another pain was beginning. The grip on his hand tightened as her eyes

239

closed against it and she became tense with the surge of the contraction. He held her hand and was silent until the pain passed and she opened her eyes.

Breathlessly, she whispered, "Really, Ross, maybe you should wait in the other room. Martha will call you if we need you."

The sweat stood on her forehead and he reached for the towel to wipe it away. "Are you sure? I would like to stay."

"I'm sure. It'll be a while yet. Martha will fix you something. I'll be all right. Then you can sleep until," she paused uncertainly, then finished, "until Martha calls you."

He raised the cold fingers to his lips and smiled. "All right. But I'll be right outside if you need me."

She smiled weakly back, and he bent to kiss her lips and whispered, "I love you."

He turned to leave, but Martha stood solidly on the other side of the bed and Marlette ordered her, "Martha, please, get something for you and Ross to eat. I'll be all right. You're both here and I can call you if I need you."

Grudgingly, Martha followed him into the kitchen, neither of them saying anything as she prepared the food. His own heart was pounding as if he had been running, and when Martha did set a steaming plate of potatoes and venison before him, he wasn't hungry, but forced himself to eat, as she ate across from him.

Finally he asked, "How many women have you midwifed for?"

"Several."

"Then you could tell by now if anything was happening that shouldn't be?"

She looked at him then—a long, hard look—and he thought he saw respect and even something close to affection in her look. "Yes. She's coming along just like she should." Then she did something he would never have expected of this woman, who had disapproved of him for so long. Her hand came across the table and rested on his. "Don't worry about her. I love her as I would my own. Even more, if you want to know. I won't let anything happen to her."

"I know you won't, Martha."

She removed her hand and got to her feet with a sudden move that indicated her embarrassment at revealing a soft side to him. She bustled around in the kitchen getting water on the stove to heat while he finished eating. Then she returned to Marlette's room, and he was alone with his excitement and his anxiety. He was tired, and the warmth and the food made him sleepy, but he wanted to fight off sleep. He didn't want to miss a moment of the birth of his child. He tested the water on the stove and found it warm enough to wash the dishes in, and finished what Martha had started. Then he went to the front room and built the fire up, trying to keep his mind functioning. It was too great an effort, and he finally lay on the rug before the fire and slept.

Marlette's cries awakened him and he scrambled to his feet half-asleep and lurched toward the bedroom. He pushed the door open and stopped as Marlette cried out again with another contraction, the hair rising on his neck and sweat springing to his forehead. The scene was somehow more unnerving than any battlefield of death.

Martha looked up and growled, "This is no place for you. Get out of here!"

"I'm not leaving. What can I do?"

Marlette gasped, "No, Ross, please. I don't want you seeing me like this."

"It's too late. I'm staying. Now give that cloth to me and you take care of," he paused and finished lamely, "down there."

Martha handed him the cloth and turned to get more cloths as Marlette gasped and strained again. The water broke and flooded the bed around her. Ross held her clenched hands and mopped her hot face as she panted like an animal, her eyes rolling wildly. Gently, but firmly, he said, "Breathe deeply, Marlette, or you'll pass out. Come on, breathe—deeply." He was so tense himself, he felt light-headed and breathed with her.

Another contraction shattered her deep breathing, and he had to urge her even more sharply as her head thrashed and she tried to keep from crying by biting her lip until it reddened.

Martha said, "I can see the top of its head. Next contraction you push as hard as you can, honey."

Marlette gasped and nodded, and Ross smoothed back her hair. She tensed as the next pain built in her and he encouraged her with, "Take a deep breath and push."

She sucked in air and bore down with all her strength; the breath exploded from her in a long, gasping cry and she shuddered and sucked air again.

Martha cried, "It's coming, keep pushing!"

241

Ross sucked air with Marlette, as tense as she was, and felt her next contraction begin. He looked down toward Martha as the head of his child burst from between Marlette's thighs. She sighed and gasped, and he commanded, "Breathe deep, and keep pushing."

Martha held the tiny head gently so the face wouldn't be pressed against the wet cloths and said, "Once more and you'll be done."

With strength and determination, she breathed deeply and forced the infant out to where Martha could grasp the tiny form and help ease it out.

Marlette, still clutching his hand, pushed herself up on her elbows, the perspiration running from her, but her smile joyous as she saw Martha raise the child by its heels and administer the arousing slap.

"What is it, Martha? What is it?"

The infant's voice wailed in protest as Martha turned the tiny blond creature for them to see. "It's a girl."

Marlette sank back on the bed, exhausted, tears of relief and joy spilling over her cheeks. Ross turned to rinse the cloth and tenderly patted her sweat-dampened face. Softly, he said, "You have made my life complete."

She smiled at him and he bent to kiss her trembling lips.

Martha interrupted them with, "It isn't over yet. Get some more water and cloths for me. I need to get this baby cleaned and dried, and then Marlette will be needing some help with the afterbirth."

Ross reluctantly let go of Marlette's hand and hurried to do Martha's bidding. When he came back, Martha was still working with the baby. Marlette looked pale and somehow ethereal. He set the warm water and cloths close to Martha and she ordered, "Start kneading Marlette's stomach. She hasn't passed the afterbirth yet."

He went to the bed and looked down at the wrinkled and shrunken abdomen of his wife and was for once dismayed at the task he had been given.

Martha glanced at him again and said, "Ain't you seen us knead bread? That's what you do to her, and don't be too gentle."

Ross hesitated, and Martha came over with the baby in a blanket. "Here, you hold your daughter and I'll take care of this."

Gladly, he took his child and turned his back on Martha, sitting gingerly next to Marlette so she could see the child, too. Marlette's hand came up but fell away as pain passed through her eyes at Martha's ministrations.

"She's beautiful, Marlette."

"Is she all right? Does she have everything?"

Martha answered, "I counted ten fingers and ten toes." Then she exclaimed, "There! I'll need your help now, Ross. Put the baby in the cradle so you can lift Marlette up while I get some dry bedding under her."

Ross stood and turned with the baby and laid her in the cradle. She immediately set up a wail, but he turned away to help Martha. As he approached the bed, he saw what she was cleaning up and suddenly felt a little sick and shaky. He fought down the feeling and put his arms under Marlette's knees and shoulders and lifted her away from the soiled bed.

"Ross, you look pale. Are you all right?"

He smiled weakly and answered, "I'm fine. And right now I'm the happiest man in the world."

She hugged him, but the effort caused her another pain and she relaxed quickly. But it was too late; the contraction brought forth more blood.

He began to shake and said with urgency, "Martha!"

Marlette said, "Oh, Ross, I'm sorry. You're shaking! I'm all right, darling."

Martha looked up and said, "Here, put her down. Here's a dry place and I'll get her trussed up."

He lowered Marlette to the bed and said, "I'll be right back," afraid he was going to be sick. He left the room, headed out the nearest door, and stood in the darkness with the cold rain hitting his flushed face. In a few minutes the shaking subsided as he began to realize what he had just witnessed. His child had been born! And the child and his wife both lived! A swift and incredible happiness filled him, and he turned his face up to the rain and opened his eyes to thank the Great Spirit for his good fortune.

The door opened and he turned and saw Martha in the doorway. "Is she all right?"

"Yes, she's all right. What about you?"

He came back to the porch and stood at the edge of the steps. "I'm all right now."

Martha came over and put her hand on his shoulder and smiled at him. "I never thought I could see in you what she sees in you, but tonight I do. I can finally see that you do love her very much. I won't regret her coming to you anymore. Now come back inside before we both catch pneumonia, and I'll get us a cup of coffee."

"Thank you, Martha. I could use it."

"With a little whiskey in it?"

"With a little whiskey in it."

She chuckled as she went through the door and turned to him again. "You know, I don't think most men would've been able to do what you did tonight. How'd you know to do what you did?"

"I didn't. Just instinct."

"Then that was your first time?" She seemed surprised.

"Yes."

"I kind of imagined you'd seen a birthin' before."

"No. Indian women are just as secretive about it as you are."

She nodded and said, "Want to go see her now while I fix some coffee?"

"You know I do."

She smiled at him and turned for the kitchen, and he went quietly to the bedroom door. Marlette was holding the baby to her breast and Ross stopped in the doorway unobserved, his senses excited by the full bared breasts and white shoulders adorned with gleaming golden hair. His heart swelled with love at the sight of his wife and child in such an intimate, maternal scene. Strangely, another stronger, conflicting emotion overrode the first as momentary resentment filled him for the child who would now be the center of Marlette's world. No longer would she love him alone. He would have to share her love with this child and was aware that the child would now have the greater claim to her attention. The child's demands would interfere with their most private moments. If she needed something, Marlette would leave him for her, and he felt jealousy for the first time in his life. But he knew this is how it must be, and he would not want it otherwise—should not want it otherwise. He realized it could never be as it had been those few sweet days on the river four years past, when she had given herself to him the first time, and he felt a deep sadness.

Marlette looked up and noticed Ross. A faint pink tinged her cheeks, and she looked down at the baby, who was making very unladylike noises as she nursed. Dark circles stood out under Marlette's eyes, and her face looked lined and haggard in the lamplight. He came to her side and gently stroked her silvered hair. She looked at him again and smiled tenderly. He whispered huskily, "Have I told you yet how happy you have made me?"

Before she could answer, Martha came through the door with her tray of steaming coffee and stopped at the foot of the bed. She beamed proudly at them and remarked, "I never thought I'd see the day when I would think that a man should be allowed to do what you've been doin' tonight, but you know, you make it seem right and natural and . . . and beautiful."

Marlette's smile was all-knowing. "Didn't I tell you he was a beautiful man?"

Ross felt uncomfortable and embarrassed. He looked down at the baby; she was fast asleep, her mouth opened with the nipple at the edge of her contented lips. "The baby's asleep. Do you want me to put her in her bed?"

"Yes. I'm so very tired and I think I can sleep now."

Martha set the tray down and gave her a cup, saying, "You drink this down first; it'll give you some nourishment."

"What is it?"

"A little coffee and a lot of milk and sugar. Now, go ahead. Drink it."

They drank their coffee, silent and tired, but happy, a feeling of warmth flowing between them as relished as the warm coffee. When the last swallow was down, Martha picked up the cups and said, "Well, good night, or maybe I should say good morning. Do you want me to wake you in time for breakfast in a couple of hours, Ross?"

"No. I promised Marlette I'd take some time off when the baby arrived, and we all need to sleep in—and that includes you."

Martha smiled and turned toward the door. Ross followed and she turned again and said, "Good night."

He placed an affectionate hand on her shoulder and smiled as he said, "Good night, Martha, and thank you."

"The pleasure was all mine."

He closed the door on her retreating figure and undressed, blowing out the lamp before he slid into bed and gently moved against Marlette. He kissed her neck and heard her sigh, and then she carefully turned over and pressed against him for his kiss.

"I'm so happy it's over, Ross. It was so much easier than I thought it was going to be. Even the pain now doesn't seem to have been bad. I'm not afraid anymore. I won't mind being pregnant as often as it happens. Now I think I could sleep a week."

He kissed her again and said, "Then turn over and go to sleep. You need it."

He pulled her closer and pressed his lips against her hair.

Then she asked, "Who do you think she looks like?"

"Not like me. Not with that hair."

"It could get darker."

"I don't think so. She's too fair-skinned. She will look like you."

"No, I don't think so. Her face isn't shaped like mine. What do you think we should name her?"

"I haven't even thought about it."

"Would you mind if we called her Abigail?"

He was silent for a moment, completely unprepared for her request. "Why?"

"Because I think she will look like your mother. She has more of your facial structure than mine. Unless you would rather not use the name Abigail."

"No. Abigail will be all right with me, if that is what you want."

Her answer was muffled in a yawn, and he felt her completely relax against him; in a moment she slept. He buried his face in her hair, and tears squeezed past his closed eyelids to mingle with the soft, silken strands.

20. Changing Seasons—
Changing Times

ROSS AWOKE SLOWLY to the sound of birds trilling, and opened his eyes to the sunlit room. On bare feet he stepped to the window and looked out across the gently rising meadow, a deep vivid green in the liquid sun, with a soft shading of violet where the first camas flowers opened. In the woods, rising dark and deep on the hill, white snowlike patches of trillium and lamb's tongues nodded. The weather had changed. Spring had come to the valley and he could no longer stand the confinement of the house. As the sap rose into the budding trees, so was energy rising in him to be out and working—to swing an axe until his muscles ached and the tight hardness returned to his belly.

He dropped the curtain and turned, but stopped as his eyes rested on Marlette, still sleeping. A smile lighted Ross's face. The weather was not the only thing changed. He had changed and the valley had changed. He was a husband and father and guardian for his cousin's son. Three years ago, when he had left the valley to go for Marlette, he had not realized how great and swiftly change would come to the valley, though he should have realized nothing in life ever remained the same. Some of the changes in his life he welcomed, feeling content and whole again with Marlette and his child, who was already over a year old, but the changes in the valley bothered him. He had chosen to live here because this had been the place to which his vision had brought him. But that had been before the emigration started—even before the first missionaries had come with Jason Lee and settled just south of French Prairie in the valley.

Ross could not see what the future would bring for him. All he could see was civilization—people—crowding in on him, and it made him uneasy. He reached for his shirt, and Marlette awakened as he laced it and reached for his belt. She sat up, alarmed.

"Ross, what is it? Where are you going?"

He smiled at her reassuringly. "It's time for me to go to work."

Her mouth pouted. "Oh, Ross, must you?"

He bent to kiss her and gave her silky hair an extra caress. "It's not because I don't like being with you. You know better. It is just time for me to do what I need to do so I can spend time with you again next winter. Isn't that what most white men do?"

She smiled and answered, "Yes. But I hoped it would be different with you."

"It would be among my people—and it could be here, too, if you had not brought your people with you."

The smile faded from her face as she realized what he said was true. She held out her hand to him and he took it. "It is true, isn't it? What was once an untamed land is now a civilized community." She paused and smiled and continued, "It's as though I really didn't leave home at all. I brought home with me."

Without expression, Ross answered, "Yes."

The smile left her face again. "You aren't happy about that, are you?"

"No. At least I don't think I will be."

She smiled again, encouraged by his doubting words. "Oh, Ross, it will be good. I know it will, and you won't mind either when you realize how much more will be available to us and how many more advantages your children will have because of it. Just look at what you have accomplished. And Cam. Why, Cam can have so much more here than he could in New York. You will see. And your children, too."

He squeezed her hand and let it go. "We'll see. I'm going to Jacques's. Don't wait breakfast for me. I'll be back at dark."

Ross went into the next room and smiled down at his daughter, still sleeping peacefully. He kissed her pale blond hair and smiled as he softly closed the door behind him. As he left the house, he was thinking that if he were still living with Spotted Fawn, his work for the day would be no more than killing a buffalo to provide them food and skins, but here that would no longer do. Here he must really work to provide his family with the white man's necessities—most of them bought at the stores that were taking the

248

place of the Hudson's Bay Company and Fort Vancouver, which saddened him still more. The Company still remained, but their power was greatly diminished since the Americans in the valley had set up their provisional government. He had even helped weaken the company by guiding emigrants to the valley and had helped ruin their business when he had helped Adam James start his store. Perhaps he would have to accept that way of life, but he doubted he would ever feel totally free from guilt over his part in ruining the very thing he didn't want to see destroyed.

Ross crossed the log that bridged the full running creek to the little cabin they had finished for Jacques after they had built the Jessup home. Ross could hear Jacques inside the cabin and knocked lightly.

"Entre," came the hearty response, and Ross opened the door. Jacques looked at him in surprise. "Mon Dieu! You finally decide to come out of hibernation, or you and Madame have a slight disagreement?"

Ross smiled and answered, "I finally decided it was time to put you to work. You're getting fat and lazy over here by yourself."

Jacques laughed and pointed at Ross's own tight belt. "Not so much as you, my friend. I think perhaps it is you who is with child this time around. Oui?"

Ross grinned and countered, "That is from eating someone else's cooking besides yours."

Jacques winced. "Ah, you hurt me deeply, mon ami."

"Well, what you lacked for skill you made up for in companionship. I'd trade Martha for you any day, my friend."

Jacques's eyes sparkled, his teeth flashing white in his dark bearded face.

"Jacques just getting ready to fix breakfast. You eat with me, no?"

"Yes. I want to know why I'm going to go out and swing an axe all summer long instead of enjoying life."

Jacques laughed. "Now you know why Jacques never get married. Too much responsibility, too much work. Oui?"

"Oui." Ross pulled out a chair from the rough-hewn table and sat down.

Jacques's hand squeezed his shoulder. "I am sorry."

"It was my choice. I love Marlette, and my child, but I did not foresee there would be other problems."

"How could you? No! No one could have known about Madame Martha or Monsieur Cam. Or Madame Jessup and her children."

"I was hoping you would relieve me of that responsibility."

Jacques eyes grew large and flashed devilishly. "Ah, me too. But I'm afraid it will never be. She still thinks of her husband, and she still wishes for you. How do I fight a dead man and my best friend's attraction. No! It is impossible! But for her I think Jacques would suffer and swing the axe all summer, too. Oui?"

"Oui. Maybe she likes smooth-shaven men?" Ross said teasingly.

Jacques laughed as he bent to stuff wood into the tin stove. "Oui." And he went about the business of getting breakfast.

Later, as they lingered over Jacques's strong, steaming coffee, Ross thought he heard a shot.

Jacques heard it, too, and asked, "What you think, mon ami?"

"Could be Indians."

More shots sounded, and both men rose and went to the door. Cam was coming out of the kitchen door as more shots sounded and they looked toward the river. A plume of smoke could be seen rising from behind a low forested hill across the river.

Jacques said, "Maybe I should go to Liz, in case the devils cross the river."

Before Ross could answer, they heard the pounding of hooves on the road, and both men hurried across the footbridge up to the front of the house to meet the horseman as he galloped into the yard.

"Tillamooks are raiding across the river. We're raising volunteers to go after them. We're meetin' in Champoeg. Spread the word."

The horseman turned his horse around, galloped back out to the main road, and continued northward along the river.

Jacques looked at Ross and asked, "Will you go?"

Ross shook his head. "No. I may be needed here. You go on to Liz's in case she needs help."

The two men separated, and Ross headed into the kitchen just as Cam was coming out with his rifle and shot pouch.

Ross asked, "Where are you going?"

The boy answered with a defiant look in his eyes, "I'm going to join the volunteers."

They gazed at each other for a long moment, measuring each other. Ross realized he had no hold over the boy now. Cam resented him—resented the fact that he still had to depend on Ross, his fallen hero. Without emotion, Ross said, ''All right, but you'd better take more than just a gun. I'll get a saddlebag ready for you while you saddle your horse.''

Cam nodded matter-of-factly and brushed past Ross as he left the house.

Ross strode through the house and up the stairs to find the saddle pouches and make a bedroll for Cam. Marlette came from Abigail's bedroom and followed him, concern lining her face. ''Ross, where are you going? What is happening?''

''I'm not going anywhere. Cam is. The Tillamook Indians are raiding across the river, and they're asking for volunteers to go after them.''

''Oh, no! Can't you stop him?''

''I could, but I'm not going to. He's old enough to do what he wants, and he wants to prove to me as much as to himself that he is a man.''

''But he could get killed!''

''I'm sure he realizes that, but I've got to let him go. He resents the idea that I'm always there protecting him.''

''And not even the fact that he could be killed will change your mind about going with him?''

''No. My place is here with you and Abigail. Now help me get some food together for him.''

21. Elitah

CAM LED HIS horse from the barn toward the front of the house, almost deciding to leave without waiting for Ross to bring the saddlebags. He mounted impatiently and was about to turn the horse away when Ross came from the house with the heavy saddlebags over his shoulder and a bedroll across his arm. Marlette followed him out the door and stood on the porch, her face sad. He wanted to explain to her why he was leaving, but he didn't know how. He waited, steeling himself against whatever Ross might say, but Ross said nothing as he fastened the saddlebags behind Cam, and tied the bedroll on top. When he stepped back, Cam raised the reins, but Ross's voice stopped him.

"Cam."

He turned and saw Ross's hand held out to him. Hesitantly, he took it, not because he wanted to, but because his conscience would let him do nothing else.

Ross took his hand and held it, saying, "Take care, and remember, you are welcome here."

Cam nodded and put his heels to his horse, waving to Marlette, and loped down the lane to the road, turning north. He felt free and full of self-confidence. For the first time in his life, he was on his own. No more would he have to be beholden to anyone, and especially not to the man he felt such contempt for.

He reached the Jessup cabin, where the brothers were standing in the yard, the rider already gone. He reined in his horse and asked, "Are any of you going?"

Jonathan answered, "We were just decidin'. It looks like you are. Is Ross goin', too?"

"No. I'm going by myself unless one of you will come with me." His glance fell on Jeremy. Jeremy looked first at Jon, then Joseph, and said, "I'd go if Maw will let me."

252

Jonathan said, "Then you'd better ask her."

The cabin door opened and Liz stepped out onto the porch. "Why, I thought I heard you out here, Cam. What did you want to ask me, Jeremy?"

"Cam's joining the volunteers. I want to go with him."

The smile left Liz's face. "No. I already lost my man, and I'm not about to lose one of you boys. You stay right here, and if there's any shootin' to be done, you'll do it here."

She turned around abruptly and brushed by Jenny into the cabin. Jenny looked at him with pleading eyes, but he ignored her and said, "Well, guess I'd better go." He pulled his horse around, disappointed and a little less enthused, but still determined to go through with his volunteering.

He met the rider coming back before he got to the next homestead. The man, slender, sandy-haired, and not more than a few years older than himself, pulled in his lathered horse and asked, "You joinin' up?"

"Yes."

"Good. You're from the Chesnut place, ain't ya?"

"Yes. I'm Cam Galligher."

The other man smiled and held out his hand. "Glad to meet ya. I'm Custis Wood. Hey, your uncle is somethin' else. He's joinin' us, too, ain't he?"

Cam answered stiffly, "No. And he's not my uncle."

There was a question in the other man's eyes as he moved his horse forward once more. "You gotta be some relation. You look like him."

Cam turned his horse in beside the other horse and answered, "My pa is his cousin."

"Well, that explains it then. Gol dang! I sure wish he was a-comin'."

They rode past the Chesnut house, Cam looking away, silently hoping Ross would not come to join them. They moved on down the road toward Champoeg, picking up other volunteers as they neared the small settlement—originally a Hudson's Bay Post, but now a town. It was late in the day, and the volunteers made camp on the riverbank, waiting for morning before they went after the Indians.

By morning more men had arrived, and the volunteers crossed the river as soon as they could see. They rode in the direction the

253

Indians had last been spotted the day before, passing the homestead the Indians had burned. By noon they had trailed the raiding party to the camp the Indians had made for the night on the other side of the Tualatin Plains in the foothills of the Coast Range. They were traveling on foot, moving slowly, weighted by the goods they had stolen in the valley. By mid-afternoon the volunteers sighted the Indians moving up a steep, timbered mountain, almost to the summit of the range. Shots were fired, and the Indians scattered into the underbrush. The volunteers urged their horses up the mountain, flushing out Indians as they charged forward.

Cam was sure there was one moving through the underbrush before him and he raised his rifle, ready to shoot as he kicked his balking horse through a heavy thicket. He saw a flash of coppery skin, fired, and saw the flash of copper disappear into the tangle of unfolding spring greenery. His horse refused to move. A huge downed log rose in front of them like a wall, so Cam kicked free from his saddle and crawled to the top of the log, still carrying his unloaded gun. He stood on the log and hurriedly reloaded, his heart hammering in his chest as his eyes nervously peered at the dense undergrowth where any number of Indians could be hiding unseen.

He saw a flash of copper skin not thirty feet from him and yelled, "Stop! Stop! Or I'll shoot!"

The bushes stilled, and he knew the Indian had stopped, but he couldn't see him. The log angled toward the thicket where he had last seen the flash of skin, and he carefully moved toward it, edging around broken limbs, every hair on his neck prickling with excitement and fear. He could hear the rest of the men moving through the brush and getting farther away from him. Straining his eyes to see into the shaded undergrowth, he held onto a limb of the snag and leaned over as far as he could. The limb broke with a startling snap and Cam fell headlong into the thicket, his gun going off as he fell, blasting a hole through the thick undergrowth. He landed in an awkward heap on something that grunted and immediately bludgeoned him with kicks and blows as he struggled to untangle himself. Cam grabbed a handful of matted, stinking hair and pulled with all his strength to keep the sharp teeth from tearing his skin. He felt sharp claws rip his cheek, and another clubbing blow landed on his shoulder. He groaned and shoved the creature away from him, holding his cheek, feeling something warm and sticky seep over his fingers and seeing blood on his hand when he brought it away. His attacker grabbed up the useless rifle and scrambled to escape, and Cam lunged after the nearly naked Indian. He grabbed at the savage's legs and, catching a surprisingly slim ankle, realized he had a youngster in his grasp. He was about to let the boy go, feeling disgust. While the rest of the men chased Indians, he had been stalking nothing but a child. He held the boy down long enough to grab his rifle and yank it free, but as he did the little savage turned and rose to attack him again, and he was stunned to see a pair of high, round, firm breasts. In that moment of surprise, she took the advantage and leaped like a wildcat on him again, grabbing for the rifle and trying to wrench it from his hands. Her knee landed solidly against his shoulder and she almost succeeded in taking the rifle from him. But he gritted his teeth and heaved in desperation against her with all the strength he had left and she went sprawling, with Cam scrambling right after her. He caught her as she tried to bolt through the underbrush, and succeeded in getting her arm twisted behind her until she lay still.

He sat on her, his breath coming in great heaving gasps as blood ran down his face and the sharp pain in his shoulder slowly subsided. His horse was still across the log and would be hard enough to get to without trying to keep an arm on this wildcat, yet without his horse he had no rope or anything else to tie up his captive. He heard the sounds of the other men coming back down the mountain and decided to yell for help.

"Hey! Hey, somebody! I need some help over here!"

An answer came back, "Where are you? Stand up so we can see you."

Slowly, keeping the arm twisted as he pulled the girl up with him, he rose. She started kicking and flailing at him with her free arm, and he shoved her hard against the log, forcing her arm higher until she gasped and was still, her face buried in the moss. He raised his rifle and waved it vigorously, hollering, "Over here by this big log."

Two men found him shortly and grabbed the arms of the savage. Cam stepped back, relieved. One of the men grabbed a handful of the wild, dirt-matted hair and raised his knife as if to cut her throat.

255

Cam shouted, "No! Don't hurt her!"

"Her?" came the startled response.

"Yes. It's a girl."

They pulled the slender, nearly naked creature away from the log and stood staring at her. She stared back in defiance, her long legs set stubbornly with nothing but a short piece of fringed cedar bark for a skirt. The high breasts stood erect with fear and decorated with dirt and moss from the decaying tree. The fragrance of rancid fish oil turned the men's stomachs, but there was something in the face that made Cam study her more closely. The eyes! Her eyes were not the eyes of an Indian. They were light-colored and strangely shaped. The rest of her face was delicately boned with a fine nose and full but not fleshy lips.

One of the men holding her said, "God damn! Look at that! Hey! We can have a little fun with this one."

Again Cam shouted, "No! She's my captive. Nobody touches her."

The men looked at each other and laughed. The second man said, "Well, if you're going to be touchy, we'll let you have first go at her."

They laughed again and the first man added, "You ever had one of these before, kid?"

Cam winced at the word "kid" and lied, "You damn right I have. Now you help me get her tied up and onto my horse." He waved his gun suggestively, and the two volunteers saluted him and grinned. He doubted they would actually try to take her away from him, but he didn't want to take any chances. He had to save her if he could. Even if they couldn't see it now, Cam was sure this girl had to be white.

The sun had gone behind the mountain, and the slope down which he led the horse with the securely tied girl was deep in shadows and fragrant with the dampness of approaching night. Other men were gathering down in the canyon depths, cutting wood for fires and setting up their camps for the night. When he came in leading the girl, the men stopped what they were doing and came to peer at the dirty, bare-breasted girl. The joking started with his two companions, and he became a source of amusement for every man in the camp. Humiliated and angry, he led the horse and girl away from the center of the camp and found an open place on the bank by the creek at the bottom of the canyon. He reached to help the sullen girl off the horse, but she kicked at him and kicked the horse in the side. The animal jumped away in surprise and Cam leaped for the reins. The horse stumbled and slid into the creek, dumping the struggling girl into the cold water.

Cam glared at the thrashing creature, and his first reaction was to let her drown. Softly, he swore at her, "Damn you. Why did it have to be me that found you?"

He waded into the stream and yanked her out angrily. "If you pull another trick like that, I'll let you drown." He tied her to the nearest tree, both of them shivering from the wetting. Cam gathered driftwood from along the bank and finally got a fire going. He sat glaring at the girl all the time he warmed himself and ate the bread and jerky Ross had packed for him. The girl sat with her chin against her chest, her filthy hair hanging over her face and her knees pulled up to her chest in an effort to keep warm against the chill night air.

Custis Wood came to his fire and squatted down to look at the captive girl. "What you thinkin' of doin' with her?"

"I don't know yet. Maybe turn her over to the missionaries. Maybe they can civilize her."

Custis grinned. "Not likely. They ain't had too good a success so far."

"Maybe they will with her since she's white to begin with."

Custis peered closer at the girl. "White? Let's see." He reached toward the girl, and her head came up with teeth bared and snapping. Custis drew back. "Damn! She's a hellion, all right. Can't tell about the rest now, though. Too dark, and," he held his nose, "a bath wouldn't hurt her none, either."

Cam nodded. "You talk any of that Indian talk?"

"No. Bet your—I mean, Chesnut could talk to her."

Cam sighed. There it was again—Ross. "Probably." He said nothing more, and Custis got up and disappeared into the darkness. Cam looked at the girl and she was looking at him. Maybe she was hungry. He took a piece of jerky and showed it to her. She stared at it, and he got up and went to her side and held it close to her lips. Quick as a rattlesnake, she struck with lips curled, clamping her strong teeth on his hand below the thumb. Reacting to the pain without thought, he slapped her as hard as he could and broke the grip she held on his hand. He dropped the jerky and returned to his side of the fire, holding his bleeding hand and cursing her under his breath with every foul word he could ever remember hearing.

He plunged his hand in the cold stream until the bleeding stopped and the pain had numbed. He hurt all over now and felt completely tired out. He crawled into his blankets and lay staring at the hunched figure across the fire. He finally dozed and some time later woke shaking with cold. The fire was almost out and he heard the sound of teeth chattering. He got up and found more wood for the fire. Feeling sorry for the forlorn creature huddled against the tree, he picked up one of his blankets and went to drape it around her. Immediately she came alive, kicking and struggling until the blanket was almost thrown into the fire. Angrily, he picked up the blanket, shook it out, and took it back to his own bed, but it now smelled of her rancid body odor and he couldn't keep it around him without gagging. The rest of the night he sat huddled in his one remaining blanket and kept wood on the fire to keep them both warm.

At daybreak the men ate their meager breakfast and some went back up the steep mountain slope looking for loot the Indians had dropped in their flight. By mid-morning they gave up their search, loaded up what they had found, and started back for the valley. Cam brought up the rear with his captive tied to the saddle of his horse as he walked ahead, leading her, suffering from the men's teasing. The trail was brushy and steep, and Cam was several hundred feet behind and out of sight of the rest of the men when his horse let out a pained squeal and reared, hitting Cam with his legs and knocking him forward. He hung onto the reins as he was rolled over and dragged on the ground while the Indian girl tried to stampede the plunging animal, her teeth sunk into the horse's neck. Custis Wood came charging back along the trail and rescued him.

Cam sat on the ground, bruised and angry. He looked at the girl, who sat quietly now, her head down and the tangle of hair covering her face. As he climbed slowly to his feet, Custis started laughing.

"Boy! Are you a sight! If looks could kill, that girl'd be dead. What you goin' to do with her now?"

Cam wasn't sure himself. He could do like the Indians did and lead her, but that didn't seem like the gentlemanly thing to do since she was a white girl, even if she didn't act like one. His eyes caught the sight of blood in his horse's mane, and he lifted up the heavy hank of hair and saw where the girl had bitten the horse. "Got another piece of rope?"

"Sure. What're you goin' to do?"

"Well, she won't behave herself like she is, so I'll tie her so she can't cause trouble."

With Custis's amused help, Cam trussed the troublesome girl hand and foot and placed her across the saddle like a bedroll, gagging and tying her so she couldn't move. He then mounted behind the saddle, too bruised and tied to continue walking, despite the smell of her.

The volunteers spent another night camped out before they returned to Champoeg, and it was a night of sleepless indecision for Cam. He had to face the fact that he had no place to go and really no money or claim to establish himself away from Ross, especially with this new problem. She sat across from him, refusing to eat and refusing to be covered. He could take her to the mission school, but every time he looked at her and saw her firm, ripe breasts, he was overcome by a feeling—the same feeling he had felt when he and the Jessup brothers had vied for the attention of Suzannah Heely, only much stronger and more insistent. The urge to discover and fulfill his desires refused to be ignored. He wanted to take her, and would have, to prove to himself—if not to these men with him—he was a man. He felt this was the remaining barrier he must surmount to obtain manhood, but his conscience, rooted in strict Catholic teaching, shouted sin at him. No. He could not rape her and leave her, but neither did he want to marry her. He must wait until she willingly allowed him to use her, and that would only come from being her benefactor. With this in mind, he knew of only one solution, and that was to take her to Ross. Ross! Why did it always have to be Ross he must go to? But Ross could talk to her and find out how she came to be with the Tillamooks. With his help, they could do everything for her the missionaries could. And more, the fire in his groin told him. He got up and hurled more wood on the fire and sat again, angry and confused. Adultery. The breaking of a commandment. Ross, the man he had idolized and wanted to emulate, had done it, and he had judged him and now must judge himself, for he was no better. He had already committed the act in his mind. He groaned and put his head on his knees and finally slept.

259

Cam crossed the river early the next morning with his captive in a boat and his horse swimming behind. He skirted the settlement of Champoeg, afraid to be seen, and headed toward Ross's. It was still early when he crossed the little creek just below the barn, and he saw Ross riding out of the yard. Cam waited at the creek, partially concealed in the trees growing along the banks.

Ross saw him and rode to within a few feet of him, eying the bundle slung across Cam's saddle.

"What have you got there?"

"A girl. A white girl, I think. She was with the Tillamooks when we caught up with them in the mountains."

Ross's face remained expressionless as he asked, "And how did you end up with her?"

"It's a long story." He paused. "Well, maybe not so long. I saw her in the underbrush, but I didn't know she was a girl. I caught her before I found that out."

"Did she do that to your cheek?"

Cam gingerly fingered the scabbed scratches. "Yes."

"What makes you think she's white?"

Cam swung down from behind the covered bundle and said, "Here, help me and you can see for yourself."

Ross dismounted, and together they lifted the tied girl to the ground and the blanket fell from her. There was a brief change in Ross's eyes as he saw the naked girl, but otherwise he remained expressionless. Cam waited for Ross's decision.

"She isn't all Indian, but I don't think she's all white either. It's hard to tell with that layer of dirt on her. We'd better give her a bath before we show her to the rest of the family. I'll get some soap and some clothes. Can you manage her until I get back?"

"Not untied I can't. She's a hell-cat."

A faint smile curved Ross's lips, and Cam felt more grown up at the use of a man's word. There was a brief feeling of comradeship with Ross he hadn't felt since Fort Boise. "Well, do what you can, but keep her out of sight until I get back to help you."

In a few minutes Ross came back with a bundle of clothing, towels, and soap. The girl watched with sullen face and apprehensive eyes. Ross handed the soap to Cam and started speaking in the half-Indian, half-French jargon that was understood by the coast Indians. Cam understood none of it, but the girl did and her answers came in harsh gutterals with violent shakes of her head in

260

obvious refusal. Ross kept talking, his patience never faltering, until the girl finally stopped her defiant protests and dropped her head in submission.

Ross nodded to Cam. "Go ahead and untie her feet, but watch her carefully. She's not going to be very cooperative."

Cam untied the rope around the slim ankles, taking every precaution against what he knew by now could be a sudden outburst of violence. He stood up and Ross told her something, but she stood unmoving.

"You'll have to take her in," he paused, and again his lips and eyes brightened with a smile. Cam knew what he was thinking before he said, "You could stand a bath, too."

Cam frowned at them both. He wanted a bath, all right, but not in this cold creek, with his clothes on. He grabbed the girl's bound hands and pulled her toward the creek, keeping one hand wrapped in the thong tied to her ankle. She resisted and pulled back, and he had to drag her into the water. The minute the cold water touched her, she came alive and fought him, breaking away from his grasp. He yanked on the ankle rope, and she fell into the water with a shower that drenched him as well. When he bent to start soaping her, she spat a mouthful of water at him, blinding him for a moment, long enough for her to lunge into him and knock him into the water, too. He heard Ross's chuckle, then grabbed the girl and roughly proceeded to scrub her, his anger not the only thing that made his blood boil as he touched her. He knew the cold water was the only thing that kept him from giving Ross something else to laugh about, and he cuffed the girl soundly when she tried to escape his rough handling.

Ross cautioned him, "Take it easy, Cam. Don't hurt her or she'll never accept you as a friend."

Cam retorted through gritted teeth, "She's done a damn sight more hurt to me." He ducked her head underwater with a vengeance as he tried to wash the greased and matted hair, and finally he had done all he could do without touching those parts of her body that he had never touched on any woman. He pulled her to her feet and looked at Ross questioningly.

The amused look still softened Ross's face. "Give her the soap and see if she'll do it."

He forced the soap into her bound hands but she threw it into the water and Cam had to chase it, dragging her after him to where it caught in a shallow of rocks and roots. He dragged her back and faced Ross with hot eyes.

"Any other ideas?"

"You could hold it in her hands and make her do it."

Cam swallowed and forced the soap into her hands while Ross said something to her. Holding her hands firmly, and careful not to touch her, he moved them with the soap over her goosefleshed breasts. He shivered, but not just from the cold water. Then all there was left to wash was what was still halfway hidden under the disarrayed cedar skirt. He looked askance at Ross.

"Take it off before you both freeze to death."

Cam caught the skirt in his hand and pulled. She pulled away, and Ross stepped closer with his knife. Cam flung her down into the water at Ross's feet, and Ross squatted and quickly cut the fiber cord holding the skirt and stepped away just as quickly, sheathing his knife. Cam pulled the naked girl to her feet, his eyes trying to look anywhere but at the thatch of reddish pubic hair.

Ross spoke to her again, and this time she held her hands open for the soap and took it, turning away from them and bending to do her own washing, then splashing vigorously to rid herself of the burning effects of the soap on her tender skin. She rose with apparent submissiveness, and Cam followed her out of the water, still keeping the ankle thong firmly in his grip. Ross handed her the heavy absorbent sacks they used for towels, and she took them willingly, her body shivering with cold. Cam dried her back, marveling at the smoothness of the skin and her beautiful coppery sleekness. Her hair, cleaned of the filth, hung in heavy dark waves still too wet to determine color, but looking close to the same dark auburn of his and Ross's hair. Ross unrolled a bundle of buckskin, and Cam looked with surprise at the soft undecorated dress. He had never seen it before and wondered where it came from.

Ross drew his knife again, talking to the girl in soft reassuring tones, and she held her hands up for him to cut the rope that bound her wrists, and took the dress willingly to cover her naked body. Ross, looking as carefully at the newly revealed girl as Cam, continued to talk to her, she answering with less harshness or fear in her voice.

Finally, when Ross was quiet, Cam asked, "Well, what do you think? Is she white?"

"She may be, but I'd guess she has something else in her, too."

"What did she say? Where is she from?"

"Her name is Elitah, and she says she has been with the Tillamooks for as long as she can remember, which is about sixteen years. Her mother was with her, but she left or died when she was still quite small. She never knew her father."

"Elitah." Cam smiled at the girl, and her eyes met his as he spoke her name. With all the dirt and smell removed, her beauty was overwhelming—a strange, haunting, exotic beauty like nothing he had ever seen. Her eyes were green, the green of pure shallow stream water, almond-shaped and slanted and fringed with thick dark lashes with fine, highly arched eyebrows. Her golden skin—neither white nor red—was so smooth and hairless it could have been carved from marble. Her face was almond-shaped like her eyes and so delicately boned it seemed fragile now as he looked at the perfectly formed mouth, knowing the fine strong teeth behind those lips all too well. "Elitah," he repeated. "It's a pretty name. What does it mean?"

"It means slave."

The smile left Cam's face. "Does that mean she was a slave?"

"She said she was."

Cam's heart sank to the depths as another thought entered to pierce his deflating hope. "Does that mean she's not a—" but he couldn't finish it.

Ross did. "A virgin? Probably not."

Cam turned away, momentarily disappointed and wondering what he could do now with this girl. He had brought home a slave, and more—a concubine for her owner, probably. She could even be a whore or prostitute. His thoughts exploded at the word prostitute. If she was a prostitute, then there would be no guilt for him in taking her and using her as other men had.

Ross asked, "Well, what do you want to do with her?"

Cam sighed. "I don't know. Do you think we can make her civilized? Do you think she could be of any help to Marlette and Martha? I don't want to take her back to the Indians to be a slave. If she's white at all, she doesn't deserve that."

"I'll ask her if she is willing to stay here. If she isn't, I don't think we'd be able to do anything with her."

Cam nodded and Ross spoke to the girl. Cam watched her face, her eyes fastened on Ross's face with growing interest, without fear now and without sullenness. Cam felt hopeful as they talked

263

for several minutes. He was sure Ross was convincing her. When Ross smiled and Elitah smiled back at him, he was certain of it.

"Well?" he asked anxiously.

"She says she is willing to stay here, but only if we promise not to give her to anyone else and if she will be treated like one adopted into the family and not like a slave."

Cam smiled with relief. "Sure! I'll agree to that. Do you think I can teach her? Will she let me, I mean?"

Ross smiled at him. "I think so. She's not incapable of learning. And I think we can trust her now. I'll take her on up to the house while you take care of the horses. I'll have Martha fill a tub for you."

Excitement filled Cam. His heart pounded and he felt he was falling in love for the first time. This strangely beautiful girl was his, and he wanted to be the one to teach her to speak English and to write and to dress as white girls did. He could picture her now, as she walked with Ross toward the house, in a velvet gown with flowers in her hair, dancing with him at some fancy ball. Not that he had ever been to one, but he could picture it from hearing of them from Liz. He grabbed up the horses' reins and eagerly headed for the barn.

When he reached the house and opened the kitchen door, they were all in the kitchen with Elitah, watching her wolf down the plate of food Martha had set before her. His dreams of quick civilization of the wild creature dimmed immediately. Her face, so recently cleaned, was smeared again with food as she shoveled in her food with both hands, completely disregarding the knife and fork set out for her. Marlette, with an appalled look on her face, led little Abigail from the room as the child giggled and pointed at the spectacle Elitah made.

When she had stuffed down everything in sight, Ross told Cam, "Better take her outside. She'll be sick."

He saw the choked look on her face already as Ross spoke sharply to her, and he grabbed her hand and yanked her toward the back porch, and not a moment too soon. She began retching violently as soon as they stepped off the porch, dropping to her knees and finally collapsing completely as the violence of her stomach overwhelmed her. He tried to hold her and keep her from rolling in her own sickness, but it was impossible. He finally let her go and watched her with a sick feeling himself as she exhausted herself on the ground.

Ross came out and appraised the situation. "Looks like another bath will be needed. I'll have Martha fill the tub for her and start more water warming for you."

"What can we do to keep her from eating like that?"

"She'll control herself next time. I'll have Martha fix some broth for her and some tea. She'll be all right."

Cam looked at the sorry creature on the ground, still now, with eyes closed, but stinking of vomit and smeared with food. He turned away, wondering why he had not given her to the other men.

Ross came back out and said, "Let's get her into the house." Then he spoke to Elitah and she raised her head halfheartedly.

Cam took one arm and Ross the other, and they helped the girl into the kitchen, where she willingly submitted to Martha and Marlette's ministrations without violence. When they were done with her, Marlette led her into the front room, wearing one of Marlette's dresses, and Cam was again overwhelmed with her beauty.

Marlette even remarked, "Isn't she the most unusually beautiful girl?" She paused and laughed. "If we can just keep her clean. Martha has your bath ready now, Cam. We'll wait a little while before we try to feed her again."

Progress with the civilizing of Elitah was slow, much slower than Cam had imagined. Ross had thought her intelligent enough to learn, but Cam became more doubtful of that as the days passed, and she seemed not to learn anything he was trying to teach her. And it rankled Cam that she responded much more quickly to what Ross wanted of her. A new resentment grew, one that reinforced his previous resentment against Ross as he became jealous of the girl's seemingly worshipful attitude. He watched Ross closely and looked for some indication that Ross was taking advantage of the girl, but there was none. Ross treated her as if she were a daughter, and indeed he was old enough to be the girl's father, but whatever Ross's attraction for Elitah was, Cam had to admit it worked. She did learn how to eat properly because Ross wouldn't let her eat unless she used the utensils. Marlette insisted she be clean or she couldn't come to the table. But learning to speak English seemed to be the least of her concerns. She had

Ross to interpret when she really wanted something, and she found she could spend the whole day in idle play by entertaining Abigail. Abigail loved her, and at times she seemed no older than the child she played with. Abigail was picking up the Chinook jargon much faster than Elitah was English.

It wasn't until Ross refused to speak or listen to her in her language that she finally began speaking English. Cam was encouraged to find that she did seem to know more than she pretended. Reading, writing, and learning the alphabet and numbers were something else. Her attention span lasted but a few minutes before she refused to try this difficult and, to her, useless form of communication. At times Cam was so upset with her stubbornness that he would walk out in anger, until he realized that was exactly what she hoped for. He actually began to dread the days he had to spend at the house guarding the family.

Before summer arrived, word came to the valley that gold had been discovered in California, and the excitement and speculation about this discovery of easy riches so nearby was the main topic of conversation. Men hurried to get their crops in so they could rush to California and stake their claims before easterners heard about it and flooded into the country.

Cam, restless and unhappy with the way things were going with Elitah and disillusioned by what he thought living in the West with Ross was going to be, began thinking about going to California, too. When he and Jeremy worked together, they talked of little else, and Cam was sure Jeremy would go with him. He hadn't said anything about it to Ross, even though he had made up his mind to go whether Ross gave him his approval or not. But two things held him, and one of them was Elitah—or rather, the expectation of Elitah's body. The other was a feeling of running out on a debt that his conscience told him he owed but his reason tried to disprove. It was a fact that if he left before the fall rains set in, he would be leaving Ross with logging orders unfilled and with little chance of filling them with him and Jeremy gone. He couldn't even support his debt to Marlette logically. Yes, she had given him the chance to come west with her, but he had already decided to do that on his own, and he had worked every step of the way. With resentment and contempt, he admitted the bond that held him the strongest was Ross. It was the same bond that had brought him west to find Ross, the man he had made into his hero before he had met him. It made no difference now that the reasons for coming west had been wrong; the bond still existed and Cam wanted to break it.

He thought of returning home and knew he couldn't unless he went back with gold. It made his heart beat faster to think of it, until he thought beyond the initial return. After that, what would he do? Go back to farming with his father. So he continued to work, waiting for something to happen, his restlessness growing as he learned of more and more men heading for the gold fields.

After weeks of trying to teach Elitah, it was Cam who became the disinterested one. It became harder and harder for him to try to listen to her read or watch her write laboriously. She disgusted him and excited him at the same time, his immediate desire and needs incapable of seeing any other reason for her existence. True, she could eat and dress properly, but she lacked every other motivation of the industrious white women he knew, and he finally quit coming into the house for their daily lesson while Abigail took her nap.

After he didn't come in for a few lessons, the word got to Ross. When they were alone for a few minutes, Ross said, "Elitah tells me you haven't been teaching her anymore. Why?"

Cam looked away and struggled for an answer. "I don't know. She just doesn't seem to be interested."

"She says she is. Do you want me to send her to the school of the Catholics at St. Paul?"

"Maybe that would be best."

There was a strained silence for a few moments before Ross said, "Cam, I feel you have something on your mind. Do you want to talk to me about it?"

Cam looked at him squarely. "I want to go to California."

Ross's eyebrows raised, but almost immediately he said, "Then why don't you?"

Cam relaxed and smiled. "Well, I thought we had too much to do and I didn't want to leave owing you."

"You owe me nothing. If you want to leave tomorrow, you can. If you want to stay, you can, but only if you want to."

Cam saw something in Ross's eyes that made him feel guilty about his own feelings and he held out his hand quickly, apologizing. "I'm sorry. I've never thanked you for all you've done, but I want to now."

267

Ross didn't take the offered hand, his face and eyes unreadable once more. "I'll take that hand and accept your gratitude when you really feel gratitude, Cam." He turned and walked away and left Cam standing in awkward silence.

The next day, working in the woods, Cam and Jeremy made their plans. Jeremy would go in spite of Liz's wishes. The two boys went home visibly excited at the end of the day. In two days they would leave. They were to work in the woods one more day and would have one day to prepare for the trip. Marlette, of course, was against letting Cam go, and Elitah, except for mentioning to Ross that he was not teaching her anymore, had said nothing to him.

On his last day at home, he was in the barn repairing and readying his gear when Elitah came into the barn and stood watching him silently. He was unaware of her at first. It angered him to be surprised so easily, and he let the anger show in his voice when he noticed her. "Do you want something?"

She came closer and stood over him. "Why do you leave?"

He glanced up at her pouting face, then back at his work. "Because I want to."

"Take me with you."

He answered with indifference, his eyes still on his work, "I can't take you with me."

"Why not? I belong to you."

Finally he looked up, stopping his work for a moment. "Because I am going to California to work. It will be hard work and I will have no time for anything else. You're better off here anyway. You'll have food and a place to sleep and someone to teach you what you need to know."

"I know already all I want. I want to go with you."

He was losing his patience. "No. You can't go."

She dropped down beside him and put a hand on his arm. It was the first time she had ever willingly touched him. "But I am yours," she said softly, with a look that stirred him.

He pulled his arm away. "Elitah, you do not belong to me in the same way you belonged to the Indians. I brought you here because I thought you were a white girl and I wanted to give you back the life I thought had been taken from you. You don't have to belong to any man unless you want to marry him. Understand?"

"Yes. I will marry you."

"No!" he snapped. "That isn't what I meant. I don't want you to marry me. Now just get back to the house and quit bothering me."

She got up and moved away from him, the swish of her skirts conveying her anger. He ignored her and continued with his work. In a few long moments, the barn door slid shut, cutting off his light. He looked up in annoyance, an oath forming on his lips. Elitah stood in a shaft of light from one of the windows, her naked body a burnished gold, her heavy hair hanging in gleaming fiery waves over her shoulders. "I belong to you. Take me."

The blood throbbed in Cam's body, responding to the hushed seductiveness of her voice, and he rose slowly, forgetting everything but the need to discover the magic of a woman's body. Hoarsely, he whispered back, "Not here. Up there."

Her eyes lifted to the loft above, almost empty of hay, but still a more secluded tryst than where they now stood. Cam picked up the bedroll, which still lay unfastened to his saddle, and climbed up the ladder, missing rungs in his haste. He pulled himself onto the loft floor and quickly shook out the blankets on the small mound of hay. He turned back to the ladder as Elitah's head appeared, and he held out his hand to her. She took it and he pulled her up beside him, feeling shaky and uncertain. He drew her into his arms and saw the eyelids narrow over her eyes until the dark lashes touched her cheeks and her lips parted expectantly. Then his own eyes closed in embarrassment. He had never kissed a girl like this. Their lips met, and his legs turned to jelly. He steered her clinging body backward to the blankets and pulled her down with him, never releasing her lips while he fumbled to unbutton his pants, feeling a warmth rise to his face that wasn't from the touch of her body alone. After what seemed like agonizingly long moments, his flesh touched hers and he felt dizzy, shuddering from the thrill of her hand eagerly exploring him. Frantic he would not be able to wait, he clumsily covered her with his body and launched his life into her, shaking and faint with the exhilaration and wilting immediately. He lay soaked with sweat and breathing heavily, hardly realizing it was over. Elitah pushed at him and he rolled over on his back. She was getting up and he grabbed at her hand and held her. "Wait. Don't go."

"For what?" she snapped, her eyes flashing.

269

She was angry, and he felt suddenly humiliated. "Elitah, I'm sorry. Don't leave. Let me try again."

"You never have woman before?" It was as much an accusation as a question.

"No."

She looked at him with contempt and disgust. Tossing her head, she said, "If I stay, will you take me with you?"

"Elitah, I already told you, you can't go with me."

Her lips drew together in a pucker and a well-aimed mouthful of spit covered his face. Momentarily shocked, he sat wiping the saliva from his face as she rose to her feet. Suddenly he understood what she had been doing. Anger filled him and he lunged after her, yelling, "Elitah, you bitch!" He sprawled headlong across the floor with his feet tangled in his pants, but managed to grab her by the hair as she went over the edge of the loft and pulled her back. She came fighting, clawing, kicking, and clubbing him with her fists, but a summer of working in the woods had added strength to his arms, and she was no match for him now. As he held her, another strength returned to him with the desire to use her as he had been used. His lips captured hers and she bit him. He slapped her hard and she sprawled into the hay. He went after her, and she struggled to get away as he pinned her down with his body. He held her by the hair and kissed her again as she struggled, tasting blood. He forced her legs apart, his hand bruising her thigh as he held her. With determination and vengeance, he fulfilled his desire, giddy with the sensation like nothing he had ever experienced. His lips tasted her breasts, delighting in the softness of her skin against his face, nuzzling her, curling his tongue around the hard little nipples, exulting in each pleasurable touch. He reached for her lips again and felt her mouth open, but this time she didn't bite him and he was aware she was no longer struggling as he felt her arching against him. Her hands pulled him closer as the intensity of their desire overshadowed everything else.

Then it was gone. In one sweet, brief moment they emptied themselves of every throbbing desire and Cam lay in awe of what he had just experienced. Elitah slowly drew away from him and rose to go down the ladder. He didn't try to stop her. He had nothing more to say to her—nothing he could put in words.

22. Gold Fever

CAM AWOKE NOT remembering for a moment where he was or just what had happened. He heard the soft munching sound of a horse eating and opened his eyes slowly. His horse was standing above him, still saddled. He closed his eyes quickly as the light brought pain and the pain sharpened his memory. He started to turn to a more comfortable position and moaned as his head exploded in pain. He lay feeling miserable, his tongue filling his vile, cottony mouth and his throat so dry he was sure he couldn't speak. Holding his head, he slowly pushed himself up to a sitting position and groaned, resting his head on his knees. A wave of nausea swept up from his stomach and he knew he was going to be sick. Lurching to his feet, he staggered and stumbled, holding his hand over his mouth as he ran to the back door of the barn. He yanked open the door, the effort bringing an explosion of pain to his throbbing head. He half-ran, half-crawled down to the creek below the barn and sprawled on the bank, vomiting violently, his head collapsing into the cold water of the stream after each contraction.

Finally he lay in shaking exhaustion, the cold water numbing the pain in his head. He pulled himself up and, with aching eyes, saw his despicable condition. He crawled into the stream and let the chill water wash over him, rubbing feebly at the straw and horse manure clinging to his clothes and hair. When he was chilled and shivering, he pulled himself out of the water and slowly gathered his feet under him, starting back up the slope toward the barn, clutching at the trees for support.

He examined his horse and found no evidence of injury, then moved into the next stall where his pack horse waited to be loaded. With an effort, he lifted the packsaddle onto the animal's back and began tying his equipment on. The barn door opened and Ross

271

came in. Cam didn't look up, hoping Ross wouldn't see his condition in the dim light of the barn.

"Were you going to leave without saying good-bye?"

Cam didn't answer, choked by a wave of guilt and shame.

There was a long, agonizing moment of silence before Ross said, "Elitah told me what happened yesterday. I don't believe all of her story. I'd like to hear what you have to say."

Cam felt his face grow hot as he doggedly finished tying off the last of his load. Angry at his own feelings as much as at Ross, he pushed on the horse's shoulder and the animal backed up, forcing Ross to move aside or be stepped on. Ross watched him while he went into the adjacent stall to get his saddle horse, keeping his lips pressed tight together, refusing to talk, sweating in spite of his still dripping clothes.

"Jeremy is waiting for you."

Cam inclined his head in acknowledgment and led his horses toward the door. Ross's voice stopped him before he left the dimness of the barn, but he didn't turn around. He didn't want to see Ross and didn't want Ross to see him.

"Cam. What I said before, about this being your home—it still is, and you can come back anytime."

Cam stood in embarrassed confusion, his emotions working on his face as he waited to hear more, but there was no more. He broke from the barn, steeling himself against the emotions warring in him. Tight-lipped and resolute, he mounted his horse and rode to where Jeremy sat his horse in front of the house.

Marlette stood by the fence opening to the yard with Abigail. He couldn't hide his appearance from her, and his mind groped for an answer to the question he knew was coming.

"Cam! What on earth happened to you? You'd better come in and change."

He smiled halfheartedly and said, "I'm all right. I'll dry out before too long. We've got to get moving."

She came through the gate and held up her hands to him, her eyes telling him how much she cared. "Cam, I hate to see you leave like this. Please be careful."

He took her hands and held them for a moment, an honest, warm smile lighting his face. "I'll be careful."

"Good luck."

He released her hands and she turned to pick up Abigail, who was tugging at her skirts. He blew the blond, blue-eyed child a kiss and said, " 'Bye, Abigail."

A chubby arm raised and she said, "Bye-bye, Unca Cam."

He pulled his horse around, feeling emotion choking in his throat again. He had to get away quickly. He sent his horses loping down the lane to the road, with Jeremy trailing behind. Once they crossed the creek and were out of sight, he slowed down and let Jeremy catch up.

Concerned eyes looked in his and he looked away as Jeremy questioned, "What did happen last night? You look terrible."

Cam tried to grin nonchalantly, still feeling the dull throb in his head and the quiver in his stomach. "I met Custis Wood last night. He and some of the other fellows I met chasing the Indians are heading to California, too. They were having a going away celebration, and Custis asked me to go with him."

"And you got drunk?"

Cam laughed. "I got godawful drunk."

"You look like it."

"And I'm feeling like it, too. I didn't even know where I was when I woke up in the barn this morning, or how I got there. In fact I don't remember too much at all about what happened after about the fourth beer last night. All I know is my head hurts like hell and I was sick to death this morning." He shook his head in authority on the matter of drunkenness, not so bothered by the ache now that he could relate his experience to someone with less experience than himself. He suddenly felt much better, shame and guilt fading as the feeling of being a man swelled him with new confidence and vanity. He wanted to tell Jeremy about that, too, but thought better of it. Maybe later, when they were a lot farther away. For the moment it was enough to just remember the experience with Elitah, and his shoulders lifted proudly.

At Champoeg they met Custis Wood and several more eager gold hunters. Two of the men were older, and Cam knew they left behind families. The rest were like Custis, Jeremy, and himself—young, unattached, and craving adventure.

In a few miles they rode through the settlement of St. Paul. Cam looked with new interest at the school for Indians operated by Catholic sisters. This is where Elitah would be sent, and Cam felt a twinge of guilt. He wondered wistfully if he would ever see her or know the delight of her body again. He shrugged off the feeling as the buoyant group of men rode on.

By afternoon Cam was completely dry and warmed by the September sun. They passed near the new site of the Methodist Mission between the new mill site on a creek that emptied into the Willamette and the site of an impressive three-story building already being called Willamette Institute.

Three days later they were going through the canyon that Applegate had led members of the Boggs train and others through. The suffering of the emigrants following Applegate over his shortcut was well known to everyone. They had nearly given up in this deep canyon, now an innocent-looking, easy road without the fall rains swelling it to a torrent. But Cam could imagine the emigrants wading in shoulder-high water, holding their guns and powder above their heads, their women and children riding on what oxen they had left or wading if they had none.

Cam swallowed the lump rising in his throat as he saw Ross in his mind's eye arguing to keep them going on the old trail. Other pictures flashed through his mind in rapid succession as he let the memory of Ross wash over him. The man he saw was not the man he thought he hated, but the man he knew he loved, and he ached now for the times Ross had needed him and he had turned away, unforgiving. He closed his eyes, trying to shut out the picture of Ross standing before him with pain in his eyes and in his body, and felt the shame he had only begun to feel when he had left without a word.

Jeremy's voice broke into his thoughts, jarring him back to the present. "What's wrong, Cam?"

"Nothing. I was just thinking about how coming through that canyon must have been."

Jeremy looked back as they topped the hill and said, "You know, we were luckier than most."

Cam said quietly, "Some of us didn't know how lucky."

That night they camped with a small band of coastal Indians. They had come over the mountains to hunt and seemed to be as afraid of running into other Indians as the little group of white men. With signs and Chinook jargon, they hired one of the Indians as a guide, not really knowing whether the Indian understood what they wanted him to guide them to.

In the following days, it seemed to Cam they were lost and

274

going in circles, but the Indian guide repeatedly assured them he was just avoiding the hostile Rogue Indians. None of them knew for sure where they were, but a white snowcapped mountain stood to the east of them when the Indian finally stopped and said he would go no farther. He pointed them straight south and disappeared back the way they had come.

Cam and Jeremy were dubious and would have been fearful if they had not been in the company of older and more confident men. They had seen enough mountains and canyons and deep forests to last a lifetime and, though neither of them expressed it in words, they were both feeling they had made a mistake. But the older men, Custis Wood perhaps the boldest-acting but by no means the most confident, eagerly started out down into another canyon and the rest followed, Cam and Jeremy bringing up the rear.

They followed a dry streambed for a few miles until a trickle of water showed. They wondered if they were in the gold region and began stopping to search for the precious gold flakes in the tiny stream. They followed the stream down until dark without finding any gold and finally had to camp in the dense timbered canyon.

Morning came and they moved on. The canyon widened and the hills rose more gently as they moved toward another canyon. At the junction of the two streams, they found their first gold miner. He hadn't been on the stream for more than a month, but he had gold and that was what counted. Cam and Jeremy immediately found themselves on their own as the men quickly disappeared up and down the stream to find their own claims.

The two greenhorns looked at each other and Jeremy asked, "Which way shall we go?"

Cam hardly knew, but said, "Why not upstream? Maybe there'll be less competition up than down."

Bypassing the claims already being staked out by their companions, they stopped at what they thought looked like a good gravel bar. They had talked gold and mining all the way from Oregon and had some idea what to look for, but they found that in practice gold was much more elusive than they had imagined. Panning during the next few days hardly showed them any color. They needed a more efficient way to collect the gold particles they felt sure had to be hidden in the stream. With axes they split cedar into half logs and nailed together a crude sluice box. Then they dug up the streambed and dumped the gravel into the box, washing it down with buckets of water. They got some color and whooped and danced with excitement, and vigorously worked until dark, when they were too exhausted even to eat. They rolled into their blankets and slept until morning, waking to the aches and bruises from the previous day's effort. Restrained by pain, but no less eager, they put in another demanding day at the sluice and collected the small, but promising, reward in gold.

For two weeks they did nothing but shovel the gravel bar and every inch of the streambed into the sluice, hardly stopping to eat or even wash. When Custis Wood rode up the stream one day, he stopped and looked at them, hardly recognizing his two young friends. "My God, is that you, Cam and Jeremy? You look like you been shovelin' gravel for a year without stoppin'!"

They looked at each other and laughed, and Jeremy said, "It feels like it."

Custis asked, "Got anything to show for it?"

Cam answered, "Some. How about you?"

"Yeah. Got a poke full already. We was goin' down to Doll's Place and celebrate tonight. You want to come?"

"Where's Doll's Place?"

"Oh, couple hours ride downstream. They got food and drink, and Doll sings and dances. I 'spect 'fore too long they'll be a place to buy grub and a laundry place, too. You ought to come along. You look like you could use a break."

Cam looked at Jeremy and they lay down their shovels. "Sounds like a good idea. Can you wait a few minutes till we get our horses?"

"Sure. But hurry up or we won't make it before dark."

They scrambled up into the brush above the stream and retrieved their horses. Without washing or changing into clean clothes, they mounted and followed Custis down through the canyon, passing other claims, now deserted as the miners took a night off for enjoyment.

Doll's Place was, from the outside, a lot less than Cam had expected. Built on a narrow flat along the stream bank among the trees, it hardly looked like a building at all. It was partially built of rough planks, but the top third of the structure and the peaked roof were made of canvas with the glow from inside lighting the oncoming darkness. There were rows of horses outside, and among the trees it looked as if there was another building being started.

They dismounted and pushed through the wood-framed tent flaps, and Cam and Jeremy both stopped, stunned by the elaborate use of material and mirrors inside the flimsy tent structure. The walls were draped lavishly with rich blue velvet, caught every few feet into a rosette, the center of which flickered with a prism of glass. Where the sloping sides of the tent roof began, the velvet was cut and rose in gathered, billowing drapes to the top of the tent peak. The centerpiece of each wall was a large gold-framed picture of nude women reclining seductively against varying backgrounds from bedrooms to forests. They made Cam flush with embarrassment and remembrance. At the back of the tent, an elaborate staircase rose in a curve to nowhere. The bar was made out of planks on barrels and draped with more royal-blue velvet. The plank holding the rows of bottles behind the bar was also covered with velvet, and large ornate mirrors reflected the whole room from behind. In contrast to the blue on the walls, there were gaming and card tables covered with emerald green cloth along the wall opposite the bar, and plain wooden tables filling the space between.

The place was almost full to capacity with men having their beer or whiskey and enjoying the games of chance and cards. Cam and Jeremy took their small sack of gold to the bar, almost ashamed. The bartender weighed it and told them what they could buy with what they had, and they settled for the less expensive glasses of beer. Custis was already having a good time at the dice table, his laughter easily heard over the more subdued voices of the relaxing miners.

From next to the stairway, the piano broke into the buzz of talking and drinking men, and there was a decided hush in the audience as all eyes turned to the top of the stairway. In a few moments the velvet curtains parted and a woman stepped through onto the landing at the top. It was obvious the stairs did go somewhere, even if only back down the other side of the velvet wall. The woman at the top looked down on them with a big smile, kissing the tips of her bejeweled fingers as the men gave her proper adulation. Doll was dressed in a white sequined gown that hugged her fleshy figure almost to the ankles. A wide ruffle of feathers trimmed the bottom of the gown and followed the split up to her

277

thigh. What she lacked in natural beauty she made up for in elegance as she came down the stairs in a floating glide that seemed to deny there were steps at all. Her hair was reddish gold and piled on top of her head in a mass of curls. Her makeup was bright and lavish, giving her face a painted doll look that was much prettier at a distance than up close. She reached the bottom of the steps, and several of the men lifted her by her arms and demurely crossed legs onto the bar. She started to sing in a husky, earthy voice and was cheered as she moved in a slow little dance step along the bar, her hips swinging ever so slightly and her jeweled hands seductively implying and imploring. The men loved it, clapping and whistling with glee.

She glided past Cam and Jeremy, never giving them a second glance, and was lifted off the end of the bar onto the nearest table, where she continued to sing and sway. She went from table to table until she was carried back to her stairway platform, where she ended her song and bowed deeply, giving every man in the room a glimpse of her awesome cleavage and blowing more kisses. Shouts rang out for more, and the piano started up for an encore.

With unspoken mutual consent, Cam and Jeremy finished their beer and edged through the crowd of men into the dark, moonless night. They mounted their horses for the long ride back up the canyon, but it took them only a few minutes to discover it would be impossible to find their way without endangering their horses and themselves. They found a patch of grass on the stream bank, hobbled the horses, took their saddles for pillows and the saddle blankets to cover themselves against the chill night, and slept.

They reached their claim early the next day and warmed themselves before the fire as the fog rose off the water. The leaves of the sumac and maples flaming against the dark evergreens proclaimed as distinctly as the chill in the air that bad weather was on the way. They got to work after breakfast, and by afternoon, with the sun warming the canyon, they were seeing color and feeling eager again.

But after another week of hard work in cold, rainy weather, they began running low on food, so they quit early and, for the first time in days, bathed and changed clothes and trimmed the beginnings of beards. Leading their pack horses, they started down the canyon before noon, hoping to return before dark.

They did their shopping first, and their small horde of gold dwindled fast with flour one dollar a pound and other prices equally high. They had only enough gold left to buy themselves a drink apiece at Doll's Place. With an optimistic shrug of their shoulders, they stepped into the saloon and spent their last flakes of gold on two drinks of whiskey. They stood at the bar and watched the wheel of fortune turn, thinking the same thoughts as they swallowed the burning liquid. Doll sat at her private table in the shadow of the staircase, overseeing her only moderately busy saloon. The bartender came back as he saw their glasses empty and offered to pour again, but the boys were shaking their heads. Doll rose and floated over from her elevated vantage point, stopping to lean on the bar near Cam.

"Hi, boys. How ya doin'?" Her speaking voice shattered all illusions as to the elegance of her movements, but her smile was big and warm.

Cam smiled back and answered, "Fine. You've got a nice place here. Never seen anything so elegant."

"Why, thank you, honey. I'm glad you like it. How's the drink?"

Cam glanced at the half-swallow he had left, not knowing how to answer. He wasn't sure whether it was good or bad; he'd never had any before. He answered, a bit embarrassed, "Oh, good, real good."

"Then why don't you boys have another?" She waved a finger at the bartender.

Jeremy answered, "Well, we would, ma'am, but we don't have enough to pay for it."

She laughed huskily. "Oh, is that all? George, fill the boys up on me."

George sloshed more whiskey into the glasses and retreated as Doll asked, "Where you boys from?"

Cam answered, "Oregon."

"I never been there. Is there any gold in Oregon?"

"Well, we don't really know. We haven't been there too long."

The tent doors flapped open and three men strode in. Doll straightened off the bar, her attention attracted to the newcomers. "Well, you boys take it easy and come see Doll the next time you come down."

They nodded at her retreating figure and finished their second glass of whiskey, feeling flushed and dizzy. They walked a little

279

unsteadily toward the door and pushed through it, mounted their horses, and started back up the canyon in the cold wind.

The next few days it rained more often than not, and the stream rose and became murky. They continued to work even in the rain, now desperate to make back what they had spent in town. The harder they worked, the harder it seemed to rain, until one day they had to quit and take refuge in the tent as a real storm lashed the canyon with thunder and lightning and a fierce downpour. Wet and cold, they stripped off their clothes, pulled on long underwear, and rolled in their blankets.

In the middle of the night Cam awoke cold and soaked. He called to Jeremy, who sat up with chattering teeth.

"My blankets are soaked. What happened to the tent?"

"Must've sprung a leak. Can you find the lantern?"

They both fumbled for the lantern and finally got it lighted. And inch-deep stream of water was coming in under the back of the tent and gurgling out the front. They got up and dressed and carried the lantern outside. Behind the tent the bank rose about five feet to the forested and brushy higher bank where they kept the horses. They had set up the tent where a dry creek bed emptied over the bank. With the heavy downpour, the runoff from the mountain was funneling down to empty into their tent. There was no other choice but to move the tent, so they agreed to move it up on the higher bank. It took the rest of the night, and by daybreak they were ready to go back to work under a clearing sky.

At noon the sun was shining beautifully and they were almost dry. Cam scrambled up the bank to bring down their wet blankets and clothes and lay them on the gravel in the sun. The run-off had died down to a bare trickle, so the gravel mound where the tent had been was high and dry. Cam shook out the blankets, crawling on his knees to unfold them. A glimmer caught his eye, and he peered closely at the gravel by the trickle of water and saw something bigger than the flakes they had so far been finding. With thumping heart, he pulled out his knife and carefully dug away the sand and rock.

Jeremy called, "What are you doing?"

He called back, the excitement in his voice undisguised, "I think I'm finding our first gold nugget!"

Jeremy scrambled up beside him and dropped down, unmindful his knees were in the water. Cam's knife lifted out the piece of gold and dropped it into Jeremy's palm, and they looked at it unbelievingly for a few seconds, silent with unspoken hope and amazement.

Then Jeremy let out a whoop and jumped to his feet, and Cam clambered up beside him. They grabbed each other and began to stamp and shout as the frenzy of gold fever made them dizzy. Laughing and breathless, they fell back down on their knees. Tossing the blankets and clothes aside, they clawed at the gravel in search of more chunks of gold, letting out a whoop every time they uncovered a bright, tiny nugget. Their tent had been sitting right on top of the pay dirt. They grabbed up their shovels and buckets and, with adrenaline pumping, tore the gravel mound apart, reducing it to bare rock. By dark, too exhausted and aching to eat, they lay on damp ground covered with damp blankets and slept without moving until morning.

With the light of dawn, some reason and logic returned and they knew they had to move their sluice box and rebuild it to catch the runoff from the dry creek bed. Another two days of building and they were ready to run all the gravel they had not yet sluiced. In one day they made up enough in gold to pay for the two days lost rebuilding the sluice. They were in the mood to celebrate. Tomorrow they would go down to Doll's Place.

By morning they had second thoughts about celebrating. An open display of wealth would invite interest in their claim and, with the selfishness of new wealth, they became secretive. This led to the realization that Custis could ride up at any moment and see the radical change in their layout. Afraid they would be mobbed and even claim-jumped, they began dismantling their sluice and returned it to its original position nearer the creek. They decided not to move the tent. There was an obvious explanation for moving it to higher ground, but they frantically smoothed over the evidence of their digging at the old tent site.

When Custis rode up early in the afternoon, they appeared to be at work as if nothing had happened. Cam, after a few minutes of conversation, saddled his horse and rode down the creek with Custis to get supplies while Jeremy remained at the claim. This seemed to arouse no suspicion, and after a drink with Custis in Doll's Place, Cam went to the store and bought supplies— including a bottle of whiskey—still without undue suspicion, except that the storekeeper remarked at the larger grains of gold he used for payment.

Once back at the claim, he and Jeremy sat by their fire after a dinner more sumptuous than their usual fare of salt pork and beans. The storekeeper had just brought in fresh hams and bacon and a supply of vegetables, fruit, and eggs. Cam had spent lavishly for them, starved for the variety of food he had known at Ross's. Then they opened the bottle of whiskey and, with connoiseurlike restraint, savored the fiery liquid. When they felt almost too giddy to care about moving, they staggered into their tent and rolled into their blankets, still sipping the whiskey until they became so saturated they passed out and slept.

With aching heads and cotton mouths, they finally dragged themselves from stuporous slumber late the next morning.

Between retching shudders, Jeremy moaned, "Why did we do this?"

Cam answered weakly, "That's what I wondered the first time. Maybe if we keep tryin', we'll get used to it."

Jeremy collapsed on his back and groaned, "I'm not sure it's worth it."

"You wanna be a man or don't you?"

"There's gotta be an easier way."

"Yeah, but we don't have any women."

Jeremy sat up and looked at him, suddenly alert, "Hey, how do you know about women?"

Cam grinned ruefully, "I didn't tell you about that, did I? That's why I got drunk the first time with Custis. I'll tell you it beats drinking all to hell."

Jeremy was almost beside himself with curiosity. "For God's sake, Cam, tell me about it. And tell me who!"

Cam laughed, relishing Jeremy's excitement. "Elitah. She came to me the day before we left and, well, it just happened. I can't describe it, Jer, but it just feels so damn good you never want to quit."

Jeremy leaned back on his elbows in silence and gazed up at the clouds. After a long, thoughtful silence, he got up and said quietly, "Well, guess we'd better get busy. This weather looks like it's fixin' to rain again."

For the next two months Cam and Jeremy worked their claim and continued to find gold as they dug back into the bank and stripped the dry streambed. The weather became more and more wintry. Snow fell, whitening the mountaintops surrounding them like sentinels. They alternated their trips to town to buy supplies so each could bring back to camp what he hungered for. And each trip, in spite of the effect it had on them, they brought back a bottle of whiskey. Eventually, their tolerance for it increased and they became aware that it took more to knock them out and the effects were less devastating.

Soon it became impossible to work even the dry streambed as it became a live stream, carrying off the rain from the mountain behind them. Days were spent huddled inside the tent or around the sputtering fire while rain or snow soaked them. Their only relief from the weather and boredom was to ride down to Doll's Place, and that was becoming more of a task, too. The stream had been their trail, but now it was high and swift and treacherous, so they had to fight their way along the bank through the brush. They would take their tent and bedrolls and stay on the flat at Doll's Place for several days at a time, drinking, talking to the other men still trying work their claims, and even gambling as a last resort.

It became obvious after the first of the year that the outside world had learned of the gold in California. New faces arrived daily at Doll's Place—men who had traveled a continent's breadth to strike it rich in the canyons of California. The flat at Doll's Place became more than a tent saloon and a provisions post. A canvas hotel sprang up offering lodging for the miners, gamblers, and those who made their living following them. A restaurant, barber shop and bath house, Chinese laundry, and an assayer's office all followed in quick order to fulfill the needs of the miners, professional gamblers, and women.

It was a much rougher and wilder population combing the canyons than before, and killings and claim-jumping became the usual instead of the unusual. Of the men Cam and Jeremy had come with, only Custis and one other young man remained. Most of the Oregon men left as the harsh weather made home seem a castle compared to the leaking tent, especially after a long day of panning in cold water up to the waist, or picking and shoveling at rock banks. Only the rootless stayed on.

Doll's Place paled in comparison with the other saloons that sprang up on the flat—not in elegance but in activity. Cam and Jeremy ventured into the others and could only tolerate so much of the din before they would go back to Doll's Place, where Doll attempted to maintain a more subdued and tasteful atmosphere. She tolerated neither cardsharps nor loose women, and she still had a crowd every night.

Cam and Jeremy spent more days down on the flat now than at their claim. The hotel and restaurant made it easier and they felt no worry now about claim-jumping. If they couldn't weather the ride up the canyon to their claim, they doubted anyone else could either. Their trips up the canyon were only necessary when they ran out of gold to pay for their room and board and the daily visits to the saloons.

But even if they preferred Doll's Place, they were attracted to the other saloons by the women. Both Cam and Jeremy were drawn and aroused by the lascivious behavior of the saloon girls. Cam encouraged Jeremy to pick a girl to become intimately acquainted with, holding back his own desire to take one for himself. Hot and pulsing with passion, yet afraid and guilt-ridden, he hid his own disturbing feelings.

Finally Jeremy reached the point of desperation. After he downed enough drinks to overcome his shyness and lack of confidence, he surprised Cam and himself by picking a woman from the dozen or so in the saloons. As Cam watched his friend disappear with the painted and provocatively dressed woman, he suddenly felt sick. He got to his feet and pushed his way out of the crowded saloon into the cold and windblown night, recoiling from the thought of being with one of these obviously prostituted women. He felt contempt for them and the use of their bodies and was surprised by the strength of his feelings. He was even more surprised because Elitah had tried to use her body in the same way and yet he felt no contempt for her, only a longing. His memory of her ruined any other woman's image in comparison; these women were brittle and painted façades hiding jaded minds and bodies, and Elitah was still beautiful and unspoiled in comparison.

He trudged past the other flimsy tent buildings toward Doll's, seeking what Doll's represented—a gentility that he missed, even if it, too, was only a façade. He pushed through the doors, through the quieter din, and stood drinking at the bar in brooding solitude. The piano began to play Doll's theme song, and he looked up hopefully to the top of the stairway. Doll came in with a flourish of ringed hands and fluttering feathers and made her way down the stairs as her music played. Without missing a beat, she was lifted to bartop and began her song. Cam watched and drank, transfixed—and, for the first time, homesick.

Cam kept drinking until he knew he had reached his saturation point. His legs were rubbery and his eyes blurred until everything looked like one big whirling prism. He didn't want to pass out here. He pushed himself away from the bar and turned around clumsily, almost falling, clutching at chair backs as he staggered toward the door. Reaching for the last chair by the door, he missed it completely, falling headlong across a table, knocking glasses, cards, money, and gold dust to the floor in a crescendo of breaking glass. For some reason it seemed uproariously funny to him, but not to the man in whose lap several glasses of whiskey and beer and Cam's head had landed. He grinned, trying to apologize and move, but he was like a stranded whale and floundered on the tabletop until the man whose chest his head drooped against grabbed him by the shirt front.

"You drunken son of a bitch!" was the last oath Cam heard as the man's fist smashed him in the face. The rest was a haze of pain he wasn't sure was even happening. Then everything went completely black and he felt nothing.

When Cam awoke, the first thing he felt was pain—pain that throbbed in his head and down his nose, into his eyes and lips, which felt too big to open, and pain that shot in spasms along his ribs as he breathed. He tried to open his eyes and couldn't. They, too, felt weighted and sealed shut, never to open again. The only sound he could make was a hoarse animal cry in his throat. He was frightened. He couldn't move and couldn't see. He had no idea where he was; his cries went unanswered and tears of panic welled in his eyes and made them hurt worse.

Then he felt a hand on his arm, and a voice he dimly recognized said, "Take it easy, honey. You're safe. Nobody's going to hurt you now. Relax and try to lay quiet. You've had a pretty bad beating and you're broken up a bit, but you'll heal if you take it easy."

The hand lingered on his arm and his sobs of distress quieted. With calm returning, he began to use his senses and his fingers to identify his surroundings. His fingers felt the cool slickness of satin and the cushion of down. He was in a bed, an elegant bed, and the perfume he smelled he had smelled before and the voice he heard he had heard before. But he couldn't quite believe his nose or his ears. Why whould he be in Doll's bed? But he had to trust those senses for now and wait until he could discover the truth.

The soft hand patted his arm and the husky voice said, "That's better, honey. Now I'm going to lay some warm cloths over your face to help the swelling. You just lay still." Then the voice faded away.

He had no measure of time without sight, and he drifted semi-conscious for what seemed like days, knowing only when his attendant bathed his face. Another voice came and went that he knew he should acknowledge but was not able to. When he began to realize the balloon sensation was gradually disappearing from his face, he tried harder to remain aware and alert, wanting desperately to see and to talk. The throb in his head was subdued, and the pain he felt more acutely was the pain of hunger. He tried to open his eyes, but they seemed sealed. He waited for the woman to come with her warm cloths and when she did, he raised his hands to rub his eyes. She tried to stop him, but he was desperate and finally broke the crusts that sealed his lids. Dimly, through smarting eyes, he saw her.

She was not the Doll he expected to see. This woman was without the mask of makeup and high-piled hair, and wasn't tightly corseted and richly gowned. This woman's hair hung loosely about her shoulders, and her skin was fair, almost pale, without the blossoms of rouge on her smooth cheeks. The lips, too, were almost colorless, but smiled at him as she stood by the bed in a loose velvet robe, looking shorter and heavier than the Doll he knew.

She reached out and put a hand on his forehead and said, "It'll be all right, honey. Go ahead and cry. The tears will help."

He blinked with difficulty, trying to clear away the tears and sharpen his vision, but there still seemed to be something in the way and he finally gave up and closed his eyes, weak from the effort.

He heard another voice in the background, and he heard Doll say, "Come in, honey."

The voice he recognized as Jeremy's asked, "How is he?"

"Better. He opened his eyes. That soup smells good. Let's see if we can get some down him."

Cam opened his eyes, recognized Jeremy, and raised his hand.

Jeremy took it and said, "Hey, Cam, I'm sure glad you're better. You really had Doll and me worried. Guess I better not leave you alone again."

Doll took the bowl and filled a spoon, and he smelled the tantalizing fragrance of food.

When the bowl was empty he spoke, his voice sounding strange and his mouth feeling even stranger as he said, "Thank you. I was hungry."

Doll patted his arm. "Of course you were, honey. We'll bring you more later, but we'd better take it easy or you'll get sick."

Through a mouth still sore and swollen, he asked carefully, "What happened? All I remember is falling across a table."

Doll laughed in her husky, hearty voice. "Well, honey, you just picked the wrong table to fall across. They were playing for big stakes, and you ruined one hell of a pot for the man who bashed in your face. Not to mention the help he got from the rest of the party."

Cam was thoughtful for a moment, then said to Jeremy, "Better get my clothes and get me out of here, Jer, so Doll can have her bed."

Doll laughed again and shook her head, keeping a restraining hand on his shoulder. "You ain't goin' nowhere, honey, in your condition. Not for a while at least. You just stay where you are until your ribs have a chance to mend. I got a perfectly lovely couch over there I can sleep on."

Jeremy said, "Well, guess I'd better take these things back to the restaurant. I'll see you later, Cam. Don't worry about a thing."

And for the next few days Cam didn't worry. It was easy to lie in the comfort of Doll's bed, the wind and rain peppering the tent ceiling above his bed while he watched Doll dress and make up for her customers. It was easy, too, after his initial embarrassment, to lace Doll into her corsets and massage her aching feet between performances.

He mended quickly and strength returned, and it wasn't many days before he could walk with Jeremy's help. He was shocked when he first saw his face in the mirror, hardly recognizing the scarred eyes, the broken nose, and the cut-up mouth with broken and missing teeth. Doll had kept him shaven, but now that he could get up she left that chore to him, and he decided to let his beard grow to hide the ravages of the beating.

As he grew stronger, his restlessness and guilt increased at doing nothing to repay Doll for her kindness. One evening after he had helped Doll dress, he dressed himself and paced the room, waiting for her to return. As she came through the door, he stopped and faced her.

She looked at him with his boots on and asked, "Where you going, honey?"

"Out to work, if you'll let me. I'm going crazy in here."

She laughed, and waved him to the settee, saying, "Come on and sit down and rub my feet and we'll talk about it."

He followed her to the settee and sat down as she kicked off her high heels and raised her feet into his lap and he began the ritual massaging. She sighed and relaxed. "And what makes you think you're able to go out front?"

"I know I can do it. Let me try."

"What can you do, honey? Can you deal cards or pour drinks?"

"Well, no, but maybe I could wash glasses and sweep. Anything!"

"Why?"

"I owe you."

She looked at him strangely for a long moment, and he dropped his eyes back to her feet and continued his careful massage.

Finally she pulled her feet from his hands and moved closer to him, her hand resting on his leg, uncomfortably close to his groin. "Listen to me a minute, Irish. You've got a body most men only think they've got. I'd like to get to know that body. I don't ask many men for that, and when I do, it's on my terms, not theirs. I'd like to teach you what to do with that beautiful body of yours. I can teach you how to love a woman in ways you never thought of. I want you to stay with me, Irish. It's as simple as that."

Slowly, he turned his head to look at her. She was serious. Her hand smoothed up his thigh, her fingers touching him with emphasis. It was an offer he didn't want to refuse.

"All right. But I have to be more than just your kept man. I want to work out front."

She laughed again, huskily and seductively, as she pressed herself against him, raising her lips to him. He turned to hold her, feeling the pull in his ribs, but he didn't care as she filled his arms and closed his eyes with her kiss.

288

23. *The Terrible Returning*

As THE DAYS passed, Cam's competency behind the bar increased just as did the competency he was acquiring under Doll's feather quilt. He was happy and untroubled, discovering new facets to his character he had not known before. The Irish charm and humor belonged to him, just as they belonged to Ross and Ross's father. Doll cultivated it, drawing it out of Cam as she nurtured his self-confidence and fertilized his ego with praise and admiration, encouraging his virility. Most of all, she let him know how much she needed him.

By the end of March, Jeremy was out of gold dust again and, in spite of Cam's insistence that he stay and use Cam's gold—Doll had insisted on paying him despite his desire to work for free to repay her—Jeremy refused, buying what supplies he had gold for and heading for the claim. The weather was clear and much milder. The snow was creeping back up the mountains, and the creek was high as it boiled down the canyon, and Cam trusted Jeremy's judgment. Jeremy was his father's son. He was quiet and cautious and sensible. Cam was confident Jeremy would return in another week with enough gold to buy all the whiskey and women he wanted.

The first week in April passed without Jeremy returning, and Cam became concerned. It was raining again, and when the clouds lifted temporarily, there was new snow on the mountains. Custis had come down from his claim as soon as the weather had changed and had no word of Jeremy. As Cam's anxiety grew, so did his guilt at having let Jeremy go alone. He had been well enough to join Jeremy, and his guilty conscience told him he should have. It began affecting his relationship with Doll. He was restless, and the pleasure he found in his education with her was diminishing noticeably.

Two weeks from the day Jeremy had headed up the canyon, he was so distracted that he couldn't concentrate on what he was doing as he held Doll. "I'm sorry, Doll. I guess I'm not in the mood today."

She laughed good-naturedly. "Sure, Irish. Tell me what's botherin' you? Your friend?"

"He's been gone two weeks. He should've been back by now. I'm worried about him."

She rose on one elbow to look down on him, her fingers trailing across his smooth, hairless chest. "He'll be all right. Miners are a tough bunch. You should know."

"I'd feel better about it if I could go up there and see for myself if he's all right."

She shrugged, unconcerned. "Whatever you think, but I think you'd be risking your neck unnecessarily. He's either all right or not, and your going up there won't change it."

He was surprised by her lack of feeling and sat up, his choice made clear. "I'll be back in a few days."

Her voice was soft but brittle as she said, "If you go up there, you don't need to bother about coming back."

He turned to look at her in even greater surprise. "What do you mean by that?"

"Just what I said. I told you no man stayed with me under any terms but mine."

He was dumbfounded and filled with realization at the same time. He had been so naive. "You mean I have to make a choice between you and my friend's life?"

She nodded, unsmiling.

Suddenly he laughed and shook his head. He didn't realize it at the moment, but it was the first sign of real maturity. He realized how he had been used and how easily he made the choice. He stood up and started putting on his clothes. She was off the bed and encircling him with her arms, pleading, "Irish, don't go. Please don't go."

He paused in his dressing. "Why? You don't need me. Jeremy does."

"I do need you. I don't say that to just anyone. You're worth more than all the others to me. You've got so much to give and so much to learn yet. Don't go. Let me teach it all to you."

He stood uncertain, tempted by the experience he already had with her. She sank to her knees in front of him, her hands sliding down his sides to caress his thighs as she placed her mouth against him. He was paralyzed with a flood of sensation as his body thrilled and responded to her, but only for a moment. Then he felt revulsion for her. She really knew how to get to him, but he realized the web she bound him with was one of his own choosing and he knew he had to break it or never be his own man again. All his Catholic decency descended on him and he pushed her roughly away, shaking and feeling shamed. He pulled on his pants and boots, gathering up his few things while she watched from where she had retreated behind her little table, her robe wrapped around her.

He turned to her as he put on the fur-lined buffalo coat, another reminder of Ross. He leaned on the table, aware of how really forgettable-looking this Doll was, knowing in time he would not be able to remember at all what she looked like as she sat there, so devoid of expression and color. The Doll he would remember was the one everyone saw, painted and elegantly gowned, singing and dancing sensually.

"Thanks, Doll. I don't think I'll ever forget what happened to me here, in this room with you. You gave me a lot, and you took a lot. For what you gave me, I'll always be grateful. I want to thank you, too, for what you took, not because I realize now that I should appreciate it, but I probably will, once I'm gone from here and have had time to think about it. It seems to be a failing of mine, so I'm going to thank you now." He straightened up and pushed a hand into the pocket of the coat, his fingers closing around the soft leather bag of gold dust there and drawing it out. He tossed the bag onto the table. "Here. It's all the gold you've given me. I don't figure you owe me anything. You were worth every bit of it and a whole lot more. Just how much more I haven't begun to realize yet."

He turned and strode toward the door. She began laughing, and he opened the flimsy door with her laughter ringing in his ears—that deep, hearty laughter he doubted he would ever forget.

He went straight through the saloon and out the front door into the rain. He felt relieved and, most of all, free again. He saw Custis coming through the mud and met him at the side of the narrow muddy track between the rows of tent buildings under one of the few trees left standing on the flat.

Custis looked at him in surprise. "What are you doing out here?"

"I'm headed up to the claim. Jeremy hasn't come down yet."

"Are you sure? He may be with that new Chinese gal he latched onto as soon as she got here."

"He would've come in to tell me. No. Something's gone wrong and I've got to find out what."

"You want me to go up with you?"

"Thanks, but there's no use in you getting wet if you don't have to."

Custis laughed. "Hell, Cam, I've spent more days wet than dry in the past two winters. You know that."

Cam smiled. He knew. He reached out his hand and Custis took it. "Take it easy. I'll be seeing you."

Custis grinned and said, "I will. You be careful."

Cam continued on to the cluster of trees that made do as a corral and shelter for horses. He found his horses still there and led them back through the mud to the hotel, where he hoped his gear would still be. It was, for a price, and he gave up part of the small reserve of gold dust he had left. That settled, he moved on to the store and bought provisions. Jeremy had to be running low by this time. In an hour's time he was leaving the flat on his way up the canyon. It would take him what was left of the day to reach the claim. Because of the high water, he wouldn't be able to go up the creek.

It was almost dark by the time he recognized the narrow bank along the creek where he and Jeremy had worked. It looked desolate, but a horse whickered from the timbered mountainside and he had a moment of hope as he looked in vain for the tent. Then he found it, covered with boughs from the trees for protection. He dismounted and felt fear rising in him. Surely Jeremy would have a fire. He threw back the tent flap, but his eyes were useless in the dark gloom.

"Jer," he called. "Jer, are you in there?"

A weak, trembling voice answered, "Cam, thank God you're here. I'm so sick, Cam. Godawful sick."

Cam ducked inside the tent and dropped to his knees beside Jeremy, his hand going immediately to his friend's head. Jeremy was burning with fever. "How long you been sick?"

"I don't know. A couple days."

"I'll get my blankets and get a fire going."

Cam unloaded his horses and turned them loose, after hobbling them, to join Jeremy's horses. He carried his bedroll into the tent and covered Jeremy with his blankets. Then he lit the lantern and cleared an area just outside the tent to start a fire. If he could get something warm into Jeremy, he might feel better. He built the fire up as big as he dared and opened the tent flaps to the heat as he boiled water for coffee and made soup from the pork he'd brought. He got some coffee and soup down Jeremy and sat watching his friend all night, keeping the fire going and the lantern lit for added warmth. He paced in front of the fire when he got too cold to sit, and wondered what he should do. There was no doctor yet in the camp on the flat. And even if there was, he doubted Jeremy would be able to ride that far. He hoped some of his questions would be answered in the morning.

With dawn the rain stopped. Jeremy awoke and called Cam, who went into the tent and squatted to feel the still-feverish forehead.

"I gotta go, Cam. Can you help me?"

"Sure, Jer." He lifted Jeremy up, keeping a blanket around him, and helped him out of the tent.

Weakly, Jeremy fumbled at his pants. "I'm afraid I'm going to be sick, Cam."

"Just hold on, Jer. I've got you."

Jeremy's pants fell around his ankles and Cam eased him down onto a log. Everything happened at once, and Cam had to hang onto Jeremy to keep him from falling off the log in his retchings. In a few minutes Jeremy recovered and Cam helped him stand. With Jeremy leaning against a tree, he bent to pull up Jeremy's pants and saw a red rash above his groin.

"Jer. You've got a rash down here. What the hell have you been into?"

There was a weak laugh from Jeremy as he answered, "Lots. Maybe I got the clap."

Cam finished buttoning Jeremy and helped him back into the tent. "Maybe I should try to get you down to a doctor. Do you think you could make it?"

"Maybe. But I'd rather go home."

"I don't think you'd make it like you are. We'd better try to get to a doctor closer. You got any gold left?"

He nodded weakly. "I almost forgot to tell you. I hit a real pocket, Cam, back there where the dry wash begins at the base of the rocks. Got a lot out before the rain came and dumped it full of dirt again."

"You got it hid?"

"You know where."

"Yes. Do you feel like something to eat?"

"No. Just let my lay here awhile. I'll feel better in a bit."

Cam built up the fire and made himself some breakfast. He carried some hot coffee in to Jeremy and helped him sit up. When he brushed back Jeremy's hair to feel his forehead, it was covered with red spots. He covered the spots with his hand. "Hey, Jer, your fever's down now, but you've got spots on your forehead. How do you feel?"

Jeremy took the cup and sipped some coffee laced with sugar. "Better, I think. I think I could eat. Got any bacon?"

"Sure. I got some eggs, too." He placed the packsaddle behind Jeremy to prop him up and hurried to fix some breakfast. Jeremy ate with apparent relish, his eyes clearer and his voice stronger, but Cam noticed more red spots on the backs of Jeremy's hands.

"I feel a lot better, Cam. What d'ya say we pack up and head for home? I've had enough of this damn gold digging."

Cam hated to leave. He didn't have much gold of his own, but Jeremy was sick, and he felt guilty enough already about what had happened. He could always come back once Jeremy was home safe. "All right. I'll get things packed up and we'll start home. You just rest easy."

Jeremy smiled gratefully and lay back with closed eyes. Cam got the horses and loaded them. Then he took down the tent and got the gold from the tree hollow where Jeremy had it hidden. Jeremy was still weak and shaky, but Cam got him into the saddle and they headed up the canyon. It wasn't an easy trail, and Cam wondered if they would be able to get over the mountain from this canyon, but it was the shortest route out and they were headed north.

They were far up the canyon by dark. Cam shivered with cold from the wind blowing across the snow on the mountainside as he set up the tent and helped a much weaker Jeremy into the flimsy protection of the tent. He tethered the horses as best he could where they could find something to eat. Then he built a fire and cooked supper. Jeremy ate very little, but Cam was ravenous and terribly tired from having spent the previous night awake. He rolled into his blankets and slept in spite of the cold and anxiety.

There was no change in Jeremy the next morning. He drank some coffee and broth and urged Cam to lead him on. His fever was still down, but Cam didn't like the red spots on his forehead. When he helped Jeremy relieve himself, he saw that the insides of Jeremy's legs were covered with spots. Cam was more than worried, but he didn't let on, helping Jeremy onto his horse and leading the horses up the last steep slopes to the ridge of the mountains. It cleared as they crossed the snow on the ridge, and Cam could see nothing but more snowy mountains on all sides.

In two days they dropped down into a canyon where the stream appeared to be heading in a generally westerly direction. Jeremy was growing worse, almost unable to eat or drink now, as the rash invaded his mouth. Cam decided to follow the stream. Perhaps there were settlements on this river. He found evidence of an Indian encampment by nightfall and that increased his apprehension, but he had no choice but to camp. He stayed awake all night, too worried about the Indians and Jeremy to sleep. Jeremy slept, but it was a tortured sleep. His spots were swelling into pimples and Cam was frightened. He said his first prayer that night.

The next day the Indians found them, and Cam was sure they would be killed. The fierce, wild little party surrounded the hapless riders, but when they saw Jeremy's swelling pimples, they chattered among themselves and disappeared into the underbrush.

They reached a fork in the river where the main stem turned south. Cam took the other branch, which looked like it headed north, and found himself traveling ever upward in a narrowing canyon. Ahead lay nothing but snowcapped mountains, which he knew would be difficult if not impossible to cross. They camped high up in the canyon where another branch of the river came in from the west. In the morning he would have to decide which of those forks to take.

Jeremy was no better in the morning. His swelling pimples looked almost ready to pop and were filled with a clear fluid. He was again burning with fever and could hardly talk.

"Maybe we should stay here for a day or two until you've had a chance to gain some strength."

Jeremy shook his head grimly, his eyes glassy. "No. We've got to go on. Tie me to the saddle if you have to, but get me home, Cam. *Please* get me home."

Tears welled in Jeremy's eyes, and Cam lowered him back on the blankets and covered him. "Whatever you want, Jer. I'll get the horses."

Cam packed; it took less time each day as their food supply dwindled. Now he had to decide which creek to take. Ahead lay snow. To the west there was no snow, only interminable forests. He started up the west branch, climbing ever higher until they had to leave the creek to reach the crest of the mountains amid forests of giant trees such as he had never before seen. He welcomed their protection from the wind, glancing back every few minutes at Jeremy.

They dropped down into another canyon, where they camped for the night along another stream.

In the morning Jeremy was no better, but urged Cam to go on, so they followed the river as it swung northwest through the giant forests. By nightfall Cam heard a low, constant thunder. He was frightened and uncertain. When he knelt to pray that night, after Jeremy was asleep, tears ran freely from his eyes as he implored God and all the saints to come to his aid. He slept with hope that his prayers would be answered.

Jeremy was delirious in the morning. Cam tied him to the saddle and they started out. The valley of the river widened, and before Cam lay golden sand banks with a vast gray-blue ocean beyond. He led the horses forward, excited by the view, as they followed the river to where it formed a small bay and he could see the thundering waves crash against the beach.

He turned north, relieved to be out of the mountains, with the coast to follow. There would only be the decision as to when he must cross the mountains again and find the valley, but he guessed he would know the right place when he saw the Indians who lived along the coast. Elitah had been one of them.

By evening Cam was frightened again, not only for himself, but for Jeremy. Jeremy was digging at his itching sores and they were oozing a vile-smelling fluid. The sores were ringed now with bright red circles and his skin was swollen. His fever was increasing, and Cam was afraid he would go into a coma and die. He cried for water but couldn't drink, and his body was wasting away to a skeleton.

Cam bathed Jeremy in saltwater, hoping to ease the itching, and finally Jeremy slept. Cam stretched the tent over driftwood so he could build a fire under it to keep them warm and the smoke could escape. He finally slept, sitting up with his back against a driftwood log that looked as if it was from one of the giants growing on the mountains rising from the beach.

They crossed a river at low tide, the horses having to swim only a narrow channel. The hard sand along the ocean made a good and fast trail as long as they could travel it, but rugged promontories jutted into the ocean from the mountains. Here Cam had to fight the dense and dripping underbrush, knowing he was racing against time.

He had to stop before dark the next day. Jeremy was unconscious. Cam made a shelter and built up the fire. He sat with Jeremy's disease-ravaged head in his lap and cried. Jeremy was dying and he couldn't stop it, and all his prayers had been in vain. He shouted against the roar of the ocean all his anger, distress, and fear.

Cam finally fell asleep with tears drying against his face, his body wrung of every emotion and incapable of uttering another wrenching sob. When he awoke in the morning, Jeremy's head was still in his lap, his face calm and ghastly pale. He felt Jeremy's forehead and it was deathly cool. Jeremy was dead, but he couldn't help calling his name, frantically. He was alone, more alone than he'd ever been in his life, and afraid. He wept and wondered what he should do. Should he bury Jeremy here? He couldn't. Not on this wild and lonely beach. He had to take him home. That had been Jeremy's wish, and he would follow it. Somehow he had to get home. Hurriedly, he scrambled away from Jeremy. He had to get Jeremy over his horse before he stiffened, or he would have to leave him here.

He saddled Jeremy's horse and loaded him with the blanket-wrapped form, tying it securely, feeling already the resistance of stiffening flesh. He quickly took down the tent and loaded the other horses, noticing their gauntness, adding to his anxiety. Wind-whipped and rain-washed at times, Cam presented a forlorn figure with his tragic cargo as he traveled ever northward. Indians watched him pass, but stayed away as they recognized a death bundle across the saddle.

As he followed the ocean shoreline in the direction he hoped would lead him home, he was filled with anxiety and prayed constantly for guidance and forgiveness. He wondered if he, too, would get what Jeremy had had. He tried to believe it was a disease only communicable by intimacy between men and women, but the uncertainty of what it really was haunted him. Even more disturbing to him was the fact that if it was contagious, he would be taking it to the very people he cared the most about. To Marlette, Abigail, the Jessups, and Ross. Ross. He would give anything if Ross were with him now. He realized how wrong he had been to condemn Ross. He could even smile wryly as he thought of his own decadence. He remembered all too clearly what Ross had told him. From the beginning, Ross had warned him about putting him on a pedestal, but Cam had needed a hero to look up to. He saw it all too clearly for the first time. He supposed Ross could even be right about Liz Jessup, but he didn't want to think so. He understood Ross now—understood how a man could be blinded by his own ego and find himself in a position he didn't realize he was in. He had been there. He would, when he reached home, tell Ross what he felt.

He realized it wasn't Ross who had driven him away, but he himself who had created the wall between them. He had wanted so much to be like Ross, and when he had failed, he had resented Ross instead. He had resented Ross's self-confidence, his quiet strength and ability to handle every situation, even violence, with adeptness. He had even resented Ross's attraction among women. But not now. He hoped he would never again let anything come between himself and Ross.

He began seeing more Indian signs along the beaches and even rode up on some who were fishing in the rivers. He used sign language and the few words of Chinook jargon he had picked up while Elitah had been with them, and asked for the Tillamooks. The Indians always pointed north.

Another bluff rose ahead and Cam turned inland to circumnavigate this latest obstacle, fighting his way through a tangle of dense undergrowth and shore pine. When he had at last reached the top of the bluff he found his way blocked by a huge bay stretching inland for miles and surrounded by vast swampy marshes. He would have to go out of his way for miles to get around it and he wept with despair. He was beginning to feel feverish and aching. The last of the fish the Indians had given him had made him sick. He tried to believe it was the putrid smell of Jeremy's body, but he knew better, and was afraid he wasn't going to make it.

By late evening he was in the foothills of the mountains. He could see no snow ahead, only the dense, forested slopes of the mountains. He decided to go on over the mountains in hopes of finding the trail they had used when riding south to California. He reasoned it had to be somewhere across the range of mountains. He stopped for the night near a clear, swift stream where a lush meadow would provide feed for the horses. He didn't want food now; the thought of it made his stomach turn, and panic gripped him as he thought of dying as Jeremy had died.

By mid-afternoon of the next day, he crossed the summit of the mountains, still heading generally east. The country began to look familiar, and by evening he was sure the river he stopped by with its plainly marked fording place was the one they had crossed going south. He was too sick and too tired to care now—too sick even to light a fire as he left the horses saddled and loaded, and wrapped himself in blankets against the chills accompanying his fever.

In the morning his fever had subsided enough that he was able to catch the horses and get into the saddle, but he realized this river was running too deep and swift to be crossed easily at this point. Cam sat staring helplessly at the high, rushing stream, wondering what he should do. He looked upstream anxiously, and his eyes caught sight of what appeared to be a canoe. He rode toward it, dismounted, and walked unsteadily toward the hewn-log craft. Perhaps if he traded them a horse, the Indians who owned it would let him use the canoe.

He unloaded one of the pack horses and looked around for the Indians. They were hiding nearby, clearly afraid, but two of them came over in response to his signals. They examined the horse and, satisfied it was an acceptable trade, untied it and disappeared as silently as they had come. Cam breathed a sigh of relief and turned back to the canoe.

When he was ready to ferry his things across the river, he looked in the underbrush and found the canoe paddle. He unloaded the horses and put the packs in the canoe, undecided how to get the horses and canoe across. If he left the horses, the Indians could come back and steal them, but how would he have strength enough to manage both in the rushing river?

Suddenly he heard a command given in an Indian voice close to him. He looked around in panic, reaching desperately for his rifle, but what he saw put his fears to rest. The Indians were dragging more canoes out of the underbrush. The Indian who had stopped him with his command was gesturing in such a manner that could only mean they were going to help him. The canoes were brought close to each side of his, and the Indians deftly cut holes in his canoe and ran lines between it and their canoes. Three more Indians mounted his horses and urged them into the water, while Cam was motioned into his pack-laden craft. As soon as he was in, the Indians manning the canoes pushed off and the wild current caught the canoes and swept them downstream.

They finally landed on the opposite bank a good ways downstream from where they had started, and cut free from Cam's canoe, just as the other Indians arrived with his horses. They immediately jumped into the canoes and shoved off into the river again, leaving Cam with tears in his eyes as he tried in vain to make them understand his gratitude.

He reloaded his horses and wearily started north again, his agony and illness intensifying as the day passed. At dusk, when he finally had to stop, he noticed the beginnings of the rash on the backs of his hands and knew with frightening certainty he had Jeremy's disease.

The next evening, when he crossed the crest of the hills he was traveling over, he saw the Willamette Valley and could rejoice. He knew where he was now and that it was less than three days' ride to Ross's.

Two more days of riding brought him close to the settlement around the Willamette Institute. The feeling of relative well-being that had aided him to travel long days since entering the valley was leaving him. He wanted more than anything to give himself into someone's capable hands so he could collapse into unconsciousness and have this misery end. But the desperate need to see Ross one more time before he died and to fulfill his promise to Jeremy surmounted his own desire to find a place of refuge. He skirted the settlement of Salem and found a secluded woods to spend the night.

He avoided the small Catholic settlement at St. Paul, and rode on toward Champoeg, leaving the road near this larger township and returning to the road well beyond it. He was growing weaker and was covered now with a cold sweat as he clung desperately to the saddle. His horses were quickening their lagging steps, their ears pricked forward with expectancy as they neared home. Home! He thanked God he would live to see it and maybe live to tell Ross he was sorry. They crossed the shallow creek, went up the gentle slope, and turned into the lane. Marlette was on the porch before he reached the gate to her yard. She must have seen him from the kitchen window.

"Cam!" she called excitedly. "Cam! Is it really you?" She came down the steps toward him, smiling her welcome, then stopping as she got close enough to notice his appearance.

He slid from the saddle and almost crumpled, hanging onto his horse with his head partially hidden against the animal. She came toward him again, questioning, "Cam? Cam!"

He answered, "Yes, Marlette, it's me."

"Cam, what's wrong? What's happened?"

"I'm sick. Awful sick."

She moved toward him again, alarm wiping all gladness from her face.

He waved her back. "Stop, Marlette! Don't come any closer. Jeremy is dead. On the horse. He had it, too. I don't know what it is. I got it from him. I need a doctor. I didn't know where else to go. God forgive me!"

He took one staggering step away from the horse and turned so she could see him, and her face went white. "Oh, Cam," her voice choked, "let me get Ross."

She turned and went down the fence toward the barn, walking with a heaviness he hadn't seen since Abigail was born. He leaned heavily against the top rail, his elbows hooked over it so he wouldn't fall. But his head was too heavy, and he cradled his face in his hands and closed his eyes as darkness whirled at the edges of his consciousness.

He didn't know Ross was there until he heard his voice. "Cam."

Cam pulled his head up with an effort and saw Ross standing in front of him, looking at him with a tenderness he didn't think possible for one man to show another. Cam knew here stood the only

301

person in the world who would give his life to save him, and tears started down his cheeks. He mustn't let that happen. In an almost incoherent voice, he cried, "Don't touch me. Oh God, Ross, I'm sorry. I didn't know where to go—what to do. I need a doctor. I'm dying."

He felt himself sinking to the ground. Ross came around the gatepost and caught him, and the tenderness that was in his eyes was echoed in his voice. "Hang on, Cam. You'll make it. Now let's get you into the house and into bed." He lifted Cam over his shoulder, and Cam heard him say to Marlette, "Get Abigail and stay in the kitchen with Martha."

The trip into the house seemed like an eternity. Ross lowered him to the bed and Cam's eyes opened. It was Abigail's room. Her rag doll lay on the chair nearby and Ross covered the doll with the buffalo-hide coat. Cam tried to protest, but his throat was so swollen he could only moan unintelligibly. God, he was thirsty! He swayed toward the pillow, wanting to lie down, but Ross held him until his grimy shirt was off. Soon his pants and boots were off and he could lie down. Ross covered him, and he felt blessed relief and slept.

How long he slept he didn't know, but something awakened him. His eyes opened, and he saw that the door was open. He heard the sound of his heavy coat make a soft thud on the floor. Abigail was picking up her doll. His mind shouted she shouldn't be here, and he raised his head and tried to yell, "Abigail!"

Abigail started and turned to the sound of his voice. She screamed in terror as she saw him and dropped the doll and ran crying from the room. He heard Marlette's voice, and shortly Marlette came into the room to get the doll and went out, closing the door. Cam could still hear the little girl's sobbing and Marlette's voice trying to soothe her. He slept again.

Much later the door opened again, and Cam's eyes opened, but there was only blackness and he wondered for a moment if he was blind. Panic made him lurch, but then a lamp was lit, and he saw Ross and another man through a shimmering haze. He lay back and closed his eyes as they uncovered him. A voice, not Ross's, said, "It's smallpox all right. You got a heifer on the place?"

"Yes. Why?"

"Ever hear about vaccination?"

"No. What is it?"

"It's a way to try and prevent this disease. I'll take some fluid from his pox and introduce it into the skin on the udder of a heifer. In a few days she should develop a case of cow pox. When she does, I can take the fluid from her pox and vaccinate the rest of you with it. Hopefully, it will be soon enough to prevent you from getting it. Do you want me to try?''

"Yes. But what about Cam?''

"Too late to vaccinate him. We'll just have to wait and see. I've seen a few who lived. Maybe he'll be lucky. He doesn't seem to be heavily covered with the rash, other than his face and arms and the insides of his legs. I wonder who else he's been in contact with. We could have a smallpox epidemic started here if he infected anyone else.''

They both looked with questioning eyes at him. Ross asked, "Is there anyone else who might have been close enough to you to get this from you?''

The look in the doctor's eyes made Cam struggle to speak, and he rasped, "No one got close, except Indians. What can we do?''

"Well, nothing for now, except I better get out a warning to the valley people to avoid the Indians you might have been in contact with. Do you know which ones you might have infected, son?''

Cam shook his head weakly, whispering, "No. Just south end of the valley and along the coast to California.''

"Well that's some relief; at least they're not too close to us here. Now, what about the other boy?''

"Jeremy has been dead for several days, I think,'' said Ross.

"We'll have to get him buried quickly. Who's his family?''

"The Jessups down the road. I stopped there to let them know, but told them to wait until you had had a chance to come before they came for him.''

"Good. We'll have to quarantine and vaccinate them, too, just in case you took it to them. By no means must they be allowed to see the dead boy.''

"You mean I am carrying it now?''

"You touched this boy. It seems like it takes even less than that to spread it. What did you do with his clothes?''

"I gave them to Martha to wash.''

"Better burn them—and that coat, too, if it was on him.''

They left the room, and Cam lay slowly comprehending the doctor's words. Panic clutched his heart. If touching him or his clothes could pass the disease, then Abigail's doll would be lethal. Oh, God! He had given it to all of them! He started to pray, but the words were lost in the great horror blanketing his mind. He was going to die, and so was everyone else he had come in contact with.

The doctor came back, Cam didn't know when. Time had no meaning and no relativity to anything now. He was barely aware of anything for the next few days except the torture of his own body. He felt as if he were on fire, and his thirst was so great he moaned for water. He clawed at his body as the pustules swelled and irritated his skin. He wasn't even aware when they bound him, only knew he couldn't scratch anymore, and he writhed in agony. In lucid moments he knew exactly what was happening and how he looked. The terrible anxiety he had known for Jeremy was even worse for his own condition. He wanted to die. He wanted the choking, gagging stench that was filling his nostrils from the putrid eruptions to come to an end. But the greatest anxiety of all was to know that what he was going through, so would the others go through until death claimed them.

24. Jenny

CAM AWOKE SLOWLY, as if rising upward through a thick, heavy bog. He was aware that the agonizing burning had subsided. As he tentatively opened his eyes, a great blackness was all he could see and he wondered if he were dead. But as he became more awake, he could feel the comfort of the bed in which he lay and the quilt that covered him and the rags that bound his arms and the foul smell of his own scabbing body. Wonder filled him—wonder that he was alive. Hope replaced amazement as he realized that if he could still be alive, those he had infected could live, too. He wanted to let someone know he was better. He wanted a drink desperately, but his hands were still bound and he was so weak he couldn't move. He wasn't sure he could even speak and didn't try. He had no idea what time it was. They could all be asleep or, worse, sick by now. He had no way of knowing. All he could do was wait, helplessly.

He only had strength to keep his eyes open and listen. A faint light brightened the window and he rejoiced that he was not blind, as he had so often feared during the nightmare of his disease. He heard noises in the kitchen. Martha was up. The stove lid clanged as she removed it to start a fire. Soon he heard Abigail's voice. She was in Ross and Marlette's room, and she was awakening them like the chirping birds he could hear outside. Hear! He could hear! He wasn't deaf! With growing joy, he waited for them to come to him. Then he wondered with despair if they might not come. Perhaps they thought he was dead and would never open his door.

He lay a long while before the door opened and the doctor and Ross came in. They took one look at him, and the doctor laughed. "By Jove! He's made it!" He bent to feel Cam's head and announced, "The fever's gone. He's really made it!"

Ross asked, "Can we untie his hands?"

The doctor answered, "By all means. I'll do it. You get him some water. Perhaps he can drink now."

Cam tried to talk, tried to say, "Water," affirmatively, but all he heard was a strangled gasp.

The doctor patted his arm. "Easy, son. We'll get you taken care of here." Then he smiled and said, "Thank God you made it."

Ross came back with the water and they lifted his head. It took every bit of what strength he had left to get one swallow down, but it was like ambrosia. Ross raised the cup again, but he couldn't swallow the second time.

The doctor said, "Wait a bit. He's too weak."

Ross laid him back gently, and Cam could see the joy in Ross's moist eyes and feel the tenderness of his hand as he held Cam's. He knew he was loved, but he needed to know more than Ross's love. He had to know if the others were still well. With difficulty, he whispered, "The others?"

Ross heard him and answered, "Everyone is still well. The doctor has vaccinated everyone here and at the Jessups. In a few more days, we should know if we have it or not. Would you like to try the water again?"

Cam gave a feeble nod, and Ross lifted him and held the cup to his lips. He was able to swallow more this time before his throat failed him. They left him to rest for a while, and then Ross came back with a steaming bowl. "Martha's made some soup stock for you. Do you feel like eating?"

He wanted to eat more than anything else. His wasted body cried for nourishment. He nodded again, and Ross sat beside him stirring the steaming brew. He had to set the bowl down to lift Cam's head and with his other hand filled the spoon and blew on it to cool it before slipping it into Cam's waiting mouth. He swallowed and opened his mouth for more. He took several spoonfuls before he couldn't swallow, and raised his hand weakly for Ross to stop. The movement left him shaking and sweating.

In a few minutes Ross fed him more, but his shrunken stomach wouldn't hold much. He had to wave Ross away again and lay feeling uncomfortably full. He was desperate now in a new way. He'd never been able to speak to Ross about his feelings. Now he wanted to, but he was too weak. Tears filled his eyes, and Ross saw them as they spilled down his cheeks.

Ross looked at him, concerned.

"Cam, what is it? Do you hurt somewhere?"

He struggled to answer, "No," his voice shaking as much from weakness as from emotion. He lifted his hand, placed it on Ross's arm, and tried to press his fingers around Ross's strong arm. But he had no strength and the hand lay there limply.

Ross put his hand on Cam's and squeezed very gently. Tears filled his dark eyes. "It's going to be all right, Cam. Don't worry. Now try to get some rest. I'll come back in a little while and we'll try to get more of Martha's soup down you."

Cam nodded and closed his eyes.

When Ross came back, Cam was feeling stronger. He drank water and ate more soup. With the liquid soothing his tortured throat, he felt he could talk and said in a husky whisper, "Ross, I need to talk to you."

"Cam, it can wait. You'd better rest and try to get your strength back."

"No. This can't wait. A lot of things have happened to me since I left here. I've done a lot of thinking while I was riding back with Jeremy, and even before that. I realized something about myself. I realized the way I felt about you was because of the way I felt about myself. I don't resent you anymore, and if it's all right with you, I'd like to stay with you. I never learned all you had to teach me, but I think I can now."

Ross smiled and put his hand over Cam's. "I think you've learned a great deal already. You left here a boy, but you've come back a man."

Cam smiled at the words and shook his head. "No, not yet, but I'm closer than I was."

"Do you want some more soup?"

"Yes."

Ross fed him some more soup, but he was soon full again and whispered tiredly, "Enough, for now."

Ross stood and Cam said, his voice weak, "There's something else."

Ross turned and sat back down beside him, and Cam continued in a soft whisper, "I'm sorry for the way I left here last fall. Elitah came and offered herself to me. It was a trade, really—her body if

307

I'd take her to California with me. I took her, like she said, but not the first time. She wanted it. Is she all right?"

"Yes."

"Where is she now?"

"I took her to the Catholic school at St. Paul."

Cam looked away, the conflicting emotions about Elitah rising with his guilt about what had happened.

Ross asked, "Are you blaming yourself for what happened with her?"

Without looking back, Cam answered softly, "Yes."

"You shouldn't. She was using you, Cam. She knew if you left, she would have to go there. She didn't want to. I realized what she was trying to do when she told me you raped her. I don't blame you, and you shouldn't blame yourself."

Cam felt the guilt dissolve and looked back with a smile, relieved to know Ross understood. Elitah could be forgotten—there was no reason not to, except the memory of her.

Ross smiled again. "Is that all?"

Cam nodded and Ross left him, and he slept.

The next day the doctor prescribed a bath in hopes of ridding Cam of the stinking masses of drying pus encrusting the parts of his body covered with the pox. They carried in the tub and filled it with warm water, and submerged his frail and shaking body. He was only now aware of how much weight he had lost. He was no more than skin and bone. While Cam soaked, Ross removed the straw tick and soiled bedding, preparing him a clean bed. Cam climbed wearily into it.

The doctor left the room to carry the soiled bedding away to the fire. In a few minutes he stuck his head in the room and said, "A lady visitor is here to see Cam."

"Who?" he questioned weakly, afraid of the answer.

"Miss Jessup."

His heart squeezed in pain. Why had they let her come? Surely they would know he couldn't see anyone like he was now. Harshly, he said, "I don't want to see her."

But the words were hardly out of his mouth when Jenny pushed through the door, her step eager and her smile glad. He turned his head away, not wanting her to see his face. He heard her gasp, "Oh, Cam!" Footsteps moved away from him and out the door. There was silence and he thought she had gone. He turned back, and she was still there, looking white. It was Ross who had left the room. Jenny's eyes widened, and she looked stricken as she stared at his face. He saw her gag from the lingering smell of his infected flesh, and her hands flew to her mouth as she turned and ran from the room.

When the doctor came back in to remove the water from the tub, Cam asked angrily, "Why did you let her come? Don't let her in here again."

The doctor straightened up and looked at him over the tops of the round glasses that had fallen down his nose. "Take it easy, Cam. We didn't ask her to come. She came because she wanted to see you. She ignored the quarantine and her own safety. We can't send her away. She's a carrier now and a threat to the others. She'll have to stay here until we've all been through the incubation period."

Cam lay there, anger wearing his body into weakness. Damn her, he thought. Why did she have to be so foolish? Before he could answer that question, he slept.

It was a couple more days before Jenny came into Cam's room again. He didn't even hear her. He was looking out the window toward the timbered hill, watching the cows and wondering if the heifer the doctor infected had died.

"Cam," she said softly.

He turned his head with an angry jerk. "What are you doing in here? Get out of here and don't come back."

He saw the frightened, staring look on her face as if she were hypnotized by the ugliness of him and couldn't tear her gaze away. "Cam, I'm sorry; forgive me. I had to come see you. Please don't send me away. I must talk to you."

"Why? I have nothing to say to you."

"Yes, you do. You were with Jeremy when he died. I want to know how he got sick."

"Jenny, there is no point in you knowing. There is nothing you can do about it."

"He was my brother and I want to know. Please tell me. Who was he with? Who gave him smallpox?"

"A woman."

She looked horrified. "I don't believe you!"

"If you don't believe me, then you might as well leave." He didn't try to keep the irritation out of his voice.

"Cam," she cried, "why are you acting like this? I have a right to know. You took my brother to California, and you brought him back dead! Now tell me what happened. Why weren't you looking out for him?"

"Jenny, he was old enough to look out for himself."

"He wasn't that kind of man!"

"How do you know what kind of man he was? You weren't there."

"And apparently you weren't either. Where were you, Cam Galligher?"

"You see my face? You see the broken nose and the scars besides the pox? I got the hell beat out of me, and I was in no shape to follow Jeremy around for a while. Custis Wood told me the last woman he saw Jeremy with was a Chinese girl."

"What was he doing with a Chinese girl?" She seemed amazed.

"Oh come on, Jenny, you're not so dumb you don't know what a man does with a woman?"

The harsh sarcasm in his voice had its effect on Jenny, and her face flamed. She rose abruptly and ran from the room, but not before he saw her face crumpling into tears.

He lay angry and disturbed by Jenny's probing questions. He had been hard on her, unnecessarily hard, and he realized part of it had been anger at himself.

Ross came in shortly and said with a gentle reprimand, "Weren't you a little harsh with her?"

"I meant to be."

"Why? All she wanted was to be with you and to know about Jeremy. She still loves you."

"She's in love with the memory of a boy she thought she knew. She doesn't know me. Look at me! I don't even look the same."

"That still doesn't give you the right to hurt her. Couldn't you tell her about her brother?"

"I tried, but she doesn't want to believe the truth."

"Then try me. Maybe I can tell her."

"All right. She wanted to know who gave Jeremy the disease. I can't answer that. All I know is Custis Wood said he saw Jeremy with a Chinese girl before he went back up to the claim. Jenny wants to know why I wasn't with him, protecting him from women. I don't have to tell you the answer to that. For most of the

310

winter, we had nothing better to do than drink ourselves blind, or gamble. Jeremy wanted a woman, and when some finally came to the flat, he bought himself some time with one of them. The first night he did, I went back to the saloon we usually drank at and got drunk. When I started to leave, I fell across a table where some men were playing poker. I must have ruined a really big hand. I didn't know a thing after the first fist hit me in the face. All I know is I woke up in the bed of the woman who owned the saloon, with broken ribs, broken nose, and black eyes, not to mention broken lips and teeth. I couldn't have protected Jeremy if I'd wanted to. Jeremy came to see me every day for the first few days, and then he went up to the claim. By the time he got back, I was better and I was working in the saloon, but he wouldn't stay and use my money. He wanted to go back up to the claim, and when he didn't come back, I got worried and went up looking for him. I found him sick and he wanted to come home. I brought him home. It's as simple as that."

Ross was silent for a moment, then said, "No, I don't think it was quite as simple as that, but I'll tell Jenny. Maybe it will satisfy her."

"I doubt it, but you have my thanks for trying."

Jenny brought in his supper that evening, her deep blue-violet eyes wide and tender as she looked at him. "Cam, I'm sorry about this morning. I didn't stop to realize what you've been through. I was rude and unfeeling. Will you forgive me?"

He pulled himself up to a sitting position to receive the tray she held, and waved away her apology. "There's nothing to forgive."

She set the tray in his lap and, as he reached for the spoon, took his hand. He looked up at her, anger beginning again. He shook off her hand and said, exasperation in his voice, "Jenny, cut it out!"

She turned away but didn't leave, sitting in the chair instead. He ate slowly, hoping she would tire of watching him and leave, but she didn't. He held up the tray to her when he was done, but she only set it on the floor and sat back in the chair. "I'd like to hear more about what you and Jeremy did. Would it bother you to talk about it to me?"

"Yes," he answered softly.

"Please, Cam. Maybe it would help if you could talk to someone. I want so to know."

311

"Why, Jenny? Why is it so important to know?"

"Cam, don't you understand? I loved my brother. I want to know everything about what happened to him. It's all I have left of him—what you can tell me."

He looked at her as she waited expectantly, her eyes imploring, her mouth slightly parted, the cheeks highly colored and flawless, surrounded by waves of thick black hair. She was lovely—he had to admit—lovely.

"All right. What do you want to know?"

Her smile was brilliant. "Oh, thank you, Cam. I knew if you understood you wouldn't mind, and I'll try to understand if you don't want to tell me something. I'd like to hear about the whole trip—what happened on the way to California—everything."

He described their trip to California, their first attempts to find gold, and how they had eventually discovered a rich pocket. And he told her about the days they spent at Doll's Place, talking to the other miners and playing cards. He paused as he remembered what followed, but he was sure Ross had told her as much as she needed to know about that time. He finished, "That's just about all there is to know up to the time Jeremy got sick."

She looked at her clasped hands for a long moment, and he didn't know whether she was satisfied or not with what he had told her. Perhaps she, like Ross, sensed there was more. Still looking at her hands, she asked, her voice very soft and with a sweetness he hadn't noticed before, "Would you mind telling me where Jeremy died—that is, if you want to?"

Flatly, he answered, "By the ocean."

"The ocean? How did you get by the ocean?"

He sighed. He was tiring, and he didn't necessarily want to remember the night of Jeremy's death, but her question had already started the memory of that terrible trip unfolding in his mind. He turned his eyes away from her and looked out the window, saying, "We were by the ocean because there was still snow in the mountains and I didn't think I could get through any other way. It was Jeremy's wish to come home, and I followed that wish the best way I could." He closed his eyes and hoped she would leave now. He wanted to sleep and forget.

She started to cry softly, and he turned his head back toward her and opened his eyes. Her face was in her hands, her hair cascading down over her shoulders. He wondered if this was the first time she had cried for Jeremy. Perhaps hearing about his death made it real. He felt sorry for her and sorry for the way he had treated her, and he gently told her so.

She brushed away her tears and raised her face to look at him. Tremulously, she said, "I'm glad you're all right, Cam." She bent over for the tray and rose with it, leaving him alone.

Cam was able to get up in the next few days, but he was still weak and had to rest often. Jenny was constantly by his side, willing and ready to help him. He felt guilty and embarrassed by her attention, except when he could sit and watch her play with Abigail. At these times she was more girl than woman and he felt less threatened by her presence.

But these few happy days came to an abrupt end when Ross became ill, aching, and feverish as he and Jeremy had been in the first stage of the disease. Within the next two days, Marlette, Abigail, and Martha, followed by the doctor, all became sick. Cam was frightened. Only he and Jenny were well, and he didn't know how long it would be before Jenny, too, would go down.

He had to have help and knew of only one person he could ask. Jenny was at the stove, stirring a pot of broth, when he came into the kitchen and passed her on his way out the back door.

"Where are you going?"

"To get Jacques. We're going to need some help."

"Cam, are you sure you're strong enough? Maybe I should go."

"Jenny," he said irritably, "I can make it to his cabin and back."

"He's not at his cabin, Cam."

"Then where is he?" His patience was growing short.

"You don't know, do you? Jacques is living at our place now. He and Mother were married last winter."

Surprise wiped away the irritation. "Jacques and your mother! I don't believe it. How?"

"Well, when she finally realized she could never have Ross, I guess she decided Jacques was better than no man at all, and he adores her."

Dumbfounded, Cam asked, "Your mother loved Ross?"

"Well, maybe love isn't exactly the right word. She liked Ross very much. He isn't hard to like, you know."

313

He had a sinking feeling. "Even after what he tried to do at Fort Boise?"

"Oh, Cam. You still think that was Ross's fault, don't you? It wasn't. It was Mother's."

"How do you know?" He looked at her in amazement. She had only been a child of fourteen at the time. How could she have known?

"Jon told us last winter."

"But how did he know, and why would he tell you now after all this time? It doesn't make sense."

"Yes, it does. You see, Jacques wanted Ross to be his witness when he and Mother married, but Jeremy, Joseph, and I were against it because of what we thought Ross had done. Jon told us what happened wasn't Ross's fault."

"But how could he know?"

"He didn't tell us exactly. Only that he was convinced Ross did not take advantage of Mother. Surely you remember how upset she was when Father was killed? She was nearly crazy. At times I thought she was."

He murmured, "I remember," and went out the door, unable to face her any longer with the shame he felt engulfing him. Now he knew why Jon had seemingly betrayed them and showed an understanding and compassion for Ross none of the rest of them had. He was even more conscious than ever of the terrible injustice of his feelings for Ross, and all the more desperate to repay Ross for that injustice.

He saddled a horse, shaking from the effort, and mounted after several attempts. He was still far from normal. He sent the horse at a gallop along the road to the Jessup cabin. Jonathan and Joseph were in the yard cutting wood. Joseph straightened up and smiled. "Cam! What brings you here? Hey, it's good to see you."

"Thanks, Joe. I'm more than glad to see you're all right. No sickness here yet?"

"No. How about at Ross's? How's Jenny?"

"She's fine, but that's why I came. Everyone else is sick. We're going to need some help. Would you call Jacques for me?"

Joseph buried the axe in the piece of wood he was cutting and turned, but Jonathan stopped him, staring coldly at Cam. "Wait, Joe. Cam, you took Jeremy away and brought him home dead,

314

and now you've got our sister. I'll be damned if you're going to take Jacques away from my mother, too."

The door opened before Jonathan finished, and Jacques stood listening. He stepped down off the porch and stopped between Cam and Jon. "Jon! You cannot speak for me." He turned to Cam and said, "Mon Dieu! You look like you have been to hell and back." He reached for Cam's hand and Cam took it, feeling the warmth of this man and noticing a striking difference in his appearance. Jacques, the big bear of a man, had been shorn. Nothing was left of his great mass of beard; only a smartly curled mustache graced his face. For the first time his chin was visible, and it was a strong, square, clefted, and handsome chin.

"Jacques, it is good to see you. I have been to hell and back."

Another voice cut across Cam's, and the sharpness of it surprised him. "Why didn't you stay there?"

He raised his eyes and saw Liz at the door of the cabin, her eyes flashing with anger and pain.

He answered, with compassion in his voice, "I'm sorry, Mrs. Jessup. I loved Jeremy, too. I would gladly exchange places with him, but I can't."

She whirled away and slammed the door, and Cam felt Jacques squeeze his hand reassuringly. "Cam, forgive her. She grieves deeply."

"I know. Jacques, Ross is sick, and so is everyone else at the house except Jenny. I need help."

The light went out of Jacques's eyes. "I will get my horse and follow you in a few minutes. I must speak to Liz—then Jacques will come."

Cam nodded and turned his horse away without a backward glance at Joseph or Jonathan. He had meant what he said to Liz, but it did not erase the guilt he felt for having survived.

Jenny was still in the kitchen when he returned. She looked at him with questioning eyes, afraid to put into words what she wanted to know. He answered her unspoken question. "Everyone is still all right at your place. Jacques is coming."

Her smile was relieved.

"How are they?" He nodded his head toward the bedrooms.

"No change."

Cam walked on through the front room into Ross's bedroom. Marlette and Abigail lay curled together in the bed, Marlette holding the whimpering child and making shushing noises. Ross sat wrapped in a blanket, keeping the fire going, his eyes glazed with fever and his face drawn and bleak.

"Jacques is coming to help."

Ross nodded.

"Can I get you anything?"

"No. I'm not hungry. How are Martha and the doctor?"

"The same."

Ross closed his eyes, and Cam left the room. He was shaking as he walked back into the kitchen.

Jenny looked up and said, "Cam, come sit down and let me get you something to eat. You look tired."

She ladled him a hot bowl full of the rich broth she had been cooking. His hand shook and he spilled more than he ate.

Finally, Jenny came over. "Let me help you." She touched his hand to take the spoon, and suddenly he was crying uncontrollably. She held his head against her, and he wrapped his arms around her, holding her fiercely, in desperation, his voice broken with anguish as he poured out his fear. "They're going to die and it's my fault. Oh, Jenny, what can I do?"

Her voice was soft and sweet and soothing as she answered, "Cam, Cam. There is nothing you can do—only hope and pray, as I did for you, that God will grant them the same mercy He showed you."

He knew she was right. It was too late now to worry about what had already happened and could not be changed. He fought back the tears and released her. She dropped her arms from him but didn't move. He looked up at her, and her eyes were deep, expectant. There was something happening to him and he wasn't sure what it was, but he wanted to kiss her. Slowly he rose, facing her. She didn't move, her body touching his ever so slightly. "Jenny," he whispered. She stood still, her eyes wistful, longing. He touched his lips to hers and felt her arms slide around him and hold him as he held her for a few breathless moments.

The back door opened, and the magic was gone as Jacques came in.

"So!" He smiled at them, his eyes teasing and full of laughter. "What have we here?"

Jenny cried, "Jacques!" and ran into his open arms, hugging him.

"Ah, ma petite, Jacques is so glad to see you!"

Cam watched their reunion and felt the obvious affection between the man and his stepdaughter. Jacques winked at Cam, and he knew what Jacques was thinking. Impetuous Jacques was concluding that Jenny had finally won him. Cam sat back down in his chair and, with a steadier hand, began eating his soup. Jenny, her arm around Jacques, led him in to see Ross, and Cam was alone to sort out his feelings about Jenny.

That night, when the house was quiet and Cam went to his room at last, he knelt beside his bed to begin again the prayer he had started so many agonizing days ago and now wanted to finish. Not for himself, but for Ross, Marlette, Abigail, Martha—and the doctor, who had come knowing his life, too, might be in jeopardy. He crossed himself and started to pray, but a soft tapping on the door interrupted his prayer and he rose and went to the door. Jenny stood looking up at him. She was in her nightgown and robe, her hair loose about her shoulders.

"What's wrong?"

"Nothing. I just wanted to be with you—to pray with you if you would like."

He looked at her, not knowing what to say, confusion showing on his face.

She smiled. "Will praying with me embarrass you?"

He recovered his voice and stepped back, opening the door for her. "No. Come in if you want."

She stood waiting for him to take the lead, and he dropped down on his knees beside the bed, feeling his face flush. She knelt quietly down beside him, clasping her hands and bowing her head. He crossed himself again, closing his eyes, and prayed in distracted silence. He prayed earnestly, but his concentration often wandered to the girl beside him, and finally he ended his prayer, feeling it would not be answered when he could not remember the words. He crossed himself and rose to his feet and, as she straightened, he held his hand out to help her up.

She rose and faced him, not drawing her hand away but holding his hand warmly, firmly. She smiled at him encouragingly, but he made no move to take her in his arms. Instead he was looking at her as if he were seeing her for the first time and wondering why he had never before noticed her breathtaking beauty. She was more beautiful even than Elitah because it was a beauty of innocence, where Elitah's was sensuous and wild. He was awed by her sweetness and poise, but most of all by the love he saw shining in her eyes for him.

Dumbly, he said, "Thank you, Jenny."

She released his hand and said, with her color rising, "Good night, Cam."

He closed the door and leaned against it. He didn't understand how she could love him. What woman in her right mind would want to love him as he now was? He gazed at his reflection in the mirror across the bed. The face gazing back was not his, not as he remembered it. It was gaunt, with sunken eyes and bright red lumps of the healing pox across his forehead and cheeks. The nose was humped and still looked as if it were being pressed against his face. Tiny threadlike scars ridged over the edges of bone at his eyes and the ragged, jagged beard did not yet cover either the scars around his mouth from his beating or the pock marks. He blew out the lamp violently, wanting to wipe out the reflection, and sat on the chair to pull off his boots. He lay down fully clothed on the bed, drawing a blanket over him, his thoughts still on Jenny. She must not be allowed to continue to think she loved him. He had already let their relationship become more than it should by kissing her. That kiss had given her hope—hope that he was finally falling in love with her. He would have to discourage that love from now on, for her own good.

Another anxious day passed while Jenny, Jacques, and Cam cared for the sick. A grim mask of despair settled over Cam's face as he watched the people he loved suffer with the pain, nausea, and fever of the disease. He knew all too well how they ached and how sick they were. That night he prayed again, but he prayed alone.

After an almost sleepless night, he rose early and went on quiet stocking feet to add more wood to the fires to warm the sickrooms. He opened the door to Ross and Marlette's room, and his heart ached as he saw Ross and Marlette with Abigail between them in the big bed, Abigail whimpering even as she slept a feverish sleep. Cam turned to the fire and gently poked it together. He quietly laid on small pieces of wood until the embers ignited them, and then added bigger pieces.

"Cam."

Ross's voice startled him, and he turned with apprehension.

Ross was sitting up. His face was calm and his eyes looked clear. Hopeful, Cam asked, "How do you feel?"

"Better. I think the fever's gone."

Cam moved closer, his hand automatically going to Ross's forehead. It was only warm, a normal warm. "Your head feels cool." With hope rising, he asked, "What about the rash?"

"Open the curtain so we can see."

Cam went to the window and opened the curtains, letting in a flood of early morning sun. Ross bared his lower torso. There was a definite fading of the rash, which had just the day before been bright red. Cam's prayers had been answered. A miracle had happened. Ross had fought off the disease. Tears swam over the edges of his eyes and ran down his face. He felt Ross's hand on his shoulder and heard his gentle, husky voice. "Cam."

The floodgates of Cam's emotions opened, and he embraced Ross as if he were something fragile and precious. Cam, in that moment, knew just how precious Ross was to him.

All day Cam lived with renewed hope and faith. By evening the miracle manifested itself again. The doctor's fever also broke, and his rash was disappearing. Cam slept undisturbed that night, but not before he offered a prayer of thanks.

But the miracle was over. Marlette, Abigail, and Martha were worse in the morning. The disfiguring rash was spreading now to their faces and arms. Hope was squeezed dry in Cam, and the joy he had known fled his heart. Ross now spent all of his time with Marlette and his child in a vigil of love. The doctor divided his time between Martha and Ross's bedroom, administering laudanum to ease their discomfort. Jacques and Cam did the heavy work. And Jenny worked hardest of all, keeping them fed and washing bedding and clothes daily in boiling water, and keeping the house clean. Cam permitted himself to look at her when she wasn't aware of his gaze. His heart skipped beats watching her work, dark tendrils of hair falling across her forehead to be brushed away by hands roughened in boiling water and lye soap.

The days passed with aching slowness as they watched and waited for the disease to reach its outcome. Ross grew even more haggard from sleeplessness as he held his wife and child in his arms. Finally Ross let Cam sit with them, and he went to Cam's room to sleep.

Jenny came into the room and he looked up. Softly, she said, "I'll sit with you if you like."

He shook his head. "You go to bed. You need to rest."

"No. I'm not sleepy. I want to stay with you. I don't want you to be alone."

"All right. I can't stop you."

His words hurt her, and her mouth trembled briefly as she pulled up a chair and sat close by. He stubbornly refused to acknowledge her, repeating to himself that it was for her own good. Finally, after an hour, she rose quietly and went back to the front room, where she made her bed on one of the long settees. His heart twisted as he watched her go, but logic told him it was necessary.

The worst stage of the smallpox set in as the pustules ripened and broke, their purulent fluid drying and crusting into vile-smelling scabs. The women and child were delirious now, the laudanum easing their agony as their bodies wasted away, just as Cam's was beginning to fill out once more with regained flesh.

In the morning Cam was helping Jenny as she sweated over the steaming tubs of wash on the back porch. Jacques came to the back door, his face pale and his eyes distressed. Cam was the first to see him and asked hoarsely, "Who?"

Jacques crossed himself and murmured, "Martha."

He heard Jenny utter a soft cry beside him and turned just as she started to tremble and cry. He caught her in his arms, and Jacques helped him lead her inside. Jacques held her until her crying stopped. The doctor came from Martha's room into the kitchen.

Cam asked, "What needs to be done now?"

"We'll need a coffin. Can you and Jacques build one?"

Jacques answered, "Oui."

"Then there'll be the grave to dig. Someplace where it won't be disturbed for a long time, if ever. Jenny, can you help me prepare her?"

Jenny wiped away her tears and nodded. Cam and Jacques went at once to start the coffin, and by late afternoon they had dug the grave on the hillside behind the house, where the spring flowers were fading. They carried the coffin to the grave at dusk. Jenny, a shawl over her dark hair, led them in prayer in a last good-bye to Marlette's trusted friend. Jacques stayed to cover the grave by lantern light while Cam went with Jenny and the doctor back to the house, too tired from what he had already done to help Jacques.

Cam awoke the next morning and thought he heard someone crying. He listened, straining his ears to sort out the sounds of birds chirping as dawn broke. He threw off his blanket, fear gripping his heart as he yanked open his door and barged into Ross's room. Ross sat in the chair by the bed, his face in his hands, sobbing quietly. Marlette lay on the bed, pale and quiet—deathly quiet—her disease-ravaged face peaceful in death.

"Oh, God!" Cam breathed, more a prayer than an oath as he crossed himself. Ross raised his head, his face ashen and wet with tears and twisted with grief, his body shaking. Seeing his tragic eyes, Cam backed out of the room, closed the door, and leaned against it, his own face white.

Jenny sat up on her bed and asked, "What is it?"

Cam's voice was hushed and strained as he answered, "Marlette is dead."

Jenny paled and got to her feet, crying, "Oh no, oh no!" She came running to him, and he took her in his arms and they stood crying together.

It was late afternoon before Ross came from his bedroom. Cam and Jacques had the coffin ready. It had been lined with their tears. The grave, too, waited on the hillside among the trillium and lamb's tongues, close to Martha's. Jenny and the doctor prepared Marlette for her final journey. Ross, as his last act of love, carried his wife and laid her in her coffin. He watched as Cam and Jacques sealed her forever from his sight, but he was too physically and emotionally exhausted to follow his wife to her grave. They would wait and bury Marlette in the morning. Cam stubbornly insisted Ross sleep in his room while he sat up with Abigail. Ross, too tired to protest, let Cam have his way.

Cam closed the door to Ross's bedroom and built up the fire again. There seemed to be a chill in the room. The May wind had blown cold at dark, and there could be frost by morning. He turned to the pathetic form of the blond-headed child, no longer beautiful to see, no longer laughing and curious. He choked and felt his heart, so drained by grief already, break with anguish. Fighting tears, he lifted the child from the bed, her wasted body even lighter than he expected. He wrapped a blanket around her barely breathing form and sat in the rocking chair and rocked her, tears glistening on his cheeks in the firelight. The rocking soothed him, if not his unaware babe, and he eventually dozed.

He awoke with a start. The fire was low and the room was almost in total darkness, except for the small glow of the last burning ember. He was alert and fully awake, feeling a strange prickling along his neck caused by something undefinable in the room. He clutched Abigail tighter, suddenly afraid, and felt her small body shudder ever so slightly and go limp in his arms. It was incredibly quiet, and he dared not even breathe as something held him in suspension, unable to move, or think, or speak. He felt something move upward and away, brushing his beard and cheek. His eyes followed the movement, but there was nothing he could see; he could only feel the life he held being drawn away from him, and he clutched her tighter to him, even as he knew with sudden profundity he could not stop her departing spirit.

Ross found him in the morning, still clutching Abigail's lifeless body. Ross stood above him looking down at Abigail. Cam, his voice quavering as the tears started down his cheeks, said, "I'm sorry, Ross."

Ross knelt down and looked at his daughter's face and felt her cool forehead. His eyes lifted to Cam's, and the calm there frightened Cam. He cried in anguish, "Ross, forgive me! I didn't know what to do! I had no place else to go! I would have rather died than bring this to you! You have every reason to hate me. To kill me! I'd welcome it. I love you and I've destroyed your family. God forgive me." He was crying too convulsively to continue. Ross pried Cam's stiffened hands from Abigail's body and laid her gently on the bed.

He turned back and stood with his hand on Cam's shaking shoulder. And the grip of that hand on his shoulder quieted Cam until he could look at Ross. There was an enduring strength in Ross that Cam had only fleetingly been aware of, but now, looking into his compelling eyes, he could see it.

With great tenderness, Ross said, "I don't blame you for this. You made the only choice you felt right. We all have to make those kinds of choices, Cam, and sometimes we never outlive the result of them. I don't blame you, or hate you, or want you dead. My only happiness is that you lived, because you are all I have left now."

And Cam realized as he looked at Ross that Ross understood the choices of life and had already made them in exactly the same way Cam had made his choice. He, too, would carry the burden of them the rest of his life, just as Cam would carry his. The dignity with which Ross carried them was what Cam needed now. It gave Cam strength and restored peace to his grief-stricken, guilt-ridden heart, and provided him with the courage to go on.

It took only a short while to make the small coffin to hold the child's body. The four men lifted Marlette's coffin, with the small one of Abigail's resting on top, and the quiet procession started across the meadow toward the hill where the grave dug the day before awaited its residents. Cam glanced back. Jenny came, her eyes down, black hair escaping the shawl clutched over her head, carrying a Bible. The sun was high above and warm. The earth exuded the odors of growing grass, fertile soil turned and ready for planting, and the rich, sweet fragrance of the cottonwood trees.

They lowered the coffins into the ground and Jenny, without opening her Bible, softly began the Twenty-third Psalm. When she finished, Cam sank to his knees and crossed himself. There was no self-consciousness now as he began to recite the rosary, his fingers holding an imaginary one in his hands. Jacques dropped to his knees, crossing himself, and softly joined Cam. Jenny knelt beside him, too, her head bowed. Before he was done, the tears were slowly easing from under his closed lids, but he didn't care. Jacques's voice, too, was choked. There was silence for a moment. Then Jenny's quavering voice began the Lord's Prayer. Cam and Jacques joined her. She rose when she finished, and Cam and Jacques, crossing themselves, rose together, their cheeks wet but their eyes calm. Jenny walked to the mound of dirt on the other side of the grave. Bending, she took a handful of the soft forest and let it trickle through her fingers into the grave. Then she turned away and walked with deliberate steps back to the house. Ross, his face stoic, followed with the doctor. Cam went to the mound, pulled free a shovel, and cast the first shovel of dirt into the grave. Jacques lifted the other shovel, and together they covered the last resting place of Ross's wife and child.

When they returned to the house, Jenny had supper ready. They ate more from need than desire, in silence for the most part, too numb with grief to talk. Tomorrow they would unburden their hearts of sadness, but not now.

Cam arose early and went outside to bring in wood for Jenny's stove. When he came in, she was just entering the kitchen. She smiled at him, and he gave her an unsmiling nod. She lifted off the lids of the stove so he could lay the fire, and soon he had it crackling for her. It was a merry sound, and it made him somehow feel better and he permitted himself to give her a small smile. Jacques came thumping down the stairs from the loft, followed by the doctor. He threw his arms around Jenny and lifted her off the floor as she gasped and laughed. "Ah, ma petite, how would you like to go home today and see your mother?"

The doctor, who was just coming in, shook his head. "I'm sorry, but I can't let you or Jenny leave here just yet."

Jacques sobered and asked, "But why, Doctor? There is no more sickness."

"I know, but I have to make sure you will not get sick either. From the time you came here, I have been counting the days. Jenny's will be up soon and she will be able to leave, but you, Jacques, will have to stay a few days longer. I'm sorry."

Cam asked, "But what about the vaccine? They'd be sick by now, wouldn't they? The vaccine must be protecting them."

"I'm sure it is. I believe Ross and I owe our lives to it, but we must wait until the full incubation period has passed for both of you."

Ross came into the kitchen and took a chair as Cam asked, "Then if it protected you and Ross, why didn't it work on Marlette, Martha, and Abigail?"

"I can only guess at the answer to that, Cam. Maybe it was too little or too late for them. They were exposed to such heavy doses of the pox from you, and their conditions were more vulnerable than Ross's and mine. Martha perhaps because of her age, and Abigail because she was too young to have much resistance." He shrugged.

"But Marlette was neither very young nor very old. How was she vulnerable?"

"By her condition." He paused and looked at Ross.

Ross's voice continued, low and brittle, "She was carrying my child."

Cam closed his eyes against the truth of it. "Oh, no," he breathed. But he knew it was so. He remembered now when he had arrived how heavily Marlette had walked to get Ross. She had been pregnant. Cam turned away and went blindly out the back door.

Jenny found him by the creek and came up quietly beside him. "Cam, breakfast is ready. You'd better come in and eat."

He looked at her, feeling very old and very worn. He blinked slowly, clearing the numbness from his mind. "All right. I'll be right there."

He ate, but could not enjoy it or even look at Ross. They were discussing what they would do once the quarantine was lifted.

The doctor was telling them, "Before any of us leave here, we will all have to be disinfected and our clothes boiled until they are free of smallpox. And Jacques, before you can take Jeremy's horse or any of his things home, they'll have to be disinfected, too. Nothing must leave this place until it has been disinfected or boiled sterile, and anything else will have to be burned."

Ross asked, woodenly, "And what about the house?"

"I'm sorry, Ross. I'm afraid there is no other way to insure all the smallpox is killed but to burn it to the ground."

Jenny let out a soft gasp, and Jacques looked stricken. Cam didn't look at Ross. He lay down his fork and rose, a feeling of nausea creeping into his stomach. It was because of him all this was happening. He had not only destroyed Ross's family, but now his home as well. He went to his bedroom and closed the door. He wanted to leave but was a prisoner of his own doing. He would have to be thoroughly disinfected before he left or he could start an epidemic that might wipe out the valley. He sat heavily on the bed. There were no tears left, only a deep ache. He would return to California and the claim. The claim. At least he had that left out of everything else he had destroyed. Jeremy's name wasn't even on it. He had filed it one day when Jeremy was up at the claim, and since Jeremy wasn't there to sign it, he had entered it in his name, fully intending to have Jeremy sign it the next time he came down from the claim. But Jeremy had never come down from the claim. The gold that was there was all his now, and whatever it took he would do to bring it back to Ross. It was nothing compared to what Ross had lost, but it was all Cam had to offer.

There was a rap on the door and Cam raised his head. "Who is it?"

"All of us, Cam. May we come in?"

It was the doctor's voice. Cam rose and opened the door. Ross, Jacques, Jenny, and the doctor filed into his room.

The doctor smiled at him gently and said, "Ross tells us you've got a small fortune in gold. Would you mind letting us see it?"

Cam looked at Ross questioningly and saw the quiet smile. "I found it in the packs you brought home. I put it in the drawer here." He went to the bureau and took out the heavy leather bags of gold and set them on the bed. The gold spilled over the gray blanket and lay glittering like pools of water with the sun shining on them. Jenny gasped and Jacques muttered, "Mon Dieu!"

They touched it, letting it trickle through their fingers, and Cam saw the wild look come into Jacques's eyes and the doctor's. Ross stood back, watching the others without expression. Jenny straightened, and he saw something different in her eyes. It was sadness and Cam understood it.

"Jenny, the gold was Jeremy's."

"What?" she stammered, unbelieving.

"The gold belongs to you now, and your mother and brothers. It was what Jeremy panned out before he got sick."

"But," she protested, "some of it is yours, too."

"No. None of it. I wasn't there, I didn't help him. It was all his."

Ross asked, "How much do you think it's worth?"

"Several thousand, at least."

Jenny began to smile. "Jacques, do you hear that? We are rich!"

The doctor dropped a nugget back into the pile and said, "Not for a while you won't be."

"But, why?" Jacques asked.

"Because it is just as liable to spread smallpox as anything else. It'll have to stay here and be burned down with the house."

The elation left their faces. The doctor continued, "There'll be something left when the ashes cool, but I'd suggest you put it where you'll be able to find it afterward."

Ross sat on the bed and started to scoop Jenny's gold back into the sacks, and Cam helped him. Jacques led Jenny from the room, and the doctor followed. They finished and drew the strings tight, and Ross placed the sacks back into the drawer. Cam kept his eyes on Ross until he turned around, and their eyes met. But he couldn't keep his eyes lifted to Ross's. He looked away and said,

"Ross, I'm sorry. I didn't know. Not that it would have mattered. Not that I could have prevented it, but I am sorry."

"I know you are, Cam. You had no way of knowing. You were too sick to know anything."

Cam nodded, feeling little, if any, better. The guilt still weighed too heavily on him.

Ross asked, "What do you want to do, Cam, when this is over?"

"Go back to California, I guess."

"Because you want to?"

Cam looked up into Ross's deep, tender eyes. "There's more gold where this came from. If I worked all summer, you could be rich. You could build the biggest house in Oregon. You could buy all the land you needed. Anything you wanted, Ross."

"Is that what you think I want?"

Cam shook his head sadly. "No. But that is all I can give you. That is all I have to replace what I've taken away from you."

"Cam, I don't want gold. Nothing I could see or feel with my hand will be able to replace Marlette, or Abigail. To know you understand who I am and what I am is all that matters to me now. I don't care about this house. I built it for Marlette, not for me. Don't make another choice because you think it is the right thing to do for someone else. Make it because it is the right thing to do for you, Cam."

Ross left him sitting on the bed and Cam watched him leave, loving him.

In the days that followed, they began preparing the house and getting ready for Ross's move into Jacques's cabin across the creek. Everything that could be boiled and sterilized with disinfectant was saved. The horses, too, underwent their baths with strong soap, as did everything Cam had brought back from California with Jeremy.

Finally the day came when Jenny could leave. Cam expected her to be excited, but she wasn't. Far from it. She seemed reluctant to go, and her wistful looks at him made it obvious what she was waiting for. He purposely went to the barn, saddled her horse, led it to the front of the house, and tied it to the rail fence. He saw her watching from the kitchen window and turned back to the barn. He didn't want to see the hurt on her face or talk to her.

Surely she knew by now that he was not the man for her. He had tried to make it plain in every way since he had kissed her.

Jenny came storming out of the house and ran down the path toward the barn. She stood in the barn door with her hands knotted into fists on her hips and her eyes blazing.

"What do you think you're doing with my horse, Cam Galligher?"

"I put him out front for you so you could go home."

"How do you know I want to go home? You didn't ask me."

"You belong at home. Not here."

"That is my decision," she cried at him, "not yours."

"No, it isn't. There is no reason for you to stay now."

Her anger was faltering and her mouth trembled. "I thought you were reason enough. Don't you care, Cam?"

"Of course I care, Jenny. I'll always love you like you were my sister."

That was the ultimate wound, and she started to cry. "It wasn't a brotherly kiss you gave me. Why are you doing this to me, Cam? I love you!"

Her anguish hurt him, but he hid it and kept his voice matter of fact. "No, you don't. You don't even know me. I'm not the same man you knew before I left here. Even my face isn't the same. You'd be making the biggest mistake of your life to love me. Now go home, Jenny, and wait for a good man to come along—a man who is deserving of you."

"No! You can't just tell me to go home! You can't make that decision for me. I must make it, and you must convince me you are not the man I think you are."

"Please, Jenny, I can't tell you. You'll just have to take my word for it."

"You're not being fair. I love you and I want you to marry me. What have you done that is so bad you can't tell me? Is it your face? Cam, I love you. Your face is as handsome to me now as it always has been from the moment I first saw you on the banks of the Ohio. I like the man who came home from California. You have grown through all that has happened to you. I can feel it. I can see it. You used to hurt me and not care. Now I know you are hurting me because you don't want to hurt me, and it isn't easy for you to do. I can see it in your eyes, Cam. Oh!" she cried, frustrated, hearing her confused torrent. "That doesn't make any sense, but you know what I mean!"

He looked away, afraid he was showing his real feelings.

"Damn you, Cam Galligher!" Her voice was strident. "You tell me why you're not good enough for me if you want me to leave you."

He was angry now. Angry that she left him no choice but to tell her if he was to save her from him. He grabbed her arm and steered her into the barn. He would tell her as graphically as possible—as roughly as possible. Then she would leave. She would have to. She was too decent to stay.

"Cam!" she cried in surprise and pain. "What are you doing?"

He let her go and faced her, his face hard and his voice harder. "You wanted me to tell you, so I'm going to. Starting with Elitah. You didn't know about Elitah, did you?" He didn't wait for her to answer, but turned and pointed up at the loft. "You see up there? Up there is where I raped Elitah the day before Jeremy and I left. Not once, but twice. And that night I got drunk. I got so damned drunk I passed out in that stall and slept in horse manure all night. Is that how you want the man you marry to behave, Jenny?" He paused only long enough to take a breath and rush on before she could answer, her eyes wide and startled. "And that's not all. I didn't tell you what I was doing the night Jeremy bought his first woman. I went to a saloon run by a woman. I told you about her already. I got myself so drunk I couldn't stand up. We did that quite a bit, Jeremy and I. We had nothing better to do when we couldn't work the claim. We spent days down at the flat just drinking and gambling until we were bored. That's when Jeremy decided he wanted something different to do. That's the night I got the hell beat out of me, Jenny, because I was so drunk I fell into the middle of a poker game and ruined some pretty high stakes. I woke up in Doll's bed. Doll wasn't beautiful like you, Jenny, and she was at least fifteen years older than me. But she took care of me—for a price. She liked my body, Jenny. She wanted me to be her stud. I accepted her offer. Willingly. I wanted everything she was offering, and she had a lot to offer—in every way imaginable. I serviced her whenever and however she wanted it. It was a hell of a lot more fun than standing knee deep in ice water for a few grains of gold. I'd probably be with her yet if

Jeremy had come back down from the claim. But he didn't and I went up to see what happened to him, and you know the rest. Now you get the hell out of here and get on your horse, little girl, and you ride for home as fast as you can go."

He waited for her to leave, but she didn't move and he wondered if she had heard any of what he said, or whether she had blanked out his words. Her wide eyes blinked slowly, and he knew she had comprehended.

Quite softly, she asked, "Do you love her, Cam?"

"Who?"

"Doll. Do you want to go back to her?"

"No."

"And Elitah? Did you love her?"

"No."

"Then is it that you want to spend the rest of your life drinking, gambling, and with . . . with casual women?"

"No."

"Is there any woman you love, Cam, that would make it impossible for you to love me?"

His voice answered much more softly, his blood racing with the sweetness, the innocence, the blind adoration of him, in spite of what he had told her. "No."

Tears were very close to spilling over her dark-lashed eyelids. "Do you love *me,* Cam?"

Unable to fight his feelings any longer, he answered, "Yes, Jenny, I think I do."

The tears glistened on her thick lashes and dropped to her cheeks. "Then marry me, Cam. Nothing you did before me matters as long as you love me."

"Oh, Jenny," he whispered, overcome with his emotions now that he'd finally admitted them, "I do love you." The smile she gave him was ethereal as she came into his arms, and he bent to take her lips as she reached for him. He didn't need to worry now about making a decision. Jenny had already made it for him.

25. *From Darkness to Dawn*

ROSS FINISHED SPREADING the powder trail through the house and stepped off the porch. He bent to light it. As it flared into life, he moved backward away from it until he stood next to Jacques and watched with growing bitterness while the house he had built caught fire and became a holocaust. He closed his eyes against the sight of it and turned away in tortured silence, hearing the roaring blaze consume what was left to his life.

Jacques's arm held him strongly, and he knew some comfort from the gesture and how deeply the big Frenchman felt his loss. He heard the roof cave in and the resounding rush and suck of flames as they engulfed what was left, and he shuddered uncontrollably and felt Jacques's grip tighten on his arm.

With breaking voice, Jacques asked, "What you do now, mon ami?"

He replied without thinking, "Go to the cabin in the mountains for a while," and was surprised at his answer. He hadn't even thought about it and hadn't known until now what he would do.

Jacques gave Ross's arm a final squeeze and pat and let his arm drop as he said, "Come spend the night with us and have a good meal, eh?"

"No!" he said more sharply than he had intended. Now that he knew where he was going, he was desperate to get away and wanted no delay. He faced Jacques and saw the surprised look in his eyes at his vehement rejection. More gently, he said, "Thank you for asking, but I want to be alone."

Jacques nodded understandingly. "Then this is adieu, cher ami?"

"Yes." He reached to take the hand that Jacques offered in both of his, emotion clouding his eyes, and he knew a handshake was not enough for all they meant to each other. He embraced

331

Jacques fiercely for a long moment, then stepped back holding onto the strong arms of the Frenchman and said huskily, "Adieu, cher ami."

The Frenchman's eyes glistened with tears as he smiled in complete understanding. Ross turned and walked to the barn, not looking at the burning ruins of his home or at Jacques. Jacques would be gone when he came out.

He stopped inside the door of the barn and looked with mild amazement at the things he had put there. Until now he hadn't consciously realized what he intended to do, but his subconscious had known and everything was exactly what he needed to stay in the cabin in the mountains. Even new blankets, replacing those that were burning with the house, lay folded with the cooking pots and food, ready to be packed with an extra change of his first store-bought clothes. He set about packing his pack horse and, that done, saddled the other horse and led them from the barn.

Cam was coming at a hard gallop down the lane. Ross stopped and waited for him. He had hoped to be gone by the time Cam came back. Saying good-bye to Cam would be hard, and he had had too many permanent good-byes in the days just past.

Cam pulled his horse to an abrupt stop and swung down in one swift, smooth motion, but the urgency with which he had ridden in was suddenly stilled as they stood looking at each other. Ross felt a tightness in his throat and a mist blur his eyes as he looked at Cam, his heart swelling with love for the boy. But thinking of Cam as a boy was not appropriate now. He was a man in every sense of the word, and Ross felt an ache in his heart to look at Cam. If Cam had been his son, the scars of maturity would not be on his face, but properly on his chest, as were Ross's, and far less conspicuous. But Ross knew that the scars of the beating Cam had taken—already beginning to lose some of the intense color of new scars—and the brighter scars of the pox would fade in time. The beard Cam was letting grow would help hide some of the devastation. Not that Cam needed to worry about it. Even though he was not as handsome as he had been, with his broken nose and broken teeth, no one who looked into his dark, beautiful eyes, finally at peace, would notice the rest of his face. Ross was as proud of Cam as if he were his own son and had wanted to ask Cam to come with him, but hadn't because of Jenny. Cam belonged here now with the woman he loved, and Ross would not come between them by having Cam make another choice.

Finally, Cam asked, "Are you leaving?"

"Yes."

"But where? Why? You didn't say anything to us."

"I know. I didn't know until a little while ago where I was going."

"Do you want me to go with you?"

Ross's voice grew husky with emotion. "No. I don't think Jenny would like me taking you away just now."

Cam smiled briefly. "She wouldn't miss me for a while. She told me I'd be in the way until after she gets everything done for the wedding."

Ross smiled, tempted—and remembering. "I know."

"There's still a lot I want to learn and a lot we haven't done together. We never got the chance before. If only for a couple of months."

Ross's voice vibrated, and his heart ached as he said, "No. I need this time to be alone—to discover what is ahead for me."

"Do you mean your vision?"

"Yes."

Cam didn't ask again, but his eyes pleaded with Ross, and Ross gently explained, "I don't know what it is I am to do now. All I know is I ride away with another of the same color as I am. It was shown to me as two white and red horses leaving together. This is all I know." Haltingly, he bared his heart. "I would forsake my vision to have you with me, Cam, if you did not have Jenny. But I will not ask you to make a decision between her and me. Your place is here. You have this land and Jacques's cabin. It is where you belong."

"Will you be back for our wedding?"

"I don't know. I won't promise it."

Slowly, Cam offered Ross his hand, saying, "Will you take my hand now, then, if this is to be the last time I see you?"

Ross smiled and stepped forward, taking Cam's hand and gripping it strongly, his other shaking hand going to rest on Cam's shoulder. Words were unnecessary as their eyes conveyed what they were feeling.

With a trembling voice, Cam said, "If you ever come back, remember, this is your home."

With a final squeeze, Ross released Cam's hand and said, "I will." He turned and went to his horse and mounted. Cam stepped aside and watched him ride past. Ross didn't look back, afraid he would change his mind about taking Cam with him.

Fighting the tumult of emotions, he stopped to gaze at the smoldering, blackened ruins that had been his and Marlette's home. He thought it fitting that all there was left standing were the fireplaces he had built and the cook stove she had shipped from the East. The visible remains of their marriage made an indelible impression as he looked and remembered the nights the two of them had spent together, cozy and warm before the fireplace, secure in their love, with their child safely asleep nearby or cradled in one or the other of their arms. And the cook stove was the substance of Marlette's love, warming and offering all the good things she prepared for him in love. It made no difference that Martha had ruled the kitchen equally; it was still the symbol of Marlette's presence in their marriage, and he would not forget this starkly vivid picture.

The horse moved forward again, jarring him out of his shaken and dazed reverie. He hoped Cam and Jenny would someday build upon what was left. In Ross's mind, this land belonged to Cam now, even though Cam refused to acknowledge it. But he wouldn't for long. Ross had gotten the deed for the land from the office at Oregon City and signed it over to Cam. Jacques was to give it to Cam and Jenny on their wedding day. The fireplaces were blackened but unhurt, and the stove had had its paint burned off and would need polishing, but it was still usable for another home, and Ross hoped it would be a far less tragic one. He urged the horse into a gallop and pulled his eyes away as he turned his horse toward Champoeg.

He rode hard for a mile or two, but knew it was impossible to outride his thoughts and memories and questions. Lost in a turmoil of grief, he let the horse pick his own pace as he rode along the road that would take him into the mountains and to the cabin.

He rode through Champoeg without stopping to see the Jameses, hardly knowing he passed through the village, he was so wrapped in thought. He had never questioned before the tragedy that had been so much a part of his vision. He had accepted his mother's death and Spotted Fawn's death because his vision had foretold them and visions could not be questioned. But Marlette's and his daughter's deaths he had not seen. If the vision had shown Marlette would die, he would not have married her. He wouldn't have wanted that to happen to her, no matter what his vision had instructed. Not after Spotted Fawn. Nor would he have imagined he could withstand another grief like the grief he had borne after Spotted Fawn's death. There had to be a reason for it, and he wanted to know the reason. Two women had died because they loved him, and three children, seed of his body, had perished because of him. Why must everything he loved be destroyed?

When he finally reached the cabin the next day, he was glad to be there. He didn't view it as exile from life but as a place where he would find a new life. Where he was to wait and learn whatever it was his life would ask of him next.

The cabin was in surprisingly good shape. The windows were dirty but unbroken, and he smiled to remember Marlette washing them. The door was open, and the interior smelled strongly from some animal habitation and would need a good cleaning to remove the stench and offal. He thought it was possible the bear still might come here, from the size of the kills that had been consumed and the dung left. The roof would need some new shingles, and wood for the winter needed to be cut, but he had all summer and more than enough time in which to be ready for winter.

The shed would be a shelter for the horses for now, but food for them would be a problem in the winter. Perhaps he would have to construct a larger building and reap the mountain meadows of their grass to feed them. The task didn't frighten him. Work would be his only salvation and he welcomed it for now. The winter, when he would have nothing but time for thinking, was what he dreaded. But maybe by then he would know what he wanted to do. Perhaps he would even be able to return to the valley and work with Jacques and Cam again. Only time would tell.

He set about to clean his living quarters, camping outside until the cabin was livable again. He hunted and fished for his food and repaired the cabin roof. When that was done, he built a bigger building of logs to stable the horses, and as the grasses matured, he went to the meadows and cut it for hay. In his spare time he cut wood.

But still, with all that he was doing, there was too much time to think. He sat against the cabin door watching the sun go down and remembered too many happy hours spent here with Marlette.

Grief engulfed him for a time and there were nights when he couldn't sleep no matter how tired he was.

He let his hair and beard grow. He still bathed almost every day, but somehow the act of shaving was too closely associated with Marlette's memory, and he felt the drastic change would help alleviate that pain. The first day he really looked at himself in the mirror with his beard and mustache and luxurious growth of hair waving to his shoulders, he laughed until tears came to his eyes. If only Jacques could see him now! He could almost hear the big Frenchman's bellow.

When everything was done that needed doing at the cabin, he took a trip over the hill behind the cabin to the old trapping hut. He spent several days there fixing it up and cutting new stakes for the trap line. It didn't matter to him whether he caught any fur, but it would be something to occupy him, and if he did get any skins, he could use or trade them.

With the work on the trap line completed, he headed down the trail for the cabin. He stopped in mid-stride as he saw the back door standing open. He had left by the back door and had barred it from the outside.

He eased his pack off his shoulder and stealthily approached the cabin with his rifle ready. He circled around to the front and saw the door there still closed. He saw no human tracks. He cautiously approached and peered in the window. He laughed out loud as he saw Jacques's big black bear curled up on the bed in the corner. His laughter disturbed the bear, who raised his head, uttering a low growl.

Ross talked to him. "Ivan, you old rascal, it's me. Don't you recognize me?" Then he laughed at the ridiculousness of that statement. The bear wouldn't recognize him even if he could see him!

Ross went back around the cabin, and the bear came charging across the floor, rising to his full height, ready to protect his domain, as Ross entered the back door. "Hey," he called. "Slow down, old fellow. I'm your friend, remember?" The bear, still uncertain, dropped down on all fours and circled Ross, sniffing. As he remembered the familiar scent, he began to snuffle and grunt happily. Ross reached to pet him and the bear rubbed up against him.

"I'm sure glad to see you, Ivan. It's been lonely without you,

you old devil. Now I don't have to feel like I'm going crazy when I talk to myself." He chuckled at that. There was more than a grain of truth in the statement. He had been talking to himself and had begun to wonder at his sanity. He patted the bear more affectionately as he remembered other times. "Maybe I can teach you to play cards. And how about the harmonica? Can you sing as good as Jacques, my friend, or—" But his voice broke as he was about to say "dance." Tears clouded his eyes, and he moved away from the bear and put up his gun, fighting for control. The bear followed and he stroked him again. "I'm sorry, Ivan. I guess I am a little crazy." He strode back to the door and turned to the bear. "Well, come on. Let's go get my pack."

The first autumn frost touched the trees, and overnight the vine maple blazed red and gold and every shade in between. The nip in the air stirred Ross to new activity. He cut more wood and had to extend the cabin overhang a number of feet more to cover it. Accompanied by the bear, he went around the hill and placed the traps. Soon the first snow would fall and they would have little to do, but in the meantime he worked, driving himself in one last effort to purge his mind and heart of all memories.

The beauty that surrounded him only made him feel his tragedy more keenly. The sunlit days; the crisp mornings when his heart wanted to burst with the love he felt for his surroundings; the shrill penetrating call of the jay; the pungent smell of the forest; the high, thin clouds colored vibrantly at sunrise and sunset in lavenders and pinks—all accentuated his overwhelming solitude.

He knew sadness and loneliness, but he also discovered he had more left to give. He had started his journey to the mountains thinking his life should end, and now he desperately wanted his life to begin again.

He stood between the cabin and the river, feeling all these things, raised his arms to the sky and cried aloud, "God, I am ready. Show me what it is I am to do."

After a long silence, he lowered his arms and eyes and, feeling foolish, walked back to the cabin. The bear stood on the porch and Ross rubbed his head. "Ivan, I really am crazy. I really expected an answer!" He laughed and went into the cabin to fix himself a meal. Ivan lay down in the sun on the porch and sighed, and Ross echoed that sigh.

337

26. The Uninvited Guest

THE NEXT DAY he cut wood, watching the clouds building in the west and hanging low over the mountain behind him. The sun was covered with a thin haze by late afternoon. Snow would not be long in coming now. From the corner of his eye, he saw Ivan rise. The bear's hair rose on his shoulders, and Ross paused to listen, hearing now what the bear heard—the sound of a horse coming along the trail across the river.

He picked up his gun and glided noiselessly into the trees away from the cabin, hearing the low growl of the bear as Ivan moved around the side of the cabin to meet whatever company was coming. Ross could see the river now as a horse and rider slid down the bank and into the stream. Sun glinted off a long braid of fiery auburn hair swinging over a feminine shoulder and breast covered by a thin cotton dress. His breath caught in surprise. He knew that hair and that figure, even though he had not seen her for a long time. The horse scrambled out of the water, and the rider stopped between the cabin and the river, waiting, her hand on a wicked-looking knife belted at her waist. There was a rifle in the scabbard, and he had no doubt she could use it, too.

Ross stepped from the shadows and her alert eyes saw him immediately. "Elitah," he said, and felt the blood begin to heat in his veins as she looked at him uncertainly. "What are you doing here?"

"Ross?" she questioned. "Is that you?"

He smiled as he remembered his beard. "Yes. Beneath this beard."

She smiled then, and he felt her powerful attraction once again. A year had enhanced her exotic beauty. Her thick, luxuriant hair, lighter and brighter than his own deep chestnut hair, the strange slanted, almond-shaped green eyes, the petulant and sensuous

338

lips, and the golden brown skin that glowed like satin made it difficult for a man not to want to touch her. He didn't need to imagine the full breasts or slender, boyish hips; he had seen them.

"I wasn't sure for a moment. You look so different. I don't like it."

He stroked the beard and replied, "It suits me. But what are you doing here? Why aren't you at the school?"

She shrugged a shoulder in her familiar evasive manner and said, "I left. I thought Marlette could use some help and that you would let me work for you."

"But how did you find me?"

"Jacques. He told me what happened."

"Jacques?" He shook his head. The incorrigible matchmaker was up to his old tricks.

"Yes. I made him tell me." She smiled devilishly. "I said I would tell Liz he had made love to me if he wouldn't tell me where you were."

He frowned, recovering from his shock at seeing her and beginning to realize the implication of her presence. "But why, Elitah? This is no place for you."

"Isn't it?" she teased.

Anger flashed through him. "You can't stay here!"

She sobered and stared at him with those hypnotic eyes. "I thought I could help you. Don't send me away. I have no place else to go."

"That isn't the point, Elitah. And you do have someplace to go—back to the school, where you belong."

Stubbornly, with her own temper rising, she protested, "No! I won't go back there. You don't know what it was like. The sisters were harder to please than the Indians. You let Cam keep me, and now you are responsible for me, whether you like it or not."

He eyed her as hotly as she was eying him. A gust of wind stirred through the trees, and the storm that had been building broke against the mountain and sent down the first chilling spate of raindrops.

Ross capitulated. "All right. I guess I can't leave you in the rain. Let's get your horse put away. You can stay the night and we'll talk about it."

In a flash she was off the horse and smiling at him, as warm as she had been cold a few moments ago. She was both bitch and temptress, and he didn't know how he was going to handle her.

They put away the horse and carried her small pack and bedroll into the cabin.

"Oh, Ross, I love it," she cried in childlike delight. "It looks so cozy and warm. If I ever wanted a place to be home, this is it."

"Elitah! You've got to forget about staying here."

She turned on him, changed instantly from girl to woman. "Why? Are you afraid of me?"

For a moment he was speechless. Then he admitted, "Yes. I guess I am."

"Why?" she asked bluntly.

Frustrated, he asked, "Do I have to have a reason?"

She smiled. "Yes. If you want me to be convinced that you don't want me."

His anger returned. "Do you have any idea what I've been through? I came here because I wanted to be alone. When I came, I wasn't sure I had anything to live for. I'm just now beginning to think I do. The last thing on my mind is having a woman."

She was instantly remorseful. "Oh, Ross, I'm sorry. I was only trying to make you feel happy. To forget." Her eyes were liquid with tears.

He turned away in complete exasperation. "Forget it and get washed. I'll fix us some supper."

He busied himself with preparing them something to eat, his mind in a turmoil. She was so quiet he wasn't sure she was still in the room; he almost hoped she had gone. When he turned, she was sitting demurely at the table, her eyes downcast. She said nothing all during supper and, like an obedient child, put her plate next to the wash pan. She retreated to the fireplace and set about building a fire.

The fire was warming the cabin by the time he joined her in his chair. She still sat demurely, with a blanket around her, her fat braid of hair falling over her shoulder and into her lap, where her hands idly toyed with it.

He sighed wearily. "All right, Elitah, why don't you tell me why you ran away from school."

Keeping her eyes down, she answered in that disarmingly seductive voice she had, "I didn't like it there. They tried to make me into something I didn't want to be."

340

"And what do you want to be?"

She flashed those eyes briefly into his, and he thought he knew the answer and immediately rejected it.

"I don't know. But I do know I don't want to be watched constantly and corrected constantly and made to feel I am nothing because I am not white. It was almost as bad—no, it was worse than living with the Indians, because I know now I don't need to be anyone's slave."

He stared at the bent head and satiny skin. She was absolutely right. With a face and body like hers, she needn't be a slave. Any man would be more than happy to be her slave. "What did you hope I would do for you?"

"I told you. Before I heard Marlette and Abigail were dead, I wanted you to hire me to work for you. When Jacques told me what happened, I felt so bad I had to come see you. Somehow I thought I could help you." She raised her eyes slowly to his and looked at him unblinkingly. "You were always good to me. You never tried to use me. And I thought you understood me. You were raised an Indian like I was. You know how hard it is for me to be equal in a white man's world."

He had to look away from those eyes, and nodded as he looked into the fire. "Yes, I know. And you know I would take you in if. . . ." He paused, unable to say the words, and continued lamely, ". . . under different circumstances. But I hardly know what I'm going to do myself."

"I don't mind. I have no other place to go. Maybe we will be able to help each other. *Please* don't make me go back."

He stood up, uncomfortable and restless. "I'll have to think about it. Come on, let's make your bed."

He helped her spread her blankets and retreated to the loft, as he had so many winters before. He lay in tense wakefulness, listening to her roam the room below and whisper to the bear until she finally settled down in the bed. At last he slept, only to be awakened by a commotion in the middle of the night. His automatic reaction was to swing down the ladder, but he stopped himself, resisting the urge to go to her aid. It was exactly what he must not do. She was swearing softly, and he smiled. She had certainly picked up the white man's language in every respect. He sat bolt upright when he heard her start up the ladder to the loft.

"What's wrong?"

341

Her head and bare shoulders appeared above the floor. "That bear pushed me out of bed."

He groaned with indecision. Whatever he did, it would not work as he wanted. He would lose, no matter what. "All right. Come on up. You can use Jacques's bed."

She came holding her blankets in one arm, entirely and tantalizingly naked. He closed his eyes and turned his head away as she spread her blankets on Jacques's bed. He heard her get into the bed and relaxed.

"Ross." The soft voice made him turn.

"What?"

"Are you angry with me?"

He opened his eyes, feeling the anger flare in him, and looked toward her. She was sitting up with her legs and feet covered, but she was uncovered from the waist up, and the firelight reflecting from below revealed all too well the lush voluptuousness of her body. He closed his eyes and turned completely away. "No," he replied shortly. "Now go to sleep."

He heard her settle down, but he could not. His pulse was pounding with lust for her, and if he had never been one to use the white man's swear words before, he used them all now against himself and against her. She had to go, and the sooner the better for his peace of mind. He almost felt the God he had trusted to give him an answer had betrayed him and cast a she-devil in his way to more acutely torture him.

At the height of his inward rage, he heard the wind mock him and the sound of frozen rain pelting the windows. It was snowing, and now he would have to let her stay, unless he wanted to take her back himself. But as he raged within himself, so did the storm outside, and he knew that winter had come and he was trapped with this child-witch.

Morning came soon after he was finally exhausted and slept. He wasn't aware of when Elitah got up and climbed down to the first floor to rekindle the fire. It was hours later before he awoke, instantly aware of her presence, but calm and stoic.

He swung down the ladder to face her and was once again brought up short by her exquisite beauty. She was brushing her hair and watching him with those strange, pensive eyes.

He sighed. "You've won, Elitah. I can't send you back now."

Her lips curved in a soft smile. "It was meant to be."

"I don't believe that."

"Why not? Is it because you don't want to believe it?"

He sighed again, in exasperation. "Forget it. I'm not going to argue with you. Let's understand one thing. I'm letting you stay because I can't send you back or take you back in the snow. By the time this stops, it won't be possible to take you out without risking both our lives. I don't want you here, but since you are here, we have to make the best of it. You do what you want to do, but don't try to seduce me, Elitah. Keep your clothes on and act like a virtuous squaw and we'll get along fine. Do you understand?"

"Yes," she answered petulantly, and turned away. He had gotten through to her by hurting her but, at the moment, he didn't care. He was well aware why she had come, and he wasn't going to be led into thinking he loved her, or that she loved him, just because she offered herself to him. She had learned to live by her body and she was doing so now.

27. Discovery

FOR DAYS ONE storm after another rolled across the mountain behind them and kept them cabin-bound with fits of rain, sleet, or snow. Elitah did exactly as he had told her to do. She remained silent and respectful, as a good Indian squaw should, keeping her eyes downcast and, for the most part, staying curled in her chair by the fire with a blanket around her.

Every time the weather permitted, she went outside to wear off the pent-up energy that had to be controlled in his presence. He knew he was being hard on her, but he was unrelenting. The compassion that had marked most of his relationships with women would not work with her. She would view any attempt by him to be kind as an invitation, and he knew he couldn't become involved with her in any way without bringing more disaster.

An unusual storm of freezing rain invaded their mountain valley one night, and they woke up to a world of dazzling sunshine reflected off a million icy prisms. Elitah scrambled down the ladder, eager to go outside, and paused to look out the window. Ross heard her awed gasp as she viewed a world where every tree and every bush was a sparkling chandelier of ice. She wrapped her blanket around herself and hurried outside, slipping on the iced snow. Ross stood at the window and watched her as she skated on the frozen surface, gaining grace of movement as she learned quickly how to balance herself. Laughing and shrieking with delight, she whirled and danced in gliding slides, her hands touching the bushes and low-hanging branches as she passed, causing a cascade of tinkling ice to fall.

He was fascinated by her. He enjoyed watching her and felt the warmth of desire filling him. He forced the feeling down, telling himself she was a child. Tearing himself away from the window, he went to make breakfast.

344

In a few minutes she came bursting in the door, her dress soaked and clinging more revealingly than ever as cold erected the nipples of her breasts. Completely forgetting her orders, she bubbled, "Oh, Ross! I've never seen anything so beautiful. Won't you come outside and join me? I've never had so much fun."

He turned what he hoped was a cold, disapproving look on her, and she immediately withdrew to the fireplace with downcast eyes. By the time breakfast was over, she was shivering from the damp dress, but he dared not suggest anything to her and they both suffered in silence.

With the weather cleared, he eagerly packed his pack and set off for a trip along the trap line. He left without giving her one word of advice, or even telling her when he would be back. He knew she could take care of herself—and if she couldn't, it would be one less problem for him to deal with.

The weather was more than cooperative, and he could have been back from the trap line the same day with no more animals than he recovered by the time he reached the end of the line, but he needed the time away from Elitah and he took it. On his fourth day away, the weather began to change again and he knew he had to get back.

He arrived at the cabin just before dark. She opened the door for him, and whatever she was cooking smelled good. Without a greeting, she returned to getting supper and he didn't interfere. When it was ready, she set both plates on the table and waited for him to come.

"This is very good, Elitah," he had to admit in surprise.

He saw her eyelashes raise, but she kept her head down and murmured, "Thank you."

The next day he began the process of scraping and stretching the animal pelts onto frames. She watched with interest, just as Marlette had watched so many years before.

Finally, breaking the silence, she said, "You shouldn't be doing that. That is squaw's work."

He looked at her in surprise and smiled. "You forget. I have no squaw."

"You have me."

He paused momentarily and looked at her coldly. "You are not my squaw."

"You're making me act like your squaw "

345

He didn't answer and went back to his work.

Again she spoke up. "I'd like to learn how to do that. Would you teach me?"

Again he looked at her with surprise. "Why? It's hard work."

Anger flashed in her eyes as she answered, "I need something to do. And I am freezing in this white woman's dress. I need something warm to wear."

He knew it was true. "All right. I'll show you."

Eagerly, she came near him and he prepared a skin for her to work on. With surprising aptitude, she absorbed what he told her about making a prime fur from the pelts he had brought in. Before they had them all stretched to cure, he decided he would give her what was left of the deer skins from the deer he had killed earlier in the summer. Most of them had gone to make him clothes, but he thought there were enough left to make some dresses for her. She received them with wide eyes.

Stroking their soft smoothness, she said with delight, "They are so soft. Teach me how to do these, too, will you?"

He smiled. "First I'd better teach you how to make yourself a dress from them."

Smiling happily, she pleaded, "And will you teach me how your people decorated their clothes?"

"My people?" he questioned.

"Yes. The Indians who raised you."

He shrugged. "All right. If I can remember."

She looked at him seriously. "You couldn't forget, could you?"

"No. I guess I haven't."

She smiled again. "And I'll need moccasins and leggings. Didn't your people wear leggings?"

"Why does it matter what my people wore? You can have them if you want. It's probably a good idea for our winter in the mountains."

"I just wanted to know about your people, what they wore, what they were like, so that I could please you."

He frowned. So that was it. "Elitah, my people weren't Indian. My mother and father were white."

She looked at him in amazement. "But I thought. . . ." She didn't finish. She turned away from him and went to the fire and stood with her back to him.

"Elitah, what did you think?"

346

She shrugged evasively.

Inwardly, he uttered an oath and said, "How can I show you how to do this if you won't stay here and watch?"

Tearfully, she replied, "It isn't important now."

She was making him angry. "Come here!" he ordered.

Obediently, she came, with tears on her face. "Are you going to watch me or not, while I show you how to do this?" Ross asked, pointedly.

Her tears turned to temper and she blazed at him, "No! You're just like all the rest, *white man!*" And she spat on the floor.

With a temper to match hers, he slapped her, and she went staggering across the room. He was instantly sorry, but he held his ground. Inwardly shaking, he wondered what was wrong with him.

She hung onto the back of her chair and wept.

Finally, he said, "I'm sorry, Elitah. I didn't mean to do that. Now will you tell me what's wrong so we can talk about it?"

Wiping tears from her eyes and becoming a dutiful child once more, she answered, "I thought you were part Indian, like I am, and understood me, but you don't. You're like the others and just say you do."

"I do understand you, Elitah. I may be white, but that doesn't mean I don't understand what it feels like to be an Indian."

She shook her head. "You still don't understand. I thought you were a half-breed. That is different from either being white or Indian, because no one wants a half-breed."

He didn't know what to say to her. If he sympathized too much, he was afraid she would interpret it as a sign he was ready to be seduced. He picked up the skins and began to sew them together, saying, "Watch how I do this."

She sat down and watched intently, apparently forgetting about everything that had happened.

He had one seam done when she said, "Let me try it now."

He surrendered the skins and sinew to her. She worked quickly and expertly with natural ability and apparent enjoyment. Before bedtime she had the skins completely sewn together. With child-like eagerness, she put it on over her cotton dress and waited for him to comment.

It wasn't nearly as arousing as the tight cotton dress, and he nodded in approval. "It looks very good."

With eyes bright, she asked, "Will you teach me how to decorate it tomorrow?"

"Yes. But we don't have any beads or quills, or even dye. I'm not sure I can show you much."

"Do you ever catch a porcupine in your traps?"

"Once in a while."

"Then I will wait until you do. I can work on something else."

The next day she started moccasins and leggings. He was delighted with her desire to learn and amazed at how easily he slipped into the role of teacher from that of unwilling host.

He left again to check the trap line after the next storm was over, and came back the next day, missing her companionship and eager to work with her.

He had a pack full of fine furs from the trap line and delighted in showing her how each one should be worked to bring out its finest qualities. His respect for her grew daily as she proved her skill. She began to ask questions. Only a few at first—about trapping and how much the furs brought—but one day she said quite unexpectedly, "Do you remember your mother?"

Quite easily, he answered, "Yes."

"What did she look like?"

"She was very fair-skinned, with hair the color of dry grass and blue eyes."

He felt her eyes on him. "You don't look like that at all. Do you look like your father?"

"Yes. She told me I did."

She was quiet for a moment, then said sadly, "I wish I knew who I looked like."

He glanced at her briefly, but she kept her eyes on her work. "Don't you know?"

"No. I don't remember my mother too well, but I'm sure I didn't look like her."

"What did she look like? Do you remember?"

"I think she was dark. More like an Indian."

"Was she?"

"Only half. My grandmother was a white woman, I think. At least, my mother said she was and my hair looked like hers. I remember my mother saying she came from far south of here. She told my mother she had been captured by Indians and the one who took her kept her. My mother was their daughter."

348

"And who was your father?"

"I never saw him. Mother told me she was given or sold to a sailor from someplace far across the ocean. He brought her north and sold her to the Indians. They sold her when I was only five, so I don't remember too much about her or all that she told me."

He looked at her enchanting beauty and thought that whatever her parentage, it had produced something rare and unequaled, but he knew by her interest in the subject that it bothered her greatly. He would have said something to compliment her, if he hadn't been afraid it would change her from student to seductress.

She worked a while longer before she asked in a tentative voice, "Do you think white people would have more respect for me if I knew how to read and write?"

"I thought they were teaching you to read and write at the school."

"They tried to, but I wasn't interested in it then."

"And why are you now?"

"I have been thinking it might make a difference. They seem to value it a great deal."

He looked up from his work, and her eyes met his. "It will only help if it will give you respect for yourself."

"But how can that be? I respect myself. I know I am better than they think. I don't understand."

"Do you really, Elitah? Do you really like what you have been? Don't you want to learn because you want to change? Unless you feel good about yourself, no one else will either."

She looked at him with unhappy eyes. She said nothing, and he went back to stretching the fur he was working with.

"Do you know how to read and write?" she asked.

"Yes."

"Would you teach me?"

He looked up and met her wide, excited eyes. He couldn't refuse them. "Yes."

"Who taught you? Was it the missionaries?"

"No, at least not the first time. My mother taught me when I was small. When I came here, I asked a missionary's wife to help me remember what my mother had taught me."

"When can we start?"

"Right now if you like. While we're working, I can teach you the letters of the white man's alphabet."

349

And so it began. When the skins were done, they worked on nothing but schooling while the storms came and went. The only break in the schooling was when he would go out to collect the furs from the trap line, and he was as eager as she to get back to the lessons.

They were working on more difficult things as he tried to explain the white man, his religion and his government, and why things were happening as they were. He thought he could see a maturity in her as her questions became more thoughtful. Just as he had done on a day so long ago in the middle of something difficult, after a particularly long day of learning, she put down her pencil and looked at him wearily.

"Will I ever be able to learn everything you know?"

He smiled. "It depends on how long a winter we have."

She laughed. "Be serious. You know so much. You should be a teacher. Maybe if you had been a teacher at the sisters' school, I would have learned something there."

"I doubt it. You didn't want to learn anything then."

"What made you decide to live as a white man?" she asked suddenly.

"I had a vision that foretold of my mother's death and the death of my Indian wife and of my leaving the Indians to go to the white eagle's nest. After my wife died, I knew I must leave to find the white eagle's nest."

"McLoughlin?"

"Yes. The man the Indians call the white-headed eagle."

"Did you see Marlette's death, too?"

"No. After the death of my Indian wife, I would never have married again if I had been shown that she would die, too."

"Did your vision show you anything else?"

"Yes. It shows me leaving the white eagle's nest."

"And where do you go?"

"I don't know. My vision ended there."

She looked at him with her extraordinary green eyes, alive with thoughts. "What do you want to do?"

"I don't know that either."

"Do you know who you want to be?"

"Do you mean, do I want to be a white man or an Indian?"

She nodded.

"I don't know, yet." He pushed back his chair and stood up

350

restlessly. Her questions were getting too direct, and that directness was causing confusion in him. He put more wood on the fire and said, "Well, I guess we've had enough for one day. I think I'll go to bed."

He put on his coat and went out into the night as he had done years ago, in a state of unrest. The snow had almost quit falling and he hoped it would by morning. He felt the need to get away for a day or two. He returned to the cabin and climbed to the loft. After a few minutes she came up, too. She had slept upstairs in Jacques's bed since the bear had decided the lower bed was his. She wore the cotton dress as a nightgown now, and though it was better than nothing at all, it was still provocative.

In the morning she began to question him again. There seemed no end to what she wanted to know.

"Did your mother have other children?"

"I have a half brother and half sister."

"Where are they? Did they come here with you?"

"No. They still live with the Indians."

"Have you ever been back to see them?"

The questions were all too familiar. Marlette had asked the same things in this same room. "Yes. I saw them a few years ago."

"Did your mother teach them as she taught you?"

"No."

"Then there is no one to keep the white man from cheating them?"

"I wouldn't say that."

"But you were the one she taught to help them and you're not there. Don't you care?"

"Of course I care." His unrest was growing by leaps and bounds. Stiffly, he said, "I am a white man. I chose the white man's life because at the time I left they didn't need help against the white man, and my life there ended with my wife's death."

She looked at him strangely, and he turned his back on her to fix them breakfast. She ate with him in silence, but when they were finishing their coffee, she asked him, "What is that thing you wear around your neck?"

"Nothing," he lied. "Just a medallion."

"May I see it?"

He took it off and handed it to her, and she looked at it carefully. "What does this horn and feathered thing mean?"

"Nothing," he lied again.

"Who gave it to you?"

"My Indian father."

She looked at him intently. "Was he someone important to your people?"

"He was a chief."

Her eyes widened. "Then you would have been a chief?"

"Not necessarily. He wanted me to be, but I would have to be worthy of being chief."

She looked at the medallion thoughtfully for a while, then asked, "Why did he give this to you?"

"So that if I did go back to them, they would know me."

"And make you their chief?"

He laughed. "No."

Eagerly, she asked, "But they would listen to you, wouldn't they? You could teach them and counsel them."

"Just what are you getting at?"

Her eyes were bright with discovery. "Don't you see? It is the answer to your vision. You leave here to return to the Indians."

He stood up abruptly, her words only adding to the uncertainty that had stalked him for months. Action was his only escape. "I'm going out to take care of the horses."

He put on his coat and charged into the snowy wilderness, but the relief was only momentary. He could leave the questioner, but he couldn't leave the questions. They still remained unanswered, and the answers that she was bringing to his attention seemed totally unacceptable.

He went into the barn, and the horses whickered weakly at him. He ran his hands over them, feeling their gauntness, and his anxiety increased. He hadn't planned on feeding three horses over the winter and had barely enough fodder for two. He had kept them confined to conserve food, and the effects were evident. By spring they would be weak to the point of worthlessness—if they didn't die first. In desperation, he took up his shovel and hatchet and went foraging for them. He drove himself mercilessly in his efforts to bring them food. The harder he toiled, the harsher became the reality of Elitah's words. He had to face the fact that what she had told him could very well be the truth. The God who had sent him

352

the vision could have intentionally given him knowledge of the white man to better equip him to return to the Nakota and guide them. He could see the part Marlette had played and just as easily see why she had had to die. She could not have returned to the Nakota with him, nor would he have ever left her. Death had been the only way to separate them. If that was his destiny, then he could accept all that had happened. The vision showed him leaving with another of mixed blood, as symbolized by the spotted horses. Elitah was certainly of mixed blood, just as he was a blend of two cultures, but Elitah was a child less than half his age.

He returned to the cabin when darkness and the increasing snow made it impossible to do any more for the horses. Elitah had supper ready and they ate in strained silence. She kept her eyes down, and he was too mentally, emotionally, and physically exhausted to wrestle with the problem anymore. He finished his meal, climbed to the loft, and fell into bed. He heard her cleaning up and waited for her to climb into the loft, but she didn't. He closed his eyes to sleep and thought he heard the sound of her crying, but he had little desire to confront her, or even comfort her, and he let sleep blot out everything.

In the morning he woke up and turned immediately to her bed. It had not been slept in. He rose and climbed down the ladder. She was frying meat for breakfast. She kept her eyes averted, and he washed silently. When she brought his plate to him, he looked at her and saw the strain she felt clearly mirrored in her face. Inwardly, he pleaded with the white man's God for guidance, for answers, for some sign that this woman was the woman of his vision.

Elitah picked at her food and he had little appetite himself. He pushed his plate away and went to put more wood on the fire, feeling the tension mount in him. His hands locked into a fist on the mantel as he stared into the flames.

She spoke to him, her voice uncertain and trembling. "Ross, may I ask you something?"

He turned to face her. "Yes."

"Haven't I done what you wanted?"

He looked puzzled, but answered, "Yes."

"Haven't I learned everything you tried to teach me?"

"Yes."

"Then why am I still not acceptable to you?"

"You're not unacceptable to me, Elitah."

Her voice rose with emotion. "But I am! In all these months, you have not touched me! I will do anything you want—be anything you want—but most of all, I want you to touch me." Her face contorted in anguish. "Don't you know how much I love you? Are you a blind man?"

Just as heatedly, he replied, "Are you blind? I am old enough to be your father!"

She clung to the chair for support. "Do you think I care how old you are? I have given my body to men older than you!"

"Elitah!" he cried, so loudly the bear curled on the bed in the corner was disturbed from his hibernating sleep and rumbled. "I don't want to hear it!"

"But you must," she cried. "I have to tell you! You know I am not a virgin, but my love is virgin! I have never loved a man until I loved you! I have never wanted a man the way I want you! I have loved you since Cam brought me to live with you. When I heard Marlette was dead, I traded my body for that horse so I could come to you. If you don't want me, I don't want to live!"

She turned away from him and ran blindly toward the door, her hands shaking so she had difficulty with the bar. He caught her there and took her in his arms and held her, stroking the soft, waving sleekness of her hair, his lips whispering her name against the fire of that softness. She trembled against him in her agony.

Finally, she pulled her head away from him and looked into his eyes, uncertain and questioning. Her very closeness set his blood on fire. He bent to kiss her and her lips came to life under his, sensuously seeking and pleading with his, driving all resistance away. He pulled away and stared at her, his breath coming quickly in his desire for her.

"Do you want to be my wife? Do you want to go with me to the Nakota?"

There was a light of victory in her eyes as she answered, "Only if we are wed right here, right now." Her hands caressing the hair at his neck pulled his head down to hers, her body burning his. He had no intention of waiting.

It was she who pulled away with a look of distaste. "Will you do something for me?"

"What?" he asked, unable to imagine what she wanted.

"Shave off that terrible beard."